W9-AVO-806

WITCH: A NEW BEGINNING

by L.S. Gagnon
Facebook/TheWitchSeries

Table of Contents

Prologue

I kept my eyes closed as I burned alive. I waited for death to take me quickly.

I could still hear them yelling, "Burn her!" as I tried not to scream from the pain.

The camp was filled with warlocks out for my blood. They stood, weapons in hand, waiting for me to burn.

So this is how I would die, burning while those I loved were far away and safe. I couldn't think of a better way for my life to end. I would die for those who had tried to save me. It would end with me. No longer would they be hunted. No more innocent blood lost.

All of this was my fault, and now I was paying the price. How simple my world had been, so dull and boring . . . until he walked into my life that day.

Chapter 1
My Favorite Author

It was a warm fall day in Salem as the sun hit my face. I sat outside the bakery with book in hand, one of the many I would read this month, I was sure. How I loved to read. I got lost in my books, always falling for the hero who saved the day. He was so handsome— perfect, in fact—and in love with me. That's how I saw it: myself as the damsel in distress, and my hero rescuing me from the villain to guarantee a happy ending.

This daily fantasy was my escape from the real world—a world I had never felt I belonged in. I kept to myself, working in the little bakery day in and day out. I was the shy, timid, fat girl who never talked to anyone. But when I picked up one of my books, I came alive inside. My heart pounded and the blood raced through my veins. It was the only time I felt normal, the only time I felt needed and wanted.

I couldn't live without my books, the books about *him*. Each story was different, but my hero was unfailingly consistent. Even

2

though he was a fictional character and lived only in my head—only in these books I couldn't put down—he was real enough for me. I felt connected to him somehow. I had never discovered the reason I'd received a free book in the mail that day, but after reading it, I didn't question why. My favorite author had such a way with words; he could melt my heart and set it on fire.

I turned the page, hoping my hero would make another appearance. My heart ignited every time he found the girl, saved her, took her in his arms, and—

"Thea!"

Just like that, my boss snapped me back into reality. "Coming, Norm."

I hurried inside, laid my book on the counter, and reached for an apron. A stack of cake orders waited for me. "Sorry, Norm, I lost track of time."

"Read, read, read," Norm mocked. "We have more important things to do, Thea."

Norm practically lived at the bakery. He had grown up working in the place, and since he never married or had children, he had made the bakery his entire life. He'd spend the day making bread while he talked about what he'd be having for lunch.

Lunch was my favorite time of the day. It was the only time Norm left the bakery. As soon as he stepped out to the deli next door, I sat down and started reading.

I sorted through the orders. "How many more cakes you want?"

Norm rubbed his mustache. "Make six

more, then the usual."

The usual was one of my creations which Norm would place in the front window and label as the daily special. Norm pretended to be bored with my baking, but I knew he looked forward to seeing what I would come up with next: raspberry ganache, oranges and cream cheesecake, red velvet brownies. His favorite was my coconut cream layer cake. I often caught him looking over my shoulder at the ingredients. "It tastes okay," he'd say, only to have three slices when he thought I wasn't paying attention.

I hurried through the orders. It was nearly lunchtime. I wasn't particularly hungry, but I couldn't wait to get back to my book.

Norm finally headed for the door. "Want anything from the deli?"

"No, thanks," I said, turning off the mixer. "Have a nice lunch."

After I pulled the last of the chocolate cakes from the oven, I grabbed my book from the counter and sat on a small wooden stool Norm used to read his paper. "Now, where was I?" I said, and began reading where I'd left off.

There he was, saving the girl from certain death. How I loved him, or at least the idea of him. My hero would never laugh at me when I crossed a room, like I was sure other guys did. He wouldn't wish me thinner or taller. To him, my nail biting would be endearing, and my constant fidgeting, charming.

I was deep into my book when the bakery door opened. An instant later, a funny smell hit me. I jumped to my feet and ran

4

behind the counter. "What's the name on the order?" I asked, not bothering to look up. When the customer didn't respond, I looked up.

My heart sank. It was *him.*

I grabbed the counter so I wouldn't fall from the shock. How could my favorite author be standing right in front of me? He looked as shocked as I was as he gazed into my eyes. I had the sense he was happy to see me. When he stepped closer to the counter, I nearly gasped.

"Hello," he said softly.

I couldn't answer. I was completely frozen.

He spotted my book on the counter and picked it up. "How long have you been reading this?" he asked.

Again, I said nothing. I thought about pinching myself to make sure I wasn't dreaming. I felt such a strong impulse to reach out and touch him, I almost couldn't stop myself.

"I seem to be lost," he said, replacing the book on the counter. "I was hoping you could tell me where Points Place Drive is?"

It was as though my heart knew who he was, and it was extraordinarily happy to see him.

My reaction pleased him somehow. He smiled when I didn't answer. "It's been a very long time since I was last here," he said. "It seems I've come during tourist season."

I tried to answer, but could only point to the tourist information booth across the street.

He glanced in the direction I pointed. "Do I make you nervous?" he asked, looking

5

back at me.

I didn't know what to say. I couldn't believe it was really him.

For once, Norm had perfect timing. "Did Thea get everything you need?" he asked as he walked through the door.

The man smiled at me again and looked over at Norm. "Actually, I just purchased the mill house," he said. "It's on Points Place Drive. Could you direct me?"

"Ah, yes," Norm replied. "It's not far from here, if you can get past the tourists."

"Yes, I was just telling the young lady here that it seems to be tourist season."

Norm nodded. "Witch central here, ya know."

As the two men walked toward the door, the man paused and turned around. "It was very nice meeting you, Thea," he said, smiling.

I couldn't bring myself to smile back at him. I wondered if my mouth was open.

"Thank you again for your help," he said and followed Norm out the door. I watched them as Norm pointed the way to Points Place Drive. They shook hands. My favorite author nodded to me before walking off.

My heart was still racing. Was I dreaming?

Norm walked back into the bakery. "Thea, what's got into you, girl?" he asked, hands on his hips.

"I . . . I'm sorry, Norm."

"New customers are rare in this town. Once the tourists are gone, things can get awfully slow around here."

6

"We have tons of customers," I said, breaking free of whatever that was. The city was busy this time of year, but Norm didn't like to hire extra help. The less money he had to pay out, the happier he was. That, of course, meant more work for me.

"He's new in town," Norm said, "and he owns that big, fancy house. That means big, fancy parties. Next time, sell him something." Norm started for the back room.

"Yes, Norm," I answered, gazing out the window. My mind was elsewhere. I picked up my book and turned it over to stare at his picture. "It was him," I whispered. He was the author of almost all the books I had, and secretly, I imagined him as my hero. That was why I didn't happen to know my favorite author's name: it kept my fantasy about him intact. His image made me feel alive inside. And today, when I looked into his eyes, I had wanted to jump over the counter and kiss him.

What was wrong with me? Why did pictures of this man make me feel this way—as though I couldn't live without him? I couldn't help but wonder why he had bought a house here. Maybe he had come to write a book about Salem. That had to be it; he must be doing research.

I looked down at his picture again. He sat in a dark room with hundreds of books behind him, his brown hair hidden under a baseball cap. He had the most beautiful blue eyes I'd ever seen. His nose had a small scar. His thick, dark eyebrows gave him a somewhat angry appearance, but he was beautiful, and certainly not the kind of man who would ever look at me twice.

As I studied his picture, I began to notice that my favorite author possessed all of the features he used to describe the central character in his books. I frantically flipped through the pages. "Did he put himself in the book?"

"Thea," Norm yelled, "are those orders finished?"

I reluctantly set the book aside. "Almost done, Norm," I answered, resuming my work.

By closing time, my thoughts were consumed by my hero. I hurried through the nightly cleanup. "Night, Norm," I yelled, heading out the door.

The night had become cool and brisk as I stepped outside the bakery. I loved Salem this time of year, but not for the reasons Norm did. Yes, it was the witch capital of the world, and the town was crawling with tourists. Witch hunts, pumpkin patches, costumes sold in shops on every corner, and palm readers and fortune tellers enjoyed a steady supply of business.

For me, it was the beauty of the season. I loved the trees and their colored leaves; the yellows, oranges, and reds. Then, when the snow came, the trees truly came to life. They looked brilliant all covered in snow. It always took my breath away. The history of the Salem witch trials pulled in its share of tourists, but most couldn't help but be charmed by the town itself.

Once the tourists were gone, I'd take long walks and admire all the old houses, some

But Thea and I are old friends." He looked at me. "She was kind enough to assist me today."

"Old friends?" Delia asked.

"I didn't mean to intrude," he said. "I just wanted to say hello, and tell Thea that I'll be seeing her tomorrow."

"Tomorrow?" I asked, surprised.

"Yes, I'm having a dinner party for some friends. I was hoping you could suggest some good things for me to serve."

I thought about Norm, and how he would be yelling about how right he was. "Um, okay," I replied nervously.

"Tomorrow, then," he said, turning to Delia. "It was nice to meet you, Delia."

I didn't like the way he looked at her. *Does he like her?* I had never felt jealous of Delia, but at that moment, I couldn't help it. He nodded politely at each of us and walked off down the alley.

"Who was that?" Delia asked.

"Shh—he'll hear you."

"How do you know him, Thea?"

I started to tell her about the books but stopped mid-sentence as something occurred to me. "When did you give him your name?"

Delia looked confused. "My name?"

"He said it was nice to meet you, *Delia.* When did you give him your name?"

She went from looking confused to looking angry. "How did you meet him?" she asked me again.

"He came into the bakery today."

"And?"

"And nothing. He just asked for

directions. Well, after he asked me about my book."

"What book?" She seemed to be getting upset. She didn't give me a chance to answer before asking, "Was it a book you read often?"

"Yes, one of my favorites."

"Did he read any of it to you?"

"Why would he read it to me?"

She grabbed my arm. "Thea, did he touch you?"

"What?" I asked, pulling free from her grasp. "No, why would he touch me?"

"Did he say anything to you that sounded like a poem?"

"A poem? No, Delia. What are you getting at?"

She sighed and looked away. "Maybe I'm just being paranoid."

"Paranoid about what?"

"Never mind," she said. "What happened next?"

"Nothing. He just asked for directions and left."

She calmed down some, but still seemed a bit worked up. "He's a little old for you, Thea. What is he, like, forty?"

I decided to tell her the truth. I hoped she wouldn't think I was crazy.

"Can I tell you a secret?" I said. "But promise not to laugh."

"Since when do we have secrets? Don't tell me you really are old friends."

"No, it's not that. He's my favorite author. I have a lot of his books. I feel strange when I have them in my hands. Then I started

He only looks like the character because you want him to.

She was right. I was up most of the night thinking about it. I was angry with myself for being so silly. My heart didn't care; it wanted to see him again. Why?

Come morning, my thoughts were still fixed on him. I decided not to try to reason with myself. There was no point. I didn't care about the books anymore. He was the only thing that mattered. My hero was real. He had walked out of his books and into my life. He was a walking, breathing person now, and no book could compete with that. I jumped out of bed and readied myself for work.

The bakery was already filled with the aroma of freshly baked bread and coffee cakes. Norm was having his usual danish while reading the morning paper.

"Morning, Norm," I said as I tied my apron. I reached for the day's orders.

Norm looked up at me. "James stopped in after you left yesterday," he said. "He wanted to speak with you about some pastries for a dinner party."

I reached for a muffin. "Who's James?"

"You know, the guy who came in here yesterday looking for directions."

I froze, the muffin halfway to my mouth. Hearing his name sent a shockwave through my body.

"His name is James?" I asked, setting the muffin back down.

"Yes, I told him you were probably down the street at your friend's booth."

"Maybe that's how he knew her name," I muttered. I tried to imagine Norm actually remembering Delia's name.

"Knew whose name?"

"Delia's, and yes, he found me. Thanks, Norm."

I picked up my muffin, poured myself some coffee, and got to work. It was going to be a long day—numerous batches of spider and bat cookies to make. Not wanting to be reminded of Delia's harsh words, I decided to skip my morning reading break. Instead, I would try to put our quarrel behind me. I'd bury myself in work, just like Norm did.

"That's a pretty cake, Thea."

I looked up and met his beautiful blue eyes. Then his scent hit me.

"James," I whispered.

I couldn't believe I'd said his name. I wanted to jump into an oven and wait until he left.

James smiled. "How did you find out my name?"

"N . . . Norm told me."

He leaned closer. "And James, that's the name you heard?"

I nodded, and in that moment, finally recognized his pleasant scent. He smelled like one of Delia's sweet-smelling potions. Delia's always smelled so sour. I had watched her make potions on plenty of occasions: love potions, potions to grow warts, to give a rash, and even one that caused someone to lose their hair. She had used that one often, usually on bullies.

"Isn't that your name?" I finally

managed to ask.

He seemed pleased somehow, but ignored the question and stepped closer.

"You have very pretty hair," he said.

Is he out of his mind? My hair is a tangled mess. I looked down. "I hate my hair," I admitted.

"Well, I like it," he said. "I hope you never change it."

I scanned his features. He was beautiful in every way, but his eyes were definitely his best feature. Under those angry-looking brows were two huge, sparkling blue eyes.

"You like my hair?" I asked.

He smiled. "Yes, very much, in fact."

His scent made me dizzy. Something inside me wanted to touch him. I even started to lean forward.

"The party, then," he said, stepping away. "My chef has informed me that we are having duck. What do you suggest serving with duck?"

I took a fast sniff as he pulled away. His scent traveled through me, as sweet as candy. "Y . . . yes, um, a raspberry tart would go well with that." I desperately wanted to jump into his arms, kiss him, and tell him I loved him.

My reaction seemed to make him happy. "Good," he said, smiling. "Please have it delivered by six to the mill house."

I looked up and nearly reached for him. I think he noticed.

"Just ring for the butler," he said and headed for the door. Before stepping outside, he turned back. "Oh, and Thea, you should forget

17

your book more often." He smiled, a hint of mischief passing through his eyes.

He was gone before I could respond. I was dumbfounded. How could he have known I hadn't brought my book with me today? Norm came through the door as James was leaving, so there was no time to dwell on it.

I hurried through the rest of the day, thoughts of him running through my head constantly. By evening, I was eager to leave. I wasn't feeling altogether good about stopping by Delia's, but I had promised her, and I didn't like to break promises. I cleaned up, said goodbye to Norm, and headed to Delia's booth, already having decided that I wouldn't stay long.

Friday was a busy day in Salem; a mass of customers swarmed Delia's booth. I was relieved. I could keep my promise to stop in and leave soon after. "Hey, Delia," I said, making my way through the crowd. "Busy day, huh?"

A black velvet hat with gold stars and silver moons adorned her head. It was her best one yet. I couldn't help but notice she had on a very sexy black dress, and her breasts were rather exposed. Now I understood all the men around her booth.

"Hi, Thea," Delia said, handing some guy his change. "I was going to call you, see if you wanted to give me a hand today. Next!"

I had to work in the morning, but she looked so happy. I shrugged off my coat and stepped behind the counter. "Sure," I said. "What do you need me to do?"

"Just take that side, will ya? Isn't this

awesome? It's been like this all day." She seemed excited as she explained the pricing for the various items. "This one is ten dollars or two for fifteen, and the sun catchers are thirty-five. The potions are priced depending on what they need them to do, so get me for those, okay?"

"Got it." I turned my attention to the waiting customers. "I can help the next person in line." No one moved to my side. They all wanted Delia; the dress was working magic for her. I settled for handing her the things people asked for. One guy wanted to know if she sold Halloween masks, but Delia was busy with another customer. "I can help you, sir," I said, facing him.

"No, thanks, lardo," he muttered, gesturing to Delia. "I'll wait for her."

As the guy turned away from me, Delia's head shot up. "What did you call her, scumbag?" She started walking around to the front of the booth.

I grabbed her hand. "Forget it, Delia." I wanted to keep her calm. I knew how wild she could get when she got mad.

"No," she said, pulling away. "You let everyone walk all over you." She stepped face to face with the man. "I asked you a question."

Before he could answer, Delia blew some kind of powder at him and began chanting: "You leave here now a happy man, never knowing who I am. Things will grow and things will smell, but you will never break my spell." She smiled mischievously. "Okay, scumbag. Walk away while you still can." She moved back into the booth.

"Weirdos!" the guy shouted as he walked away.

"Hee-hee-hee-hee," Delia cackled, "and your little dog, too."

We shared a laugh and returned our attention to the customers. After a few minutes, I asked, "What was that—a spell?"

She flipped her hair and smiled. "Just a little something I've been dying to try. Besides, he was an idiot. I'm sure I did a lot of people a huge favor just now."

"What kind of spell was it?" I asked, taking a seat on a stool.

"We'll have to wait and see now, won't we?"

"Guess so," I replied, still wondering if any of her spells really worked.

Delia scratched her head and stepped toward me. "Listen, Thea, about yesterday . . ."

"It's okay," I replied. "Really, I'm fine."

She squatted down and placed her hands on my knees. "No, listen," she said. "I have to say this." She paused and took a deep breath. "I didn't mean to hurt you. I know you get lonely, and sometimes I forget how shy you can be. I understand your need for the books. I had no right to judge. Please tell me you forgive me."

I couldn't stay mad at her. "You're practically my only friend, Delia. There's nothing to forgive."

Delia smiled and looked relieved. "Oh, and Thea," she said, giggling, "Norm doesn't count."

We shared a laugh, and just like that, we

were us again. Shortly after, we started packing up the merchandise. It was getting late and I had to leave soon.

"So tell me about this author," Delia asked. "Did he stop by the bakery after all?"

"Yes, but get this. I left my book at home this morning and didn't mention it to anybody, not even to Norm. But after placing his dinner party order, he said I should forget my book more often."

Delia seemed bothered. "You're sure you didn't tell him?"

"I'm telling you, Delia, not a word. And remember, he knew your name. I thought maybe Norm told him, but Norm never remembers your name. He always calls you 'that girl.' And today when James leaned toward me—"

"Wait." Delia held up her hand. "He leaned toward you?"

"Yes, he told me he liked my hair."

"He what?" Delia said, stepping back.

I was surprised by her reaction, but I went on. "After he placed his order, he said to have it delivered to the mill house. He said to ring for the—"

"Wait," she said, cutting me off. "He rents the old mill place?"

"I think he owns it. So anyway, he wants it del—"

She grabbed my wrist. "Stop. Are you sure he owns it?"

I backed up. She looked so angry. "Um, yes, pretty sure," I answered, yanking my arm from her grip. "What's the big deal?"

She didn't answer me. Her eyes looked far away.

"What is it?" I asked, rubbing my wrist.

She snapped out of her trance and grabbed my shoulders. "Listen, Thea. I want you to go home. Don't stop to talk to anyone. I'll be there as soon as I can."

"Why? What's the matter?"

"I'll explain later."

I wriggled out of her grasp. "What's wrong?"

She ignored the question and chanted: "It was a day, it was an hour, it was everything within my power. The things you've seen, the things I've said, and all the memories in your head. Remember not the things that passed, remember not the spell I cast. Tomorrow you will wake and read, once again you'll feel the need."

Chapter 2
Release Me

I wondered how long my alarm had been going off. I didn't remember hitting the snooze button. "Damn," I said as I rolled out of bed. "Norm's going to be pissed." I scanned the floor, grabbed a few items of clothing, and quickly threw them on. My room was a mess. For that matter, my whole apartment was a mess.

I loved my apartment. It was on the third floor, but I didn't care. Some of the single-family homes in Salem had been turned into three-family tenements, and the third floor was usually the cheapest, which was fine by me.

I hurried out the door and ran all the way to the bakery. When I arrived, poor Norm was attempting to ice a cake due to be picked up any minute.

"Thea, where have you been?" he asked, waving a chocolate-covered spatula in my direction.

"Sorry, Norm. I overslept." I hurried to the counter and grabbed the spatula from Norm's hand. I smoothed over his jagged work and sprinkled on some shaved white chocolate.

Norm shook his head as I boxed it up. "We have to finish all these orders," he said, disappearing into the back room. "We're closed tomorrow, so these need to be ready for pickup today. You should have been here at five a.m."

I didn't like it when Norm used the word *we*, because he really meant *me*.

"I'll have them all ready to go," I said confidently. "I'm only a couple of hours behind." I already had three cakes ready for icing. I just needed Norm to step out of the way. I was glad when he finally went back to his bread dough. He was making the bread for Tony's deli today.

It took me only an hour to catch up. When I finished boxing up the finished cakes, I yelled back to Norm, "Hey, Norm, don't forget we have a few deliveries today."

"No, Thea, you have a few deliveries today," Norm shouted from the back room.

I spent most of the day hurrying. I couldn't wait to sit down and read.

"Oh, my book," I said to myself when I realized I'd left it at home. I had an overpowering desire to read today—more than usual. I was surprised when Delia walked in.

"Hi, Thea. What time are you getting off work today?" she asked.

"I have to leave by five thirty." I cast an annoyed glance in Norm's direction. "I have a few deliveries to make."

"I'll come with you," Delia said.

"Really? You don't mind?"

"It's fine. I feel like a good walk,

anyway. Mind if I wait here till you're done?"

"Not at all. You want some coffee or something?"

"Nah, go ahead and finish up. Don't mind me."

She took a seat at one of the small tables. I finished the raspberry tart and boxed it up. I had some white chocolate shavings left over from a previous order and decided to bring them along to sprinkle on top of the tart.

"Okay, I'm ready to go." I picked up a few boxes and looked over at Delia. She appeared to be lost in thought. "Hey, you—a little help, please?"

Delia snapped to attention and moved to the counter.

"Here, take this," I said, handing her the container of chocolate shavings.

It was odd how she would do as I said sometimes, without question. Even odder was that I knew she wouldn't say no.

"See ya, Norm," I yelled as we walked out the door.

Half an hour later, with all but one delivery made, we headed for the old mill house. "So, you nervous about seeing old author guy again?" Delia asked.

"I wouldn't say nervous," I lied.

"Let me ask you something," she said, facing me. "When did you first start having feelings for him?"

"I don't know. A few years ago, I guess, when I first started reading his books."

"And how did you come across his books?"

"I received a free one in the mail. I liked it so much, I ordered more."

"And had you ever seen or spoken to him before? Before the bakery, I mean?"

I couldn't understand why she was asking so many questions. "What are you talking about? I would have told you something like that."

We started walking again. "And do you read only his books, or do you read others?"

"I have the ones you gave me, but lately his are the only ones I read."

"And the book you forgot that day, the day he said you should forget it more often, was it one of his?" She was starting to sound angry.

"No, it was one of yours. Why? What is it with you?"

"It's nothing," she said. "Besides, we're here."

We turned toward the mansion. The house was a beautiful old Colonial with divided light windows. It was surrounded by a tall, black wrought-iron fence overflowing with greenery. A pair of chimneys jutted out from the mansion's steeply pitched roof, and a grand front door beckoned beyond the gate.

A piece of paper hung from the gate that read, *It's open, Thea*.

I reached for the note, but Delia's hand crossed in front of mine and forcefully snatched it from the wrought-iron bars. "Let's go," she said, pushing open the gate.

I reached up to ring for the butler as James had instructed, but Delia pushed her way in without bothering to knock. I gasped as we

26

stepped inside. The foyer was enormous, with a sparkling chandelier suspended overhead. Expensive-looking art hung on every wall.

Delia appeared unimpressed by the grand old place. She tapped her foot impatiently on the cherry-wood floor.

"Good evening, ladies," I heard James say. He stepped out from what appeared to be his office. He didn't seem surprised to see Delia.

"What's so good about it?" Delia asked.

I was mortified. I couldn't believe Delia was acting so rude.

"Sorry if I'm late," I said. "Where would you like me to put this?"

James stared at Delia, who glared back at him. *Great, he likes her.* I instantly regretted letting her tag along.

"The kitchen is through there," James answered, his eyes still locked on Delia.

I was almost to the kitchen when I remembered the white-chocolate shavings I'd handed to Delia. As I walked back to retrieve them, I heard loud whispering and stopped short. James and Delia were having what sounded like an argument.

"Of all the rotten tricks," Delia hissed. "We had an agreement."

"No, Delia," James replied. "We had a deal—one I never felt good about."

"But you agreed to it."

"I said I would try."

"Well, try harder," Delia yelled.

I stood, frozen. Was it possible they knew each other? I leaned against the wall and continued to listen.

"I told you," James said, "as long as I could stay connected to her. And you agreed."

"And I told you, it's too dangerous."

"How dare you think I'd ever put her in danger."

"Oh, please. All you've ever done is put her in harm's way."

I heard James take a step. "I never imagined she would do that. How could I have known?"

"Don't feed me that, James. You knew very well what you'd gain."

Who's in danger? How do James and Delia even know each other?

"Choose your words wisely, Delia. Now you're putting yourself in danger."

"Don't talk to me about danger. I have these to remind me."

I peeked around the corner and had to cover my mouth to keep from gasping. Delia's arms were covered in scars, as if they had been held over a fire. I suddenly became very frightened. What had happened to her? Why had I never noticed her scars before?

"And who saved you as you burned?" James asked.

Delia yanked down her sleeves. "Stay away from her, James."

"I'm afraid I can't do that," he said. "I've waited long enough."

"I'll take her away again."

"And I'll find her again."

"She won't remember you. She has no idea who you are."

"Yes, I can see the spell you've chosen," James said, smirking. "Keeping her mind occupied with reading—how creative of you. And keeping her thoughts of me at bay through *your* choice of books? Brilliant."

"Oh, and your ideas are just so much more creative," she said, rolling her eyes. "Writing yourself into your own books? Ingenious."

The tart shook in my hands as I began to tremble. Nothing they said made any sense.

"It took me years to figure out that you cast spells on the books you were giving her," James hissed. "You left me no choice."

They were talking about me. I was sure of that now. I wanted to run, but my feet were glued to the floor.

"It's not the seventeenth century, James," Delia continued. "She can't do the things she did before. We've worked hard to hide her right under his nose. She could walk right by him and he wouldn't even notice." She sighed. "Every time you pull something like this, I have to erase weeks from her memory. Can't you see that your being here only puts her more at risk? Did you forget that he lives here, too?"

Did she just say "the seventeenth century"? Too scared to move, I began to cry.

"She listens, Delia. I must go to her."

Panic rose inside of me. I didn't want him anywhere near me. I didn't even know if I wanted Delia near me. *Who is she?*

"Oh, please," Delia said, rolling her eyes. "Like I'm going to let her remember this? I

29

should have erased her little meeting with y—"

The tart fell to the floor, interrupting their heated exchange. I bolted for the door.

Delia chanted: "You will stay, not run away, not move until I say."

I fell to the floor, terrified.

"Listen to me, Delia," James said. "I will not intrude on her life. I only want to make sure she's safe."

"You're the only danger here, James. If they see you, it will be a dead giveaway who she is. Can't you understand that, you idiot?"

James was visibly angry. He stepped up to Delia and leaned his face close to hers. "Did you know it was me the other day?"

Delia looked away.

"It's one of her spells," he explained, sounding calmer. "She engraved it in my mind so I could hide. It took me years to get it right. But I did it, and it even fooled the mighty Delia. That's why I dare come now, just to be near her. It's all I ask. I'll beg if needed. It's time that I'm allowed to protect her."

Delia looked up at him. "The council might disagree."

"The council knows I'm here."

"Then it's been voted?" Delia asked, clearly taken aback.

"Yes."

Rage washed over Delia's face. "There's a reason she did all this. You shouldn't be here."

"I'm not leaving, Delia."

"If they see you, they'll go after her." Delia gestured in my direction. "James, they'll try to kill her."

He looked at me and back at Delia. "Just answer me this: Did you know it was me at your booth the other night?"

She stared at him for a long moment before looking away. "No," she said quietly.

I could tell he'd won.

"You have five minutes," she said to James, and walked toward the door. "Enjoy your moment, judge." She slammed the door behind her.

I could hear him breathing as he approached. He squatted down in front of me and I closed my eyes, terrified.

"Don't be frightened," he said softly, holding out his hand. "I'm not going to hurt you."

I couldn't move; Delia's spell had paralyzed me. I looked at his hand and shook my head.

"I would die a million deaths before I would hurt you," he said.

"I . . . I can't move," I replied, my voice shaky.

He understood that Delia's spell was keeping me down. He seemed to be deciding something as he looked toward the door, then back at me. "I want you to do as I say. Close your eyes and think of chains breaking, then say the words, *Release me.* Understand?"

I looked at him, confused.

"It will break her spell," he explained.

I nodded.

"You have to believe they're really breaking, feel them falling off you."

I nodded again and closed my eyes. I imagined the feeling of big, heavy chains wrapped around my body and forced my arms against them. My body tingled as I said the words: "Release me." In an instant, I felt lighter.

"Yes, very good," he said, smiling. "You're doing wonderfully, querida."

Instinctively I knew he had given me a tool, one I could use to block her spells, and his. I wondered if he had done it intentionally.

He held his hand out again. This time, I took it. He helped me up and quickly put his hand on my shoulder. "I'm sorry we only have a moment, but I need your heart to hear this. I don't understand why you gave me the orders you did, but I'm back. I need you to tell me if you got my message in that book. I need you to give me a sign somehow, tell me if you know I have it."

He was trying to leave some kind of clue in my head before Delia wiped my memory clean, but nothing he said made any sense. How could I possibly know the answers to his questions?

He looked toward the door again and back at me. "I think I know where they're keeping the crystal. I'll have to rejoin them to retrieve it. I won't let this turn into a witch hunt again. And I won't let them find you, understand?"

I nodded. My voice still shaky, I asked, "Who am I?"

He smiled and stepped back. "You are the most special witch of us all, my love."

"And who is she?" I asked, glancing toward the door.

"She's your most loyal friend and guard."

I sensed he wanted me to ask him who he was. Instead, I asked, "And her burns?"

He thought for a moment. "They believed it was you they had captured. They thought they were burning you."

My knees felt weak. I tried to focus. "But she looks nothing like me."

"They saw what she wanted them to see," he explained. "She gave you the only gift she could—a way to escape."

"Why did they want to burn me?" I wasn't sure I wanted to hear the answer.

"Please don't ask me that."

"Okay," I agreed. "Why am I in danger?"

He didn't answer and glanced at the door. "I'm sorry," he said, reaching for me, "but we have so little time." He pulled me into his arms. "Forgive me for this."

Then he crushed his lips to mine.

I quickly panicked. *Release me!* I screamed inside my head. But this was no spell; he was really kissing me. I knew I would never get a chance like this again, so I pressed myself into him and kissed him back.

Without leaving my lips, he whispered, "Querida," and kissed me harder.

Every question I had was forgotten. My dream was coming true. Every book, every single word I'd read, all came down to this moment. The way I touched him was well planned out in my head. Years of putting myself in these moments had me well prepared. I touched his hair, his face, his lips. Everything that was within my reach would not escape my touch. The shy, fat girl had vanished; now this passionate woman was being held in her hero's arms. I was lost in this kiss.

"Every moment, every hour," he whispered in my ear.

A spell—I hoped my plan would work. *Release me!*

"Everything within my power," he continued. "I put you back into your life, and watch over you, my lovely wife." He kissed me again.

Release me, rel—wait. Did he just call me his wife?

The door flew open. "Of course she responds to you," Delia said. "She always did have terrible taste in men." She looked at the two of us, unable to mask her disdain. "We have to go," she said as she reached for my hand. "I only have a short time with her in a daze, ya know."

I quickly sorted through my head. I could remember it all, especially that kiss. Delia didn't seem to notice I was no longer frozen. I wasn't sure how to act right now, so I was glad to hear her say I would be in a daze.

James kissed the top of my head and handed me off to Delia. "Thank you for giving us this moment," he said.

Delia shot him a dirty look. "I didn't do it for you."

We headed for the door.

"Delia, wait!" James called. He walked over to us. "How did you figure out it was me today?"

Delia laughed. "Oh, please. I knew you'd come back here, so I put a spell on the house. Anyone can rent it, but only you could buy it."

When she turned toward the door again, James reached for me. With my hand still in Delia's, he kissed me again.

"Oh, come on," Delia said, yanking me away.

I didn't know where she was taking me. She kept muttering to herself. I repeated the words *Release me* in my head on the chance she might be casting more spells on me.

My mind was bursting with questions, making it impossible to focus. Exactly how old was I, and why hadn't I aged? Was James really my husband? Why would I give him orders? If I was a witch, why didn't I have any powers? What was so special about me that I needed a guard? Was it really possible I was a witch—a real witch? I didn't even believe in witches.

Who am I?

One thing I did know: Delia was a true friend, and she loved me. But my guard? How many times had she erased my memory? Who were they hiding me from? *Why* were they hiding me?

Delia mumbled to herself nonstop. We had walked to the shore and were heading toward an old pirate ship—one I knew well. It was only open during tourist season, a sort of floating restaurant. We passed the closed ticket house and stepped onto the boat. Delia chanted as we climbed aboard. We walked down a narrow corridor to what appeared to be the captain's quarters.

Delia threw open the door. "You dirty old hags!"

Four women jumped up from a small wooden table, scattering a mess of papers about the room. The women gaped at Delia, turned to me, and immediately started chanting: "Hear no more as you stand, until my voice commands."

Release me!

"Why wasn't I told about this?" she shouted. "You voted without me?" I'd never seen Delia so angry. "You dirty witches. Some council you are."

One of the women stepped forward. She looked young, and could have easily been mistaken for a tourist. She had beautiful blond hair, green eyes, and was slender like Delia. "Now wait just a minute," she said to Delia. "Just because you form part of the guard doesn't give you the right to—"

"It gives me every right, Helena!" Delia said, cutting her off. She pointed at me. "See her there? She gave me the right. She put her life in *my* hands, not yours." Delia held her fist to the witch's face. "And when we find the crystal and get the rest of her powers back, we'll see how much longer you sit on this council."

The rest of my powers?

"Forgive us, dear," an older witch said. "But we didn't know it was him until he showed his true form. And I don't really see the harm."

"He can do whatever he wants," Helena said. "No one will know it's him."

"She's right, dear," the older witch continued. "He would have gone unnoticed, even by you. We shouldn't anger him. He's her husband. You have to accept that."

Delia laughed. "Don't tell me you old fools fear him."

The witches looked at each other, clearly not sure what to make of Delia's attitude.

"She never gave him that gift," Delia said. "You fools! He's no better than we are."

A third witch spoke up. "She hasn't given him the gift yet, but she will."

"And she can make him more powerful than any of us," added Helena.

"Yes, yes, yes," Delia said, waving her arms dramatically. "She picked him, blah blah blah. But until then, you will not vote without me, or her—even if she won't remember it." Delia headed back to me.

"Wait," the third witch said. "You must stay close to him. We need to know what he's up to."

"You know I can't be near him without her," Delia replied. "I can't break her spell, not even with a thousand witches helping me."

"You are her guard," they all chimed together. "Find a way."

Delia looked at the witches for a moment and grabbed my hand. As we headed out the door, Delia shook her head and muttered, "Idiots."

I knew what was coming and prepared myself. By the time we reached my apartment, I was exhausted. Repeating *Release me* over and over inside my head had worn me out. I was glad to have seemed in a daze when she put me in bed.

Delia chanted one last spell before she left: "Sleep well, my dearest friend; I'm with you till the end, and may this day be like a ghost, and dream with whom you love the most." She kissed my head and left.

I wanted to get up and write down the incantation, but I didn't want to chance Delia seeing me awake. I lay in bed, my mind spinning with the day's unbelievable events. What should I do tomorrow? Go about life as usual? I had to be careful. I couldn't let them know that my memories were still my own. It was going to be difficult. Delia and I were so close.

One thing I planned to do was sit in on the council meetings and find out all I could about my true identity. As luck would have it, Delia couldn't be near James—my husband— without me.

Did I know this would happen? James seemed to think so. He asked for a clue about a message, something he had written in one of those books, something he wanted me to read. I would start there, with James's message. I would comb every word in those books until I found it.

That's a lot of books.

I felt more exhausted than ever. I pulled the blanket up over my head and fell into a deep sleep. I dreamed about the person I loved the most, but not because of Delia's spell. I wouldn't allow spells to control me anymore.

I dreamed of him because I loved him. I loved him before I knew who he was, before he ever walked into the bakery.

Chapter 3
The Message

I opened my eyes and prayed it hadn't been a dream. I was happy I didn't have to run to the bakery; I didn't feel up to working today. I lay there thinking of Delia, and how all this time she really had been a witch, not just an eccentric.

My best friend was my guard. I thought about how long Delia had been in my life. She was a part of nearly all my memories—what memories I had left, that is. I remembered all the years working for the bakery, getting up at the crack of dawn, day in and day out. But when I tried to remember my childhood, my mind drew a blank. Did she erase that, as well?

What about James? I smiled as I thought of him. "My husband," I whispered, amazed at the thought. Why did he love me, of all people? I was shy, ugly, and fat, although Delia had always referred to me as "full-figured." I had felt James's love yesterday. I didn't think about my weight when he held me. Somehow I knew it didn't matter to him. He loved me as I was. He even liked my tangled mass of hair. In his arms, I felt beautiful.

I remembered what he'd said about the message in the book. I had to find his message and unravel this mystery. I had to do what I could to help find this crystal. I rolled out of bed and shuffled over to the small mountain of books piled on my desk. One by one, I picked them up and perused the different titles. Maybe one would jump out at me. When that didn't happen, something occurred to me: *I'm a witch.* Maybe I had powers, even if I couldn't remember them.

I stood up and stared down at the books, hoping this was going to work. I took a deep breath and shrugged. "It's worth a shot."

I felt a little silly as I held out my hand and closed my eyes. I focused on James's message and said, "Come to me, book." I gasped when a book came flying into my hand.

"I did it!"

I ran to the mirror. "You're a witch, Thea! You're really a witch!" I scanned the room, looking for something to command into my waiting hands. "Come to me, glove." In an instant, my glove flew through the air and into my hand. The sound of my own laughter filled the room as I summoned item after item into my hands.

I briefly wondered why I didn't need incantations like Delia, but I quickly pushed the thought aside. I didn't really care why. I was too excited about my newfound powers to give it more than a passing thought.

I jumped on my bed, searching the room for more objects to bring under my control. As I surveyed my mess of a room, a thought began to occur to me. I drew a deep breath and concentrated. "Apartment, clean yourself up."

I cheered as my clothes began to fold themselves and shoes lifted off the floor and returned to the closet. When I heard a noise coming from the other room, I leaped off the bed and bounded into the living room. Chairs were pushing themselves in at the table. Dishes rinsed and dried themselves and neatly stacked themselves into cabinets. I stepped aside as pillows floated by and landed gently on the sofa.

I moved to the bathroom, where my towel was hanging itself up on the rack. I looked into the mirror; I wanted to see the witch I now was. As usual, my hair was a mess. "Hair, do something with yourself." Nothing. I looked directly into the mirror. "Please?" Again, nothing.

My mood darkened. "Why won't it work?" I whined, trying to run my fingers through the tangled mass. I looked into the mirror again, sighed, and said, "brush yourself, hair." Instantly, knots loosened and detangled as my hair began to groom itself. "It has to be a specific command," I said to myself, making a mental note.

I glanced into my room. I spotted the book that had removed itself from the pile. In all my excitement, I had tossed it aside. It now lay in the center of my neatly made bed. I stepped into my room and picked up the book.

This was going to be easy—just one simple command. "Show me the message." I waited for the pages to reveal themselves. To my surprise, the book remained closed. I held it out in front of me and tried again: "Book, show me the message." Again, I waited. Nothing.

What am I doing wrong?

A thought occurred to me. "Show me my husband's message, book," I ordered. Instantly, the pages began to turn. I remembered that James had taken precautions. Only a command from his wife would work. "And that would be me," I said aloud, smiling.

I sat on the edge of the bed and began to read. The hero was saying good-bye to the girl. This book was among my least favorites because it didn't have a happy ending. The two were standing outside a train station, and the girl was crying:

> *"You promised me you'd never leave this way," she said with tears in her eyes.*
>
> *He took her in his arms and whispered in her ear, "For the time that we're apart, within myself I hold the heart, and until you wake, I will keep safe."*
>
> *He kissed her on the head and left.*

The rest of the page suddenly went blank. I quickly flipped through the entire book to find that all of the words, save for the ones I'd just read, had been erased. I knew I had found James's message. I had no idea what it meant, or how I could get word to James that I'd found it. But I would think about that later. I was too excited about my newfound powers. I walked back to the bathroom mirror and laughed at my reflection. My hair had already managed to revert to its usual form.

"Thea, you really are a witch," I said, a smile spreading across my face. I began dancing around the room. I felt so free and alive. My life finally made sense. I felt the need for some air and decided to go for a walk. That was nothing new for me, so Delia shouldn't think twice about it. I knew I had to be careful around her.

I pulled on some neatly folded clothes from my drawer, grabbed my coat, and ran down the stairs. When I stepped outside the main door, I found a gorgeous day waiting for me—warm for this time of year. I walked in the direction of the pier. It was still early enough in the day to avoid the tourists. Once at the pier, I could clear my head and think about what to do next.

As I walked toward the water, I was suddenly hit with a repulsive smell. A man, clearly the source of the stench, was walking toward me. It was the man from Delia's booth, the one she'd cast a spell on for being so rude to me. I covered my nose and stepped back as he approached.

"Y . . . your friend," the man said, "she

did this to me. I'm sorry about the other day. I shouldn't have said that to you. Please, you have to tell her to help me."

He looked horrible. His pants looked as though he was carrying around two bowling balls inside of them. My mouth gaped as I realized what had grown. Large, red blisters covered his body. As they popped, they released a hideously foul odor.

"I'm begging," he pleaded, "please ask your friend to make it go away." He was practically on his knees.

I looked around, making sure he was alone. I couldn't leave him this way. His suffering was getting to me.

I placed my hand on his shoulder and said, "Release him." As an afterthought, I added, "And erase Delia and me from his memory."

I stepped back and watched as the man's blisters healed. I avoided looking down at his pants. I turned my head to the side and released a small giggle.

"What are you laughing at, heifer?" he said, looking almost normal again.

I shook my head and walked away. His words had no power over me. I felt nothing but pity for him.

Some of the shops near the pier were getting ready to open. Fortune tellers had their signs out. I thought of how Delia often made fun of them, calling them "silly humans." I walked along the pier until I found a bench. The cleansing ocean air hit my face as I sat. I thought of how much had changed in such a short span of time. I marveled at how different I felt. I closed my eyes, then felt something shocking my hand, a small, sharp zap. It wasn't enough to hurt, but enough to catch my attention. I glanced around but saw nothing.

Maybe it was just the wind.

I directed my face to the sun again, leaned back, and closed my eyes. Zap! This time I stood up and looked out in all directions. I crouched down and looked under the bench. I couldn't find anything out of the ordinary.

Maybe this is what happens when you use magic.

I looked around one last time and sat back down. There it was again; this time, it zapped the back of my head. I jumped to my feet and spun around. A short, bald man stood behind me. He was dressed like he was on the way to the office, with a suit, tie, and all.

He looked me up and down repeatedly. "I've never seen you do magic before," he said, stepping closer. "Don't you work in the bakery?"

He'd been watching. He had seen me remove Delia's spell from the blistered man.

"Magic?" I replied. "What do you mean, magic?" I didn't know who he was, but my gut told me I shouldn't be talking to him.

"What you did over there," he said, pointing. "Magic."

I struggled for a way to explain. Telling him the truth seemed too dangerous. Suddenly, I felt a strange presence inside of me and instinctively knew what to do. "Erase," I said confidently.

The man looked lost for a moment and looked up at me. "Oh, I'm sorry," he said politely. "Is this bench taken?"

It worked! "I was just leaving," I said, smiling.

As I passed him, the wind shifted and I noticed an odd smell. I thought perhaps it was Delia's potions again, but this was different. The smell burned my nose and made my eyes water. I felt anger building inside of me. I turned back to the man. I was about to say something when I heard another voice.

"Good morning, Thea."

James. What was he doing here?

"Ah, James, there you are," the short man said.

James glanced at me and smiled before he turned to shake the man's hand.

"Great dinner party, James," the man continued. "Everything was wonderful."

"Thank you," James said. "Thea here made the pastry."

I had dropped it on the floor. James must have fixed it with a spell.

"Ah, yes," the man said. "I've seen her in the bakery." The man turned to me. "It was exquisite, young lady."

"Thank you," I said, looking away from James.

"Thea," James said softly, "I believe your friend Delia is looking for you. You should go and find her."

I wanted to throw myself into his arms and kiss him. "Oh, okay," I replied.

"Have you been waiting long?" I heard

James say to the stranger as I walked away.

Moments later, I saw Delia walking toward me. She was out of breath and seemed nervous. "Hey, Thea. What are you doing out here?"

"I felt like a walk," I said, glancing back at James and his friend.

"Did you go out walking with author guy?"

"No, he showed up after."

"Who's that guy he's with?"

"I don't know," I said, shrugging my shoulders. "You want to grab some breakfast?" I felt the need to get out of there as fast as possible. The man's scent was making the witch inside of me furious; I wanted to cause him pain.

"Yeah, let's get out of here," Delia said, looking at James and the stranger.

As we walked away, I wondered who the stranger was, and how he knew about magic. What were those little zaps I felt? Spells? Was he attacking me? When I looked back again, he and James were sitting close together. They were obviously deep in conversation.

"What's wrong?" Delia asked.

"I'll tell you over breakfast."

Just then, an idea came to me. If Delia believed my memory had been erased, I could get away with asking a question or two. If I was careful, she wouldn't know her spells were having no effect on me.

We walked to one of my favorite mom-and-pop restaurants where we could sit outside and enjoy the beautiful day. We sat down at a small table and waved over the waitress.

"Delia, querida." The waitress nodded at me. "Mistress."

Delia cleared her throat. "Ahem, yes, Maya. Some coffee, please."

That word again. I had to know what it meant. "Delia, that word the waitress just called you, what does it mean?"

"Querida? It depends on how you use it. Mi querida means *my lover*, but just querida, well, that's more tender. It means *my love*." Delia smiled, gesturing to the waitress. "She calls everyone that."

James called me his love. The thought of it made me happy.

"Is she Spanish?" I asked, glancing toward the waitress. She was beautiful, and full of curves. She looked so sensual in her tight blue dress. Her nails were painted bright red to match her lips.

"I think she's Mexican and Portuguese," Delia replied. She looked at me. "She kind of reminds me of you with all those curves, except you wear loose clothes, which makes you look bigger than you are."

I didn't know what Delia was thinking. I looked nothing like that beautiful woman.

"You ready to order?" Delia asked.

"Yeah," I said absently, still looking at the waitress.

After Maya served our breakfast, I decided it was a good time to ask questions, but Delia beat me to it. "Who was that guy on the pier?" she asked, leaning back in her chair. "Did he talk to you?"

"Um, yes, a little," I said, taking a sip of coffee.

She leaned forward. "What did he say? It didn't sound like a poem?"

"No, he asked if the bench was taken." It wasn't exactly a lie.

"Nothing else?" she pressed. "He didn't ask you anything?"

"No, just about the bench—why?" I couldn't tell her what he really said. I would give myself away. She studied my face. For the moment, she seemed satisfied with my answer.

"It's nothing," she said, returning to her food. "Eat your eggs."

I had to lighten the mood before I could begin asking my own questions. "Hey, what's the difference between a potion and a spell?" This was nothing new. I often asked Delia questions about being a witch.

"Oh please," she replied. "Everyone knows potions wear off, but spells can last forever." She took a bite of her pancake. "Potions can be reversed by any witch, but spells can only be broken by the witch who casts it."

"So witches can't remove each other's spells?" I asked, wondering why I was able to remove hers.

She looked up at me. "I only know of one who can."

"What is she?" I asked. "A grand witch or something?" I couldn't believe how well it was going, it was like our usual chit-chat.

Delia let out a little laugh. "Sort of," she replied. "More like a ruler of witches. There are many grand witches, but this one is extra special." She looked at me. "Take me, for instance. I'm a grand witch, but I don't have near the powers she has."

"So this top witch, is she like your boss?"

Delia laughed and shook her head. "Yes, Thea, she's kind of like my boss."

"Where is she now?"

"I'll introduce you to her one day," she said, still shaking her head.

I pressed on. "So what about the powder you blew in that guy's face, what was that?"

She paused before answering, eyeing me curiously. "That's just to freeze someone so I can finish my spell." She picked up her fork and looked down at her food. "Why, you want to freeze author guy so you can kiss him?" she said, giggling.

I was relieved to hear her laugh. She had started to appear suspicious. I decided to back off on the questions for the time being.

"So what are we doing today?" I asked.

"I have to stop by my house for just a moment," she said, waving for the check. "Then we can decide."

I sat, taking in what she'd just said. *Her house?* I sifted through my memories and found nothing. I didn't know where Delia lived. How could that be?

"Where do you live again?"

She ignored my question and just smiled. "Come on, let's get out of here."

I got up and followed her about three blocks to an area of Salem I knew well. We stopped at an old house I'd seen many times before. The house was flanked with many large trees; the yard looked like a forest. The gray, three-story house with red trim appeared to have been built in the seventeenth century. It looked like an old barn that had been converted to a house. Its small windows were covered with dark curtains. I couldn't imagine how this structure was still standing.

Delia opened the wood gate and motioned for me to follow. I felt a touch angry with her, knowing I'd been here before and couldn't remember it. I didn't stay angry for long.

"Wow, you live here?"

She turned to me and laughed. "You always say . . . yes, this is where I live."

She had almost slipped. I suppressed a giggle.

"Come on, I'll show you the inside," she said, leading the way. I began to follow her in, but before we reached the door, a voice called out.

"Delia!" I heard a woman yell.

We both turned. I knew the voice. It was one of the witches from the council.

"Give me a minute," Delia shouted back. "Thea, wait here, okay?" She walked over to the woman.

I wasn't willing to wait. I needed to know what the witch wanted. I closed my eyes and thought of how I could listen. "Ears, be like Superman and listen." It was the only thing I could think of, and I giggled as the words left my mouth. Moments later, I heard voices.

"I must speak to you now," the witch said nervously.

"So speak," Delia replied.

"The sands moved, Delia. They moved." I opened my eyes and looked over at them. I could see the witch trembling. Delia gasped and grabbed the witch's arm. "When, you stupid witch? When?"

"This morning," the witch replied.

At once, they both turned to me.

"Quick, come inside," Delia said, pushing the woman through the gate.

I chanted in my head as they approached me.

"Thea, let's go inside," Delia ordered.

"Um, okay."

As we stepped inside, Delia turned to cast her spell on me. Again, I was prepared. When she thought she had me safely under her spell, she turned to the witch. "I knew there was a reason James was here," she said, banging her fist on a table. The only other furniture I saw in the old place was a simple dining table and a few chairs.

"What does this mean for us?" the witch asked. "We still haven't found the crystal. We'll be killed if she remembers."

"Shut up, Vera," Delia yelled. "We have to gather everyone quickly. If the sands run out, we'll have to fight. The boys have been preparing for this."

"But why have they moved?" Vera asked. "How much time did she set it for?"

"Four moons, but not enough time to find the crystal." Delia started to pace. "That idiot! He knows something, and he's not telling us." She walked over to me, her expression angry. "What does he know, Thea? What orders did you give him?"

I knew it wasn't a question she expected me to answer.

Delia turned to Vera. "I'm going into her memories."

"But you can't—not without her," Vera replied. "It's not possible."

"I have to try." She looked at me, fury in her eyes. "You had to have him, didn't you? Look at us! We're sitting ducks without you here!" To my surprise she began to cry. I'd never seen Delia break down this way, she was always so strong.

Vera hurried to her side. "We're doomed, sister."

"Get off me, you fool," Delia said, pushing Vera away. "I have to think. I have to run away with her. I'll take her away and hide her. I can't let them find her. They'll kill her."

"And leave us here to die?" Vera cried.

Delia turned to face Vera. "I don't know what else to do." She dropped to the ground and began crying.

This was my fault. I could see that now. It was time for me to learn the truth about who I was. I stepped forward. "Then maybe it's time to tell me everything."

They looked at me and gasped, eyes wide.

Chapter 4
The Memory Clouds

Delia jumped to her feet. "It's a spell. She's bewitched." She pulled a handful of powder from her pocket and blew it at me.

I held up my hand. "Stop," I yelled. It sounded like sand when it dropped to the floor.

Vera chanted at me as she ran for the door.

"Stay," I whispered.

Vera froze, one foot in front of the other.

Delia chanted: "Leave her now, you evil spell, all your magic I repel."

"Wall!" I shouted.

She flew into the air and slammed high against the wall. I wasn't sure what to do next. I didn't even know how I had done that. It was as if someone was inside of me, helping me—the same presence I felt at the pier.

I hadn't expected Delia to react like she did. She didn't think it was me just now, that part was clear. I looked up to where she hung. "Delia, I—"

"How dare you speak my name, witch!" she yelled, cutting me off. "What did you do with her?"

"Delia, it's me, Thea. You have to let me explain."

"I will kill you if it's the last thing I do, scum," she said, glaring at me.

"Delia, you put a spell on me at James's house so I wouldn't run, remember?"

She didn't answer.

"When you left the house, I couldn't move. James told me the words to say so I could break free of your spell."

"That's impossible. I left you . . ."

I eyed her intently. "You said you knew of only one who could."

I could see it in her face—she was putting it together.

"James told me what words to say, and it worked," I explained. "When he chanted his spell at me, I used those words, and I've been using them ever since. You have to believe me, Delia. Plus, something awful is happening, right?"

She stared at me for a long moment and looked down. "Yes, Thea. Something very bad."

I had gotten through to her. "So, can I put you down now?"

She nodded and looked away from me. I could tell she was bothered by the forgotten spell.

"Release," I whispered.

Delia gently floated down from the wall.

Vera ran and threw herself at my feet, wrapping her arms around my legs. "Forgive me, mistress," she pleaded.

nervously.

"Like I said before, because you helped us, because you stood by our side. You demanded that they respect us. And you did so by casting fear into their hearts. Their fear of you kept them from treating us like slaves."

"Why in the world would they fear me?"

"Because you're special, Thea," Delia said. "You're something our world has never seen before, something the warlocks would kill to be." She paused and took my hands. "You're the daughter of a pure witch and a powerful wizard. You don't need spells or potions, just the wave of your hand. Like your father, you can sense the future, which is why no one doubted your orders. Your spells are ten times stronger than a warlock's spell. You have real powers—no potion could ever do what you can."

"I'm half wizard?" I said, amazed.

"And half witch, too." Her lips turned up in a small smile.

"And what are you?"

Delia's smile faded. "I'm half human and half witch, like all the others you protected, male and female. We need spells and potions to use our powers."

"Male witches?" I asked, confused. "I thought a warlock was a male witch?"

"Warlocks don't consider half-human men warlocks. They consider them trash. If you were born half human, then you're nothing but a witch to them—woman or man."

"Is James a warlock?" I asked.

She laughed. "He wishes. He's half

human just like me, just like most of us around here. He also has limited use of his powers, although you taught him some extremely potent spells."

I sensed she wasn't telling me everything, as though I had to pry the information from her. "Delia, if I can wave my hand, then tell me what to do to fix things. I don't know what's going on, but I'll make it go away."

She looked away. "I'm afraid that's not possible.

"Look at me," I yelled. "Tell me why!"

When she looked back, she seemed nervous. "Because you don't have that kind of power anymore, Thea."

"I don't understand. Why not?"

"I was hoping you could tell me why. Why you did it. Why you put us all in danger like that, for him."

"For who?"

"James," she yelled.

I didn't know what to say. I had no idea what I had done or why. "What the hell did I do?" I asked. "Please tell me."

"I would have to show you, and it's too dangerous."

"I don't care. I want to know what happened. Why I did what I did. Why I would put any of you in danger. I have to know, Delia."

"You may not want to know, Thea. Many of us were burned alive because of your choice." She paused. "And that's the easy part to hear."

My eyes filled with tears. If this was my fault, I didn't care if I died. I welcomed death if others had suffered because of me. Why would anyone want to protect me if I had done so much harm?

"Don't cry," she said, brushing a tear from my cheek. "If ever there was a witch with a reason, it would be you."

"Then tell me what I did. Why do they hate me?"

She stared at me for a moment. "Wait here."

When she returned, she held a small gold box in her hand. It was covered in sparkling rubies and sapphires. It looked like treasure. "I'll show you, but you must do as I say."

"What is that?" I asked, looking at the box.

"Your memories," she replied. "Every memory you asked me to keep safe."

"This is where you put my memory?" I asked.

"Not your memory, Thea. Just the memories you asked me to save."

I reached for the box and she jerked it away. "Before I show you what's inside, I must explain something first. Inside this box are memories you may not want me to see. But the only way I'll show them to you is if I'm present when you see them. You still don't remember who you are, and we must keep it that way—for now, anyway."

"Why?" I asked.

"Because if you remember who you are, they'll know where to find you. The hourglass would give away your location. I can't allow you to remember before the sands run out. You set them for a reason, Thea, and I won't change that. But I'll stall them for a while so you can learn the truth."

I looked at the box, not knowing if I wanted Delia to see my secrets. I realized I would have never given them to her if I didn't trust her completely.

"Show me."

"Just one thing before we begin," she said. "I'm going to start out slow, not show you too many at first. We have to be careful that they don't shock your memory back. If I see any signs of that, I will pull you right back out, understand?"

There had to be a reason I did all this. If I'd had her erase my memory, I would have to keep it that way. "Can you promise me, if you see my memory coming back, that you won't erase everything that's happened up to this point?"

"Thea, you can order me, you know. I have no choice but to listen."

"No, I want your promise as my friend, as someone who loves me."

"Then yes, my friend, I promise."

"Then I'm ready."

She smiled and stepped to my side. "Give me your hand. I'll be able to hear you, and vice versa. If you see something you'd rather not, just squeeze my hand, okay?"

I nodded.

As Delia carefully opened the box, crystal-clear clouds floated out of it. They looked like soap bubbles as they hovered above our heads. The clouds were filled with moving objects, which I quickly realized were people.

"Which one do you want to see first?" she asked as we both watched in amazement.

I spotted James leaning on a tree, smiling. "Show me that one," I said, pointing.

Delia rolled her eyes. "Of course you'd pick that one."

She reached for the cloud, which stuck to her skin like a soap bubble, and carefully brought it down to eye level. Before I knew what was happening, we were inside the bubble.

A breeze blew back my hair as the sun hit my face. Birds chirped, and I could smell the forest around us. I saw no houses, cars, or roads—only trees. It all felt so real; I was compelled to touch something. I reached for a tree.

Delia swiftly pulled me back. "We can't touch or change anything about the memories. We can only watch. They won't be able to see or hear us, so you can ask me questions." Then she pointed toward James.

He was leaning against a tree, arms crossed, clearly enjoying himself. He looked so young, his hair a bit longer, and he wore funny-looking clothes. His nose looked different, too; the scar was missing. His blue eyes sparkled. He looked so happy.

I turned to see what he was looking at. "It's me."

"Yes," Delia said. "You came here often, to pick wild mushrooms. Well, that was why you started coming here, anyway."

"What do you mean?"

She gestured again to James. "He's watching you. And you're pretending not to know he's there."

"I know he's there?"

"Shh," she said. "Just watch."

"I thought they couldn't hear us?"

"They can't. I just don't want you to miss anything."

The girl held a small basket in one hand as she dug around the base of a tree with the other. She looked at James through the strands of her long hair, and quickly looked back at the ground, smiling. Her soft curls were well-combed and shiny. She glanced in his direction again, and again quickly looked away. James smiled when he caught her looking his way.

As she worked, two men emerged from the trees directly behind her. They appeared to be hunters. They walked toward the girl, but she was too busy looking toward James.

"*Thou art pretty, little maiden,*" one of the hunters said.

The second hunter spoke. "*Yes, brother, and there is plenty for us both.*"

They laughed and stepped closer to the girl.

Startled, she dropped her basket and turned to face them. "*Noble lords, thou hast frightened me.*"

One of the men stepped behind her and sniffed her hair. "*She smells of wildflowers, my brother. What a treat this will be.*"

The girl raised her hand as if to wave it, but seemingly thought twice as she looked toward James.

"You could have taken care of them both in an instant," Delia said, rolling her eyes. "But you didn't want to scare away your admirer with your magic."

I looked to where James had been standing. He no longer leaned against the tree.

One of the men began unbuttoning his shirt. *"What say you, my brother? Shall I go first?"*

The other man came up from behind and grabbed the girl's arms. *"Where art thou going?"* he asked.

She struggled to break free of his grasp. *"Today thou shalt die, my lord,"* she said.

The man laughed, and his brother stepped closer.

Out of nowhere, James appeared and tackled the first man to the ground. The other man roughly threw the girl into a tree and ran to the aid of his brother. The girl looked on as the two men overpowered James, kicking and punching him as he tried to fight back.

The girl looked for a chance to help, to wave her hand and blast the men, but she couldn't get a clear shot at the two offenders without risking hitting James. As the three men wrestled, she took a chance. She waved her hand and managed to clip the shoulder of one of the men, but James's face took most of the hit.

"So that's how he got the scar on his nose."

"You knew he had that?" Delia asked.

"You can see it?"

"Yes, how can you miss it?"

We turned our attention back to the fight. James had been thrown back from the blast, but was now on his feet. He was obviously an experienced fighter, holding his own with the two men.

"We need to talk, Thea." She rolled her eyes as she watched the fight. "What a show-off."

"What do you mean?" I asked.

"Oh please," she said with annoyance. "Can't you see?" She gestured to the ongoing struggle between the three men. "He knows who you are and that you don't need his help. He's just trying to impress you."

"He knows?"

"Yes, and now you're going to pretend to faint, making him think he saved the day."

I watched as the girl waved her hand again, this time finding her mark. One of the men flew off James and landed on his back a few feet away. The other struggled free, pulled his brother to his feet, and together, they ran.

James stood watching as the two men disappeared into the forest. He looked back at the girl. "*My lady, thou bleeds,*" he said, walking toward her.

She placed her hand to her head, her fingers covered in blood. She let out a small gasp, then pretended to faint. Delia laughed as James ran to the girl, catching her before she hit the ground.

"*Thea!*" he said, reaching for her.

"He knows my name?"

"Of course he does," she said. "I told you, he knows who you are—all the male

68

witches do."

James held the girl, gently brushing the hair away from her face. "*My lady,*" he said, gently shaking her. His eyes tender, he touched her lips and continued stroking her hair. "*Upon this moment, I know I love thee,*" he whispered, then kissed her.

My heart raced as I thought of our passionate kiss—the first kiss I could remember.

She opened her eyes. "*To me thou speak of love, my lord?*"

Embarrassment flooded his face as he helped the girl to her feet. "*Forgive me, my lady,*" he said, stepping back.

"*Do I forgive thy words, or thy kiss?*"

He seemed genuinely surprised, as though he truly hadn't expected her to wake and realize what he'd done.

"*Perhaps a kiss is my lord's price for rescuing me?*" she asked.

He took a step closer and smiled. "*If this price thou pays willingly, then may a million hunters find thee.*"

Her eyes lit up. "*I will search the forest, my kind lord, and dance in danger's face if it will bring thee to me, if it will prompt thee to kiss me again.*"

He smiled and stepped closer. "*If danger shows not its face, what say thee to the price then? What then, maiden? Wilt thou still pay with a kiss?*" Without giving her a chance to answer, he took her face in his hands and kissed her.

She threw her arms around his neck and

kissed him back. "*My lord is hurt,*" she said between kisses.

"*But thy kiss will heal me,*" he said, never leaving her lips.

My heart raced faster, and my head began to spin.

Suddenly, I felt air blowing from somewhere behind me. In an instant, we were back in Delia's house. The memory clouds still floated over our heads.

"I was afraid of that," Delia said, letting go of my hand. "You have to keep your emotions in check, Thea. You were shaking."

My heart pounded as I thought of our kiss. "He loves me," I whispered, turning to Delia. "You said I still didn't know who he was."

"Now, how did I know you would ask me that?"

"Tell me," I demanded nervously. "Who is he?"

"He was one of them, one of the many who hunted us."

I started to ask a question, but Delia raised her hand. "Relax. He didn't know they were killing us. He actually started helping us." She sat down at the table and motioned for me to sit.

"I don't understand," I said. "Why don't you like him?"

She seemed uncomfortable. "It's not important. Besides, I don't like anyone. You know that."

I looked at the memory clouds still floating in the room. "I have too many questions. I think I'd rather see for myself now that I know you can show me."

She tapped the table. "We have to talk first."

"What is it?"

"You said you knew he had that scar on his nose—can you see it?"

I leaned forward. "What do you mean, can I see it?"

"What color are his eyes, Thea?" she asked, raising her voice. "What color hair does he have?"

I didn't understand the reason for her questions. "His eyes are blue. His hair is dark brown. Why?"

"And how old is he?"

I stared at her, bewildered. "I'm not sure, but he looks to be in his early twenties." I was starting to lose patience. "Why?"

She ignored my question and walked out of the room. Moments later, she returned with a pen and a piece of paper. "When I say his name, what do you hear?" She handed me the pen. "I want you to write it down."

I looked at the piece of paper, confused.

"Just do it, Thea. It's important."

I wrote the name *James* and set down the pen.

Delia snatched the slip of paper and read it. Her eyes widened, her face turning red. "I knew it!"

"What?" I asked. "What did you know?"

"You are a clever witch, Thea. A very clever witch, indeed."

"What are you talking about?" I asked,

more confused than ever.

She hurriedly wrote on the piece of paper. "When I see James, I see a slightly overweight, thirty-nine-year-old man with blonde hair. And when I say his name, this is what comes out of my mouth." She pushed the piece of paper toward me.

Delia had written the name *Steve*. "I don't understand."

"You clever little witch," she said, shaking her head. "You knew he'd be back, didn't you?"

I didn't answer and kept looking at the paper.

"Don't you see?" she asked. "You made sure you'd always know it was him."

"You think I had a good reason for doing that?"

She looked at the clouds and back at me. "I don't know. You ready to go find out? Do you think you can keep your emotions in check?"

"Yes," I replied.

"Are you sure? Because it only gets worse."

I was thinking about James, but tried to focus. We didn't have much time. I stood up. "I'll be fine."

I followed Delia back to the memory clouds. I looked at my friend, my trusted guard. "Which one do you think we should go to next?" I asked.

Delia surveyed the crystal-like bubbles carefully. "I think this one might help." Again, I felt wind blowing. I closed my eyes and waited. Moments later, I heard someone speaking.

"*I see no valid evidence brought before this court,*" the voice said.

I opened my eyes. "A courtroom?"

"Yes," Delia said. "There's a woman being accused of being a witch." She motioned with her head to where the woman stood. The woman's hands were secured in front of her with ropes. Her head was down, her clothes dirty and torn.

"*This woman be not a witch,*" I heard a familiar voice say. A man, dressed in black and wearing a long white wig, sat high on a bench with three others at his side. As I focused on his face, I saw that it was James.

"He's a judge?" I asked, turning to Delia.

But the voice of another man diverted my attention. "*Who brings forth this woman?*"

My mouth fell open as two familiar figures emerged from the back of the courtroom—the hunters. I turned to look at the girl whose hands were bound. She lifted her head.

"It's me," I gasped.

"Yes, and do you recognize the prosecutor?" she asked, motioning.

My heart sank. "The short man from the pier."

"The very one," she said. "The one we're reasonably certain is Simon. He's persuaded them to accuse you of being a witch. They burned people they thought to be witches back then. Sometimes they stoned them to death."

"Why did I allow them to capture me?" I

asked. "Why don't I just wave my hand and get out of this?"

"Because you can't," she explained. "You stored half your powers in the crystal and no one knows why."

I looked at the girl—at myself. She looked at James with a deep sadness in her eyes. "Why would I do that?"

"That question has haunted me for four hundred years," Delia replied.

"*She's a witch,*" one of the hunters shouted, pointing at the girl.

"*My brother speaks the truth,*" the second hunter chimed in. "*And a friend have she to help her.*"

"*What be his name?*" the short man asked.

My heart raced. I was sure they would point to James. It was then that I realized that James looked different from the way he looked in the other memory. "They don't recognize him, do they?" I asked.

"No," she said. "That was weeks ago. Besides, they never got a good look at him."

James spoke again. "*What did she of witchery?*" he asked. "*Thou hast yet to show proof.*"

The short man banged his hand on the table. "They witnessed firsthand her witchery," he shouted. He walked to one of the hunters and pulled the shirt down from his shoulder. "For here is her mark," he said, scanning the courtroom.

The room filled with gasps as the hunter slowly walked around the court, parading his wound, eventually resuming his place beside his brother. "*It was a flying dagger thrown by the witch,*" he said, once again pointing at the girl.

"*She casts evil spells on us,*" the other man yelled.

"They're lying!" I said to Delia.

"Of course they are," she replied, rolling her eyes. "They also said you flew through the air. They have no idea," she said, shaking her head.

One of the three men sitting near James spoke. "*It is the mark of witchery,*" he said angrily. "*Burn her!*"

"*No,*" James said, rising to his feet. "*This maiden is not a witch.*" He turned to the girl. "*Do something!*" he yelled.

The girl just bowed her head and began to cry.

"*She burns, then,*" another man said, banging his gavel.

"*No!*" James yelled again, still looking at the girl. "*Why are you just sitting there?*"

One of the men jumped to his feet and stepped in front of James. "*She burns!*" he said, jabbing his finger into James's chest. "*You will do well to agree with us.*"

"*Thou art mistaken,*" James said.

"*Take her away!*" the short man yelled.

My body trembled with rage as I raised my hand to help James. Delia blocked my arm. I pushed her hand away, realizing we were back in her house. I was so confused. Why didn't James grab me and run? I struggled to breathe. "Why was I there? Why didn't he help me? Why didn't he do something?"

Delia hurried to my side. "Because he didn't know what you had done with the crystal. He thought you could just wave your hand and save yourself."

I pushed her away. A sharp zap shook my body. Flashes of light rushed through my head as I felt another zap. Images raced through my mind. I shook my head, trying to cast them off, but it didn't help. I pushed against the wall in horror as I saw needles piercing my feet. I saw James, still wearing his robe, cutting ropes from my wrists. Then the vision changed, and James was dragging me out of a hole in the ground. I was covered in blood, and half my hair had been pulled out. I gasped as I realized what was happening; I was remembering who I was. I turned to Delia for help.

Powder blew into my face. I couldn't move or see, but I could hear Delia chanting: "These last five minutes I erase, leaving calmness in its place. I put these memories back inside, the truth for now we'll have to hide."

I didn't block her spell this time; it was too soon for me to remember. I allowed the calm to wash over me as my mind drifted away.

I heard Delia calling someone as I collapsed to the floor. "Get over here," she said, and slammed down the phone.

I could sense myself drifting. I could no longer feel the floor. Delia frantically ran around the house. Her feet blurred as I finally lost consciousness.

Delia's voice roused me from an odd dream. "Thea, you awake?" she asked, gently shaking me. "You're home now."

I opened my eyes and found myself in my own bed.

Delia looked worried. "You okay?"

"What happened?" I asked, trying to get out of bed.

"Get some rest, now," she said, gently pushing me back down. "I just wanted to make sure you were okay." She began taking off her shoes. "I'm staying here tonight. I think I should stay close to you from now on." I noticed she'd already made herself a bed on the floor—a bunch of blankets piled on top of each other.

I tried to think of how I came to be in bed, but couldn't remember anything. "Are you going to tell me what happened?"

"After you passed out, a witch from the council called in a panic because the sands moved again." She looked at me. "I think you're making them move, Thea, and that they're causing these flashbacks. I think your memory is coming back, and you're the one who's making it happen."

I pushed the blankets off. "I had a flashback?"

"Judging by the look I saw in your eyes, I'm fairly certain."

"What about the hourglass?" I asked. "I thought we stalled it."

"Do you remember when I told you that you could sense the future like your father did?"

I nodded.

"Well, I think you knew when you would need your memory to come back. It seems the sands won't be stopped, even by you." She got up and walked over to the window. "I think you're trying to hide something—not from me, but from them." She looked at me. "I had to erase what you saw in that flashback, because it was restoring your memory."

"Was it bad?" I asked.

She stepped away from the window. "That's not important right now. You get some rest. We'll try again after work."

"Work? Are you kidding me?"

"No, Thea. It's best you go to work. James might come looking for you if you aren't following your usual routine. I still don't trust him."

"Why don't you like him?"

"I told you," she said, slipping into the blankets on the floor. "I don't like anyone."

"Delia, thanks for keeping your promise and only erasing what you needed to."

She was quiet for a moment. "I wish I could erase all the bad things that happened to you, Thea, but I know one day you'll remember it all."

"Just don't ever erase him. I can handle everything else, but not that."

She sighed. "Get some rest, Thea."

I switched off the light and tried to sleep. I thought about how I was able to control the objects in my room. I couldn't have put too much of my magic into that crystal, because I still seemed to have a great deal of power. I was driving myself crazy wondering what Delia had erased today. Whatever it was, it made her nervous. I couldn't fight the nagging feeling that she was holding something back, glossing over things. I vowed to pry the truth from her tomorrow.

My mind thoroughly exhausted, I closed my eyes and drifted off.

Chapter 5
The Flashback

I nearly stepped on Delia as I dragged myself out of bed. It was still dark outside and too early to leave for work. I flipped on the bathroom light and surveyed myself in the mirror: dark circles under swollen eyes, hair messier than ever. Although the thought of going into the bakery was daunting, Delia was right; I should go about life as usual. James would come looking for me if he suspected something was wrong.

Despite the early hour, I decided to shower and ready myself for work. As I closed my eyes and allowed the hot water to hit my face, I felt a sharp zap. I pushed myself against the shower wall as vivid images rushed into my mind.

~~~

"How dost thou open it?"

I knelt before a wooden barrel filled with water, my hands bound behind my back. I held my breath as my head was forced into the barrel and held under. Moments later, my head was wrenched out of the water. I gasped for air before I was pushed under again. Two men stood on either side of me, eyes closed, chanting spells to block my own. The rope around my neck pulled tighter, and again, my head was yanked from the barrel.

"Tell me the chant that opens the crystal!" the man ordered me.

Another man spoke up from behind me. "Remember, Simon," he said, "thou must not allow her to touch the crystal."

"Silence!" the man called Simon yelled. He leaned closer, his lips brushing my ear as he spoke. "I shall find a way—with or without thy help, witch."

He ordered the man to pull on the rope. My neck burned as I gasped for breath. I wanted to scream, but I vowed to remain silent. I would not give him the satisfaction.

Simon grabbed a fistful of my hair, pulled it out by the root, and deposited it into a black velvet bag. He stepped aside and instructed his men to follow suit. As handfuls of hair were viciously torn from my scalp, my pain was no longer manageable.

Simon smiled as I screamed. "The sound of thy cries gives me pleasure, witch," he said, stroking my face. "And I plan on being pleasured all night."

Simon produced a long needle and held it before me. He reached down, lifted my leg at the ankle, and smiled as he drove the needle into my foot.

"No!" I screamed.

Simon reached for another needle and repeated the torture. Every time I screamed, he

*smiled. "Perhaps next time thou wilt pick
another husband," he said, inserting another.
He turned to one of his men. "Bring me the
longer needles!"*

~~~

The sound of my screams filled my head.
I clamped my hands over my ears and sank to
my knees.

"Thea! What's wrong?"

Delia's voice drew me out of the
flashback. She turned off the water, wrapped
me in a towel, and helped me out of the shower.

"She's fine," I heard her say to someone
standing at the bathroom door. "Go back
downstairs."

"Thea, why were you screaming?" she
asked, leading me back to my room.

I sat on the bed, shivering, tears
streaming down my face. I leaned my head on
Delia's shoulder. "This is too much for me,
Delia. I don't know if I can handle it," I said,
going into a complete sob.

Delia took me in her arms and rocked
me. She didn't say another word until I'd cried
my last tear. "I'm here, my friend," she said.
"I'll never let them hurt you again." She rubbed
my back. "Hey, I didn't know you were such a
crybaby," she teased. "I didn't even know you
had tears." She rose to her feet. "Now, let's get
you some clothes, shall we?" She walked to my
closet and opened the door. "So, what was with
all the screaming?" she asked, pulling out a pair
of jeans and handing them to me.

I grabbed the pants from her. "I think it
was a flashback," I said, choking on a fresh

bout of sobs. "I was being tortured."

Delia sat down next to me. "Do you want me to erase it from your memory?"

I shuddered from the horror of the memory, but I didn't want her to erase it. I needed to know everything that had happened to me, no matter how disturbing. "No," I said, rising from the bed. "I can handle it."

Delia smiled and jumped to her feet. "That's my good little witch. I'll walk with you to the bakery," she said, slipping on her shoes. "And I'll pick you up after work."

I finished getting dressed, and we headed to the bakery. The day was going to be difficult, but I felt the truth getting closer. The memory of Simon and his men flashed through my mind. Delia seemed to be avoiding the subject. I was afraid to learn more, but I couldn't hide from the truth.

"Delia, can I ask you something?"

"What is it?"

I took a deep breath. "What else did those men do to me?"

Delia continued walking, staring straight ahead.

"I can handle it," I said. "I need to know."

She sighed and looked at me. "Why? How will it help?"

"Because if I understand my past, I stand a better chance at fixing what's happening now."

She refocused her gaze on the road ahead. "I've often wondered what they did to you. It took James two days to find you, and when he did, you were nearly mad." She looked at me. "You should be happy you can't remember it."

"They had me for two days?" I asked, stunned.

"Yes. At the end of that day in court, James set you free. They almost killed him for releasing you. He practically lost his mind when you went missing later that same day. When he finally found you, you were covered in dirt, and your entire body was black and blue. You gave us orders to wipe your memory clean, and ran about casting spells on things—the hourglass, for one." She stopped walking and faced me. "You wouldn't tell us why, and you made us promise to obey your orders.

"Then you did something I still don't understand," she said. "You sent him away. He begged you not to, but you cast a spell and made him leave." She paused. "You told me repeatedly not to let him near you."

"James?" I asked, shocked. "I made James leave?"

She nodded. "He pleaded, but you wouldn't back down. And your magic was stronger. He had no choice."

We started walking again.

"After he left," she continued, "you told me never to leave your side, and to erase your memory. You asked me to keep your thoughts occupied; giving you books to read was the only thing I could think of."

"So it was James who found me when I went missing?"

"Yes, but you forgot one thing," she said.

"Before you went missing, you'd put half your powers into the crystal. No one knows why you did it."

"What would make me do that? What reason could I have possibly had?" I stopped and turned to Delia. "Why do you think I did it?"

She looked at me. "I think you did it for James," she replied. "But let's not get into that right now. I don't feel like getting upset."

"Where is the hourglass now?"

"It's on the ship, safe. We cast numerous spells on it so it can't be moved."

"The pirate ship?" I asked.

Delia laughed. "It's not a pirate ship, Thea. It was the only home we had at one time." She shook her head. "I'm sorry. I keep forgetting this is all new to you."

"I thought Simon had the hourglass."

"No. He did cast a spell on it, though. We don't know how he was able to get close to it, or how he even found out about it."

"Is my memory in that hourglass?"

"No one knows. You put a spell on it and told me to guard it with my life."

"Maybe James knows," I said. "We should ask him."

"How about we don't," Delia snapped.

I still couldn't understand her disdain for him. "Delia, why don't you like James?"

"I don't think you want to hear the answer to that question. I have nothing nice to say about him."

The mere thought of her saying something bad about James made me want to hurt her. I decided to leave it alone for now, but vowed to get to the bottom of Delia's hatred for the man I loved. We walked the rest of the way to the bakery in silence. It was still early; Norm hadn't arrived yet. I pulled a set of keys from my pocket and let myself in. "This is weird. I'm never here before Norm."

Delia walked in and headed straight for the coffee machine. "How do you work this thing?"

I turned on the ovens and focused my gaze at the machine. "Coffee, make yourself." I winked at Delia.

Delia started giggling and suddenly stopped. "Thea, you just gave me an idea," she said excitedly. "Do you think Norm would let you leave early if all the work was done?"

I knew what she was thinking. I scanned the bakery, my eyes coming to rest again on Delia.

"How should I do it?" I asked.

"Just say exactly what you need—seems to work."

"Look out for Norm," I said as I perused the day's orders. "I need a hundred dozen spider cookies and twenty-five chocolate cakes, boxed up."

I finished reading the long list of orders, grabbed a cup of coffee, and sat down across from Delia, who sipped from her own mug. We watched in delight as flour poured from sacks and eggs cracked themselves over waiting bowls. We giggled as pastry dough rolled itself out and cut itself into squares, and cakes floated into ovens.

"Why do you suppose Norm isn't here yet?" Delia asked, looking out the window.

I stood behind the counter and ordered some muffins out of the oven. "I don't know," I replied, concerned. "He's never been this late."

The phone rang, and I picked it up.

"Thea?"

Finally! "Norm, I was worried."

"I'm fine," he answered. "Well, mostly. I'm feeling a little under the weather today. Can you close the bakery early, after all the orders are picked up?"

I couldn't believe my luck. "Are you sure you're okay?"

"I think it's the flu," he replied. "Don't close until the orders are picked up, okay?"

He hung up before I could answer. I relayed the news to Delia.

"You're stuck here, then?" she asked.

"Well, I can close early, but not until all the orders are picked up." I looked over the long list of orders for pickup.

"What are we going to do now?" Delia ran her fingers through her hair. "I know! I'll go and get the box. We can open it in the back room."

I glanced in the direction of the back room. "Is it safe?" I wasn't altogether comfortable with the idea, but I trusted Delia.

To my surprise, Delia pulled a cell phone out of her bag. "I'll call Vera over. She can deal with the customers. Just make sure everything's boxed up and ready to go."

"Since when do you have a cell phone?"

"Since yesterday," she answered, waving

me off.

Delia usually rejected modern technology. That she possessed a cell phone at all was surprising, but even more so was that she knew how to use it. I observed her curiously for a moment as she spoke into the phone, but I didn't want to waste any more time. Now, more than ever, I wanted to visit my memories. I resumed my commands and supervised as the cake boxes folded themselves.

I heard Delia's phone snap shut. "I'm going to have to go and speak to Vera in person," she said with annoyance. "Stupid witch thinks I'm calling her over here to turn her into something."

"Can you blame her?"

Delia was all business. "Not sure how long I'll be. Stay put till I get back, okay?" She turned and walked out.

I wondered again how safe it was to open the box in the bakery. I didn't know what others could see when we were in the memory clouds. I spent the morning making sure all the orders were completed and ready to be picked up. Delia was taking longer than I had anticipated. I decided to get a jump on cleaning up the place to keep myself busy until she returned. I was sweeping behind the counter when the door opened and an odd scent hit me. An unfamiliar man entered the bakery.

"May I help you?" I asked.

He walked to the coffee machine and poured himself a cup. "Just a cup of coffee and a doughnut," he said, stepping up to the counter.

I leaned over and opened the display

case. "Any kind?"

When he didn't answer, I looked up to find him staring in the direction of the back room, his mouth open.

Puzzled, I glanced over my shoulder. My heart leaped into my throat. I had completely forgotten I had things moving on their own. Cakes were boxing themselves up, and muffins were flying out of the ovens. Before I could look back at him, he jumped over the counter and grabbed my neck with both hands. I fought to free myself as he tightened his grip. He punched me, and panic flooded my body as I struggled to think of a command to stop him.

He blew a fistful of powder at me. I tried not to inhale. His face was right up against mine, and I could feel his breath on my lips. He quickly chanted: "Tell me now, tell me fast, are you the witch lost from the past?"

I blocked his spell, but felt myself blacking out. I couldn't think straight. With his hands still on my neck, he pushed me toward the back of the bakery. "I'll make you talk, witch," he hissed, as he kicked my feet out from under me.

I struggled to breathe as he dragged me away, my mind losing focus. I hit his hands with all my strength, but he was stronger. He threw me onto a table and started pounding my head. Then everything that had been moving stopped. Cake-filled boxes, on route to the counter, dropped to the floor. Ovens were shutting down.

"Tell me the chant that opens the crystal, witch!"

He squeezed my neck tighter, and I began to slip into darkness. I was able to breathe when he suddenly removed one of his hands from my neck.

"How do you open it?" he said, punching me. "Tell me now before you die, witch."

I knew I was about to die. I could hardly keep my eyes open. He threw me to the floor and dragged me toward the back door. I knew he wanted to get me out of here, maybe take me to Simon. Then something flashed in front of me, and all at once, the force on my neck was gone. Though his hands were still around my neck, I was no longer choking from his grip.

Suddenly, Delia was at my side. She chanted at the hands to release me. It was then I realized that the hands around my neck had been severed. The man's body had fallen to the floor. Horrified, I began to scream, but the sound of James's voice quickly silenced my cries.

"Beg like you once made her beg!" James shouted.

James was holding a gold whip in his hand and cutting the man to pieces with it. The man screamed with every lashing. He tried to drag himself away, but James kept pulling him back. "Is this what you were going to do to her?" James yelled as he whipped the man again.

The man went quiet and still. Then the hands around my neck turned to dust. I looked to where the man was hunched on the floor, and the rest of him also turned to dust. James looked at me, the whip still in his hand. He shook the weapon and it, too, vanished. James now held what looked like a small knife.

My eyes filled with tears, and I dragged myself away from Delia and James. Huge, choking sobs escaped me as I rolled into a ball in a corner.

In an instant, James was at my side. He held up his hand to Delia, signaling her to back off. "She's frightened," he said, sliding the knife into his pocket. "Stay where you are."

When he knelt in front of me, I backed up and buried my face in my hands. My face was bloodied, and my throat burned.

"Thea, it's over, sweetheart," James said softly. "He's gone." He slowly inched toward me.

I shook my head and backed farther away from him.

"I'm here, my love. You're safe now." Again, James moved closer. He reached out and brushed the hair away from my face.

I looked into his eyes and threw myself into his arms. The moment we touched, I felt safe, and something inside of me rejoiced.

He wrapped his arms tightly around me and kissed my head as I cried. "I'm here, my love," he whispered. "I've got you." He loosened his embrace and lifted my head. He looked pained as he examined my battered face. His eyes closed as he pulled me back into his arms and began stroking my hair.

Delia stood a few feet away, clearly shaken. "I'm so sorry," she said quietly, and walked out of the room. I knew she felt guilty for leaving me alone, but it wasn't her fault.

James started to lift me up into his arms.

"No," I said, my voice hoarse. "I'm too heavy."

"You're in pain," he said. "Don't talk." He lifted me into his arms and walked out of the back room. He stopped at the counter where Delia stood in a daze, staring out the front window. "Are you coming, or do I need to use one of my spells?"

I understood that he was asking her if he needed to use a spell of his own to erase my memory. He still had no idea that I had the power to stop the spells.

Delia shook her head. "Don't bother. I even messed that up."

"What do you mean?" he asked.

She looked toward the back room. "I'll clean things up here and join you both later after I close the place." Without another word, she walked into the back room.

"Can you stand?" James asked me.

I nodded, and he set me down.

"Wait here," he said, following Delia into the back.

"What kind of guard am I?" I heard Delia say as James stepped through the doorway. "This is my fault. I even forgot about the spell I put on her back at your house."

James cleared his throat. "I suppose I should explain how she was able to free herself from your—"

"I know all about it," she said, cutting him off. "Thea told me. Did you know she used it on you, too? She remembers everything you told her."

"I don't understand. I—"

"She knows who she is, James. She knows who you are, too."

He looked halfway over his shoulder. "It appears we need to talk. I'll take her home and wait for you there."

I heard Delia sniff back tears. "I'll be there as soon as I can. Vera should be here any minute to help. Don't leave her alone," Delia warned. "She's scared to death."

"I understand," James replied. "Just hurry, so you can explain what's going on. I need to know exactly just how much she remembers."

I quietly inched away from the counter and peered into the back room. I was surprised to see that James had his hand on Delia's shoulder. "There was nothing you could have done to prevent this," he said.

She looked up at him. I was shocked when Delia threw herself into James's arms and sobbed. I understood her need for comfort, but couldn't shake the uneasiness I felt at the two of them sharing such a tender moment.

"You've been more than a guard to her, Delia. You've been like a sister." He tipped her chin up with his fingers. "You can't blame yourself for what happened today."

She looked into his eyes for a moment, then quickly pushed herself away. "Go to her," she said, turning her back on him. "She needs you."

"Delia—" he said, stepping forward.

"Just go," she cried. "Please."

He sighed and looked down. "I'm truly

sorry, Delia. Sorry for any pain that—"

"Get out of here!" she yelled. "Please leave."

James slowly turned and left the room. I didn't ask him any questions when he returned. I didn't need him to explain what I could see for myself: Delia loved him. It was clear something had happened between them—but what?

"Let's get you home," James said, putting his arm around me.

I glanced over my shoulder. Delia stood in the back room doorway, her backed turned to us.

"I'll be waiting for you," I said to her.

She waved her hand over her head, and James and I walked out of the bakery.

In the car, I noticed we weren't headed in the direction of my apartment. "Where are you taking me?" I whispered, my throat still burning.

He flashed me a smile. "Why, I'm taking you home."

I looked at him, confused.

"Your real home," he said, reaching for my hand. "We'll get you cleaned up when we get there."

Moments later, his phone rang. He glanced at the number on the screen and flipped it open. "Yes?" A long pause. "I see." He looked over at me. "That's good to know—and it works?"

I eyed him as he spoke. I couldn't believe he was my husband. I was still staring at him when he thanked whoever it was and snapped the phone shut.

"Who was that?" I asked, my voice cracking.

He set down the phone and took my hand again. "Please don't talk. Your voice sounds terribly strained."

When we reached his house, he opened the car door and swept me up in his arms. "Welcome home," he said, smiling widely.

How is he able to carry me so easily?

"William!" James yelled as he walked inside and set me on the couch.

"Yes, master?" a voice said.

"Bring some tea and towels, please," James ordered.

"Right away, master," the butler replied. "Is the girl hurt, sir?"

"All is well, William. But she needs some healing tea."

"I'll bring it at once, master."

I couldn't see the butler, but I could smell him.

"I'm going to give you something for the swelling," James said, gently examining my neck. "There's a lot of bruising on your face, as well." He sat next to me. "Are you in pain, querida?"

I shook my head and looked down at my hands. "I like it when you call me that."

He smiled. "I've spoken nothing but Spanish for the last hundred years. I have to keep reminding myself where I am, but that word always makes me think of you."

I was about to ask him why, but the awful smell hit me again.

"Your tea and towels, sir."

James took the towels from the butler. "That will be all, William."

But the butler didn't leave. "What happened to the girl, master?"

James rose to his feet and stepped in front of me. "The girl is fine, William. Please prepare a room for her." He motioned with his head for the butler to leave.

"As you wish, master."

William stared at me for a long moment, turned, and left the room.

James sat down again and offered me the cup. "It will help your throat," he said. He looked above my head and nodded. I attempted to glance over my shoulder to see who he was acknowledging, but he grabbed my chin gently. "Drink," he said, pushing the cup toward my mouth.

I took a sip of the tea and set the cup down. James picked it up and handed it to me again. "Please, drink. It will help with the swelling."

Again, I took the tea from him, this time drinking the entire cup. The room began to spin, and my vision blurred. The cup slipped from my hand as James lifted me into his arms.

"Why?" I asked before everything went dark.

Chapter 6
The Heart

I opened my eyes, and the smell hit me. I jumped out of bed and looked around.

"Is madam well?" the butler said from his seat in the corner of the room.

"Where is James? And what are you doing here?" I asked.

"Forgive me, madam," he said, getting to his feet. "I was told to watch over you." He bowed his head. "I will go and tell master that you are awake."

He shuffled to the door and turned back. "Is madam feeling better?" he asked.

I held my hand up to cover my nose; his foul odor was much stronger than that of the others. "Yes, better," I said, realizing my throat was no longer sore.

He nodded once and left the room.

I ran and locked the door behind him. I didn't know what to make of him. My heart still pounding, I leaned against the door. "Where are you, Delia?" I said out loud.

Seconds later, I heard footsteps in the hall. I double-checked the lock and backed away from the door. Someone knocked, and I jumped.

"Thea?"

I threw open the door. "Delia!" I cried, falling into her arms.

Delia seemed surprised. "Are you okay?"

"They gave me something, and I fell asleep. The butler, he was in here, just staring at me."

Delia chuckled and pulled away.

"Why are you laughing?" I asked, annoyed.

She shook her head and walked past me into the room. "I'm just not used to you being so—so nervous. It's okay. James needed you to sleep so his healing potion could work quickly." She pointed at my neck. "It feels better, right?"

I rubbed my neck and nodded.

"James asked William to stay with you while he and I talked downstairs." She walked over to me. "Thea, James would never leave you alone with someone he didn't trust completely."

I bit my lip. "I was rude to him—the butler."

"That's the least of our problems," she said, taking a seat on the bed.

"What do you mean?"

"Like I said, James and I talked. He told me what's been happening on his end."

I sat down next to her. "What do you mean—his end?"

She sighed. "You know how I don't see James the way you see him?"

I nodded.

"Many years ago," she said, "James killed one of Simon's men. He then acquired the dead man's identity, and has since been passing himself off as the man to gather information from the others."

"So they see him the way you see him?" I asked.

"Yes," she replied. "It was a spell you taught him. Unlike Vera's potions, the spell can't be broken. It took James a long time to get it right. But that's not the important part, Thea." She withdrew a piece of paper from her pocket. "They sent him this today. He received it just before he went looking for you."

She handed me the note. A strange feeling swept over me when I touched it. I held the note up to my nose and quickly pulled it away. The offensive odor was so strong it made my eyes water.

"What's wrong?" Delia asked.

I didn't answer and read the note.

Smile, my brothers, for today the crystal shines once more. Her memory comes soon, and we must wait and listen for the hourglass to lead us to her. Soon we will have the power within the crystal. Soon she will be dead, and we will have reason to celebrate.

"They know I'm starting to remember?" I asked, shocked.

"I think so," Delia answered.

I read the note again. "Why is the crystal shining?"

"I can answer that," James said from the doorway.

My heart raced as he walked in the room, but not because I was happy to see him. It was something else.

"How is our patient feeling?" he asked, smiling.

I touched my neck and smiled back. "Much better. Thank you."

He examined my neck and seemed pleased. "When Delia told me about your flashbacks, I finally understood why the crystal was glowing. I believe the crystal can feel its owner coming back. The glow is how it helps you to locate it."

I rose from the bed. "Then I should go and find it. Open it and get my powers back."

Delia laughed. "Now why didn't we think of that?" she asked sarcastically.

James shot Delia a look. "I'm afraid it's not that easy, Thea," he said.

"Why not?"

"Because you transferred half your powers into the crystal," he explained. "And without your full powers, Simon's men could kill you. The crystal is well protected. Simon has many men expecting you to walk in. They've been training for hundreds of years to fight you." He glanced at Delia. "Some assume you did it for me, to give me half those powers when you reopened the crystal."

Delia snorted. "Some still assume that," she said, giving James a dirty look.

James ignored her. "If you remember who you are now, not being fully prepared, Simon's spell would lead them directly to you. They could force you to open the crystal and steal your powers."

That strange feeling swept over me again as James gently brushed my cheek with the back of his fingers. "They can steal the powers from the crystal?" I asked.

"Once opened," he said, "you can give the powers to whomever you wish. This is why so many assume you did it for me. Your powers would make me stronger than a warlock."

"And is that why I did it?" I asked. "To give them to you?"

"Yes, James," Delia spoke up. "Tell us, is that why?"

James seemed hurt and was obviously uncomfortable with the question. "I never wanted that from you," he said. He looked at Delia. "And despite what you might think, I would have never taken that gift from her, even if she'd begged me to."

Delia laughed. "Oh please, James. You would have been on cloud—"

"Stop it," I snapped, cutting her off. "I believe him." I looked at James and took his hand in mine. Again, I felt that strange feeling as I touched him. "I don't care what others assume. I believe you."

"Thank you," he answered. "But you did have a reason for placing your powers into that crystal, and we need to find out what it is." He walked toward the door. "I think it's time for you and Delia to visit some more memories.

Maybe you'll find some answers."

Delia pulled out the box.

I held up my hand. "Wait," I said, looking at James. "You said you would have magic like mine if I chose you. What makes them think I'll give them my powers?"

James looked at Delia. "Why haven't you explained this to her?"

Delia remained silent, seeming suddenly nervous.

"Thea," James said, "what you did with the crystal can only be achieved when certain moons are aligned. It sometimes takes hundreds of years for the proper circumstances to present themselves. We're fairly sure that it can only be opened in the same way. This particular crystal is rare, and is used to give the gift of magic. Only someone like you can use it or understand how it works—how it opens and closes. It's what you can't remember that's kept you alive."

"I still don't understand why I would have placed half my powers into it."

"No one knows," James said. "But you must have had a very good reason, especially considering how long it takes to reopen it." He paused and looked into my eyes. "Thea, Simon wants those powers. Someone betrayed you and told him what you'd done with the crystal. They took it to him after you had transferred your powers to it. When Simon realized he couldn't open it himself, he began hunting for you."

What James told me didn't make sense. "If only I know how to open it, why would they think I would just hand over my powers?"

"Simon doesn't realize that only you can

open the crystal," James explained. "He thinks he only needs to know the spell you used on it. He believes that once he's performed the spell, he would have access to your powers. This is why he's so hell-bent on finding you—to get you to reveal the spell."

"Is my memory in that crystal?" I asked.

"I don't know," James replied. "I don't even know why you transferred your powers to it."

"Why do you *think* I did it?"

He looked into my eyes, seemingly searching for an answer. "I've been asking myself that question for hundreds of years," he finally replied.

"What was going on in my life at that time?" I asked. "Did something happen?"

James didn't answer. He looked down at the floor.

"You're not going to tell me, are you?"

He finally looked up. "I think it's best that you visit the memories you asked Delia to keep safe. Perhaps you'll find your answers there."

I looked at Delia. "Why didn't you tell me any of this?"

She looked down at the box. "I'd planned to tell you," she said. "But things kept happening, and you seemed so overwhelmed. I didn't want to scare you."

She was lying. I felt it. Before I could question her, we were interrupted by a knock on the bedroom door. James opened it.

"Master, you have a phone call."

"Thank you, William," James replied.

"Give me just a moment. I'll be right down."

William nodded and walked back down the hall. I could still smell him as he walked down the stairs.

"Why does he smell so much stronger than you guys?" I asked, waving my hand in front of my nose.

James and Delia exchanged confused glances.

"Smell?" James asked.

"Yes, smell," I replied. "His smell is more pungent than the two of you put together."

Delia looked at James. "I have no idea what she's talking about."

"What exactly do you smell, Thea?" James asked.

"Mostly, I smell rotten apples," I said, turning to James. "But your scent is different—sweet, pleasant."

"You can smell us?" he asked, confused.

"Yes, I can smell all of you," I replied. "Why, can't you smell each other?"

"No," James said, looking away from me.

Delia walked over to me. "Thea, did you smell that guy at the bakery today?"

"Yeah," I replied. "Like I said, I can smell all of you."

Delia looked at James. "What do you think this means?"

James ignored her and remained focused on me. "And you're saying that William smells stronger than we do?"

"Yes, and also that man you were with at the pier that day," I answered. "And I also felt these sharp zaps whenever he stood near me."

James stepped closer. "Zaps?" he asked, his face reddening. "You mean like electric shocks?"

"Yes," I answered.

"You never told me that," Delia said.

I struggled to recall the conversation. "I must have left that part out," I offered. "Why, what was it? Was he attacking me or something?"

"Delia," James said, ignoring my question, "I think it's time to visit Thea's memories. I'll be back a little later." He walked out of the room and closed the door behind him.

Suddenly, flashes of James darted through my head. I felt as though I was seeing the future, a vision of what was to come. I closed my eyes. Two men beat James and threw him into the water. The scene changed, and I saw three men chanting, summoning a traitor. Instantly, I knew that this was where James was headed. I wasn't sure why, but I knew I couldn't let him go.

"It's about time," Delia said, pulling out the box again.

I ignored her and ran from the room. "Wait!" I yelled.

James was walking down the stairs. He stopped and turned. "Is everything okay?"

Another vision entered my head. The men were beating him again and forcing him to drink a potion. They celebrated because the spell had worked, and James had shown his face. I tried not to panic. I didn't want him to see how nervous I was.

James walked back up the stairs. "Thea, is something wrong?"

I looked up at the ceiling as tears rolled down my cheeks.

"Don't be frightened," he said, alarmed.

But it wasn't fear for myself that was troubling me, it was fear for him. The note—from the moment I touched it, I felt something inside of me wake up. It carried the same scent William emitted, and it made me feel angry. Whoever had written that note wanted James dead. I threw myself into his arms and cried.

"Thea?"

I tried to regain my composure. He was in danger. The witch inside of me knew this. I had to talk him out of leaving. I held him tightly and drew in a deep breath. "You came into my life in a book," I began. "Even then, I knew I loved you. Even then, my heart belonged to you. I never thought of my weight or my looks when I read those books."

He pulled away, looking a little angry. "You silly girl . . ."

"No, please, let me finish," I said.

He pulled me into his arms again and kissed the top of my head.

I looked up at him. "When you walked into the bakery that day, I thought I was dreaming," I said. "Never in a million years did I think you could ever love me, and when you kissed me, I felt that my life finally made sense. But if I lose you now, if something happens to you, I won't care who finds me, or if I die."

He wiped the tears from my face and smiled. "May I say something now?"

I nodded.

He pulled away. "You wonderful, silly creature," he said. "How can I explain how beautiful you really are? I don't know what spell makes you think otherwise." He pulled me into his arms again. "How can I put into words how much I love you, how I've never understood what you see in me?"

I held him tighter. "Then don't go," I pleaded. "Don't leave me—please."

He sighed. "Thea, there are things I must do to keep you safe until your memory returns."

I pushed myself away from him. "I can live without my memories, but I can't live without you."

He stared at me as if mystified by my behavior. "Only you can see who I really am," he said. "I assure you, I am perfectly safe."

I wiped my tears and stood my ground. "If you leave, I'm going with you."

He looked into my eyes. "What are you not telling me, Thea?"

I decided to tell him the truth. There was no other way. "If you go, they'll kill you."

He shook his head. "I understand that you're worried, but I'll be fine. I will come back to you." He kissed my cheek and quickly walked off.

I started to run after him, but stopped when I felt a sharp zap. Flashes of the past filled my head; I collapsed when I heard someone yelling.

~~~

"How dost thou open it?"
Simon sat facing me in a dimly lit cellar.

His hands were covered in blood—my blood. I was on the edge of death. His men dragged me across the room and chained me to a pole. Simon wiped his hands and ordered his men to bring him more needles.

A man entered the room with a woman in tow.

"Why?" I asked her.

Simon spun on his heel and struck my face with the back of his hand. "Thou speaks only when spoken to!"

I spit in his face. "Is that the best thou canst do, Simon?" I could barely see my skin from all the blood.

Simon slapped me again and turned to his men. "What say you?" he asked. "Be it true of James?"

"It be true, my lord," the man replied. "This witch says he wed her three days ago."

Simon made a fist and turned to face me. He swung with such force that I was surprised the punch didn't knock me out. "He was my servant!"

"My lord," the woman whispered, "if thou dost kill her, thou wilt never know how to open the crystal."

Simon slapped her. "Do not speak to me, witch," he hissed. "Lies are all thou brings."

She dropped to her knees. "My lord, it was I who brought thee the crystal. It was I who told thee its purpose."

He grabbed the woman by the hair and pulled her to her feet. "And dost thou know how to open it?" he yelled. He pushed her away and turned to look at me. He leaned forward and

108

wiped the blood from my eyes. "I want you to see the head of thy husband, for today he dies, and his head I shall bring to thee. And I shall also kill thy friends, and anyone who loves thee."

I tried to kick him away, but it only made him laugh.

Simon looked at the woman. "Lead my men to the traitor, and bring him here to me."

The woman stared at me, tears in her eyes.

Simon stood over me. "Bury her," he told his men. "Bury her in her father's grave. Perhaps in two days, we will have the answers we seek." He looked back at the woman. "Find him, witch, and bring him here to me. For I shall have his head today!"

She looked at me one last time before leading five of Simon's men out of the room.

"Stay away from him!" I screamed, as they dragged me from the room. I had to find a way to escape, to help James. "I shall kill you all!"

Simon's men burst into laughter.

"And how shalt thou kill us, witch?" One of the men kicked me. "Wave thy hand now," he teased.

The men laughed louder. They threw me into the back of a carriage where two more of Simon's men waited. The horses galloped toward their destination as one of the men cast spells at me and the other blew powder in my face. "Keep her mind free of spells, may nothing hurt us as she yells."

From his place at the front of the

carriage, Simon handed one of the men a black velvet bag. He smiled malevolently as his men covered me with straw.

The carriage stopped. I tried to struggle free of my constraints, but the ropes were too tight. Someone grabbed my feet and pulled me from the carriage. The men laughed as I fell onto the ground. They dragged me to a dug-up grave, opened the wooden coffin that lay inside, and threw me in.

"Bring me her mother's heart," Simon said.

Simon removed a dried-up heart from the velvet bag. He held it up and began to chant: "I put thee into darkness, to search inside her head, gather all her memories, and present them when she's dead." He tossed the heart into the box, a wicked smile spreading across his face as his men filled the grave with dirt. "Now every time she remembers, my brothers," he said, "we shall be closer to our dreams."

Panicking, I tried to clear my mind; I could feel the enchanted heart stealing my memories as I lay there dying. I couldn't allow Simon to see why I had placed my powers into the crystal. I writhed desperately against the ropes. I could still hear Simon and his men talking when it hit me: if I had no memories, there would be nothing for the heart to take. I struggled to keep my mind occupied, to shield my memories. I attempted to reverse the spell Simon had cast, but my magic had no effect.

"Leave her in darkness for two days," I heard Simon say. "Then bring to me the heart so it can reveal its secrets."

110

I screamed and kicked at the walls of the coffin. I couldn't let Simon win. I was terrified that it had already taken my deepest thoughts. If that were so, everyone around me was in danger. I had to find a way out of this; I had to save them. I tried again to free my hands from the ropes, twisting my wrists until they bled.

"My lord," I heard someone say, "this heart will truly take her memories?"

It was getting harder to hear them as more and more dirt covered the coffin.

"It shall work, my brother, no matter how far from her it be. A mother's heart will always search for its child." Simon's voice was fading. "We have searched the world for this spell. She cannot destroy it, or her own heart dies." Simon began another spell, but I couldn't make out the words.

I screamed, realizing I was going to die.

~~~

"Thea!" I heard James say. "Delia, something is wrong."

Flashes of my past continued to race through my mind. Panicked, I opened my eyes. "Erase my memory!" I shouted. I slapped my hands to my head to stop it from spinning, and turned to James. "What hast thou done?"

Without hesitation, James threw powder in my face. He and Delia chanted in unison: "Erase the time from before, when she took a step outside this door. May she rest, may she sleep, allow her not these memories to keep."

I had the sensation of flying as James lifted me from the hallway floor. "Thank the heavens you told me this might happen," I

heard him say to Delia before darkness filled
my head.

Chapter 7
Regrets

My eyes opened to the sound of shouting. I could not recall how I came to be lying on the bed. I remembered wanting to stop James from leaving, but had no idea what had happened after I had dashed from the room. The powder on my face revealed that a spell had been performed. They had erased my memory—why? Not wanting to alert James and Delia that I was awake, I remained silent. I closed my eyes again and pretended to sleep as I eavesdropped on their conversation.

"What did you say to her?" Delia asked. "Something you said must have prompted the flashback."

"I told you," James replied. "She didn't want me to leave. As I was walking down the stairs, I turned back and saw her shaking." He sounded stressed.

I opened one eye and stole a glimpse of the two of them. James sat in the corner chair, running his hands through his hair. Delia paced, the box still in her hands. It was obvious I'd had a flashback, and from the looks on their faces, it

113

was a bad one.

"What do we do now?" Delia asked James. "Do we keeping visiting the memories? She seems to be remembering on her own."

She looked in my direction, and I quickly closed my eye. "Did you see her face?" Delia asked. "Did you hear the fear in her voice?"

"Yes," James said, raising his voice. "Do you think that's the first time I've seen her like that? Do you think I didn't see her face when I pulled her out of that grave?"

Shocked, I opened my eye again.

James was standing now, his hand on his forehead. "You were not there when she was gasping for air. You didn't see what those animals had done to her!" He walked to the fireplace and leaned his hand against the bricks. "I've thought of nothing else. If it wasn't for that witch who told me where she was . . ." He shook his head.

The revelation that I'd once been buried alive made my skin crawl. I was also curious about the witch who disclosed my whereabouts.

"Don't torment yourself, James," Delia said, stepping closer to him. "You found her; she's alive because of you." She rested her hand on his back.

He turned to face her, a look a deep sadness on his face. "If she did it for me, then she's doomed because of me." He spun around and punched the wall. "Why did she do it? I never wanted any of it!"

Delia stepped back, her eyes filled with tears. I could see she wanted to comfort him, but I sensed she feared that he would push her away. "You'll wake her," she warned.

James looked toward the bed and I quickly closed my eye again. "I regret the day I walked into her life."

I heard his footsteps as he stormed from the room.

My eyes burned with tears forming behind closed lids. I opened them in time to see Delia following James out the door and close it behind her. I was relieved to be alone. I sat up in the bed, covered my mouth with my hand, and silently cried.

James regretted walking into my life. I heard him say it. My heart heard him say it. I threw off the covers and ran to the window, opened it, and looked down. I trembled as I wondered if I would survive the fall. I wanted to run, to leave this house and erase his regret.

I had climbed onto the sill when I heard the bedroom door open. "Is madam leaving?" the butler asked.

"Stay away from me," I cried, turning my face to him.

He took two steps toward me. "If madam jumps, I can assure her that I will jump after her."

"I don't believe you."

"If madam prefers, I can jump first." He smiled and took another step forward.

I stared at him, confused. "What?"

He smiled and offered his hand. "It seems madam is confused as to who will jump first. Shall we discuss it then?"

I glanced at his hand and out the window again. Without warning, I flew through the air and into his arms. I opened my mouth to scream for help, but he waved his hand and my voice was gone. I pushed myself away from him and tried to run for the door. Again he waved his hand, stopping me in mid-run. How was this possible? He didn't chant, just simply waved his hand.

"Thea," he finally said. "You are costing me precious energy."

I looked at him, stunned.

He smiled. "I'm not going to hurt you, child," he said. "You have no reason to fear me." He reached out and placed his finger on the end of my nose.

Instantly, I was filled with comforting warmth. My voice was restored and I could move again, but I didn't try to run. I looked up at him. "Who are you?"

He smiled and stroked my face. "Let's just say, I'm alive because of you."

He emitted such tenderness, as though love itself was embracing me. I reached to hug him but he stepped back.

Before I could question, the door opened behind me. "William, what are you doing in here?" James asked.

William looked into my eyes. "I was asking madam if she wanted some tea, master." He looked back at James. "I was just about to close the window—madam was cold." William glanced at me again and turned to the window. I didn't know who he was, but I knew this: I felt a tender love for him.

"William," I said, not bothering to acknowledge James's presence. "I think I'll take that tea, thank you."

He smiled, his green eyes twinkling. "Splendid, madam. I will bring it at once."

I felt I'd looked into his eyes many times.

William walked toward the door, but James blocked his way. "William, is everything okay?"

"Yes, master," he answered. "Madam was only asking about regrets." He stepped around James and walked out of the room.

The look on James's face revealed that he understood what William meant.

"Thea," he said. "Please let me explain."

"Are you sure you want to? You might regret it."

He grabbed my arm and pulled me toward him. "How can you think I could regret loving you? I said that because of the pain I've caused you."

I pushed him away and tried to walk out.

He pulled me back to him. "You stupid girl," he whispered, then pulled me to his lips.

I tried to pull away, but his lips were sweet. I gave in, kissed him back, and threw my arms around his neck. I moaned as his tongue found mine.

He put one hand on my back and drew me into him. "How can I regret this?" he asked between kisses.

How could I have ever thought he meant anything else? Never again would I jump to conclusions about James. I had allowed my own insecurity to make me think the worst.

The sound of someone clearing their

throat jolted us from our passionate embrace. "Your tea, madam." William stood in the doorway, a tray in his hands. "I'm glad to see madam is feeling better," he said, walking between us. "Perhaps master should come with me now?" He placed the tray on a table.

James looked embarrassed. "Yes, of course," he said. "I was just clearing up a little misunderstanding."

William looked at me. "And does madam understand, now?"

I suppressed a giggle and glanced at James. "Yes, William—perfectly."

It was odd how my feelings about William had changed completely. I trusted him, and somehow knew he would keep my secret. I also noticed that James felt the need to explain himself to William, as if he'd been caught with his hand in the cookie jar.

James had turned to follow William out of the room when I suddenly remembered the visions I'd had when he was getting ready to leave earlier. "Wait," I said, tugging on James's arm. "I had a vision of you being hurt."

"Just now?"

"No, before, when you walked out of the room. I saw a vision of a group of men. They were chanting spells to lure a traitor."

"Can you remember the spell?" he asked.

I searched my tattered memory. "I think so." I tried hard to remember every word: "Be it James or be it Mike, bring the traitor here tonight. Of the two, just send one, make only the traitor come."

James looked at William. "They grow

suspicious."

"This is why I told master that madam should return to work. They will be looking for those who are missing."

James glanced at me and back to William. "I can't allow that," he said.

"The matter has been taken care of, master."

I observed them talking as if I wasn't there. "Who's Mike?" I asked.

"The man who attacked you at the bakery," James replied.

"But didn't you kill him?" I asked, confused. "Why would they think he's the traitor?"

"They don't know," James said. "They believe him to be missing. Perhaps they think he fled. Maybe I can use this to my advantage," he told William.

William remained silent. He looked at me and smiled. "Will madam excuse us, please?" he asked.

I was instantly upset. Why would they exclude me from their conversation? I decided not to push the issue. I already had a plan of my own in mind. "Where's Delia?" I asked James.

"Ah, yes, I almost forgot," he replied. "She was on the phone with your boss."

I had completely forgotten about Norm, as if I was living in an entirely different world now. "She's talking with Norm?"

"Yes, we thought it best for you to stay here and not work anymore."

"The matter has been resolved, master," William said. "The girl will be more than safe."

James finally conceded to William. He told me he would see me at dinner, and he and William left the room. I was putting on my shoes to go looking for Delia when she appeared in the doorway.

"Hey, I was just about to go looking for you," I said.

"Well, look no further," she said, smiling. "How you feeling—rested?" She started to close the bedroom door.

"Don't bother," I said, gesturing to the door. "We have some snooping to do. Come on."

"What are you talking about?" she asked.

Without answering, I walked out the bedroom door and scanned the hallway. "Do you know your way around here?" I asked, wondering which way they had gone. The house was huge. We were on what appeared to be the second floor, and I could see that the grand staircase continued up. I remembered the day Delia and I had delivered the tart. James came out of a room downstairs adjacent to the foyer. I headed in that direction.

"Thea, wait," Delia said, hurrying behind me. "What are we snooping for?"

I ignored her and headed down the stairs. When Delia caught up with me, she grasped my arm. "Thea, hold on," she said, pulling me back.

"Let go of me!"

She stepped back with a look of shock. "Thea, what's gotten into you?"

I didn't know. I only knew that rage grew inside of me, my frustration coming to a head. "I'm tired," I said. "I'm tired of being lied to, tired of my questions being ignored. I'm tired of you erasing my memory."

She folded her arms across her chest and tapped her foot. "You forgot one little thing, witch."

"Oh, that's a surprise. What?"

She rolled her eyes and pushed her face up to mine. "You seem to have forgotten that we're only doing this because you told us to." She turned on her heel and walked back up the stairs.

My anger churned as my eyes followed her up the steps. "So you're just going to walk away from me?"

"That's what it looks like, witch."

"Don't be a coward, Delia," I said, trailing her. "Tell me the whole story. You know you want to punish me with the truth."

She spun around. "Coward?" she asked. "You dare call me a coward?" She walked back down several steps, closing the gap between us. "You want the truth, witch?" She pulled the box from her pocket. "Well, you got it." She opened the box, reached up, and drew one of the clouds toward us. In an instant, we were inside of it. "No more kid gloves, Thea."

When my eyes finally adjusted to the darkness, I saw a small cottage standing alone in a deeply wooded area. "Where are we?" I asked.

"Why don't you go find out?" she said brusquely.

I surveyed the cottage, its windows illuminated by candlelight. "Who lives here?"

"I'm not sure," she said. "Maybe the

coward does."

I wanted to tell her I was sorry, but I was still so angry. I walked cautiously toward the little house, Delia on my heels.

I heard the voice of a girl, obviously petrified, as I approached. *"Please, mistress, who art thou? What shalt thou do to me?"*

I spotted the scared girl through the window. It was me, and I was covered in dirt and blood. I sat in a chair beside a little table watching Delia mixing something in a large cup. I looked at the present-day Delia questioningly.

"You had already sent James away," she explained. "I had just erased your memory. I brought you here to hide you."

My past-self trembled as Delia added more ingredients to the cup and chanted: *"Fill the air, fill the night, make me look like her tonight. Let them see what I wish, blind their eyes from this witch."* She dashed out the door and carefully poured the contents of the cup along the ground around the outside of the little house. When the cup was empty, she ran back inside and repeated the entire ritual. Fog-like smoke began to rise from the ground where Delia had deposited the contents of the cup.

I began to cry. *"Please, my lady, I—"*

"Silence, witch!" Delia walked to me, cup in hand. *"Drink this,"* she ordered. *"It will calm thee."* She held the cup to my mouth.

I tried to turn away, but she persisted. *"Thou shalt drink,"* she said, tipping the cup to my lips and forcing the liquid into my mouth.

Moments later, five men arrived at the

cottage on horseback. I recognized the short man from the pier, the man Delia called Simon, right away. When Delia saw them through the cottage window, she hastily threw a blanket over me, ran to the door, and cracked it open.

The five men dismounted their horses. *"Search for the witch, Delia,"* Simon ordered. *"And bring her to me."*

Outside the cottage, Delia pulled me away from the window. "Move back, Thea," she said. "They're going to drag me outside."

I stepped back, but could still see inside the cottage from where I stood.

Two of the men rushed inside. *"This be a good day,"* one of them said. *"We come to find the witch, Delia, and find our prize instead."*

When the men dragged Delia out on her knees, Simon's eyes lit up. It was clear he was seeing *my* face. A wicked smiled formed on his lips as he strode to where the men restrained Delia. As he approached, the men grabbed Delia's hair and yanked her head back so that she was looking directly at him.

"Thou hast been a very bad witch," Simon whispered. *"Who has taken thee from the grave?"*

Delia remained silent, her scared eyes darting in all directions.

Simon moved closer, his lips nearly touching Delia's as he spoke. *"If thou shouldst refuse to answer my question, thou wilt burn."*

Delia's chest heaved. She looked as though she might faint. *"I have taken myself out of it,"* she cried.

Simon turned to the other two men.

123

"Search the house and find the heart. Kill the witch, Delia, if ye find her. Somebody removed this witch from the grave." Simon turned back to Delia. *"What be of James, witch? Where shall I find him?"*

Delia, now trembling uncontrollably, didn't answer. Simon struck her face, forcing her backward.

The present day Delia reached for my hand and held it tightly. She looked so scared, as if she were reliving the pain. I looked through the window at the men searching the cottage. They had already managed to tear the place apart. Furniture had been turned over, and drawers and cupboards had been emptied, their contents thrown about. Not once did they look in the direction of where I sat, hiding under the blanket. I could see me, but it was clear that they did not. Delia's spell had not only made them see me instead of her, but had made me invisible to them. The two men exited the cottage and motioned to Simon that they found nothing.

Simon looked down at Delia. *"Burn her,"* he ordered. *"I have no use for her. The heart has already taken what I need to know. We will surely find it after she is dead."*

The men tied Delia to a nearby tree and pitched straw and wood at her feet. A panic-stricken Delia screamed as they set fire to the debris.

Simon and two of his men mounted their horses. *"We shall return when she is dead so that we may look for the heart,"* he told the two men tending the fire. He rode away, one man on either side of him.

I wanted desperately to help her and began to run toward the fire.

The present-day Delia blocked my way. "No, Thea," she reminded me. "You can't change what's already happened."

I watched in horror as the fire raged, Delia's screams ringing out into the night. I saw a man on a horse, and at first I thought Simon had returned. I was relieved when I saw that it was James. He dismounted quickly and brandished his whip, striking and severing the legs of Simon's men. He slashed Delia's restraints, carried her to a barrel full of water, and threw her in.

James walked back to the men who were dragging themselves along the ground, crying out in agony. He raised his whip and struck each of them. They did not turn to dust; instead, blood flowed swiftly from their bodies. I turned my head as James finished them off.

When things were finally quiet, I looked up. James was helping Delia out of the barrel. "*Where is Thea?*" he asked, setting her gently on the ground.

Delia, writhing in pain, was unable to answer him. She began to weep.

James chanted: "*Heal these burns, make them well, give her calmness with this spell.*" James removed his shirt and covered Delia's half-naked body. "*Delia, where is Thea?*" he asked again.

Present-day Delia spoke up. "We've seen enough," she said nervously. "Let's go back."

I ignored her, pulling my hand away as

she reached out.

James continued to question Delia as to my whereabouts. Delia opened her eyes and reached to touch his face.

James tilted his head back and lifted her into his arms. *"Delia, is Thea safe?"* he asked.

Delia's burns were beginning to heal. She pushed her lips against his as he carried her.

He stopped and set her down. She clung to his neck and continued to kiss him.

I noticed that the present-day Delia had stepped behind me and turned her back. I said nothing and returned my attention to the memory.

James removed Delia's hands from his neck, sighed, and pushed her away. He spoke slowly, intently. *"Where is my wife?"*

Delia stumbled back, her mouth agape. *"Thou hast wed her?"*

"Yes," he answered.

Tears streamed down her face as she turned her back on him.

He stepped forward. *"Say to me now that she is safe, Delia,"* he pleaded.

After a moment's silence, Delia spun around, fury in her eyes. *"Thea is well,"* she said, *"but hast told me she does not love thee."*

I couldn't believe what I was hearing. I looked behind me. "Did I really tell you that?"

Delia didn't answer. She kept her back turned as if she didn't hear me.

I returned my attention to the scene. Delia looked so angry. *"Hast thou forgotten I loved thee first?"* she asked. *"It was I who professed her love to thee, not her."* She stepped

126

closer to him. *"It was I who made but a fool of myself for thee. Why love her and not me?"*

James looked away. *"I never asked thee to love me,"* he said. *"I never asked thee to lie in my bed."*

She raised her hand to slap him, but James blocked it.

I felt air under me as Delia grabbed my hand and pulled us out of the memory.

I wriggled from her grasp, and she closed the box. "I knew you loved him!" I yelled. "But why wouldn't you tell me? Why wouldn't you tell me you'd been in his bed, Delia—why?"

She put the box away and flipped her hair with the back of her hand. "I can't answer that."

"Why?" I asked. "Because it's still going on?"

Silence.

"Answer me!"

"I told you," she said. "I can't answer that."

I stared at her for a long moment and decided it was time for me to leave. "I'm going home now," I said. "I would appreciate it if you wouldn't follow me." I ran down the stairs.

Delia called to me as I reached the front door. "Oh, real nice, Thea. Just run away, why don't you."

I didn't turn around. I stepped outside, slamming the door behind me.

Chapter 8
The Boys

I ran from the house with no clue as to where I was running. I wanted to go home, but I knew that my apartment was the first place James and Delia would think to look for me. I couldn't fathom seeing or talking to either one of them right now. Delia could have James all to herself. There was no confusing his words; he had slept with her. They'd had a romance and kept it from me, maybe because it hadn't ended. *You're such an idiot, Thea!*

Did I know this was going on between them? Could their relationship have something to do with why I placed half my powers into the crystal? I felt foolish for thinking James could ever love me the way he pretended to. But why would he pretend to be in love with me? Was this part of their plan—to get a hold of my powers and escape together? The idea of them plotting against me made my heart ache. I ran faster, tears streaming down my cheeks.

Regaining my memory meant nothing to me now. They could keep it and find their own way to open the crystal. What if the memories I saw were false—an attempt to scare me into working with them? *That's it!*

By the time I reached the park near James's house, I had convinced myself that Delia and James were using me. I decided I would go to the bakery and spend the night there. Norm would be delighted to see me at work bright and early the next morning.

As I crossed the street toward the park, a gust of wind swept up, and I froze. I could smell them—James and Delia. They were close by and surely looking for me. I bolted from the middle of the street and dove into a bush. The pungent odor grew stronger. I tried desperately to calm my breathing. I couldn't risk giving myself away.

I heard James's voice first. "If something happens to her, I will kill you with my bare hands," I heard him say to Delia.

"I told you," Delia replied, "she ran off before I could explain."

She was lying. She had never tried to explain anything.

"I'm going back for the car," I heard James say. "I'll try her apartment first and then the bakery."

I bit my lip, frustrated. *Now where am I going to sleep?*

I heard James's footsteps running away from the park. I didn't hear Delia follow him. I remained still and waited. I could still hear her breathing. I heard her take a few steps and stop. I peeked out from the bush. Delia was sitting on a bench, face in her hands, weeping.

I heard a car. Delia lifted her head as the

lights hit her face, but James drove right by without bothering to stop. She watched him pass, buried her head in her hands, and sobbed.

It suddenly occurred to me that Delia and James had been together without me. I thought about what she'd said to the witches on the boat about me having to be present in order for her to be near him. Was that a lie, too?

I suddenly heard Delia's shaky voice. "Why didn't you let me explain, you stupid witch?"

It was getting late, and I had no coat. I wrapped my arms around myself to keep warm. Delia's tears tugged at my heart. Against my will, I was starting to feel sorry for her, and waited patiently while she wept.

I shivered against the night chill, but Delia showed no signs of leaving. Tears spilled from her eyes as she removed the box from her pocket and turned it in her hands. To my surprise, she opened it. Her eyes followed the memory clouds as they drifted up out of the box. She drew one close, held it to her head, and closed her eyes. "Take all of my memories," she said through her tears. "I don't want them anymore."

I quickly jumped out of the bush. "Delia, don't!"

Startled, she looked at me. "Thea," she said, looking relieved.

I walked over to her and pulled her hand away from her head. "Trust me, you don't want to be in my shoes."

Slowly, she closed the box, the clouds funneling back inside of it.

"Right now, those shoes don't seem so bad," she whispered.

I began to walk away.

"Please, let me explain," she pleaded, grasping my arm.

I pulled away. "Explain what? How you and James had this whole thing planned? That you've both been lying to me?"

She was clearly taken aback. "What is it that you think we planned?"

"Oh please," I said. "It's obvious you and James lied about all of this, that you want the crystal so you and he can be together."

She was stunned for a moment, and then began to laugh. "And I suppose we had some guy attack you at the bakery, too? Had him almost kill you so we, as you put it, could be together?" She walked toward me. "Is it also obvious that James is losing his mind because he doesn't know where you are?"

I was about to answer when Delia reached for my hand and opened the box. She quickly reached up, and before I knew it, we were encased in another memory.

"Where are we?"

"You asked me a question," she said. "Well, here's your answer."

The room was dark. I could see a bed with someone in it, but couldn't make out who. "What do you mean, here's my answer?"

"Thea, I couldn't answer your question because I didn't know the answer."

"What do you mean?" I asked, frustrated.

She looked over to the bed. "I'd erased this memory from my mind because it

131

tormented me, humiliated me to the core."
Tears rolled down her cheeks. "But you're
giving me no choice. You're jumping to
conclusions about James and me, and you need
to know the truth. I was recovering this memory
when you appeared from the bush."

"So how is this going to explain
everything?" I asked, looking toward the
bed. She bowed her head. "You'll see."

An exhausted-looking James entered the
room and tossed some rolled-up papers onto a
table. He removed his boots and lit a candle that
sat on the table. He began to undress. I glanced
at Delia, who was averting her eyes.

When I returned my attention to the
memory, James was naked. The sight of his
bare, muscular body made my heart race. He
was so fit, I couldn't take my eyes off of him.
James walked to the bed and was about to get in
when he noticed the obvious lump under the
covers. He grabbed the blanket and pulled it
back, revealing a naked Delia. For a moment, I
thought he was going to slide into bed with her.

"*Hast thou lost thy mind?*" James yelled.
He moved away from the bed and hurriedly
pulled his pants back on. "*I could have killed
thee! What business hast thou here?*"

Delia stood and walked over to him.
"*Does my lord not crave the love of a woman?*"
she asked, running her fingers over his chest.

He backed away. "*I bid thee forgiveness,
maiden, if I have implied anything to make thee
act in such a way.*"

Delia spoke from behind me. "I tried to
make him take me," she confessed. "I noticed

the way he'd been looking at you. It was my last, desperate attempt to bond him to me."

I looked at her, confused. "Bond him to you?"

She looked at herself in the memory and shook her head. "If he would have taken me, we wouldn't be here right now. He would have been connected to me forever."

I looked at the two of them. James was wrapping his shirt around Delia.

"*Indeed, thou art a beautiful woman.*" he said kindly. "*But my heart loves another. I will not lie with thee.*"

Delia raised her arms, and the shirt slid to the floor. "*Thy friend knows not of who my lord is. She offers not what I offer thee. I have loved thee for months. I have wanted thee every day. Why would my lord want a child when he can love a woman?*" She paused and looked into his eyes. "*I can make thee happy, my lord.*"

He reached out and stroked her cheek. "*Be it true, I have had my choice of lovely maidens,*" he said, smiling. "*I have even had my share of human women. But it is the witch with the golden smile that has captured my heart.*"

She slapped his hand away. "*Then my lord is foolish,*" she snapped. "*For she will never love thee back—her heart is already taken.*"

He smiled and looked to where Delia's clothes lay on the floor. "*I am afraid I must bid you good night, maiden.*"

"Can we leave now?" Delia asked from behind me.

I turned to her.

"Don't worry," she said flatly. "He's about to kick me out."

I wanted to spare her further humiliation, and so reached for her hand. "Let's get out of here."

In an instant, we were back at the park. A shiver ran through me. I looked at Delia, unsure of what to say. I felt foolish as I thought of all the conclusions I had made about her and James. Delia had relived a painful memory for my sake, and I was grateful to her.

"Delia . . ." I said.

She held up her hand. "Let me go first. I have to say this before James finds us." She sighed. "I want you to know that if you had loved him by that time, I would have never done what I did. I thought he only wanted you because you could give him the gift everyone wanted from you. I thought if I could bond him to me, he would grow to love me."

I wanted to ask her about this "bonding" she kept mentioning, but this wasn't the time. "I know it was extraordinarily difficult for you to show me that," I said, taking her hand. "Thank you."

She put the box away and sighed. "No, Thea. I've been a complete jerk. I've been making things so hard for James. I guess I was punishing him." She pulled out her cell phone. "He even got me this thing so I could call him if I ever needed him." She smiled. "For anything to do with you, I'm sure."

"Who are you calling?" I asked as she pressed the speed dial.

She rolled her eyes. "God, you are so

slow in this day and age." She spoke into the phone: "I found her." She snapped the phone shut and looked at me. "We okay?"

"Only if you promise me something," I said.

She smiled. "Anything."

I pointed to the box in her pocket. "Don't tell James you showed me that memory. And don't tell him the crazy stuff I dreamed up about you and him, okay?"

"Okay," she agreed. "If you promise me something in return."

"Sure, what is it?"

She walked over and put her arms around my waist. "That you'll never run away like that again."

I hugged her back. "You know, I didn't get a chance to thank you for risking your life for me," I said. "You nearly burned alive."

"I only got a taste of what they had already done to you," she said, pulling away.

I gently pushed up her sleeves, revealing her scars. "But I didn't burn like a marshmallow, did I?"

She tugged down her sleeves. "No. It's a pity you can't remember what a confident witch you once were. Now I'm stuck with you like this."

I laughed. "Well, you're the one who erased my memory."

"Yeah, but I'm the one who has to put up with you now."

It felt good to be normal with Delia, laughing and joking about each other. "Am I really that bad now?" I asked.

"Oh please," she said. "Don't get me started." We walked back toward the house.

"It's horrible the way you think of yourself now," she said. "I don't know why you made yourself so insecure."

"Maybe because I'm so fat?"

Delia stopped. "What world do you live in?" she asked. "Why do you think you're fat? Because you're not skin and bones like me? Look at you. Your curves are beautiful. Do you not see the way men look at you?"

We began walking again.

"You were never like this back then, Thea. I wish you could remember that about yourself."

"Tell me, Delia, how was I?"

"Actually, I'll do better than that. I'll show you. Besides, you need to know who they are."

I looked at her, puzzled.

She pulled out her cell phone again. "Hold on." She took a couple of steps away and spoke into the phone. "How far are you from the park? What? Oh, she was hiding in a bush." Delia looked at me. "No, everything's fine. I'll meet you back at the house." She rolled her eyes and continued talking. "I think we can manage walking two blocks, there's no reason to—"

She pulled the phone away from her ear and eyed it. "You are so stubborn," she muttered, putting it away. "He's almost here."

"Delia, you said I need to know who 'they' are. Who were you talking about?"

She looked up and down the street and

took out the box. "He'll just have to wait," she said, opening the box. "Come on, this won't take long."

I grasped her hand and looked up. "Won't someone see us?"

She chuckled. "You really think I'm that stupid?" She reached for one of the clouds and pulled it toward us. "You ready?"

I nodded.

Immediately, the smell hit me. "Delia, someone has a strong scent here." I looked at our surroundings.

"You can smell them, even in the memory?" she asked.

"Who's 'them'?"

She smiled and gestured to an open field.

I noticed five boys—teenagers—running about wildly. "Who are they?"

Before Delia had a chance to answer, I spotted myself emerging from the forest. I laughed and threw pieces of fruit at the group.

One of the five ran to my side and pointed out targets. "*Fish threw the last one, mistress,*" he yelled, pointing to one of the others.

"*He lies, mistress,*" the boy named Fish said, running right by me. "*I threw them all!*"

I laughed. "*Samuel, find me a rotten apple. I shall make him eat it!*"

Samuel ran ahead of me and told the others to help him capture Fish.

"They're all so young," I said.

Samuel was handsome. I wasn't sure, but I think he had green eyes. He was tall and slim with short dark hair and a nice build.

137

Two of the boys chased Fish. I noticed a tall, gangly redhead lagging behind.

"That's Joshua," Delia whispered. "The ones chasing Fish are Javier and Cory."

As I watched them run, a smile spread across my face. "Who are they?"

"They're your friends and guards," she said. "And you love them to pieces."

"These kids are my guards?"

"Yes, and they wouldn't have it any other way. They adore you. They begged for the honor of protecting you and wouldn't take no for an answer. " She paused. "They're still looking after you."

"Why haven't I ever seen them before? Like I've seen you, I mean. Where have they been?"

Delia sat on the grass and motioned for me to join her. "They've always been close to you, Thea. They were mad at themselves for missing our little friend at the bakery."

I sat next to her and surveyed the group. The one named Javier looked Latin and was very handsome, with light brown eyes. He sported a Mohawk and had the body of a wrestler.

I noticed that all of my guards looked extremely fit. "They're just kids," I said as I watched Fish throw more fruit at me.

"You're no older than them, Thea," Delia said, smiling. "And you might not want to refer to them as kids; they don't like it."

We watched as Joshua and Cory threw Fish into the nearby lake as I rolled on the ground, laughing. They all cheered as Fish popped out of the water with a fish in his mouth. One by one, the others dove into the lake.

"Samuel is the hothead," Delia said. "Javier is the charmer. He likes to think he's a ladies man, and he loves human girls," she said, rolling her eyes. "And Fish, well, you can already see that he's the comedian."

I giggled as I watched Fish spit the fish out of his mouth.

"The handsome one is Cory," Delia continued. "He's also the level-headed one, sort of the leader of the group. Joshua is your big red teddy bear."

I watched the boys swim in the lake while my past-self gathered the strewn fruit and put it into a basket. The expression of happiness on my face was unmistakable. The red-headed Joshua came out of the water to help me. The one named Cory also came to help. I watched as Cory strode out of the water, his clothes sticking to his body. He was tall, and I could see his muscles through his wet shirt. Delia was right; he was very handsome. I couldn't take my eyes off of him.

"Close your mouth, Thea," Delia whispered to me playfully.

I quickly looked away, embarrassed.

"I'm surprised you noticed him like that. You never did before. Look at you, clueless to the beautiful man in front of you. That's who I always thought you'd fall for. Everyone thought you two would marry one day."

I watched as Cory scooped up the basket. He had impossibly long eyelashes, and his big blue eyes reminded me of James's eyes. All of his facial features were striking. His nose was a little big, but somehow it suited him. He had thick, straight brown hair that he repeatedly shook off of his face. His dashing smile was irresistible.

He helped me to my feet and handed me the basket. He shook his head, splashing me with water. I grabbed a piece of fruit from the basket and lobbed it at him. He tackled me to the ground when I tried to run.

"Look at you," Delia whispered. "You don't even notice how much he likes you." She snorted. "I don't know why it was James that you finally noticed. Before him, you never gave anyone a second glance."

I returned my attention to the scene. The others, now drying themselves on the shore, cheered as Cory tried to throw me into the lake. A wave of my hand sent them all flying into the water. *"Have I taught my lords nothing?"* I shouted from the shore. *"It will take more than five of you to get thy mistress into the water."*

"Watch this," Delia said, pointing toward some trees.

I turned and saw several men walking toward the group, carrying what looked like fishing poles. They didn't look happy.

"You there," one of the men yelled. *"Be on thy way, this be our fishing hole."*

Cory grabbed me at once and headed for the trees.

"Why is he taking me?" I asked.

"Those are Simon's men," Delia said. "And Cory knows you."

Puzzled by her explanation, I looked back at the scene unfolding before us. Samuel was walking out of the lake. *"It seems thy fishing hole is full this fine day,"* he said to the men and pointed down the lake. *"There be fine fishing just a ways from here."*

Joshua and Fish walked up and stood on either side of Samuel.

"We are very fond of this spot," Samuel said, crossing his arms.

The men started laughing and laid their poles on the ground. *"It seems today we will be teaching these kids some manners,"* one of the men said.

Samuel smiled mischievously as they approached him. *"Prepare to learn some manners, my lords,"* he said, looking from Joshua to Fish.

One of the men stepped up and punched Samuel in the face. Fish and Joshua jumped in at once. I saw Cory run out from the trees. He pulled a man off of Fish and punched him. The men spat into their hands.

Spells! I got to my feet and started to run.

As usual, Delia held me back. "Just watch, Thea. You can't change this."

I saw myself come out of the trees and wave my hand toward the men. Their bodies, now glued together, formed a circle. I strolled around them as I held my hand up to stop the boys. *"Be well, my lords, for it seems these men like picking on young boys."* I turned to Samuel. *"Why should they not feel how wonderful the water is?"*

Samuel smiled. *"Why not, indeed, mistress."*

"Filthy witch," one of the men said. *"I will tell the town's people to burn thee."*

I turned and walked over to the man. *"Really? And what about thee, my lord? Shall they burn thee, as well, for being a warlock?"*

"They will not believe thee," he answered.

I smiled and touched his head. *"But I am hoping they will believe thee, my lord."*

He looked up at me, seemingly dazed.

"What shalt thou tell the townspeople, my lord?" I asked.

"That we fished, and nothing else," he answered.

"Yes, and thou, what shalt thou say?" I asked, touching the man beside him.

"That there were no fish to be caught," he replied.

"Good, and thou?" I asked the next man. *"Who didst thou see today?"* I watched myself as I touched each of them, erasing their memories and placing one of my own choosing into their heads. When my task was complete, I waved my hand. All of the men flew into the lake. *"Happy fishing, my lords,"* I called as the boys laughed.

Delia stood. "We'd better go," she said. "James is waiting."

I didn't answer. I watched myself leave with the boys as Delia pulled us out of the memory.

"Sorry we took so long," she said, letting go of my hand.

I looked at James and smiled, but he turned and walked back to the car. He opened the door. "It's getting late," he said, avoiding my eyes.

"He knows why you ran away," Delia whispered.

I bit my lip and walked to the car. I couldn't bring myself to look at him as I got in. I noticed Delia didn't follow me.

"Aren't you coming?" I asked.

James closed the door and walked around the car.

"No, I'll see you tomorrow."

James got in and slammed his door. He placed his hands on the steering wheel and stared straight ahead. "Please, don't ever do that again," he said.

"I'm sorry," I whispered. "I never meant to worry you. I guess I just don't understand what you see in me—why you love me."

Without warning, he threw open his door and stormed around the perimeter of the car. He opened my door, pulled me out, and took my face in his hands. "You listen to me, Thea Hawthorn, I don't know what spell or potion has you believing that I'm the lucky one. But inside this silly head of yours is the woman I love, the woman I married. I don't know why you think the way you do, but you need to stop."

He pressed his lips to mine, but I couldn't concentrate on his kiss. I kept hearing my name over and over inside my head. *Thea Hawthorn, Thea Hawthorn, Thea Hawthorn.* I felt a sharp zap and heard my name again.

~~~

"Thea Hawthorn, get back here at once," a woman shouted. "Thy father wishes to speak to thee."

"Coming, Vera."

"Ah, there thou art, my child." My father, smiling, held out his arms. He reminded me of someone. "Come. The time has come for me to give thee a gift."

Vera walked back into the house as my father sat me next to him.

"Hello, Father. I was playing with Cory from next door."

He laughed and put his arm around me. "I see that thou chooses thy friends well." He tapped my nose and smiled. "We have something to discuss, Thea. I have been waiting for thee to come of age so that I may give thee a gift."

"Thou hast a gift for me, Father?" I asked excitedly. "Is it my year's end already?"

He laughed again and hugged me. "No, my child. Thou art still but twelve. But soon thou wilt begin to see those boys thou plays with differently, and I wish thee prepared to choose wisely." He reached into his pocket and revealed a shining crystal.

"What is it, Father?" I asked, taking it from him.

A cluster of white crystals surrounded a distinct green one much bigger than the others. Some rock remained stuck to it from the place where it had been dug up.

"It is a channeling crystal, Thea," he explained. "And a very rare one, at that."

I looked up at him. "It is very pretty, Father. Thank you."

He smiled and took it from me. "Very pretty, indeed, my daughter. A crystal like this comes along only once in a lifetime. I myself had never seen one before I found it. It is something wizards like me only dream of, and it is something others would kill for if they knew its purpose. They would even kill someone like thee, Thea."

I looked at the crystal again. "What does it do?"

He gave it back to me and put his arm around my shoulder. "One day, thou wilt have a need, a reason to keep something safe or hidden. Perhaps thou wishes to use it to share the powers thou wert born with. As you know, not everyone is like us, and thou canst use this crystal to give a loved one some of thy powers."

I held the crystal up to the light. "I can give away my magic?"

"Thou canst do more than that, my daughter. Dost thou see how the green one is surrounded by the small white ones?"

I nodded.

"These crystals are normally all white," he explained. *"And they are used to pass information along, almost like a messenger. Thou canst take a thought and pass it along to someone else, using these white crystals."* He touched the green one. *"But this one—this one is special. It should not have grown with the others. No one knows why this happens, only that it is very rare. It was a great wizard friend of mine who first discovered its true powers. It*

was he who told me of its existence. He was able to hide something very dear to him inside of it and release it hundreds of years later."

I looked at him, surprised. "Hundreds of years? Why did he wait so long?"

He sighed and stood. "This is why thou must choose wisely. Whatever reasons thou may have one day, thou must be prepared to wait for the crystal to release it in its own time; it might be days, it might be years. And only thou canst know why thou used it, and only thou may open and close it. Once thou dost claim it and make it thine, it will open for no other."

He knelt down in front of me. "Thea, there are others who will want this crystal. They understand that people like us can use it to give them the gift of magic. This is why thou must claim it, make it work only for thee. This is a gift to thee, my daughter." He stood. "Hold the crystal next to thy heart."

I did as I was told. The crystal felt cold against my chest.

"Thou wilt repeat my words, understand?"

I nodded and bowed my head as he chanted: "Feel thy blood, feel thy heart, feel thy soul when we're apart. Just thy voice, just thy smell, thou wilt not open with a spell. Feel thy touch, feel thy hand, only open with my command."

I repeated my father's words. The crystal began to glow as if a light had been placed inside of it.

"It now belongs to thee," my father whispered.

It was still glowing as I pulled it away from my heart. "Will it always shine like this, Father?"

He took it from me, and it stopped glowing at once. "I do not think so, Thea."

~~~

"Do my kisses no longer interest you?" James asked.

I opened my eyes. I sensed that only moments had passed, but it seemed like hours to me. "I'm sorry," I said. "I'm just cold."

He removed his jacket and put it around my shoulders. "May I take you home now?"

"Yes, please," I said, slipping my hands through the sleeves.

He tilted my chin up. "Can you promise me something? Promise me you will never speak of yourself that way again."

This was a promise I intended to keep. I had gotten a glimpse of who I really was. I wanted nothing more than to find that confident girl within myself before my memory returned. "I promise."

He smiled and kissed me again. I was about to throw my arms around him when a man suddenly appeared behind us.

"Good evening, James. A word, if I may?" The man glanced at me as he crossed the street and waited for James.

"Wait in the car." He opened the door, and I got in. "Lock it," he ordered before crossing the street to join the man.

Chapter 9
The Traitor

Curious, I discreetly cracked the car window.

"I see you've developed a taste for human girls," the man said.

James shot him a look. "She's none of your business, Jack."

The man turned my way. "It seems she's fond of you, as well. At least you don't have to worry about becoming bonded."

James took a step forward. "I told you, she's none of your concern."

The man smiled arrogantly. "All is well, my brother. I only meant to say that you seem to like them young."

"What do you want, Jack?" James snapped. It was obvious that James didn't care for this man.

"There's still no word from Mike," the man said. "I think it's safe to assume that he's the traitor, that he's helping the witches."

This news seemed to relax James a little. "I told you there had to be a reason why he left," James replied. "I never trusted him."

148

They looked my way, and the man smiled again. "When you're done playing, we've gotta run patrol. I was just told that the crystal glowed again tonight."

James glanced my way. "And what exactly are we patrolling?"

"The witches. They'll be gathering soon to wait for her. We need to find the place where they've arranged to meet. The witch, Delia, hasn't opened her stand for two days; that must mean something. We need to keep an eye on her." Jack lit a cigarette. "I'm not a babysitter, James. That's your job. I want reports of where she goes and who she's with." Jack looked my way again and smirked. "Maybe your toy will come in handy. Seems the witch is her friend."

"Old age is slowing you down, Jack," James replied. "You're not giving me any ideas that I haven't already thought of myself."

Jack took a drag from his cigarette. "Touché, my friend. Then I will let you get back to work."

Jack walked away as James returned to me. He got in the car and pulled out his cell phone. "I know you were listening," he said. He hit the speed dial and started the car.

I noticed we weren't headed in the direction of the house. "Where are we going?"

"A safe place to talk," he replied, holding the phone to his ear. "Hello," he said to someone on the other end. "Meet me at the bakery. Yes, now." He snapped the phone shut. "What did you remember today? I know you remembered something. The crystal only shines when you have flashbacks."

I was instantly on edge. I feared he'd want to erase what I had just seen. Looking down, I didn't answer.

"Thea, do you not trust me?"

I nodded. "You'll erase it."

He sighed. "I've only done that once, when I thought your memory was back." He reached over and took my hand. "If I promise not to, will you tell me?"

"Yes."

"Then I give you my word."

"I saw my father giving me the crystal. He told me how rare it was, and what it was for."

"What did he say?"

I remembered my father's words: that only I should know the crystal's purpose. James was already aware that it could be used to transfer my magic, but I wasn't prepared to tell him the rest. "I don't think I can tell you," I answered.

He sighed with frustration. "I'm only trying to find out what else you could have used the crystal for."

I wrung my hands nervously. "It's not that I don't trust you. I just can't remember what he told me." I felt bad for lying to him, but if my father gave me specific instructions, he must have had a good reason.

"I see."

"Why are we going to the bakery?" I asked, hoping to change the subject.

"Because it's a safe place to talk."

The bakery was dark when we pulled up. James got out of the car and opened my door.

"Stay close to me," he said and took my hand.

We walked around to the back of the bakery. Delia was waiting for us in the alley. "The others are already here," she told James. She opened the bulkhead we used to receive deliveries.

We followed Delia inside where the witches waited. I recognized Vera and the other three witches from the boat. The blonde one looked me up and down and sneered. The witch standing beside her, a brunette, smiled. I wondered if they were sisters; they certainly looked alike, aside from their hair color. An odd sensation began to arise inside of me, and I wasn't sure I liked it.

I'd never spent much time in the basement delivery area. Norm was always kind enough to bring things up for me. The atmosphere in the room sparked anger within me that grew the longer I stood there. The sounds of chains clanking and distant screams brought me to a revelation: this was where I had been tortured. This building sat over Simon's old property. I wanted to run, but the witch inside of me wasn't having it.

"Has something happened?" one of the witches asked James.

With her petite frame and eyeglasses, she resembled the stereotypical schoolteacher— save for her hair, which was a mass of tangles like mine.

"It's Thea's memory," James replied. "I think it's coming back. We need to talk."

She looked at me. "May I speak with her?" she asked, looking back to James. He nodded and she walked over to me. "Your mother was my dearest friend," she said. "I'm honored to be able to protect and look after you in her place." She touched my face and smiled. "You look so much like her, my dear. She was so beautiful, and you were the world to her."

My eyes filled with tears. I leaned over and hugged her. "Thank you."

"Sharron, we don't have much time," James said.

My mother's dear friend pulled away from me. "Yes, of course," she said, composing herself. "What can we do for you, James?"

Vera was staring at me. I smiled at her but she looked away.

"Delia, you have to open your booth," James ordered. "They've noticed it's been closed. It's best to continue your normal routine. I want you there tomorrow, doing what you usually do."

"You dare give these witches orders?" I said, surprising everyone, including myself.

James stared at me, shocked, but continued on. "Sharron, you need to find a different venue for your council meetings. They're watching the ship."

"So let them watch," I said. I didn't like what was happening to me.

James ignored my comment and looked at Vera. "Vera, we'll need one of your changing potions, in case Thea needs to take it."

Vera, who appeared extremely nervous, nodded, and glanced at me from the corner of her eye.

"What's going on, James?" Delia asked.

"I was told to follow you," he explained. "Give reports on where you go. They think you're searching for a safe place to meet Thea." He paused. "You all need to be extra careful."

"Okay, Mr. Hawthorn," Delia said sarcastically. "What else do you need us to do?"

James shot Delia a dirty look. "Don't push my buttons, Delia," he warned. "Never call me by her last name again."

"Please continue, James," Sharron said, flashing Delia a disapproving look.

"Thea will be returning to work. And I need you to join her."

"Yes, of course," Sharron answered.

James addressed the group. "I'm still not sure what the crystal looks like, but I have a good idea of where they're keeping it. When Thea's memory returns, we'll need to be prepared to get her there fast. I'll—"

I interrupted. "You don't know what it looks like?"

"No, you only told me it was a gift from your father. We discussed what you wanted to do with it, but as you well know, I wanted no part of that."

I looked at Vera. "You never told them what it looks like?"

An expression of disbelief washed over Vera's face. "M . . . me?" she stammered. "How would I know what it looks like?"

"You were there the day my father gave it to me," I said. "You went back into the house after you called for me, but I saw you; you were standing in the doorway, listening to our conversation."

Delia walked across the room and faced Vera. "Why didn't you tell us you were there?" she asked suspiciously.

Vera took two steps back. "She's mistaken," Vera lied. "I never knew anything about it. You're the one who told us about the crystal."

"No!" Delia shouted. "Everyone knew her father had given her that crystal. I only told you what she had done with it."

Vera's eyes darted nervously around the room. "She has no memory. How could she know if I was there or not? She's wrong. I know nothing about it."

I walked over to Vera. "You were there when I was speaking to my father," I said angrily. "He held up the crystal, and I saw your reflection in it. You were looking right at it."

Vera's face reddened. She quickly removed her hand from her pocket and attempted to blow powder in my face.

Delia grabbed her and threw her to the floor. "Stupid hag!"

The other witches blew powder in Vera's face and chanted: "Be as still as the night. Do not scream, do not fight."

Vera cried as she dragged herself closer to me.

Delia kicked her. "Stay away from her, you traitor!"

Vera lifted her hands toward me. "I never knew they would treat you that way. I only thought they wanted the crystal." She dragged herself closer.

James pulled me toward him and stepped

154

in front of me. "Don't get any closer, or I'll kill you."

"Mistress, please," Vera said, reaching for me. "It was I who led those men away from James. It was I who told him where they had buried you."

"And it was you who told them where to find her," Delia said, kicking Vera again.

"There's no need for that, Delia," James said, pulling her away. He knelt in front of Vera. "Why did you do it?"

"They told me they'd use the crystal to bring my husband back."

"But he was dead, dear," Sharron said from behind me. She walked over and knelt beside James. "Did they promise to bring him back from the dead? You know that's not possible."

Vera reached for Sharron. "I was frightened," she sobbed. "It was too late to take back what I'd done. I didn't know what they were going to do to her. I swear to you, I didn't know."

I felt sorry for Vera. My heart knew she was telling the truth. My mind began to hatch an idea; a way for Vera to redeem herself to me. I instinctively knew that if there was anybody in this room I could trust right now, it was her.

"Is this why you keep changing what you look like?" Sharron asked.

Vera nodded and looked at me. "Forgive me, mistress," she cried. "I beg you to forgive me. I'll do anything you want—die, if you wish it so."

As I started to walk to her, James tried to stop me.

"It's okay, James," I said. "I can take care of myself." I pulled my arm from his grasp and knelt before Vera, who was shaking and crying uncontrollably. "I understand what a woman will do for the man she loves. I believe it was your pain that made you to act as you did." I took her hand. "I also believe that you had no idea this would go so far. I forgive you, Vera."

"What?" Delia shouted. "How can you forgive such treachery?"

I looked at Delia. "We've all done foolish things for the love of a man."

Delia's mouth snapped shut. She glanced around the room and looked down.

Vera began sobbing again and threw herself at my feet. "I will never betray you again, mistress," she wailed. "I do not deserve your kindness. I will do anything you wish me to."

I motioned for James to help me pull Vera up from the floor. Once standing, Vera flung herself into my arms.

"I need to speak to you in private," I whispered in her ear. I scanned the room to make sure no one had heard me. James and Delia kept staring at me.

"Is something wrong?" I asked.

"Did I miss something on the way here?" James asked. "It's almost as if your memory is already back."

Delia chimed in. "Yeah, it's as if the old Thea is guiding your actions."

156

Sharron walked over to James and whispered something in his ear.

"Agreed," he replied.

Vera tugged on my finger. "Okay," she mouthed, her eyes finally dry.

I winked at her discreetly.

"Come, dear," Sharron said, taking Vera's hand. "We have much to talk about."

Vera slipped free of her hand and hugged me again. "You won't regret this, I swear." Before walking out with Sharron, she turned toward me one last time. "Thank you."

"You're making a big mistake," Delia said when they had left. "What makes you think she won't go running to them again?"

"Delia is right," James added. "We can't take these kinds of chances. It's too dangerous."

"And what you're doing isn't dangerous?" I asked James. "Are you not with them most of the day? Can they not discover who you really are at any time?" I looked at Delia. "And you," I scolded. "Don't tell me you're not in danger. How long have you been putting your life on the line for me? It's obvious that woman is tormented with regret. Whatever her reasons, I forgive her."

The witch who had smiled at me earlier stepped forward. "Vera lived for her husband," she said. "When he died, Vera tried to poison herself. Everyone knew of her anguish; she was an easy target for them."

"That's no excuse," Delia yelled. "I know the two of you have been friends for a very long time, but how can you—"

"Stop it, Delia!" I shouted. "What's done

is done. We can't change what happened. Besides, all of this is my fault. I will deal with the repercussions."

Delia and James glanced at each other.

Delia took a step forward. "Are you sure your memory isn't back?"

I ignored her question and looked at James. "Take me home," I ordered.

His eyes hadn't left me; I wondered what he was thinking.

"Mistress," the smiling witch said. "My name is Amanda." She gestured to her right. "This is my sister, Helena."

"It's Helen," the sister corrected. "We live in the twenty-first century now."

"Helen, then. I just thought it would be nice for you to know our names." She glanced at Delia. "So you didn't have to call us hags."

I smiled as Delia rolled her eyes. "It's nice to meet you both, although I'm sure we already know each other."

"Will you be coming to the council meeting?" Helena asked me.

"What a stupid question," Delia said. "When has she ever not been there?"

I shot an irritated glance at Delia. "I'll see you there," I said to Helena and Amanda.

Amanda smiled and motioned to her sister. They gave Delia dirty looks as they walked out of the building.

"Good night, hags," Delia called, waving behind them.

"Delia, why do you treat them like that?" I asked.

"Oh please. Those witches never liked

you—especially Helena. Oh, I mean, *Helen*."
She rolled her eyes.

"Enough!" James yelled. "I will not stay
here and listen to you witches gossip." He
stormed out.

The odd, angry feeling I'd had vanished.
I couldn't understand what had come over me. I
sensed the witch inside of me was trying to
show me something, but I couldn't understand
what.

"You're acting really weird, Thea,"
Delia said.

"I'm fine," I replied, following James out
the door. "I'll see you tomorrow."

James was already in the car. I got in and
looked at him. "Are you angry with me?"

He looked straight ahead and didn't
answer. He started the car and pulled away from
the curb. We didn't say a word until I realized
he wasn't taking me home, but to my apartment.

"We're not going home?" I asked.

"You are," he replied. "I have things to
do."

"I don't mind waiting for you," I said,
hoping he would take me with him.

He pulled up in front of the building, his
eyes still fixed straight ahead.

"It's getting late, Thea."

"Aren't you coming in with me?"

"Like I said, I have things to do." He
turned and gazed out the driver's side window.

I sat, confused, trying to make sense of
his cold demeanor. After a moment, I stepped
out of the car and ran into the building. I ran
into my apartment and slammed the door

behind me. I heard his car drive away, and I slid down the door in tears. "James," I cried.

Suddenly, I felt sharp zaps all across my body. I knew the witch inside of me wanted to show me something. I closed my eyes and drifted into my memory. I saw an image of James and me in a small cottage deep in the woods. We were arguing.

~~~

"I can take care of myself," I shouted.

"I know thou canst," James yelled. "But why must thou make me look foolish? Dost thou not understand that I am a man? That townspeople laugh at me and call me the witch's toy. Dost thou not see what that does to me? How it makes me feel?"

"I will not allow thee to be hurt because of me," I said.

James pounded on the table. "If thy precious Cory or any of the other boys had tried to help, thou wouldst have allowed it. Why dost thou not have that same faith in me?"

"I need not the help of any man to save me," I said indignantly.

"And I need not the help of a woman to save me," James shot back. "Dost thou want a man or a servant?" he asked.

"How dare thee speak to me in such a way. Thou dost know of my love for him."

"Then treat me like thy husband."

"And allow thee to order me? Thou dost not own me."

He threw a candle across the room, sighed, and looked into my eyes. "Asking thee to let me take care of thee is not ordering thee. I

160

am thy husband. I have a right to take care of thee."

"I do not need to be taken care of."

He grabbed my arm and pulled me to him. "If there be a way to take back my love, to have never loved thee, to have seen then what I see now . . ." He pushed me away. "Thou wants not a husband, but an obedient servant. I wish not to own thee but to love thee. But not like this." He turned and walked out.

"My servants would never leave this way!" I shouted from the doorway as he disappeared into the trees. I slammed the door and threw over a table in protest.

It was clear his words had cut deep into my heart. My arrogance had driven him away. I dropped to my knees, lifted a floorboard, and pulled out a bag. I sobbed as I opened the bag and removed the crystal. The white crystals were gone, leaving only the green one. "A curse be these powers without him," I cried. The crystal began to glow as tears streamed down my face. "Thou wouldst take back his love for me. I shall fix things, my love," I said, holding up the crystal. "I shall be as you."

I was ready to relinquish my powers to the crystal, for they were interfering with my love for James and his love for me. My domineering attitude, my wish to protect him at all costs, had chased my husband away.

I saw myself raise the crystal, I knew what I was about to do. Then I saw myself trembling and slowly lower my arms. I knew at once she was having a vision. I couldn't see what it was, I could only see myself looking into space. Then something made me smile, after a moment, horror washed over my face. "No!" I heard myself shout.

I watched myself stand and lift the crystal, my hands shaking as I chanted: "Open now, open here, help me with the things I fear. Take thy powers, keep them safe, no matter of the time it takes."

I held the crystal against my heart, and it glowed brighter. The cottage filled with light, and all at once, the light vanished. I carefully slipped the crystal into the bag and returned it to its place under the floorboard.

"James!" I yelled as I ran out the door. I disappeared into the forest, calling his name.

When I couldn't find him, I returned to the cabin. I instantly noticed the floorboard where I had hidden the crystal had been disturbed. Before I could check for the crystal, I was distracted by noises outside. I quickly looked out the window.

Vera had arrived at the cottage, accompanied by five men. She was trying to hold them back. "My lords," she cried. "I already brought you what you wanted. Why do we come back here?"

"Silence, witch," one man shouted. "Or I will kill thy mistress."

They shoved Vera to the ground, kicked open the door, and dragged me from the cottage. Vera ran to the edge of the trees, crying. She trembled as she watched the men kicking me.

"Thou art accused of witchery!" they yelled as they dragged me into the woods.

I waved my hands repeatedly, but my powers were no longer strong enough to save me.

The men laughed at my failed attempts. "So it is true," one man yelled. "She has lost her powers." He looked at the other men. "Let us fear this witch nevermore, for today justice shall be served."

I screamed as the men dragged me farther into the woods.

~~~

The sound of my screams filled my head. I couldn't stand to hear it. What were they doing to me? I clamped my hands over my ears. "No!" I shouted.

"I've got you, Thea," I heard a voice say.

I opened my eyes. Cory was sitting beside me, his arms wrapped around me. I threw myself into his arms and went into a complete sob. "I don't want to remember anymore," I cried.

I heard someone walk in, but couldn't bring myself to look up.

"Go back downstairs," Cory said, picking me up. "I'll take care of this." He tried to lay me down on the bed, but I wouldn't let go of him. He sat on the bed, the two of us locked in an embrace. "It's okay, Thea," he said, rubbing my back. "Don't be scared."

I pressed myself into him. "Don't leave me," I cried. "Don't let me think."

He squeezed me tighter. "I'm not going anywhere, sweetie."

I sobbed, my face buried in his chest,

163

trying to erase the painful images. I now understood why those men were so cruel, why they hated me so much. It wasn't self-confidence I had witnessed at the lake, it was pure arrogance. How many people had I hurt? I cried harder as I thought of those men dragging me away. They had no compassion for me, only hate. They said they would never have to fear me again. What horrible things had I done to them? How could anyone even love me, much less risk their life for me?

James's wish to take back his love cut through my heart. I wanted to crawl in a hole and die. Now I knew why I had looked at him with sadness that day in the courtroom. We'd had a fight, a horrible fight. I wondered if I had lost him again. He didn't seem to care about the danger when he had driven away earlier. He had seen the old me tonight, and it must have thrown him.

"Let me get you some tissues," Cory said, trying to break away.

I wrapped my arms around his neck and begged him not to let me go.

He sighed and scooted us farther onto the bed. He leaned his head against the headboard and pulled me close. "Does this mean you remember me?" he asked.

"No, but I know who you are." I looked up at him and got lost in his eyes. They were as blue as James's.

He tilted his head to the ceiling and sighed. "I think I'd better go now."

I grasped him tighter. "Please, don't leave me."

He stroked my hair. "Okay, Thea. I'll leave when you're ready, all right?"

I nodded and closed my eyes. I felt safe—not like with James, but safe nonetheless. "I was a horrible person, wasn't I?"

Cory didn't answer. After a few minutes, he pulled me closer. "You weren't that bad," he finally answered. "Your whole life, you were told how special you were, how different. That's bound to change a person."

I didn't like hearing that. It cemented what I already thought of myself. "How can any of you even stand me?"

He looked down at me and smiled. "You were never like that with me or the boys, but that's because we all grew up together."

"But I was so conceited and mean," I said, choking on a sob.

"Come on, now. You shouldn't think that way. You were just trying to look after everyone. Everyone looked to you for answers. I think you acted the way you did so you could be strong for them."

"Thank you for seeing that in me, Cory. Even if I don't deserve it."

"Thea, things were different back then. It was another time. People were controlled by fear—fear of things they couldn't understand. And they didn't understand you."

"Oh, they understood," I said. "They knew I was a mean person. They hated me." I couldn't stop thinking about James. It had taken me so many years to find him, and here I was again, without him.

Now that my eyes were finally dry, I found myself exhausted.

Cory held me as I drifted off. I felt him kiss my forehead. "I love you," he murmured as I slipped into a deep sleep.

Chapter 10
Fido was a bad dog

I heard the building's main door slam, waking me up. I was still safely in Cory's arms.

When I looked up, he was smiling at me. "Good morning," he said. "I was wondering how long you were going to sleep."

"What time is it?" I asked, turning to check the clock.

"It's time for you to get to work." He pushed me toward the edge of the bed, stretched his arms, and shook the hair from his face.

"I'm sorry about last night," I said, feeling bad for the way he had to sleep.

"Are you kidding me? This morning was worth it." He winked and jumped off the bed. He walked to the front door and whistled loudly into the hallway. "I know it's a little late to ask, but do you know my name?"

"Yes, Cory," I said, smiling. "And I know the names of the other boys, too." He rolled his eyes playfully. "You'd better not use the word 'boys' in front of them, or you'll never hear the end of it."

I heard someone running up the stairs.

"You're still alive, bro!" Samuel said as he arrived at my door. "Thought it was going to get ugly." He smiled at me. "Hi. You feeling okay now?"

"Do you live here?" I asked.

"We all do," Cory answered.

Samuel walked in. "First and second floors," he said, sitting down next to me. "We sleep on the first floor, train on the second." He looked around the room. "So what did you two lovebirds do last night?"

"Shut up, Samuel," Cory said, throwing a sock at him.

"Man, I already told you to call me Sam—just Sam."

"I'm going to start calling you *stupid* if you don't shut up." Cory opened the door for Samuel to leave.

Samuel rolled his eyes and walked toward the door. "He was pretty pissed, so you might want to think of what to say to him."

"How about I say nothing?" Cory asked, pushing Samuel out the door.

Cory turned and waved. "See you later. I'll let you get ready now."

After he left, I could hear the boys on the other side of the door. One of them was upset because he didn't get to say hello to me. "You'll see her later, Fish," Cory said. "We have to go."

I wondered who Samuel could have been talking about. Maybe one of the other boys was mad at Cory for staying here last night. Why would Cory need to think of what to say? There was no time to worry about it. I jumped up and got into the shower. I couldn't believe I was actually looking forward to going to work. I wanted to keep myself busy so I wouldn't have to think of James.

I decided I would visit the boys after work, maybe spend the day with them. I quickly dressed and ran out the door. The hallway was empty; the boys had gone. A sudden thought occurred to me: If they had lived here all this time, why hadn't I smelled them? I pushed the thought aside and hurried out of the building. I thought I saw James's car parked out front, but the car was gone before I could get a good look inside.

As I neared the bakery, I saw a delivery van parked outside. "What the heck?" When I walked in, I couldn't believe my eyes. The place was crammed with people, and boxes were stacked practically to the ceiling.

Norm smiled as I approached him. "Thea," he said with his hands in the air. "You see? You see how hard work pays off?"

I was speechless. I'd never seen Norm so happy.

"It started two days ago," he said. "I even had to rent a delivery van."

I looked out the front window and smiled. "Yeah, I saw it."

"How are you feeling?" he asked. "That girl told me how sick you were. I had to hire extra help to keep up with the orders."

"I feel fine, thanks." My eyes drifted to the woman standing next to Norm.

Norm followed my gaze. "Oh, this is Sharron. She's working the register."

"Hello, dear," Sharron said, winking at me.

I smiled at her, not knowing what to make of all this.

"And your trainees are in the back," Norm continued. "So chop chop, Thea. Let's get those boys working." He gave me a gentle push toward the back room.

I shook my head and smiled. "Yes, Norm, right away." I waved at Sharron and wondered what kind of spell they had put on the townspeople to make them suddenly want pastries.

I grabbed an apron and walked into the back room. To my surprise, I found Cory, Samuel, and the rest of the boys wearing aprons and rolling out dough. They stopped when they saw me. You could hear a pin drop as we looked at each other. Cory gestured with his head, and they resumed their work.

Fish, with his innocent face and a devilish smirk, kept stealing glances at me from the corner of his eye. I smiled and walked over to him. He had dirty-blond hair and green eyes. His face was that of a fifteen-year-old.

"I'm sorry I didn't get to say hello this morning," I said to him. "I had a rough night."

"You did?" Fish said, smirking at Cory. The other boys laughed as Fish put his fingers over his lips. "I thought you were praying when I heard you saying 'Oh God' last night."

Cory chucked a piece of dough at Fish and the other boys laughed harder.

"I thought I heard her praying a few times," Joshua said from behind me.

When I looked over my shoulder, he bowed his head quickly. "I'm sorry," he said, his face reddening. "That was rude."

"Ah, my red-headed teddy bear," I said to him.

He looked up and smiled. "You remember me?" he asked eagerly.

I turned and threw my arms around him. "No, but my heart does."

Joshua lifted me into a bear hug. "Ahem!"

I turned to find Javier, arms folded across his chest.

"Are you ready to hug a real man?" he asked, his eyes playfully meeting mine.

"You're the charmer, right?" I asked, walking over to him.

"I'm your favorite, and the best-looking one of all these losers." He leaned over and kissed me on the cheek. "I missed you, mama."

"Boo, don't listen to him," Samuel said, stepping forward. "Everyone knows I'm your favorite. He wishes he was good-looking." Samuel pushed Javier out of the way and hugged me. "I didn't get a chance to do this earlier."

As I looked around at each of their faces, I felt my soul fill with happiness. "I know I can't remember you," I said, "but I saw all of you in one of my memories. I feel nothing but joy having you all around me."

"What did you feel last night?" Fish asked, flashing a devilish grin.

Cory rolled his eyes and threw more dough at him. "You'd better not burn the bread again. You're going to get us all fired." Cory looked at me. "You have to be careful with Fish," he warned. "He's always up to no good."

I walked over to Cory and put my hand on his arm. "Thank you again for last night."

"I think we gave Fish ammo for the next four hundred years," he replied.

We both laughed as I tied my apron and began showing them what to do. For the rest of the day, anytime I said the words "hard" or "long," Fish giggled and said, "Enough about Cory, what do we do now?"

The day flew by. I laughed so hard my stomach hurt. It felt good to let go and enjoy life for a while. I had so little to be happy about these days.

Despite the joyful distraction, James was still on my mind. I couldn't get his words from the memory out of my head.

We were hard at work when I heard Sharron out front. "Good afternoon, James. What can I do for you?"

The boys stopped working and looked at Cory.

"She's in the back," Sharron said.

A few moments passed. "Hello," James said as he entered the back room.

I kept my back to him, not wanting to face him. The boys were still looking at Cory and waiting to see what he would say.

"Hello," Cory said to James.

The boys followed Cory's lead. "Hey," they all said to James.

I could feel James behind me. "Thea, may I speak to you, please—alone?"

I looked over my shoulder and nodded.

Cory motioned for the boys to leave. He removed his apron and threw it onto the table. "I'll be right outside, okay?" he told me.

I nodded.

Cory smiled widely at James. "And how was your night, James?" he asked, brushing James's arm with his own as he passed. "Because mine was real nice."

"Yes," James said, turning to him. "I had the privilege of seeing you sleep very soundly."

"Best night's rest I've had in a long time," Cory said.

"I wouldn't get used to it," James shot back. "It would be a pity to see Thea so sad."

Cory faced him, the boys already in a stance. "It's not over till it's over, my friend."

"Oh, it's been over for quite some time," James replied, stepping closer to him.

Sharron walked in. "Boys, I have some deliveries for you."

Cory stared at James for a long moment before walking out. Each of the boys glared at James as they filed out of the back room behind Cory.

"She might be a little tired," Fish said, and the rest of the boys laughed.

I suddenly realized that James had seen me and Cory this morning. He was the one who had slammed the door. I turned to him, feeling nervous. "James, last night, I . . ."

Before I could get the words out, James was kissing me. I didn't know what to do, but my heart did. I threw my arms around him and kissed him back.

"I'm so sorry," I said when our lips finally parted.

"And why, may I ask, are you apologizing to me?" He gently kissed my lips. "It is I who should be on bended knee." He held me tighter and kissed me again. "I behaved like a monster last night," he said into my ear. "Can you ever forgive me?"

"James, last night I was—"

"You have nothing to explain," he said. "But had I known you needed company, I would have come up." He paused. "I was parked outside your building all night."

It was James I had seen driving away this morning. "You were? Why didn't you come inside?"

He ran his fingers along my face. "Like I said, I behaved like a monster."

I wanted to explain why I was in Cory's arms this morning. "James, last night after you left, I—"

He cut me off again. "Shh," he said, placing his finger to my lips. "I'll be the only one explaining anything."

James was obviously not bothered, so I decided to leave it alone.

"Have you seen Delia?" I asked.

He smiled mysteriously. "She's doing me a little favor."

I stared at him for a moment and decided not to ask. In fact, I decided to stop questioning everything he did. I wanted to show him that I had complete trust in him.

"Will I be seeing you later?" I asked.

"I should say so. It's a very important

day."

I leaned back in his arms. "It is? Why?"

"You'll find out tonight," he said, kissing my head. How I loved when he did that. It felt like such a tender act of love.

I was about to ask him where we were going when Sharron walked in. "James, a word, please."

He nodded and pulled away from me. "I'll pick you up around eight."

"Okay," I replied. Sharron gave me a smile as she followed James out of the back room.

I resumed my work and began removing things from the ovens. I wondered where he was taking me. *What's so special about this day?*

I was closing one of the ovens when the smell hit me. It was so strong. I looked around and saw no one, so I walked to the front of the bakery. Jack, the man James had been talking to the night before, was standing at the counter. There were six men with him, all milling about the bakery. I glanced around for any sign of James or the boys. I couldn't think of where everyone had gone off to; the place had been packed earlier.

"M . . . May I help you?" I asked nervously, walking up behind the counter. I tried to push down the panic that was rising inside me.

"Your friend's car is parked outside," Jack said, "but I don't see him. You happen to know where he is?" He leaned against the counter. The other men walked to the door and stood in front of it as if trying to block it.

"James left a few minutes ago," I answered.

He leaned closer and looked into my eyes. "Tell me something: Does he follow you around like a puppy dog?"

I took a step back; his smell was overpowering. I started to feel dizzy. "Excuse me?"

"You must give him some very good treats," Jack said. "I mean, to keep him parked outside your house all night. He's a good little watchdog, huh?"

"What do you want?" I asked, moving farther away from the counter. "I already told you, he left a few minutes ago."

Jack looked at the other men. "You hear that, boys? Fido already left."

The men laughed, and Jack turned back to me. "I wonder if Fido is done playing with his toy yet?"

I was horrified as he leaned farther over the counter. He smiled wickedly. "I like playing with toys, don't you, boys?" The other men stepped up behind him. Jack reached over and stroked the top of my hand with his fingers. "Do you have any special treats for us? James is my friend, and friends share everything."

I pulled my hand away. "Don't touch me."

He laughed. "Looks like she's got a little bite in her, boys. I think Fido's been holding out on us." He walked around the counter.

I stepped back.

"I wonder what would happen if I broke

Fido's toy?" he said. "Maybe that would help Fido better concentrate on his duties." He reached toward my face.

I slapped his hand away. "Don't touch me, pig!"

I tried to push him back, but he grabbed me and threw me over the counter. As I hit the floor, his men picked me up and slammed me against the display case.

Jack jumped over the counter and put his face up to mine. "I can't afford for Fido to have any distractions. You see, Fido has been a very bad boy. He chose you last night instead of doing his job. We can't have that now, can we?"

He tried to touch my face, but I quickly turned my head. He grabbed a fistful of my hair and yanked my head back. "I think it's time to put Fido's toy away."

He raised his hand to strike me, but was stopped by a sudden foot in his face. I spun around to find Cory landing on his feet. He crouched quickly, and Fish used his back as a launch pad, flying across the bakery and hitting one of Jack's men square in the face. Another man grabbed Fish and slammed him to the ground. Fish swiftly rolled over and jumped to his feet. Cory was on his feet again when another man grabbed him from behind. Cory tilted forward and sent the man flying over his back.

"Bring it!" Samuel called out as he ran up the wall. He back-flipped onto one of the men's shoulders and twisted the man's head until it snapped. I ran to the corner as Fish

fought two of the men. Cory ran to help and
flicked his arms forward, propelling two shiny,
sword-like weapons out of his sleeves. He
swung at one of the men, cutting his head clean
off. One man started for the door, but Joshua
was coming in. He grabbed the man by his neck
and threw him to the floor. He crushed the
man's face with his foot. Jack, finally back on
his feet, ran toward me, but Cory cut him off
and tackled him, sending the two busting
through the counter.

"It's her! She's the witch!" Jack yelled.

Another man started for me, his face
twisted in rage. Javier came out of nowhere and
pushed me out of the way. He wrapped a mesh-
like chain around the man's head and spun
around him. I watched in horror as only the
man's body fell to the floor. Javier pulled on the
chain and it rolled back into his hands.

Cory and Jack were behind the counter,
wrestling amongst the broken glass. Jack was
on his back. Cory straddled him, uncovered his
weapons, and raised his arm to stab Jack.

"Stop!" James yelled, blocking Cory's
arm. James was holding his whip, while the rest
of the attackers lay about the bakery in pieces.

"Traitor!" Jack yelled.

Cory flicked his arms again and the
blades disappeared. He punched Jack's jaw,
knocking him unconscious.

"Guess we won't need that sleeping
spell," Fish said.

"Defending your friends?" Cory said to
James as he got to his feet.

James ignored him and ran to me. "Thea,

are you hurt?" He helped me up.

I was trembling and angry with myself. Once again, I had been gripped with fear and did nothing.

"Oh my goodness," Sharron said, running to me. "Are you all right, dear?"

"I . . . I'm fine," I said, bursting into a sob.

James pulled me into his arms. "Don't cry, my love. It's over."

Cory walked over and got in James's face. "You want to explain why you didn't let me kill him?"

I tried to step between them, but Sharron pulled me aside.

"And then what?" James replied. "Sit here and wait while they figure out we've been picking them off? You really think they're not going to notice one of their main gorillas is missing? You think they don't know that he was headed here?"

"Let's just kill him and get it over with," Samuel yelled to Cory. "We can deal with those fools ourselves."

"Yes, and why don't you just place Thea in the middle of the street?" James said sarcastically. "Maybe she can wear a sign that says she's the one they've been looking for. You can't kill him." He gestured toward Jack. "They'll be waiting for him."

"Then what's the plan?" Cory asked.

"We'll erase his memory of this and replace it with one of our own—one that can help us."

"What about the men he came here

with?" Cory asked.

"Delia can take care of that," James said, taking his phone from his pocket and stepping away.

Cory looked at me. "You okay?"

"I'm fine," I said, wiping the tears from my face. I overheard James telling Delia to bring the box.

He closed his phone and walked back to us. "Delia's around the corner. She can put some fake memories in his head." He put his arms around me and kissed the top of my head. "It's going to be okay, my love."

Cory gave James a dirty look and walked away. "Fish, you, Sam, and Javier go and grab a couple of brooms and sweep up this dust."

I watched as Fish and Samuel swept up. I hadn't even noticed when the men had turned to dust.

"He'll be in the basement," Joshua said, dragging Jack away.

Cory chanted at the counter, ordering it to repair itself.

Sharron offered to help him when the counter didn't come together quite right. "Why would he use that spell?" she said to herself.

I looked up at James. "They were looking for you. I think they wanted to hurt you."

"What did they say to you?" he asked, pulling away.

I bit my lip. "They said I was distracting you."

James's eyes narrowed.

I wrapped my arms around his waist and

closed my eyes. "If anything ever happened to you, I would never forgive myself."

"I'll be fine, Thea," he said. "It's not me I'm worried about."

Delia walked in. "You'll do anything for attention, won't you?"

"Where have you been?" I asked.

She rolled her eyes. "Oh please, like I matter right now. Are you hurt?"

I shook my head and buried my face in James's chest.

"We have something to attend to in the basement," he told Delia. "We'd better get started."

"Where are the boys?" she asked.

"Fish, your girlfriend is here!" Samuel yelled as he walked out of the back. "Hey, Dells. You missed the fun."

"So I hear," she said, giving Samuel a kiss on the cheek.

Fish stormed out of the back room. He slowed and smiled when he saw Delia. "Did they tell you how manly I just was?" he asked.

"Yes, they did," she replied, smiling.

Fish's eyes lit up. "Josh is in the basement. Javier is getting rid of the dust."

"We'd better get started then," Delia said, looking at James. "You'll have to be very specific about the memory you want replaced. Do you just need me to pull out the memory from today?"

James looked shocked for a moment, but then his face lit up. "Delia, that's brilliant!" He released me and grabbed her shoulders. "Is it possible to extract a few and show them to me?"

Delia's mouth was open. "All these years, why didn't we ever think of looking through their memories?"

James looked at Cory. "Care to take a walk down memory lane with me?"

Cory nodded and called the boys over. "Help Sharron clean this up," he ordered. "Then keep Thea in the back with you. You know what to do if you need me."

They nodded, and Cory disappeared into the basement with Delia and James. I felt helpless. I wanted to go with them. I wanted to see the memories they were going to pull out. I began to think of all the harm I'd caused, how one simple choice I'd made had altered the lives of everyone around me. Now, more than ever, I needed to know what it was. In the memory, I'd had a vision, but I couldn't see what it was. What would make me take such drastic measures?

I started to walk toward the basement.

"Where you going?" Samuel asked.

"I have to know, Sammy," I replied. "I need to go with them and watch these memories."

"Listen, Thea, I get it," he said. "I want to be down there, too, but if you see anything that brings back your memory, we'll have twenty times the guys in here in an instant." He paused. "And without your powers to help us, we'll all die."

His words stopped me in my tracks. He was right; I would only make things harder for them. They would fight, I knew that now. They would fight until they were dead, if necessary.

"Your memory is coming back faster than you think," Samuel whispered.

"Why do you say that?"

"Because you just called me Sammy," he said with a wink.

I looked into his eyes, then put my head down in shame. "I'm sorry I did this to you."

"Did what, dear?" Sharron asked, walking into the room. "It wasn't you who made those warlocks want the power they seek. It was Simon who betrayed your father's trust."

"What do you mean?"

"Simon was your father's best friend," she explained. "Your father took him under his wing in England. He was with your father when he found the crystal."

"He was my father's friend?" I asked, shocked.

Sharron looked at the Samuel and the others. "Gentlemen, can you give us a moment, please?"

"Come on, guys," Samuel said. "We'll watch the front for Sharron."

I waited for them to leave. "Delia never told me Simon was my father's friend."

"No one knew, dear. Only Vera knew who he was when he returned."

"Returned? I don't understand."

"Even before your memory was gone, Simon was looking for a way to take your powers, hatching a plan to steal the crystal."

"Did I know that?"

"You knew what your father had warned you about. Every time Simon came around, he tried to romance you, but you always saw through his disguises. His spells never fooled you."

"Spells?"

"Yes," she said. "Changing spells. He changes what he looks like. We think he uses some powerful potions, as well."

"Did he kill my father?"

She shook her head and sighed. "Your mother warned your father repeatedly about Simon. She never liked him. He was—is—unkind to humans. He considers himself above them, and most of all, above us."

"But why?"

"We're half human. We represent the half of the world he hates." She paused. "Half of who he is. No one claims to know why he despises humans so much, but I've often thought that your father may have known the answer."

"Simon is half human?" I asked, stunned. "I knew he needed spells, but I didn't realize it was because he was half human."

"Yes, dear," Sharron said. "I believe it's why he was so fascinated with your father. He was a wizard, after all. Simon had never been around someone like that. He envied your father's powers. When your father told him stories about a crystal that could give the gift of magic, Simon saw a way to have what he always wanted. But he knew your father would never give him that gift. I think your father finally saw through him." Sharron smiled. "When you were born, there was no doubt as to who would eventually receive the crystal.

Simon knew this, of course. So, he waited—waited for you to come of age, and promptly asked for your hand in marriage."

My eyes widened. "What?"

"Yes, dear. You were only six years old, but he wanted to claim his prize before anyone else could. He planned to wait it out, thinking once you and he were married, you would give him the gift he so desperately wanted. But he never expected your father's reaction."

"What happened?"

"Your father nearly killed him that day, but to your father's surprise, Simon was prepared for battle. Simon had learned some powerful wizard's spells from your father. They were friends and had spent many years together in the wizard world—a world your father left when he fell in love with your mother. Simon desperately wanted to make the wizard's world his home."

My legs suddenly felt weak, and I sat down at one of the tables.

Sharon placed her hand on my shoulder and continued. "Simon fled. Your father cast a spell to slow your aging. He knew you had to be twelve before he could give you the crystal, but he wanted to make sure Simon wouldn't return before that. You remained the same age for many years, until your mother died."

"How did she die?" I asked.

"She was poisoned, dear. When we found her . . ." She choked back a sob and turned her back to me.

"What? Please, tell me."

She sighed and turned back to me.

"Someone had cut out her heart."

I clamped my hand to my mouth, and my eyes began to fill. "Why?"

"We don't know," Sharron replied. "Your father went nearly mad with rage. The pain of losing her drove him into a deep depression for many years. I thought he would die of a broken heart." She sighed again and looked into my eyes. "He began to let you age again. He would disappear with you, sometimes for days. I don't know where he took you, but you always seemed wiser and more mature when you returned." She paused, a tear rolling down her cheek. "Eventually it was time for him to give you the crystal, and after bestowing it upon you, he joined his wife. Before he left, he warned us all about Simon."

"He warned you?"

"Yes. He said Simon would return one day. He had searched for him for years, but Simon had developed a talent for changing his appearance and moving around constantly. Your father said he had run out of time and that certain things had to happen, that he couldn't change them. He said you would meet Delia and the two of you would become great friends. He gave me instructions to pass along to her when she turned twenty. He also told me to stop your aging when you turned eighteen." She tilted my chin, and I looked into her eyes. "He spent two days putting spells on you before he departed. He gave me the recipe for the potion we needed to stop your aging, but as you can see, we've all used it, too."

"Sharron, why wait until now to tell me all of this?"

She revealed a small hourglass and set it on the table. "This is why."

I gazed at the miniature timekeeper and picked it up. "Did my father give this to you?"

"No, dear. You did."

"*I* gave this to you?"

She nodded. "You told me to tell you what I just told you. You said I would know when."

"And today you knew?"

She nodded again.

I examined the hourglass and turned it in my hands. It had very little sand in it. "Where has all the sand gone?"

"Portions of it seem to disappear whenever I talk to you. That night in the basement of the bakery was the first time I noticed it. That's when I knew."

"It still has a bit of sand in it."

"Because I'm not finished, dear."

Chapter 11
The Bond

I watched, mesmerized, as the sand floated inside the glass. Sure enough, each time Sharron spoke, more of it disappeared.

"We had no idea Simon had returned," Sharron said. "No one knew what he looked like. Even now, we can only guess who he is. The short man you told James about seems to give all the orders."

"The man from the pier. He had a very strong scent. I almost felt the need to touch him when I wiped his memory."

Sharron smiled. "Trust me, dear, if Simon had known it was you for even a split second, he never would have allowed you to touch him."

"But he looks the same. Even in my memories. I think it's him, Sharron."

"He could have already changed what he looked like by then; your father warned us about that. The moment your memory returns, we must be certain it's him. You see, dear, the one thing your father never shared with him is the fact that only you can open the crystal."

"Who do you think he is?"

"Well," she said, pausing, "at first we thought it was James. But he's done nothing but love and protect you, so our suspicions went unfounded."

"Delia still doesn't trust him."

"You have to understand, dear, everyone thinks he convinced you to give him half your powers. We thought he planned on giving them to Simon once they were in the crystal."

"I really tried to give him some of my powers?"

"Yes, but he never wanted that from you." She smiled. "He only wanted to love you."

"Why do you suppose that is? Why me?"

"Only you know the answer to that, dear. I didn't even realize the two of you were in love, much less getting married."

I was confused about James. I still couldn't understand his love for me. "I wonder why he wanted me," I whispered to myself.

"What, dear?"

"Nothing. I was just wondering why I never told the others I knew him."

"Because they didn't trust him," she explained. "And I think you wanted to spare Delia a broken heart."

I looked at her, surprised. "I knew she loved James?"

"We can't hide things from you, dear," she said, giggling. "You can tell when someone is lying to you."

"I can? How?"

"I'm not exactly sure, but you always

knew when one of us was hiding something."

She was right; I had a strange feeling about Delia. I knew she was holding something back. "Sharron, can I ask you something?"

"Of course."

"Why do you think I did it? Put my powers into the crystal, I mean."

"Well, I know you had a vision of the future. You saw something that would have put us all in danger."

"How do you know that?"

"That, I can't tell you."

A few sprinkles remained inside of Sharron's tiny hourglass. I looked at her. "You're not finished."

She reached into her pocket and pulled out a ring. "You must be waiting for this."

"Whose is it?"

"It was your father's. You gave it to me the night we wiped your memory clean."

I took the ring from her and turned it in my fingers.

"I don't think you should wear it," she warned. "Your father never took it off. I believe it was his wedding ring. Anyway, someone might recognize it."

"His wedding ring?" I asked, examining it. It looked like glass with tiny stones embedded in it. I looked closer and realized the stones were actually floating inside the ring. "It's beautiful," I whispered, hugging Sharron. "Thank you." I carefully placed the ring into my pocket.

Delia strode through the back room door, followed by James and Cory, who were supporting the still-unconscious Jack.

"We don't have much time," Delia said. "Everyone, get into place. Thea, get behind the counter."

"Come, dear," Sharron said, taking my arm. "Let's get this over with."

James and Cory leaned Jack against the counter. I stood behind it, wondering what was going to happen. James stood next to Jack. Cory walked to the back and whistled for the boys, who were still outside, to join him. The five guards noisily resumed their work.

"Sharron, can you grab a tray of doughnuts and fill the display case?" James asked.

"Yes, dear," she said, heading into the back.

"What do you need me to do?" I asked.

He looked at me intently. "I need you to cry. Like I just broke your heart."

I focused on the memory of James telling me he wanted to take his love back, but I couldn't cry a single tear. I tried again— nothing.

"Great," Delia said, rolling her eyes. "Now, of all times, you can't cry." She sighed and chanted: "Make her weep, make her cry, there doesn't need to be a reason why."

She slipped quietly into the back as tears instantly brimmed in my eyes and began to spill over.

James laughed. He gave Jack a pat on the back as if he had said something funny. "It's true, my brother," James said. "The younger, the better."

191

Jack opened his eyes and looked at James. He seemed confused for only a second before the fake memory streamed through his head. He laughed along with James and looked over at me. "At least she keeps you warm, my brother," he said. "I wouldn't toss her out just yet. But let us not forget our mission."

James stopped laughing. "Yes, brother, you're right." He walked over to the counter. "Please don't cry," he said to me. "I was just joking. My friend and I were only having a little harmless fun."

I did as James instructed: I cried.

Jack leaned over and whispered loudly in James's ear. "Maybe we should leave now. You can talk to her later and work things out. We still need to know what the witch, Delia, is up to."

James nodded, and they turned to leave. Jack put his arm around James's shoulder as they strolled toward the door. "I still can't believe she likes you, old man." They laughed again. James glanced at me from the corner of his eye as he and Jack stepped out of the bakery.

They were gone, but I couldn't stop crying.

"They're gone, dear," Sharron said.

Delia walked in and chuckled. "I wonder how long she'd stand there and cry."

No one laughed.

Delia cleared her throat. "Uh, yes," she said, and chanted: "Stop the tears, stop the weeping, her eyes will now stop their leaking."

My crying ceased just as suddenly as it

had begun. "Very funny, Delia," I said, wiping my face.

"I think it went well," Cory said, peering out the window. I hadn't heard him come out of the back room. "Okay, Thea. We're on now."

"What do you mean?"

"We're heading to the park," he explained. "You need to look upset when we get there. I'm supposed to comfort you so Jack thinks I'm moving in on James's territory. James thinks it will help keep them away from you."

"What are you talking about?" I asked. "How can that help?"

"Jack doesn't like to lose," Delia replied. "He thinks he and James are great friends now. He won't like seeing you with Cory, even if he thinks you're just James's toy." Delia sniffed. "It's a guy thing, and Jack's head is full of it. He looks at you as their property now."

Cory shook his head. "No, Delia. It's a warlock thing. They think Thea is human and see her as being marked by James. Jack's in the brotherhood. He sees Thea as James's prize— one not to be shared. I still don't agree with this, but if it will keep him from bothering her, then I'm willing to try." He walked to the door. "We have to go, Thea. James will be waiting."

"Be careful," Sharron said, looking at Cory. "Both of you."

"We'll be fine," he assured her. "The boys are already on their way."

I wasn't altogether comfortable with what we were about to do, but I was willing to try anything that would help keep Jack at a distance. Cory took my hand, and we slipped out the door. It was just starting to get dark.

"What exactly am I supposed to do?" I asked Cory.

"They won't be able to hear us, so we can talk about anything. It just needs to look like I'm comforting you."

"Where will James be?"

"He'll be with Jack, somewhere in the park. Our job is to discreetly spot them and sit somewhere close, but not too close."

There were tourists scattered all around the park. A pumpkin-carving contest was in progress. Food venders were busy serving customers. I spotted James and Jack under the gazebo. As we came into view, they looked in our direction.

Cory found an empty bench and we sat down close together. He put his arm around me. "You cold?" he asked.

"Not too bad. How long do we have to stay here?"

He glanced over his shoulder. "When they leave, we can head out." He rubbed my back from time to time and leaned close to me as if we were talking intimately.

I felt silly, not knowing if this little act was going to help. "It's busy here tonight," I said, watching the tourists mill about.

"Yep, always busy this time of year."

"You guys ever get out and join the festivities?"

"Javier does. He loves this time of year—lots of human girls around."

"What do you guys do for money?" I

asked. "Delia only works seasonally."

He laughed. "What do we need money for? There isn't anything we can't get with a spell."

"A spell to make money?" I asked, surprised.

"Money has no value in our world, Thea. As long as we have a place to live, we have everything we need."

I thought for a moment. "Then why does James have money?"

He shrugged. "You'll have to ask him."

I was starting to feel uncomfortable and hoped we didn't have to do this much longer. "Where did you guys learn to fight like that?"

"He's looking at us," Cory said, scooting closer to me. "Sorry, Thea. James said to make it look believable."

I just smiled and looked away. "You didn't answer my question."

"Well, we've had hundreds of years to practice, for one thing. We also got some good ideas from watching movies."

"Really? Delia hates television and computers, and any sort of modern technology."

Cory laughed and shook his head. "You should have seen her when James gave her that cell phone. She had no clue. We had to show her how to use it. Fish kept calling and leaving spells on her voice mail."

I laughed at the thought of Delia trying to check voice mail. "What kind of spells would he leave for her?"

"Love spells," he said, rolling his eyes. "What else?"

We shared a laugh. "He's a little stinker," I said. "But he definitely cracks me up."

"He's a handful, all right," Cory replied. "Never a dull moment when Fish is around."

"Tell me about Sam."

"Well, he's the complete opposite of Fish. Total hothead—quick to throw a punch. But he's brave. He would fight an army alone if he had to. Kid's got a lot of spirit."

"And Joshua? Delia said he was my tender teddy bear."

"Yes, but don't let that fool you. Josh's got unbelievable strength and a heart of gold. He'd give you the shirt off his back."

"What about Javier?"

"Javier, well, he's the Romeo of our time—or so he thinks." Cory smirked. "He's got a silver tongue with the ladies, and has a taste for human girls because they can't bond to him."

There it was again. "Cory, what is this bonding thing? I've heard Delia talk about it, too."

He scratched his head, searching for the words to explain. "Well," he said, looking a little embarrassed, "when a witch gives herself to a warlock, or vice versa, there's an instant bond between them. Even if there is no love shared between the two, they will forever be bonded to each other."

"What do you mean?"

"When they bond," he said, scratching his head again. "You know, sleep together? The witch will never have feelings or urges for another man. For the man, well, he'll never get the response he needs from his body to perform for another woman. That's why, back in our time, a lot of the warlocks turned to human women. That way, they couldn't become bonded, and remained free to seek out other women."

"The warlocks don't recognize you as one of them, is that right?"

"That's right." he replied. "Even though I'm male and a warlock, they consider me only a witch because I have one human parent."

"Are there many like you?"

"Yeah, but we can't spit spells like the purebloods can. We can only chant them. It's guys like Javier that keep making half-human witches. Some of the humans walking around here don't even know they're witches. But that's what happens when guys like him don't want to be stuck with someone they may not love."

"Are you bonded?" I asked. "What's your story?"

"Oh, I'm a lost cause. I waited too long. I thought she was a sure thing; everyone thought we would marry one day. So, I took my time and played the field with human girls and never saw it coming."

"What do you mean?" I pressed. "What didn't you see coming?"

"She fell in love with someone else. By the time I was ready to make my move, it was too late." He leaned back. "But there's still a little hope."

"Is she not with him anymore?"

"No, it's not that," he said. "She's not bonded to him yet. The way I see it, she's still fair game." He sighed. "And I don't plan on making the same mistake twice."

"Well, I wish you luck. I hope she sees what a great guy you are."

He looked at me and smiled, his blue eyes sparkling. "What else do you think of me?"

"Are you kidding me?" I asked, giggling. "Where do I start? You were there for me last night when you didn't have to be. You're risking your life for me right now even though I don't deserve it." I looked over at him and smiled. "And you're pretty."

He laughed and shook his head. "Sorry, I don't mean to laugh. It's just that I've never been called 'pretty' before."

I looked away, embarrassed. "I can't believe I said that."

"No, Thea. Please don't be like that. I liked it. I like that you think I'm pretty."

He was more than pretty; he was beautiful. I couldn't believe a guy like him didn't have a girlfriend. I looked over my shoulder. James and Jack were still under the gazebo. "They haven't left yet. What's taking so long?" I was getting cold and wanted to get back to the bakery. I wanted to get ready for my date with James. I couldn't wait to find out where he was taking me.

Cory looked across at the two men. "Well, we've been laughing the whole time. You were supposed to look upset. Jack has to feel that James is losing his conquest, and he doesn't look too convinced." Cory looked thoughtful for a moment. "I think I know how to fix this."

I turned to ask him what his plan was, but found his lips instead. He placed his hand on my back and pulled me toward him. Before I knew it, he was pulling me to my feet as he kissed me. I tried, in vain, to push him away.

Cory pulled me closer. "This will help James," he whispered.

I looked into his eyes and let him kiss me. I felt the heat from his body as he wrapped his arms around me. His heart raced, pounding against mine. He lifted me off the ground and kissed me harder. His kiss was strange, not at all like James's. My heart wasn't racing and my knees weren't giving out. I wanted him to stop.

When he finally pulled away, he looked into my eyes. "This is how it should have been," he whispered. He leaned forward again, crushing his lips against mine.

This time I felt my heart race, but in protest. I opened my eyes as he was kissing me and glanced toward the gazebo. James and Jack were gone. I pulled my head back. "They're gone," I said, nearly breathless. "We can stop." I pulled away from him.

He stepped back, looked around, and smiled. "I thought that might work," he said, seemingly satisfied with himself. He took my hand, and we walked back to the bakery. It was completely dark now, and I was shivering from the cold.

"About time," Delia said as we walked in. "What took so long? We almost went looking for you."

The boys followed us inside. "Thea was choking on something, and Cory was trying to dislodge it with his tongue," Fish said, walking up to Delia. "Want me to show you how?"

She eyed me suspiciously. "What happened?"

"They wouldn't leave," I explained. "Cory thought it would help if he kissed me."

"Did he?" she said, smiling at Cory.

He smiled back and shrugged. "James said to make it look convincing."

Fish stepped closer to Delia. "I think I need convincing."

The boys laughed as Delia hugged Fish. "If you ever decide to age again, I might just think about it."

James stormed in and headed straight for Cory. "What the hell was that?" he yelled. "Do you know what I almost did?"

The boys instantly got into a stance, but Cory held up his hand. "You wouldn't leave," he explained. "She was getting cold. So, we gave you a little push."

"James, please," I said, reaching for his arm. "He's telling the truth. It was a last resort, nothing more."

"It was a last resort for you, but a golden chance for him." He jabbed a finger at Cory.

"I thought you had nothing to worry about," Cory said. "You seem pretty worried to me."

"Don't confuse my actions with jealousy, Cory," James shot back. "And don't ever touch my wife again." He grabbed my arm and practically dragged me out of the bakery. He was pulling me toward his car, his hand tight around my wrist.

I yanked my arm from his grip and stopped on the sidewalk. "You're hurting me."

He turned on me, rage in his eyes. He pinned me against the building, leaned in, pushed my arms above my head, and held them there. "How did it feel when he kissed you?" he asked. "Did it feel like this?"

His tongue entered my mouth forcefully as he pressed his lips to mine. He paused for just a moment before his lips began to travel. My heart was on fire as he kissed my neck. He pressed his body into mine and thrust his tongue into my mouth again. Cory's kiss was nothing like this. I thought my heart would explode.

Suddenly, he stopped, sighed, and let me go. He turned his back and bowed his head. "Forgive me. I feel like a complete animal."

I stepped forward and put my hand on his back. "Are you angry with me?"

He turned and put his arms around me. "No, my love. I'm angry at myself. I didn't mean to hurt your wrist. Please forgive me."

"Take me home," I whispered.

"I understand," he said, pulling away. "I don't blame you for being upset. Of course I'll take you back to your apartment."

I looked up at him and smiled. "No, James. I meant take me home with you."

I melted as he looked down at me with those big blue eyes.

He pulled me back into his arms and kissed my head.

"Don't ever stop doing that," I said, squeezing him tighter.

"Never," he said. "As long as you never forget you love me."

I rested my head on his chest. "I only kissed him to help you."

"Just don't ever forget you love me," he repeated, and kissed my head again. "Let's get home so we can celebrate our special day."

I looked up and began to ask what we were celebrating.

He placed his finger to my lips and smiled. "You'll see." We walked to his car and drove home.

William was waiting for us when we walked in. "Good evening, madam," he said, bowing to me. "How is madam this evening?"

I threw my arms around him. "I'm happy, William. Very happy."

William didn't move. He seemed shocked that I was touching him.

"It's okay, William," I whispered. "I understand now." I felt my soul connect with his.

He slowly pulled away from me, a hint of a smile on his face. "I'm happy to hear that, madam." He took two steps back. "There is something in the room for madam," he said, extending his arm toward the stairs.

I looked into his eyes and smiled. "Thank you, William." I smiled back at James and ran up the stairs.

"Do you think she knows?" I heard James ask William.

I didn't turn around. I smiled to myself,

feeling happy that soon I could tell William that I knew who he was.

Once in my room, I sighed and looked around. I hadn't noticed before how beautiful it was. The bed alone took my breath away. Above the bed was a painting which I only now realized was of me. I was sitting in a garden with a flower in my hair, smiling and holding a bouquet of flowers on my lap. I looked closer and noticed a wedding band on my finger.

"A friend of mine in France painted that for me," James said from the doorway. "I cast a spell on him so he wouldn't miss a single detail. You were so happy that day." He walked across the room to me. "That image of you has been engraved in my mind for more years than I can count."

"It's beautiful, James. Am I looking at you?"

"Yes, you were asking me to come and sit by you. But I was too busy admiring my new wife."

"Why did you fall in love with me?" I asked, looking into his eyes.

"The question is, my love, why did you fall in love with me?"

"No, really, tell me about it," I pressed. "Why did you fall for me?"

"It's that important to you?"

"I don't know why, but yes."

"If it will make you happy, then I will tell you." He sat on the bed and motioned for me to sit beside him. We both looked up at the painting. "I was walking home one day when I heard someone singing in the woods. I'd seen you in town a few times, but you were always surrounded by so many people. I walked through the trees and saw you. You were dancing around and putting flowers in your hair. You had a basket sitting on the ground nearby, with mushrooms in it. Your hands and feet were dirty. I followed you at a distance as you made your way to the lake. You looked around and began to remove your clothes."

He took my hand. "I should have turned away—it was such a private moment—but I couldn't take my eyes off of you. The way the sun hit your hair, and the sight of your naked body . . ." He sighed. "It was more than I could take. I wanted to touch you, feel your silky skin. I had to hold onto a tree as you slipped into the water. After that, I took the same route home every day, hoping to see you again. You seemed so free and pure. I'd hide in the trees and wait for you to appear, and you never disappointed me. I always wondered if you knew I was there."

"I knew," I told him. "Delia showed me the memory."

He smiled. "And why do you suppose you fell in love with me?"

I looked up at the painting. "Look at my face," I said. "I look so happy and complete. I think you made me feel like the person I wanted to be. I think you made me feel like a real woman, not just a witch." I walked up to the painting. "How will I ever be able to show you how much I love you if I can't remember?"

He touched my face. "You've already shown me." He kissed me.

I felt the heat from our bodies burning between us. I wanted to tear off his clothes and touch every part of him. I wrapped my arms around his neck and pulled him closer.

His kisses became more passionate. He picked me up and carried me to the bed. His lips never left mine as he lay me down.

I pulled him toward me. When he slid his hand under my blouse, I started to tremble. "James," I whispered.

He reached under my leg and pulled me closer. "So long, I've waited," he said as he kissed me again. He removed my blouse and flung it across the room.

I smiled as I unbuttoned his shirt. "Is this what we're celebrating?" I asked.

Suddenly, he stopped. He looked into my eyes for a moment and scrambled off the bed. "Forgive me," he said, picking up my blouse.

I couldn't understand what I had done wrong.

He handed me the blouse and looked away. "Please get dressed, Thea, before I can't stop myself."

I took the blouse from him and began to cry. I felt so humiliated and rejected.

In an instant, I was in his arms again. "Thea, my love, please don't cry. It's my fault. I lost my focus on why we're here."

I tried to stop them, but the tears kept coming. I pushed him away and stood. I hurriedly buttoned my blouse and headed for the door.

He grabbed me and turned me around. "You think this doesn't drive me mad? I'm married to you and I can't have you."

"What do you mean?" I asked shakily.

"Thea, I'm a man," he replied. "You have no idea how difficult it was for me to stop myself just now."

"Then why did you?"

He looked into my eyes and pulled me into his arms. "I'm afraid only you know the answer to that."

"What do you mean?"

"You were adamant when we last spoke, just before they wiped your memory. Before you sent me away, you specifically told me not to touch you like that." He lifted my face. "Maybe one day you can explain it to me."

"I don't know what to say," I replied.

He smiled and kissed my head. "I'm sorry I lost control. I got caught up in the moment."

I squeezed him and closed my eyes. "I'm sorry I act like a child sometimes."

"Let's not talk about this," he said. "Not tonight, okay?"

I nodded.

He stepped to the closet, opened the double doors, and stepped in. "I have a surprise for you."

I wiped my tears and tried to fix my hair. I was sure I looked a mess.

James came out of the closet holding a beautiful dress. "Delia will be here soon," he said. "She'll help you get ready." He laid the dress gently on the bed.

"Where are we going?"

He shook his head playfully. "No

questions." He leaned over and kissed my head.

There was a knock at the door, and James turned and opened it.

"Master, we have deliveries arriving," William said.

"Yes, thank you, William. Is Delia here yet?"

"She's on her way up, sir."

James looked at me and smiled. "I'll see you downstairs."

Chapter 12
The Fake James

I lifted the off-white dress from the bed and admired its flowing sleeves and pearl buttons running the length of the back. Delia and I had seen similar dresses while browsing the medieval fairs. I happened to notice that it closely resembled the dress in the painting. The corset waist made me nervous; I wasn't sure it was going to fit.

"Pretty, isn't it?" Delia asked from the doorway.

"Yeah," I replied. "I wonder why James is making such a fuss."

She rolled her eyes and walked into the room. "Will you just play along? He went through a lot of trouble today. You'll find out soon enough." She stood back and scrutinized me. "Thea, you're a mess," she proclaimed. "What have you been doing?" She grabbed my hand and led me to the bathroom.

When I stepped out of the shower ten minutes later, Delia was plugging in all kinds of styling devices. I couldn't help but laugh; she obviously had no idea what she was doing.

"Are you planning on opening a salon?" I asked.

She looked at me and rolled her eyes. "I promised your husband I would help you get ready, and I don't know any spells strong enough to fix that mess you've got going on up there."

I giggled and walked into the bedroom.

"You think this is funny?" she asked, following me. "I'm the one who has to make that gnarled mass of I-don't-know-what look beautiful tonight."

"What kind of hairstyle were you going to give me?"

"I don't know," Delia whined. "James said to make it look like the painting."

I looked at the painting. "Hair, make yourself look like it did in the painting." At once, my hair began to untangle and brush itself. A flower flew from the vase on the dresser and landed behind my ear. Portions of my hair were pulled straight and moments later, soft curls bounced back.

I looked at Delia and smiled. "How's it look?"

She sighed. "You look beautiful, Thea. I don't think I've ever seen your hair look so neat."

I walked to the mirror, and my mouth dropped open. It was like I was seeing myself for the first time.

"Have I always had curls like these?"

Delia stepped over and gazed into the mirror from behind me. "Yes, and you've always been beautiful, too."

I could see my features clearly now. My thin nose, brown eyes, and my hair—it was so long. "Who are you?" I asked the person in the mirror.

"She's you, Thea," Delia said. "She's been there all the time, waiting for you to notice her." Delia held up the dress. "Now, let's get this on you, so you can notice the rest of you."

I eyed the dress apprehensively. "I don't think it's going to fit, Delia."

Delia released an exasperated sigh. "What kind of spell did you put on yourself? Why did you make yourself so insecure? Look at your curves, Thea. In what world do those equal fat? Now let's get this dress on before James comes up here looking for you."

I stepped carefully into the dress. To my surprise and delight, it seemed to fit okay. Delia pulled the corset tight, then tighter.

"I can't breathe," I protested.

She yanked on it again and tied it. "Isn't that the point of these things?" Delia walked around me, inspecting my appearance. When she came full circle, her eyes lit up. "There they are!" she said excitedly, pointing at my breasts.

"What?" I ran to the mirror to find my breasts popping out of the top of the corset. "They've never looked so big before," I said, panicking. "Maybe it's too tight?"

"No, Thea. It's perfect. Trust me." She reached for the shoes, sitting on the floor next to the bed, and set them in front of me. "Here's the final touch."

I looked down. "Delia, I don't know how to walk in high heels. I'll break my neck."

"Put them on, Thea. You'll do fine."

I slipped my feet inside the shoes and stepped back for Delia to examine the final product.

"Gorgeous," she said, a tear running down her cheek. "This is the witch I remember." She walked to the door and opened it. "Let's go. He's waiting."

I walked to the doorway and paused. "What's waiting for me down there?" She gave me a gentle push into the hallway and closed the door behind her. "It's time to go find out, my friend."

I walked toward the staircase, butterflies fluttering in my stomach. At the bottom of the steps, James waited, looking handsome in his tuxedo. My heart raced as I beheld this beautiful man waiting for me.

He turned when he heard my footsteps on the stairs. His eyes lit up at the sight of me. He was practically beaming when I reached him, and he gently pulled me into his arms. "Beautiful does not suffice for what I wish to say right now," he said. "You look breathtaking, my love." He leaned down and kissed me.

In that moment, nothing else mattered.

"It's a good thing you weren't wearing this dress earlier," he whispered into my ear. "I'm afraid we'd still be in the room."

"We can go back up if you wish," I said playfully.

He smiled and held his elbow out to me. "Come. I want to show you something." I took his arm, and he walked me to a set of double doors. I could smell flowers and scented

211

candles. "I never had a chance to celebrate these two occasions with you, and I've waited four hundred years to celebrate this one." He opened the doors.

I walked into the room slowly and gasped. The room was lit with hundreds of candles of all sizes. Tall vases filled with flowers lined the walls. Three huge, sparkling chandeliers hung overhead, and beautiful white drapes adorned the massive windows. I gazed around the room in amazement. It felt like a scene from one of my books.

"Happy anniversary, my love," he whispered in my ear.

I looked at him, my eyes filled with tears. "Anniversary?"

"Our first one together." He held out his hand. "May I have this dance?"

Music began to play. I looked across the room and saw a small stage with a violinist and a cellist. It suddenly dawned on me that we were standing in a ballroom. The musicians played a waltz as James led me to the dance floor. He took me gently in his arms and we began to dance.

I was relieved that I was able to dance in my high-heeled shoes. I smiled, wondering if Delia had put a spell on them. "This is the happiest day of my life," I said. He pulled me close and kissed my head. I looked up into his blue eyes. "How I love when you do that."

"I feel as though I'm kissing the witch inside of you when I do that," he said. "I feel compelled to kiss you both, if that makes sense." He looked into my eyes and touched my face. "How I've missed you, Thea. How my heart has ached to hold you in my arms again."

I smiled as tears streamed down my cheeks. "I love you, James."

"And don't you ever forget that."

Nothing could have prepared me for this perfect moment, not even his books. The musicians had begun playing another song when James's phone rang. He sighed and pulled away from me. "I'm sorry, but I have to answer this." He flipped the phone open and stepped away. "This had better be important," he said to the person on the other end.

I looked around the room. A small table for two had been set near the stage. I smiled and walked over to it. It looked so elegant, with silver settings and long-stemmed roses in a crystal vase. I pulled out a chair and sat, wondering what could have been so important as to interrupt our dance.

Moments later, James flipped the phone shut, pitched it across the room, sighed, and walked over to me. "I can't believe I'm going to say this, but I have to leave."

"You have to leave? But why?"

"After what happened at the bakery today, I can't say no. I'm being summoned."

I stood up from the table and threw my arms around him. "Be careful."

"I am so sorry, my love," he said. "I'll make it up to you."

"Don't worry about me. Just be careful, please."

"I'll have Delia drive you home." He kissed my head and left the room.

After a moment, I heard James open and slam the front door. Delia walked in and shrugged. "Sorry about your night. Did he even get a chance to tell you happy birthday?"

"Birthday? It's my birthday?"

She walked across the ballroom and sat across from me. "That's why I'm still here. I was supposed to wait for his signal so I could come down and help him present his gift."

"Gift?" I asked, curious.

She raised her hand. "No way. I'm not telling you anything. You'll have to wait." She turned to the musicians. "Thank you, gentlemen," she said graciously. "You can leave now." After they left, Delia pulled a bottle from her pocket and handed it to me. "Here, drink this."

"What is it?" I asked suspiciously. "And why am I drinking it?"

"It's so you won't age. James was going to explain. You take it every year on your birthday."

I eyed the little bottle curiously. "I've never taken this."

"Trust me, you have."

I tried to remember my past birthdays, and nothing came into my mind. How could I have no memory of my birthdays?

"Sharron said you all take it, too."

"We don't have to," she explained. "It's a choice we made when everything happened. Some might choose to age again when all this is over."

I downed the potion. "How old am I?"

"I'm not sure, somewhere around five

hundred."

"And them—do they take it, too? The bad guys, I mean."

"Yes, but they turn to dust when they die; we figured out that much when our first little friend visited you at the bakery. We think they're mixing the potion wrong." She smiled at me. "Don't you want to know how old I am?"

I smiled and nodded.

"Well, I'm younger than you, old lady," she said, winking. "I'm still in my early four-hundreds. You were already taking this potion when I met you."

We both laughed.

"But your father," she continued, "I heard he was over a thousand years old—at least, that's the rumor."

"Did you know him, Delia? What was he like?"

"No, I didn't. But I've heard stories about him—how he used to advise kings, and how his magic didn't need spells."

"Did I have powers like that?"

"God, yes. Even warlocks were scared of you."

"Why do warlocks hate half humans so much?"

"Simon," she replied bitterly. "He made them hate us, he made them hunt us. He's the reason that James and the boys aren't considered warlocks."

"But Simon is half human. Why don't they hate him?"

"We don't know."

I thought of the boys; they were such

good fighters. I wondered if they could compete against a warlock. I winced at the thought of any of them getting hurt—or worse. "So, is that why the boys learned how to fight like that?" I asked. "Because they have no powers?"

"I wouldn't say that," she replied. "They have the power to cast spells, and have cast spells on their weapons. As for the fighting itself, they learned that for you—to protect you."

"Where did they get their weapons?"

"They made them," she said matter-of-factly. "They've been training for years. Did you happen to notice all those muscles on them?"

"How could I *not* notice?"

"Especially James, right?"

I felt my face flush. "Fish is good-looking, too."

"Yes, he is." A secret smile spread across Delia's face. "But Cory gives James a run for his money. Have you noticed the way girls look at him?"

I felt guilty for even noticing how handsome Cory was, but she was right. I had noticed plenty of heads turning at the park.

"He's always had an eye for you, Thea. James might need to watch his back."

"James is my husband," I reminded her. "He has nothing to worry about." I didn't like where our conversation was headed and decided to change to subject. "What else can you tell me about my father?"

"Well, I heard that his powers were ten times stronger than yours. They said he could turn day into night. Also, I heard he once killed an army of men with just a blink of his eye."

"Do you know what happened to him?"

"No one knows for sure. I do know that he told Sharron your mother was calling to him, something about her heart drawing him to her."

A familiar sensation surged through me. Although her lips were still moving, I could no longer hear Delia's voice.

Horrific images flashed through my mind. Instinctively I knew they were of the memory I'd begged Delia to erase. The witch inside wouldn't have it—she needed me to know. I leaned back and gave in to the memory.

~~~

I lay on my back in darkness, gasping for breath inside the coffin. I had somehow managed to free my hands. My bruised and bloodied wrists ached as I tried to hold up the broken box which had cracked in several places. I feared that, at any minute, it would collapse and fill with dirt.

Blood dripped from a wound on my head onto the bones lying beneath me. I startled as they began to vibrate. As more and more of my blood trickled down, the bones started shifting as though they were putting themselves back together.

When my blood reached the dried-up heart that Simon had enchanted, it appeared to be bringing it back to life. I screamed in horror, nearly using up what little air I had left. My movements slowed as the oxygen in the box diminished.

I heard James yelling above me. "Dear

God, no!" He chanted: "Lift the dirt from this grave and allow me my wife to save. Give her air, give her light, make the earth for her shine bright."

The coffin lit up, and breathing became a bit easier. The bones had formed a hand, and the hand was holding up the heart.

I could still hear James shouting from above. "Thea, hang on! Please, don't die!"

Dirt flew up and out of the broken box. I could hear James's labored breathing as he frantically dug and pushed the soil away from the grave. When he finally reached the coffin, he pulled up the broken pieces of wood and lifted me out. "My Thea," he cried. "What have they done to thee?" His eyes filled with horror as he brushed the dirt from my face.

I looked at him through swollen eyes. Most of my hair had been pulled out, and my neck felt badly bruised. The skin on my wrists had been rubbed to the bone, and my feet ached from the deep bruises left from the needles. My entire body was black and blue from where they had beaten me.

I noticed Vera standing beside James. She had changed her appearance, but somehow, I knew it was her.

James trembled as he held me, tears streaming down his face. "Forgive me for leaving you."

My heart ached for him; he blamed himself for what they had done to me.

He kissed my head and chanted a healing spell: "With all my strength and all my soul, I command these bones now to be whole.

*May every break and every cut, heal themselves
and be sealed shut." He continued chanting one
healing spell after another. I closed my eyes,
and in time, I felt them working.*

*"Thea," James said as I opened my eyes.
"I'm here, dearest. I'm here." He brushed more
dirt away from my face.*

*I looked up at him. "Thou wouldst take
back thy love for me?" I whispered. "I wish not
to be saved if thou doth not love me."*

*He pulled me closer and began to cry.
"Forgive thy words, my love, for you will find
no truth in them. If thou hadst died today, I
would have buried myself with thee."*

*He resumed chanting, and my body
gradually responded. As movement became less
painful, I looked down into the grave. Panic
overcame me as I remembered the heart and the
spell Simon had placed on it. I looked back at
James. "The heart!" I screamed. "Get it out of
here! Take it far, far away. Let it not be near me
ever." I scrambled to the grave to search for it.
"Thou must take it—now!"*

*As I fumbled around in the dirt, James
jumped in to help me. "What heart dost thou
speak of?" he asked. He turned over the coffin,
and we both jumped back and gasped.*

~~~

"Thea, are you even listening to me?" I
heard Delia say.

My heart was still racing as the vision
faded away. I inhaled deeply, trying to catch my
breath. I smiled weakly at Delia. "I have a
headache, is all."

"Maybe I should get you home, then,"

she said, standing up from the table. "I'll go upstairs and get my things."

I tried to calm myself, but I was still reeling from the terrifying memory.

"Is madam leaving?" William asked from the ballroom doorway.

I stood and walked across the grand room. I looked into William's eyes and smiled. "Yes, William." I threw myself into his arms. "I'm not wrong, am I?" I whispered in his ear. "It's really you."

He leaned back and smiled. He didn't seem surprised.

Our conversation was disrupted when we heard Delia in the foyer. "Oh, hey, James. We were just about to leave. Do you want us to wait?"

William stepped into the foyer. "Good evening, master," he said. "I was just asking madam if she needed anything else."

I stepped into the foyer behind William to greet my husband, but was startled to find a stranger standing between Delia and William. I looked beyond the man, but James was nowhere in sight.

"James," Delia said, addressing the stranger. "Are you hearing me? Do you want us to wait, or what?"

I remained silent as I tried to make sense of what was happening.

"Hey, it wasn't my fault you had to take off," she said huffily. "So don't be mad at me."

I looked at Delia and back to the man she was calling James. He was staring at me intently, waiting for my reaction. I couldn't let him see that I knew he wasn't James. Panic mounted inside of me. *What has he done with James?*

I tried to stay calm. I had to get Delia out of here before she said anything damaging. I also needed to warn William.

I smiled at the stranger and looked at William. "Thank you for everything, William," I said, trying to keep my voice steady. "I'll see you tomorrow." I leaned over to kiss his cheek and discreetly whispered, "That's not James."

As I pulled away, our eyes locked for a split second. William glanced at the stranger from the corner of his eye and gave a slight nod. "Yes madam, I'll see you very soon." He turned to Delia. "We should give them a moment," he said, offering his elbow. The two walked to the staircase and quickly ascended.

I drew a deep breath and tried to think of what to say. "You're quiet," I began. "Are you angry because our special night was interrupted?"

He took two steps toward me. "I have a lot on my mind," the stranger said. "It was a long night." He stepped closer.

My heart rate accelerated, my breaths becoming shorter. My impulse was to step back, but I fought it. I couldn't let on how nervous I was. "Well, you said those friends are very important to you," I lied. "That's why you never say no to them."

"Did I?" he said, taking my hand. "And does that bother you?"

It was a test. They wanted to know if James was hiding something. "Why should it?"

I replied as calmly as possible. "It never has before." I slipped gently from his grasp. "Do you have to go back to them again tonight?"

I turned my back to him as he extended his arm toward my face.

"That depends," he said, grabbing a handful of my hair. "Are you staying here tonight?"

I closed my eyes in disgust as he sniffed my hair. I felt his breath on my neck as he leaned closer. "I'd think twice about leaving again if you were staying," he whispered into my ear. "My friends can wait. You're more important."

He placed his hands on my shoulders and turned me around to face him. My stomach churned as I waited for the inevitable. I closed my eyes as he lifted my face to his. To my great relief, his hands suddenly slipped away from my face. A loud thud filled the room. When I opened my eyes, William was standing over the stranger.

Delia ran into the room holding the box. "We have to hurry," she said. "They might be waiting for him." She opened the box and held it to the man's head. Memory clouds escaped and floated above him.

I looked into each of the clouds. "I need to know if James is safe," I said. "Let's find him and go into that one first."

Delia looked up and shook her head. "You're not going anywhere," she said. "The boys are on their way." She pulled down the man's memories and began to sort through them.

I eyed the box intently; I knew I only had one chance. I reached down and snatched it from Delia, who gasped and looked up at me in disbelief. Before she could react, I scanned the clouds, quickly spotted James, and pulled the memory toward me.

Cold air hit me at once. I was down at the port. I quickly spotted the man who was posing as James. He was walking toward an old storage shed. I followed him closely as he walked inside.

Boating equipment and fishing gear hung from the ceiling and walls. The man walked over to a small canoe that was leaning against the far wall and tapped it lightly. The boat slid to the side, exposing an entryway. The smell hit me at once. I followed the man through the secret door and hid the box in the sleeve of my dress. I wasn't sure how I was going to pull myself out of the man's memory, but I couldn't leave until I knew James was safe.

As we descended a long staircase, the odor grew stronger. I heard voices as we reached a door. James's imposter tapped on the door six times.

"What comes first? What comes last?" someone asked from the other side of the door.

"To find the witch and take her past," the man answered, completing the spell.

The door opened, and we stepped inside. The smell was overwhelming, the strongest scent I could recall. I looked around the room and spotted James right away. He stood near the short man who everyone believed to be Simon. The room was filled with familiar faces, many of which I had seen in the bakery over the years. Why hadn't I smelled them? I stood behind as the man walked to the middle of the room. I inched my way toward James as the man addressed Simon and the group.

"*I've searched everywhere,*" the man said. "*There's no sign of Mike. It's like he disappeared into thin air. Perhaps someone is hiding him.*" The man turned to James. "*There's one place we haven't yet checked. It's possible there's more than one traitor.*"

"*I have proven myself to you,*" James replied. "*What more do you want from me?*" He looked at Simon. "*I've done everything asked of me. I've shown nothing but loyalty to you.*"

Simon smiled wickedly. "*Then you will not be opposed to us visiting your home, James. If you have nothing to hide, that is.*"

"*I'll take you there myself,*" James answered.

Simon smiled and turned to one of his men. "*Give him the potion,*" he ordered.

The man stepped forward, glass in hand, and gave it to James's imposter, who still stood in the middle of the room. Immediately after consuming the potion, the man's features began to change, quickly forming an image of James's face on his own.

When James realized what was happening, he snapped his head toward Simon. "*This is not necessary.*"

"*You must understand, brother,*" Simon replied, pacing the length of the room, "*we are preparing to fight the most important battle of our lives. We cannot take any chances.*" He stepped up to James, leaving only inches between them. *"If you have nothing to hide, then no harm will come to those who live in your home."* He paused. *"But I cannot ignore the fact that several of my men have gone missing since you arrived in this town. You'll just have to forgive my lack of trust."*

"I stand by this man," Jack called out. He walked over to Simon. *"I'm certain you'll find he has nothing to hide. I find your distrust insulting."*

"No stone will be left unturned," Simon replied. *"No man overlooked."*

"And when does it end?" Jack asked. *"When we prove our worth with our very lives? This man saved my life once, and he's done nothing but obey. What else do you want from him?"*

"Enough!" Simon bellowed. *"If he has nothing to hide, then he has nothing to fear."* Simon looked into the middle of the room. *"Go to his home,"* he ordered James's imposter, *"and talk to whoever you see there. Lay with the girl if you must. Let us see what secrets she holds."*

"She has nothing to do with this!" James yelled.

Simon tilted his head and smiled his wicked smile. *"I find your attachment to this girl fascinating, James. Have you fallen in love with this human?"*

"It's taken weeks for her to warm up to me—she trusts me now." He gestured toward the pretender. *"He's going to destroy all my hard work in one night."*

Simon laughed. He walked to the phony James. *"Do not hurt the girl,"* he said. *"But do try to determine what our Romeo here has told her. Search the house and acquire anything that looks suspicious."*

The man nodded and turned to leave.

James called out to him. *"If you touch her, I will kill you!"*

"Go," Simon said to the man. *"Leave now."*

Simon strode over to James. *"It seems you have allowed your heart to grow soft for this human. I assure you they are disgusting creatures. We are above such trash, do not forget that."*

As the imposter waited for the door to open, he flashed a malevolent smile toward James. *"You know why I like human girls?"* he asked. *"Because you never have to worry about becoming bonded to them."*

James ran at the man, but Jack stopped him in mid-stride. *"Be well, my brother,"* he said. *"He only means to upset you. Let him go and ask his questions, so that Simon can, once and for all, be reassured."*

Madness crept into James's eyes; he was desperate to stop what was happening. A moment later, he smiled and relaxed. Perhaps it was then that James realized I'd be able to see through the imposter.

Air began to blow around me.

"It worked," I heard Delia say. "Quick, grab the box from her."

Chapter 13
Delia's Secret

Delia withdrew her hands from the man's head. "Are you crazy?" she yelled. "Do you have any idea the damage you could have caused?"

"Thea, what did you see?" William asked.

I looked away from Delia and relayed the memory to William. He became upset when I told him the man had been ordered to search the house.

"Young Delia," William said, turning to her. "It seems the memories you placed in Jack's head are working as we hoped. Do you think you can do it again?"

I returned the box to Delia's waiting hand.

"I'll have to first find out the questions he'd planned on asking, but yes, I can do it again."

Seconds later, the boys practically crashed through the front door, weapons at the ready. "What's going on?" Cory asked. "Are you okay, Thea?"

"She's fine," Delia snapped. "She just wanted to be a hero, that's all." She looked at me, sighed, and turned back to the boys. "Help me drag this guy to the sofa. I need to hurry." She reopened the box.

I wanted to be able to apologize, but I wasn't sorry. I had grown tired of standing aside while they did all the work. I wanted to help, not just be the damsel in distress.

Fish and Cory carried the man over to the sofa, tossed him onto it, and laughed. "He feels like a bag of rocks," Fish said.

Delia quickly sorted through the man's memories. One at a time, she drew down the bubbles, scanned them, and flicked them back. Finally, she smiled and closed the box. "Okay, boys," she said. "You have to hide now. I'm going to let him walk out of here on his own." She looked at me. "It's time for you to play hero again. He's going to think he already asked you all the questions he was supposed to." She turned to William. "He's going to think he talked to you, as well, and that he's already searched the house."

"What was he looking for?" William asked.

"Nothing specific," she explained. "Simon is just trying to make sure that James isn't a traitor." She glanced at me. "He planned on passing himself off as James . . . for the entire night."

Cory walked over and kicked the man.

Delia rushed to his side. "Don't leave marks on him," she scolded. "He has to leave as he came."

Cory shook his head and looked at Delia. "You didn't, did you?"

"I had to," she replied, unbuttoning the man's shirt. "It was the one thought I couldn't remove. He had his mind made up already."

When I finally realized what Delia and Cory were talking about, I ran over and shoved her. "And what do you think James is going to do when he thinks this man raped me?"

Delia pushed back, and Cory stepped between us. "Do you think I'm an idiot, you stupid witch?" she yelled. "He's not going to tell him." She pushed Cory out of the way and glared at me. "Why don't you go looking for the memory where you opened the crystal, and tell us why we're all living this way."

"I did!"

The room went silent as everyone turned to look at me. I knew they wanted an answer, but I didn't have the answer they wanted.

"Delia," William said soberly, "let us first deal with the problem at hand."

She stared at me for another long moment and motioned for the boys to hide. She turned and flicked the man in the head. "He's all yours," she said sourly as she walked past.

The room quickly cleared. Cory hid behind a large rubber tree plant, blades exposed. I heard the man stirring and turned around. He smiled as the replaced memory took effect. I glanced over my shoulder, hoping the boys wouldn't jump the gun and give themselves away.

The man laughed, buttoned his shirt, and walked toward me. He stood in front of me, obviously pleased with himself. "I was a bad boy," he said, touching my lips with his finger.

I turned my head and stepped back.

"Ah, did you not enjoy that, precious?" he asked. "And here I thought you loved me." He roughly pulled me into his arms.

"That's all you ever wanted from me," I replied, pushing him away. "You got what you wanted, now leave me alone."

"Don't be angry, precious," he said in a sickeningly sweet tone. "I'll be back shortly. I'm sure I'll be a changed man." He slid by me and walked out of the house. I wiped my lips as the door closed behind him.

Delia applauded as she entered the room. "Bravo!" she said sarcastically.

"Why are you so mad at me?" I asked.

She held up the box. "Because you have no respect for this!"

"You were going to leave me behind," I shot back. "I wanted to help."

She stepped up to me and shoved her face into mine. "What were you trying to do when you opened that crystal?" she asked.

I turned my back on Delia.

William stepped forward. "Even if she wanted to share that information, she could not. Only she can know the reason for using the crystal."

"Well, isn't that convenient for her?" she snapped.

William shook his head and put his hands on Delia's shoulders. "Young Delia, the crystal would close itself forever if she shared her reasons with you. You must understand that."

She ducked away from him. "I understand that she didn't care about the rest of us. She thought only of herself."

Her words cut through me, my anger flaring.

"She didn't care who she hurt," Delia continued. "She didn't care that James turned into a shadow of the man he used to be."

I spun around and slapped Delia hard across the face. She fell to the floor, holding her cheek. Rage grew inside of me as I eyed her. "If thou dares to repeat those words, I shall tear thee apart. I shall make you beg like a dog, if thou speaks of my lord ever again."

I felt all eyes on me as Delia returned to her feet. She stumbled back as I stepped closer to her. The witch inside had taken over, and she was furious. I stood inches from Delia's face. "Pray that my reasons have nothing to do with thee," I hissed. "Or anyone else thou says I never thought of."

The boys surrounded me, weapons exposed. They peered around the room as if expecting someone to burst through the door at any moment. "Where the hell is James?" Cory yelled. "He's the one who knows where the damned thing is."

Delia took off her belt, threw it into the air, and chanted: "To my blade I command, come flying back into my hand." A long blade with a glass handle flew into her hand. She stepped in front of me, faced the door, and ordered William out of the room. "We don't need you in the way when they get here," she told him.

I glanced around, confused. "What's going on?" I asked, and then it hit me. They thought my memory had returned.

"I . . . It's not what you think," I stammered. "I still don't remember anything." Delia spun around. "Then why were you speaking to me like that?" "I don't know."

Samuel looked at Cory. "I say we get her out of here, anyway, just in case."

"Agreed." Cory took my hand. "She'll be safer at our place."

"Wait. I told you, my memory isn't back." I pulled my hand from Cory's grip and turned toward the living room.

"We have to hide you," Cory yelled. "At least until we're sure."

William walked back into the foyer and reached for my hand. "I agree with the young man here. I believe it is best you leave with them. I will explain to James when he arrives."

But I didn't want to leave. I wanted to make sure James arrived home safely. I looked at the boys. "Will one of you stay behind and wait for James, so you can tell me if he got home safe?"

"I'll stay, Thea," Javier said. "I'll head for home as soon as he arrives, okay?"

I nodded and Cory grabbed my hand again. We headed out the door without another word. When we got back to the apartment, everyone was quiet. Delia hadn't said a word to me the whole way home. She sat as far away from me as she could in the car, never looking at me once. By now, everyone was convinced that my memory hadn't returned. Cory seemed to relax a little.

Before leaving my apartment, the boys checked every room. Cory even checked the closets. "I'll be right downstairs, Thea," he said. "Tap on the floor if you need me." Delia stayed behind, but I wished she had left. Things were so awkward between us. She refused to even look at me. She sat in a chair in the corner of my living room with her back to me.

I thought of telling her how sorry I was, but she still seemed tremendously upset. I decided to leave her alone for now. I sat on the sofa and waited for Javier to return. I would feel better once I knew James was safe at home. My mind wandered as I waited. I began to think about things I hadn't noticed before—like Delia's weapon. When had she gotten that? I realized how prepared they all were, and how I hadn't a clue how to defend myself in a fight. I planned to talk to the boys about helping me.

I glanced at Delia. The light from the moon was streaming in through the window, hitting her face. Her cheek was swollen from where I had slapped her. I felt bad. I didn't know where the rage had come from. I loved her too much to ever hurt her like that. When the witch inside came forth, I seemingly had no control over her actions. I resolved to change this, to change who I once had been.

A tear rolled down Delia's cheek. I had to at least try to talk to her, even if she ignored me. I walked across the room and knelt in front of her. She continued gazing out the window.

"Delia, I am so sorry for what happened. I didn't—"

"Stop it, Thea," she snapped. "Just leave me alone."

"Please, I love you. I feel dreadful about what's happened."

"I don't deserve your love," she said. "It was my fault. I had it coming. I should have never said that to you."

I took her hand. "Delia, your friendship has been one of the most important things in my life. It's I who doesn't deserve your love."

"Can I tell you something?" she asked. "Something that might change your mind?"

"What do you mean?"

She looked down, tears streaming down her cheeks. "Do you remember how at first I didn't tell you everything about the crystal? How I didn't give you all details about it?"

"Yes, what about it?"

She pulled the box from her pocket. "There's something I've been hiding from you. Something from the past that I placed inside this box." She looked into my eyes. "It's the reason I was so angry when you took it from me today. I was afraid you would learn my secret."

I eyed her curiously. I couldn't begin to imagine what she had been hiding from me.

"I was walking home one day after spending the afternoon with you and the boys and Vera at the lake. I wanted to get home fast because I was wet, and so I cut through the woods." Her eyes filled and she looked down.

I rubbed her back. "It's okay, Delia. You can tell me."

She wiped her tears and continued. "I don't remember what happened, but when I woke up, I was lying on the ground, covered in powder. In the days following, it happened three more times. I tried never to be alone after that. I would have Vera walk me home whenever I visited you.

"One day I found Vera lying in the woods, beaten half to death, covered in powder. I took her home and cleaned her up. She began acting strangely after that." Delia broke into a sob. "Oh, Thea," she cried. "I've been horrible to her, and for no good reason."

"Don't torment yourself, Delia."

"No, there's no excuse for my behavior." She covered her face with her hands and looked up again. "She would go missing, sometimes for days. No one even bothered to ask why because she was always so sad about her husband, and had been known to slip into the shadows from time to time. After it happened to Vera, it never happened to me again. A few weeks afterward, you went missing." She cried into her hands.

I still didn't understand why she felt so bad. It wasn't through any fault of her own that this had happened. "Delia, why didn't you tell anyone? Why didn't you come to me?"

"I couldn't," she replied. "Not after what he did to me."

"After who did what to you?"

She drew in a deep breath and tried to control her tears. "The last time I woke up in the woods, I realized I had become bonded to someone." She swallowed hard and looked at me. "I was bonded to him."

I finally realized what Delia was trying to tell me. "Simon," I said, nearly choking on his name. "He raped you."

She turned her head and stared out the window.

"I'm so sorry," I said. "Why didn't you tell me?"

She shook her head as tears ran down her face. "I was too ashamed," she cried. "I was bonded to a monster. I felt shame for wanting him, for wanting to protect him from you." She paused and looked at me. "I didn't want you to hurt him. I was terrified he'd find out it was me that day, the day they dragged me out of my house. I thought he would feel the bond and know it was me and not you, but he clearly felt nothing."

"What do you mean? He can't kill you?"

"I'm fairly sure," she replied. "And I can't kill him. That's why your father gave Sharron special instructions for me."

"I remember her mentioning that," I said.

"He said you would one day kill the man I was bonded to, and that I shouldn't be near you when you kill him." She looked away. I could see the thought of Simon dying bothered her.

"I know he has to die, Thea. I know it's not love that makes me want to protect him. When he dies, so will our bond, and my heart will be free. But until then, I don't want him to die."

I couldn't imagine how she felt; how much pain she'd carried with her all these years.

"Delia, can I ask you a question?"

"I'm sure you have a lot of them."

"Why have you never used your bond to help locate him?" I asked.

"It doesn't work that way. Even if I wanted to, I couldn't. The bond is that strong. That's why I've never gone into hiding—I *want* him to find me. The bond compels me to put myself out there for him. I believe Simon planned it that way, so I could lead him to you."

"But we're always together," I said. "How can they not know it's me?"

"They don't see a witch in you. You look and act like a human. The spell Sharron cast was a strong one; I presume your father gave it to her."

"But my face," I said. "Don't they know what I look like?"

"God, you're slow," she replied, a hint of a smile creeping onto her face. "Spells, Thea. We cast spells on you—they see what we want them to see. They don't think twice about us being friends. It's not unusual for witches to be friends with humans."

"What about James? You kissed him that night, the night they tried to burn you. I didn't notice any bond between you and Simon. You wanted James."

"When Simon rode off, obviously feeling nothing for me, I thought our bond had perhaps been broken. I kissed James, hoping to desire him again. When he told me he had married you, I was mostly just offended." She smiled. "But that's all behind us now. You and James belong together."

I smiled and hugged her. "You've been carrying a huge burden, my friend. I wish I could take it away."

She smiled and turned to look out the window again. Everything about Delia made sense now. Her bitterness and anger, and why she never had a boyfriend. I presumed this was the reason she was always creating new potions: she was trying to create one that would break her bond with Simon. I wanted to take her pain away, and I understood that I had to kill Simon to do it.

We were still talking when there was a knock at the door.

"That must be Javier," Delia said, getting up.

"I'll get it," I said, motioning for her to stay put. My heart soared when I opened the door and found two beautiful blue eyes looking back at me. "James!" I yelled, throwing myself into his arms.

He wrapped his arms around me. "Thea."

"I'll be downstairs with the boys," Delia said, ducking past us. "I need to speak to you before you leave," she told James.

James nodded and closed the door behind her.

"Kiss me," I said, grabbing his face.

He grinned. "Yes, ma'am!"

"I was so worried," I said between kisses. "Did they hurt you?"

"Not a scratch." He kissed my neck. "But I hear you weren't yourself today. Is everything okay?"

"What answer will keep you kissing

me?" I asked, tilting my head back. His tongue grazed my neck. His breath was sweet as he found my lips again. "Stay with me tonight," I whispered. "Don't leave. Don't leave me alone, please."

He leaned his head against mine and sighed. "I don't know if that's a good idea. I don't know if I can be a gentleman."

"Then don't be," I said, kissing him again. I pressed myself into him and ran my hands through his hair. "Take me," I whispered.

James abruptly backed away and leaned against the door, his hand on the doorknob. I feared he would leave. Before I could beg him to stay, he stepped toward me and took my face in his hands. "Damn your rules. You're my wife."

He kissed me again. The room spun as he took me in his arms. I had waited so long for this moment, to feel our bodies close together, to see my husband lying next to me when I opened my eyes in the morning. He lifted me into his arms and carried me to the bedroom. He gently laid me on the bed and began to remove his shirt.

I sat up and ran my fingers across his chest. "My lord, thou art so beautiful," I said, looking up into his eyes.

He stepped backed, eyes wide. "What did you say?"

"I said you were beautiful. Why?"

He stood silent for a moment, grabbed his shirt, and put it back on.

"What are you doing?" I asked. "Why are you getting dressed?"

"I have to leave, Thea," he replied as he buttoned his shirt. "This wasn't a good idea. I can't stay here tonight."

I felt my heart breaking into a million pieces. I jumped out of bed and clung to him. "What did I do?"

He sighed in obvious frustration. "You have no idea how sorry I am right now. Every part of me wants to stay here with you, but I have to leave." He kissed my head and walked out.

I had to stop myself from running after him. Once again, his rejection cut through me. I knew he hadn't intended to hurt me, but my heart couldn't help but to feel unwanted. When I heard the door close, I slipped to the floor, leaned against the bed, and burst into sobs. I couldn't understand why he had changed his mind. What had I done to make him leave? I cried harder as feelings of foolishness washed over me. All of my old insecure feelings flooded back. I wanted to crawl back into my shell and never leave.

I didn't want any part of being a witch anymore. There was so much pain in this world. I knew James loved me, but the pain of his rejection was more than I could take. It made me feel as if he didn't care about me, even though I knew that wasn't true. I buried my head in my knees and cried for all I couldn't understand.

I felt someone touching my hair. "Please don't cry."

I looked up to find James standing over me. "You came back."

240

He sank down beside me and put his arm around my shoulders. I leaned my head on his chest and reached for his hand. He squeezed it and held it to his heart.

"I want you to know that I'm suffering with you," James said. "I've thought of little else but holding you again." He kissed my hand and pulled me closer. "I'm staying with you tonight. A thousand men couldn't pull me away."

"Are you sure?"

"I needed a moment to think it through. But yes, I'm sure."

We sat on the floor holding each other. I looked at his hand and was alarmed to see that his knuckles were bloody. "What happened?"

He pulled his hand away and smiled sheepishly. "Just a little stress release."

I looked into his eyes. "You have the most beautiful blue eyes I've ever seen."

"And they will forever remain blue for you, Thea," he said. "Only death will turn them brown again."

I stared at him, puzzled. "What do you mean?"

"It's just something that happens to us male witches. When we fall in love with a witch, our eyes turn blue for her, and only her."

My heart warmed. It was such a beautiful sentiment.

"My guess is that Cory's eyes appear blue to you, as well."

"His eyes aren't blue?" I asked, surprised. "What color are they?"

James chuckled and threw back his head.

"That's what I thought."

"Oh," I said, realizing what he meant. "So your eyes are really brown?"

"Yes. But tell me, how do I look with blue eyes?"

"Beautiful."

He kissed the top of my head. "And so is your hair."

"There is nothing beautiful about my hair."

"Not true," he protested. "And you'd better never change it."

We talked all night and into the wee hours. I didn't even care that I had to work the next morning. It was such a joy to laugh with him, to hear him muse about the differences between the two worlds: the one we had come from, and the one we lived in now.

Technology amazed him. He laughed when I told him about Fish leaving spells on Delia's voice mail. "Do me a favor," he said. "Tomorrow, ask Delia what color Fish's eyes are."

We laughed heartily until I was reminded of Delia's tragedy. "That's so sad," James said when I told him her story. A faraway look washed over his face. "Well, it certainly explains a lot. I arrogantly assumed she hadn't taken a partner because of me. I've always felt so guilty about what happened between us."

I leaned my head on his shoulder and closed my eyes.

He stroked my hair and kissed my head. "Don't ever forget you love me, Thea."

I opened my eyes and pushed away from

242

him. "Why do you keep saying that? How could I possibly ever forget that I love you?"

He looked into my eyes but didn't answer. He just kissed my head and pulled me into his arms again. We talked until I drifted off. I felt him lift me up and lay me on the bed. He snuggled in beside me for a little while before he left. I had gotten my wish. James and I had held each other until the sun came up. I smiled as he kissed my head and started for the door. "Never stop doing that," I said dreamily.

When I woke, he was gone, but his sweet scent lingered. I breathed him in and thought about our special night.

I was broken from my reverie by a knock at the front door. I hurried from my room and threw open the door, expecting to find Delia.

My heart leaped into my throat when I saw him. James's imposter was staring down at me. My mouth suddenly dry, I struggled for words. I wanted to slam the door in his face, but knew that wouldn't be wise. After all, I wasn't supposed to know what he looked like, or even who he was. I forced a smile and tried to act natural.

"I'm sorry to bother you," he said, "but does James happen to be here?"

"He's in the shower," I lied. "I'd be happy to let him know that someone is looking for him." I began to close the door.

The man stuck his foot inside and blocked the door. "You mind if I come in and wait?"

"He should be out any minute. I'd prefer you to wait outside." I began to close the door again.

The man forced his way in. "I don't think so," he said, striding into the apartment. "You see, I have a problem. James doesn't know that I've been a bad boy." He smiled. "This may come as a surprise to you, but you and I know each other very well."

My heart thumped in my chest. I stepped back and tried to think.

"I can't have James finding out about our little secret," he said, closing the gap between us. "But I don't see why we can't have a little fun before I kill you." He reached toward me.

I stumbled back. He tackled me and pinned me to the floor.

"Wall!" I shouted.

The man flew up and away from me and smashed into the living room wall. He hung, suspended, a look of shock on his face. "Impossible!" he yelled. "You're not a witch!"

I smiled. "Says you." I scrambled to my feet and slammed the door. The witch inside was delighted. "What would you say I am, then, my lord?"

He stopped writhing and eyed me intensely, a look of acknowledgment on his face. "Welcome home, witch. My friends will be awfully glad to see you."

I stepped closer to him. "I can't have them finding out about our little secret," I said, my smile growing wider. "But I don't see why we can't have a little fun before I kill you."

I heard footsteps on the stairs. The boys were on their way. What had taken them so long, and how had this jerk gotten by them?

244

The man kicked at me. "Not if I kill you first," he threatened. "And when I'm through with you, I'm going to tear your boyfriend apart slowly, piece by piece."

The man assumed my memory was back, and that I was her.

The door flew open. Cory seemed surprised to see me. "What are you doing here?" he asked.

Before I had a chance to answer, Cory spotted the man hanging on the wall. "What the hell is going on?" He crossed the room and punched the man's face, knocking him out.

"So, what was the noise?" Sammy asked, stepping in from the hallway. His eyes quickly drifted to Simon's minion. "What the hell happened?"

"Why didn't James tell us he didn't take you with him?" Cory asked as he walked over to me.

"What do you mean?" I asked. "Take me where?"

"He told us last night that he was going to take you to work himself."

"That must have been this guy," I said, gesturing toward our prisoner. "He's the same one who impersonated James last night. He came here to kill me."

Samuel spun around and punched the still-unconscious man. "You came here to kill someone, fool? Looks like you're the only one dying today."

"What are you guys doing?" Delia said as she came through the door. She swiftly scanned the room. "What's going on?"

"Looks like the memory you put in this guy's head backfired," Cory replied.

"What do you mean?" she asked.

"It means you're going to teach me how to fight," I answered. "I'm tired of not knowing what to do when one of these guys gets me alone."

Samuel laughed. "Thea, you don't need to learn how to fight," he said. "That's what we're here for."

"Really?" I snapped. "Because I don't think this guy knew that."

Samuel stopped laughing and bowed his head.

The other boys entered the apartment. "What's going on?" Fish asked.

I ignored his question and looked at Samuel and Cory. "You can teach me how to fight, or I can learn from him," I said, pointing at the man. "I'm sure when he wakes up he'll try to come at me again."

The boys looked at each other.

"We already have a tool," Cory said to Delia. "We can make it work."

Delia looked at me and back at the boys. Samuel spoke up. "I say we do it."

"I'm in," Javier said from the doorway.

Fish walked over to Delia, grinning. "I'll teach her all my manly moves," he said. "You're welcome to watch if you can keep your hands off of me."

Delia stifled a giggle. "I'll try to restrain myself."

"Okay, get Thea to the bakery," Cory ordered. "I'll be right behind you."

"What about Simon's toady here?" I asked.

"Don't worry about him," Cory said. "We'll take care of it. Just order him off the wall for me, will ya?"

"He knows, Cory," I said. "He knows I'm a witch."

He chuckled. "Yeah, I figured that when I saw him hanging there. It's going to be fine, Thea. Just go to work and I'll be there shortly."

Chapter 14
Fish's Hooks

All day long, as we rolled out dough and baked, the boys and I discussed a plan for my training. "What about a weapon?" I asked.

"That depends on you," Javier answered. "What do you think you can handle?"

"I don't know. I've never thought about it."

"What about James?" Samuel asked. "Are you going to tell him about training with us?"

"No," I said, shaking my head. "He can't know about this. I don't want him worrying about me."

The boys honored my wishes and decided it was best if Delia accompanied me to practice. James would assume we were just out and about. Fish was thrilled about Delia joining us.

I happened to notice Fish's green eyes, and a thought occurred to me. "Hey, what happens when you guys fall in love with a witch and your eyes are already blue?" I asked. "What color does she see then?"

Fish's eyes lit up. "What color are Cory's eyes?"

"Shut up, Fish," Cory yelled from the ovens. He walked toward Fish. "Don't answer that, Thea."

"What?" Fish asked, playing dumb. "I was just wondering if she's colorblind."

Cory smacked him on the head with an oven mitt and walked back to remove the latest batch of cinnamon rolls. "Ask something else," Cory said, glancing at me over his shoulder.

"Okay, what about us?" I asked. "Do our eyes change color?"

The boys looked around at each other and then over at Cory. "Don't even go there, guys," he told them, "or I'll stick all of you in this oven." He walked over to me. "Can we change the subject?"

I nodded, but wondered why Cory was so uncomfortable. It seemed like a simple enough question. I respected Cory's request and didn't push the issue. Instead, I asked, "How long are we going to practice?"

"As long as you want, Thea," Joshua said, pulling out his weapon. "Here, I want to show you how this works."

"What is it?"

"On the surface, it's a bow and arrow, but this particular one searches for organs to rip apart." Obviously proud of his weapon, Joshua admired it for a long moment before carefully returning it to the storage area under the counter. "Have you seen Fish's yet?"

Fish was smiling. "She'll never guess what it is."

"It's not hard to guess," Joshua said. "It's how he got his nickname."

I looked at Fish, confused. "I thought they called you Fish because you can catch fish with your mouth."

"I can do a lot of things with my mouth," Fish said, winking.

"Fish, don't be rude," Cory yelled at him.

"I was just going to show her how I whistle," Fish answered.

The rest of the boys hurled chunks of dough at Fish as we all laughed. I felt so happy around them; they made me forget about the horror I was living. We hurried through our day. They seemed just as eager to begin my training as I was.

"I'm the best jumper," Samuel said as we cleaned up after the baking was done. "I can show you how to run up the walls—my spell works great."

"What if there are no walls?" Fish asked him. "Should she run into the air?"

"Very funny," Samuel replied. "You know she can run up anything."

"Will you guys shut up already?" Cory said. "She's going to learn the basics first."

"What's the big deal?" Fish asked. "She can learn from all of us."

Cory rolled his eyes. "You guys have been practicing for hundreds of years," he said. "Thea can't remember that she knows how to fight. Maybe the basics will jog her memory."

"I know how to fight?" I asked, surprised.

Fish burst into laughter and shook his head.

"Why are you laughing?" I asked.

Cory flashed an angry look at Fish. "Fish doesn't know when to shut his mouth," he said, lobbing another chunk of dough at him. "Don't listen to him."

Fish was still laughing when Delia walked in. "What's so funny?"

Fish spun around, smiled, and strode over to Delia. "Hello, Delia. The guys were just begging me to show Thea my awesome moves."

Delia looked at me and giggled. "You're in the best possible hands."

"Do you want to be in the best possible hands?" Fish asked her.

I could tell Delia thought Fish was sweet. Her eyes lit up when he flirted with her. She always catered to his ego, making him feel special whenever she could. Fish was very good-looking. He was younger than her, but no more than four years or so—at least, on the surface. He had dirty-blond hair and a boyish face, but there was nothing boyish about his body. He had muscles everywhere, just like all the boys.

I'd caught Delia staring at Fish more than a few times. Her eyes practically devoured him, but she always looked away when he tried to catch her eye.

Delia clapped her hands together. "So, you guys almost ready?"

"Hey, where's this going to happen?" Cory asked.

"The lake," Delia replied. "Plenty of

trees and bushes to shield us from human eyes. It should be safe to train there."

"I love that place," Javier said, excited. "We never get to go there."

"I wonder if it still looks the same," Joshua added.

We finished cleaning up and headed to the lake. When we arrived, I had the feeling of having been there many times before. "I know this place," I said.

Joshua smiled. "It's our lake, Thea. We used to come here all the time, but not so much anymore. Delia says it's not safe."

"If it's not safe, then why are we here?"

Delia ignored my question and addressed the boys. "You guys get started," she said. "We'll sit and observe for a while. I want Thea to have an idea of what to expect."

They nodded and ran to an open field.

"I had to tell them that," Delia whispered, "or they would have been here all the time."

"Why don't you let them come here anymore?"

"Because Simon doesn't know what they look like," she explained. "If they spent a lot of time here, it would be a dead giveaway."

"Simon has never seen them?" I asked, surprised.

"He never paid attention to them," she replied. "They were just kids."

We sat on the grass and watched the boys practice. I watched as Fish practiced running up Cory's back. Javier wrapped his mesh chain around a rock. I watched as he spun the net and released the rock, sending hundreds of pieces scattering. He spun the net again and caught every piece. By the time he'd repeated the maneuver several times, only sand was flying out of the net.

"Go get the fruit from the car," I heard Cory tell Fish.

Fish ran, grabbed a bag out of the trunk, and returned with it.

"Watch this," Delia said, smiling.

Cory took the bag and pulled out a melon. Fish ran across the field and faced him. "I'm ready!" he yelled. Cory threw the melon as high as he could and ran. Fish spread his arms wide and flicked them once. A hook, attached to what looked like very thin cable wire, popped out of each sleeve. Fish swung his arms toward the melon and the hooks flew across the field and into the melon. When he pulled his arms back, my jaw dropped. The melon, still whole, had fallen to the ground without the peel.

Cory walked over and picked it up. "You missed a spot," he yelled to Fish.

"How did he do that?" I asked Delia.

"Spells," she replied. "They put spells on their weapons."

I looked at the boys and wondered why they used such brutal weapons.

Delia seemed to know what I was thinking. "They're not expecting a fair fight. They can't afford for the first strike to miss."

"How many men does Simon have?"

She looked down. "We're not sure. James seems to think he has at least a hundred, if not more."

"And how many do we have?"

"We have the boys, James, and about forty witches—most of whom don't care what happens to you."

My eyes filled as I realized how high the chances were that these boys would lose their lives. Guilt bubbled up inside me when I thought of the price they would pay because of a choice I had made hundreds of years ago.

"I don't know why I did it, Delia," I said, sniffing back tears. "I saw myself opening the crystal, and I still don't know why I did it."

Delia took my hand. "Can you tell me about it?"

I nodded. "For one thing, you were wrong about James wanting my powers. I wanted to transfer them to the crystal because they were tearing us apart. But before I could do it, I got a vision. Something I saw scared me half to death. I saw horror in my eyes, and I still don't know why that was," I said, going into a sob.

Delia cried with me. "I'm so sorry, Thea, for every word I have ever spoken against James."

"I didn't do it for him," I cried. "I swear to you, I didn't."

She placed her arm around my shoulder. "I know, sweetie. I know."

I wiped at my tears and stood, composing myself. "I won't let any of you die. I don't know what I saw in that vision, but I'm not going to let any of you pay for the choice I made. It's time for me to learn to fight."

Delia jumped to her feet and smiled. "That's my good little witch."

As we joined the boys, Fish ran to my side. "Me first!" he yelled.

"Shut up before I throw you in the lake," Cory said, giving Fish a playful shove.

Cory stepped up to me. "I'm going to grab you from behind. Show me what you would do." He turned me around and wrapped his arm around my neck. "Okay, Thea, what would you do?"

I reached up and tried yanking his arm away from my neck.

"Wrong," he said. "You're not using the most important weapon you have." He stepped in front of me. "He's going to be stronger than you. You'll never get his hands to release you by doing that. Remember this: he can't fight your commands."

Cory stepped behind me again and grabbed my neck. "Show me, and be creative. How could you get me to let go?"

"I might hurt you."

"Don't worry," Joshua said. "Delia knows what to do. We do this all the time."

"Just do it," Cory whispered in my ear. He squeezed my neck tighter.

I hesitated, trying to think of what to say.

"Remember, be creative," he said. "Use commands that will help your next move." Again, he tightened his grip.

I closed my eyes and yelled, "Break!"

Cory yelped as he fell to the ground.

"Wow, I think I heard something actually break," Fish exclaimed.

Delia ran to me, clearly excited. "Thea, look at Cory and say the word *heal*."

"What?"

"Look at Cory and say *heal*," she ordered.

I looked down at Cory, who was wincing in pain. "Heal."

Seconds later, we all watched as Cory's arm reset itself. He stood and stretched it out. "That's much faster than waiting on a spell." He paused and slowly looked over at me as though a light had switched on in his head. "This just may work," he said, smiling at Sam. "Show her how to jump," he ordered. "Put the spell on her shoes." He looked at me again. "Thea, if you can keep yourself separated from them as you shout out commands, we have a good chance of winning this."

"What do you mean? Like I did just now?"

"Yes, but we need to keep you away from them," Samuel said. He motioned for me to remove my shoes. I pulled them off and handed them over. He set them on the ground and chanted: "Give her speed, give her height, give her quickness in a fight. Climb the trees, climb the walls, may she climb anything at all."

"All right," Javier exclaimed, high-fiving Fish. "This is getting good."

The boys showed me everything they knew. We spent hours running up trees and jumping off enormous rocks. The jumping spell made it easy for me to climb the massive maples. I felt alive as I jumped. At one point, I knocked Javier to the ground. "This is exhilarating!" I yelled. For the first time since I could remember, I didn't feel helpless.

"Jump higher, Thea!" Fish yelled.

Several hours later, Delia began gathering her things. "We'd better leave before James comes looking for you," she said. "I don't want him angry with me for keeping you out too late."

"So let him get mad," Cory answered. "We're doing important work here."

Delia gave Cory a knowing look and began walking away from the lake.

"What?" Cory asked. "Why are you getting mad?"

Delia stopped and turned back. "He's her husband," she said, and resumed walking toward the car.

"What, are you and James best friends now?" Cory asked sarcastically.

Delia stopped again. She stood motionless for a moment, spun on her heel, and approached Cory. "I've moved on, Cory." She glanced at me and back to Cory. "Maybe this will help you move on: he never left her apartment last night. They were together the entire night."

Before Cory could respond, she turned and started again for the car. "Come on, Thea. I should get you home."

Cory was like a statue, his jaw clenched. He wouldn't even look at me.

I was tempted to tell him that my night with James was not what Delia was insinuating, but I thought it best to let it go. If James was right about Cory being in love with me, then

Delia had done the right thing. I didn't share Cory's romantic feelings. He would never be more to me than a dear friend.

I followed Delia to the car and got in. "You know nothing happened last night, right?" I asked, closing the door.

"It doesn't matter either way. Cory needs to move on."

I knew she was right. Cory told me he didn't plan on making the same mistake twice, but my heart had already chosen.

I changed the subject. "So tell me, what color eyes does Fish have?"

A slow smile spread across Delia's face. "Blue. And I wish my hair was a mess for him."

I looked at her, confused. "What do you mean?"

"It's our sign," she explained. "It shows other males that we're very much in love and taken."

I was shocked. "They know by our hair?"

"Yes," she replied. "Why do you think you can't keep yours neat for more than five minutes?"

"You mean to tell me that they get beautiful blue eyes when they fall in love, and we get this . . . rat's nest?" I said, grabbing a strand of hair.

"Yep, only difference is, we're the only ones who can see their blue eyes, but everybody can see our messy hair."

"Well, that's the most unfair thing I've ever heard of," I said indignantly.

"Oh, put a spell on it," Delia said, rolling

her eyes.

We exploded into laughter. I touched my hair and thought of how James had told me never to change it.

"Funniest thing is," Delia continued, "until we figured out that we could use a spell, we used to wear these ridiculously enormous hats to cover up the mess."

"Oh, Delia," I said, stifling a giggle. "Please tell me you're not referring to the quintessential Halloween-costume witch hats."

Delia became annoyed. "At least we have a spell for it now. I'll have to teach it to you. Look at that thing you call hair. I'm surprised I didn't try to put a spell on it long ago."

"Why didn't you?"

"Because it has to be you."

"What about black cats? I've never seen you with one. Oh, and do you have a broom?"

She shook her head. "You are so clueless. The things you can't remember."

The boys made it to the car and got in.

"Where's Cory?" Delia asked.

"He's walking home," Fish replied. "Said he'd see us later."

They all glanced my way. I knew they were wondering if I knew how Cory felt about me. I decided to keep that information to myself, and would ask Delia to do the same.

"Hey, let's order pizza," I said. "I'm hungry."

"If we're going to order pizza," Delia said, starting the car, "let's try to find Cory and pick him up. I have a feeling I know which direction he's headed."

"Delia, when are you going to get a new car?" Samuel asked. "This wagon is practically as old as we are."

"I think I can hear it crying," Fish added.

"This wagon belongs to you?" I asked. "I thought it belonged to the boys."

The boys burst into laughter. "She never wants to drive it," Javier said. "She makes us take it home and keep it there."

"Yeah, and she had to put a spell on it just so it will start," Joshua added.

We all laughed, and Delia made a huffing sound. "Hey, it got you here, didn't it?"

We were all still laughing when Delia pulled up next to Cory, who was walking along the lake road.

"Get in," she said. "We're ordering pizza."

I was surprised when he opened the door and climbed into the front seat without arguing. "Keep driving," he said. "I think we were being watched."

I snapped my head around and looked out the back window.

"Don't, Thea," he warned. "I don't want them to know I saw them."

"How many?" Delia asked.

"I'm not sure," Cory said, glancing into the rear view mirror. "I think two. I think they might follow us. Stop by that picnic table. We'll get out and sit there for a minute."

The boys whispered to each other excitedly about the possibility of a fight. After Delia parked the wagon, we got out of the car and sat on a table.

"You guys pretend to talk," Delia said. "Cory and I will take a look around. Listen for the whistle."

Cory put his arm around Delia. They smiled at each other like two lovebirds taking a walk. I became anxious as they disappeared into the trees.

"What do we do?" I asked. "We can't just sit here."

"We're not just sitting," Samuel said, glancing over his shoulder. "We're making sure there are only two of them."

I couldn't calm my nerves. I felt like I might throw up. I reached for Joshua's hand.

"Don't be scared," he whispered. "We're all here with you."

I hated how easily I became overwhelmed when faced with danger. The training wouldn't do any good if I just wanted to shrink away in fear.

Javier bowed his head and closed his eyes. He looked as though he was taking a nap.

"Javier," Samuel whispered. "Stay alert."

Javier didn't answer. He kept his head down, his eyes still shut.

Joshua gave him a small shove. "Javier?"

Javier fell sideways and hit the ground with a thud. Samuel jumped down from the table and rolled him over onto his back. We all gasped at the sight of a knife sticking out of Javier's chest. Samuel whistled loudly, and the boys immediately brandished their weapons. They surrounded me as they scanned the area.

"Stay put, Thea," Sammy yelled.

Delia and Cory ran toward us, Cory's blades at the ready. Joshua pointed his arrow toward the trees.

Something inside of me took over; I knew exactly what to do. I eyed Joshua's arrow. "Find," I commanded.

Joshua released the arrow and instantly drew another.

"Find."

Joshua released the second arrow.

The boys ran into the trees as Delia chanted spells at Javier. I decided to join the boys. I ran as fast as I could. I wouldn't allow my fear to hold me back this time. I jumped off trees and anything else that was standing. I even passed the boys as I climbed and jumped off an enormous oak. The spell on my shoes made me feel like I could fly, jumping nearly twenty feet into the air.

I came to a stop when I saw Joshua's arrows sitting atop two piles of dust. When the boys caught up to me, I held the arrows in my hand. Such a strange sensation it was to feel the witch inside of me coming out. Suddenly, I felt drawn back to where Javier lay dying. I dropped the arrows and ran back to find Delia still chanting, to no avail.

"Silence, witch," I ordered. "Stand aside so that I may save him."

Delia shot me an alarmed look and hurriedly moved aside.

I knelt down and chanted: "Thy heart still beats, thy blood still flows; until they stop, thy soul won't go." I took a deep breath and withdrew the blade from Javier's chest. "Heal,"

I said, placing my hands on his chest.

Moments later, Javier coughed. He looked up at me. "What happened?"

I felt all eyes on me as I got to my feet.

Samuel stepped slowly toward me. "Mistress?"

"Yes, Sammy?"

"Is that you?"

"If you mean, is it me, Thea, then yes."

"Looks like the odds just got better," Fish said, high-fiving Joshua.

"She's coming back," Joshua added.

The boys helped Javier to his feet and hugged him all at once.

"What's all this for?" Javier asked, chuckling.

Samuel held up a sort of metal crossbow. "Because of this, my friend." Samuel turned to Cory. "We found it back there," he said, gesturing toward the woods.

"What the hell is it?" Fish asked, reaching for the strange weapon.

"Looks like it shoots blades," Samuel replied, pointing at another one on the ground.

Cory looked around. "We have to make sure they were alone," he said, heading for the trees. "We'll go back to where I first spotted them."

"Can I keep the crossbow?" Joshua asked. Fish handed him the weapon, and we all followed Cory. When we made our way back to the area where we'd been practicing, we found a campsite with two sleeping bags.

"It's like they were hiding," Cory said, looking around. "But from who?"

"Not hiding," Delia said. "Waiting. I think they were waiting for orders."

Cory searched the bags as the boys checked the rest of the site for clues. They uncovered some odd-looking money, every bill a different color.

"James might know where these are from," Delia said. "I see Spanish words printed on them."

Cory shoved the bills into his pocket. "We need to clean up the area," he said. "Get rid of this firewood. Make it look like no one was here."

We cleared away anything that seemed out of place. Cory ordered Joshua to destroy the crossbow. Joshua wasn't happy about it, but he threw it onto the burn pile.

I could feel Delia staring at me. "What?" I finally asked her. "Why do you keep looking at me like that?"

She shook her head. "It's just that I can't always tell when it's you or when it's her."

"Her? You talk as though I'm two people."

"Well, you sort of are," she replied. "But the two of you are becoming one. She wants out. I can see that now."

"Then we'd better hurry and get me ready so I can welcome her home."

"Just don't lose my friend, okay? I kind of like her."

We brought our findings back to the car and loaded them in. "We'll burn everything tomorrow," Cory said. He looked at Delia. "We'll need a batch of your stuff."

"How many square feet?" she asked.

"What are you two talking about?" I asked.

"A potion," Delia replied. "So no one sees the smoke."

"Oh," I said, nodding absently. I found myself preoccupied by Delia's earlier comment about not losing her friend, and feared I wouldn't be able to separate my two personalities. More and more, I felt the witch controlling me.

"Get in, Thea," Delia called from the driver's seat. "It's getting dark."

I climbed into the car and heard the boys telling Javier what had happened. He reached for my hand and kissed it. "Thank you."

I rested my head on his shoulder, closed my eyes, and thought of how happy they all made me. I knew I couldn't let these boys die for me.

"So, can we still get pizza?" Fish asked.

We all burst into laughter. It felt good to resume our earlier mood. Cory hadn't said two words to me since we'd picked him up. He made a point of sitting up front with Delia, leaving me in the back with the boys.

"What time is James coming?" Delia asked when we arrived at the building.

"He's not coming over today," I replied. "He said he had things to do."

"Let's order in, then," Fish suggested. "Dinner at Thea's."

Delia smiled and told me she needed a moment alone with the boys. "Order the pizzas, and we'll be up shortly."

I nodded and headed upstairs, wondering what Delia wanted to talk to them about. I was searching for the phone when I noticed a note sitting on my bed. I was about to open it when the boys walked in.

"What kind did you order?" Joshua yelled from the living room. "Because I don't like pepperoni."

I folded the note and slipped it into my pocket. "I haven't ordered yet," I yelled from the bedroom. "I was waiting to see what y'all liked."

Chapter 15
The Walking Stick

After Delia and the boys went home, I retrieved the note from my pocket. Vera wanted to meet with me.

This situation could end only one way: with me. Vera was the only one who could help me. I would have to arrange for a discreet meeting. I scratched out a reply on the same piece of paper and placed it on the bed where Vera had left it, hoping she would know to come back.

Exhausted but restless, I decided to read. It had been days since I picked up a book. I propped myself up in bed and reached for the last paperback Delia had given me. Moments later, I heard a soft tap on the door. I presumed it was one of the boys, coming to check on me.

The stench hit me as I neared the door. I froze in my tracks.

Another tap, then, "James, are you in there?"

I recognized Jack's voice immediately. "James, it's me, Jack."

My heart raced. Why was Jack looking

for James? I slowly pulled open the door.

Jack seemed relieved to see me. "You're home," he said, seemingly surprised. "Is James with you?"

"No," I replied. "I thought he was with you."

My answer didn't please him. He sighed heavily, concern washing over his face.

"If he stops by, tell him I'm looking for him."

Jack turned to leave, and I grabbed his arm. "No, wait. Come in." I couldn't believe I was asking him into my apartment, but he seemed genuinely worried about James, and now, so was I.

Jack stepped inside. "Did you tell him what that idiot did to you?"

"No," I replied, shaking my head. "Not a word."

"When was the last time you saw James?" he asked.

"Last night. He stayed here with me." I couldn't believe how open I was being with him, but his concern for James compelled me to continue. "He was supposed to meet me tonight, but he never showed. I think he might have found out what happened to you and went looking for that jerk. They're both missing." He handed me his cell number. "Call me if he shows up," he said and headed for the door.

"No, wait," I said, grabbing his arm again. "Do you think something happened to James?"

"I don't know," he said, walking toward the stairs. "I have one more place to check. I'll call you if I find him."

As panic set in, I knew I couldn't let him leave. I had to know where he was going, and if James was safe. I swallowed hard. "Freeze!" I yelled as Jack began walking down the stairs.

I hurried into my apartment and threw on some warmer clothes. I passed the frozen Jack on the stairs and ran down to the boys' apartment. By the time Cory opened the door, I was in tears.

"What's wrong?" he said, quickly pulling me inside. He peeked up and down the hall.

"I'm not being followed," I said. "It's James. He's missing. Something is wrong, I can feel it." I relayed Jack's concerns, and Cory agreed that it was odd for James not to have told anyone where he was going.

He pulled out his phone and called Delia. I hadn't even thought about calling her. She had James's cell number and might be able to reach him. I bit my nails as Cory and Delia spoke. I had to keep myself from grabbing his phone and asking her myself.

Cory closed his phone. "She's on her way," he said. "She doesn't know where he is."

"Did you tell her to call his phone?" I asked. "She needs to call his phone." I was starting to feel desperate. "Tell her, Cory. Call her back and tell her to call James—please!"

"Calm down, Thea. She's calling him right now." Cory placed his hands on my shoulders and looked into my eyes. "We'll find him."

"What's going on?" Fish asked as he

walked out of the kitchen. "What's with the tears, Thea? Did you see Cory naked?"

"Shut up, Fish," Cory snapped. "Get ready. We're leaving with Thea."

Fish locked eyes with me for a moment and disappeared into one of the bedrooms. He returned a few minutes later with the other boys in tow.

"What's up?" Samuel asked. "Where are we headed?"

"Did Jack tell you where he was going?" Cory asked.

I opened the door and pointed up. "He's still here, frozen on the stairs."

"Wait here," Cory ordered. "I'll be right back."

"Did you freeze him in mid-air?" Fish asked.

I was in no mood for his humor right now. I ignored his question and kept my eyes on the hallway. I heard the door to my apartment close and Cory's footsteps on the stairs.

"We have to move fast," Cory said as he came back into view. He turned to me. "We'll wait outside while you release him, then we'll follow him." He stepped out of his shoes. "Everyone take off your shoes and put them in a pile—hurry."

I removed my shoes and set them next to Cory's. "What are you going to do?" I asked.

"If we're going to follow him," he explained, "we have to be as quiet as possible."

"So we're going to follow him with no shoes on?"

Fish laughed, and I shot him a dirty look.

"Sorry, Thea," he said, stifling a giggle. "I just thought by now you'd have caught on. We cast spells on everything."

Cory gathered our shoes, traced a circle around them with his finger, and whispered, "Together." He pushed the shoes closer to each other. Just before he began the spell, another pair of shoes landed on the pile.

We looked up to see Delia smiling down at us. "Not leaving without me, are you?" she asked, holding a strange-looking stick in her hand.

Cory looked back down, traced another circle with his finger, and again whispered, "Together." He pushed the shoes closer again and chanted: "Find his steps, find the way, on his trail make sure we stay. Keep our steps soft and hollow; allow him not to know we follow." Cory snatched his pair out of the pile and replaced them on his feet. The rest of us followed suit. "Put them on and wait outside," he instructed. "We'll follow behind him a good few yards."

When I finished tying my sneakers, Delia handed me the stick. "Here," she said. "You might need this."

"What in the heck is it?" I asked, taking it from her.

"If my old friend shows her face tonight, you'll know exactly what to do with it, because it's yours."

"This is mine?" I turned it over in my hands.

"Yep."

It resembled a staff, like the ones I'd seen at the medieval fairs. But this one looked particularly old and rustic. It felt familiar in my hands. I could see impressions from my own fingers on it. My hands slid right into place when I held it.

"Okay, let's go outside and find a place to hide," Cory said. "If he gets into a car, get ready to run. The spell won't allow us to lose his trail."

The boys jogged outside and waited.

"When should I unfreeze him?" I asked Cory.

"Wait until we get outside and behind that big willow. We still don't know which way he's going."

I nodded, and we walked outside. I couldn't see the boys, but Cory gave a soft whistle as we stepped behind the willow tree. "Ok, Thea," Cory whispered. "Release him."

"Release," I said quietly. I held my breath as we waited.

Seconds later, Jack came running out of the building. We were relieved to see that he was on foot as he ran down the street and disappeared around the corner.

"Okay, let's go," Cory ordered.

Delia and the boys disappeared into the trees. I stayed with Cory as we ran behind Jack. It quickly became evident that Jack was heading toward the lake. He appeared frantic as he neared a huge stable. We watched as he looked through a small broken window and pulled out a long knife. My throat went dry; he had seen James.

"He's in there," I whispered. "I know Jack saw him."

"Wait for him to walk in," Cory replied. "We still don't know what's going on."

Unable to contain my worry, I attempted to run toward the building.

Cory grabbed my arm and pulled me back. "Stop. You can't just storm in there. This may just be one of their meetings."

I heard Delia behind us. "I can sense James is in there, all right," she said. "But why does Jack have his weapon out?"

A blood-curdling scream rang out into the night, startling us all. *James!* He was in pain. The witch inside of me came alive. I spun around and pushed Cory out of the way. As I ran for the stable, I saw Jack burst through its door.

"Who are you!" someone shouted. "Show us who you really are!"

"What the hell is going on?" Jack yelled. "Why is he hung up like that?"

"He's a traitor," someone yelled.

"Cut him down at once," Jack ordered. "He's on our side, you fools."

I was almost to the door of the building when Cory grabbed me from behind and clamped his hand over my mouth. "Not like this," he said. "We have to be smart."

When Delia reached us, she helped Cory drag me back. "We have to count them first," she explained. "We don't know what the odds are yet."

Again, we heard voices coming from the stable. "This man is not who he pretends to be."

Cory put his finger to his lips. "I'm going to take a closer look," he said. "Stay behind me."

The boys stealthily worked their way toward the stable and waited for Cory's signal.

"What are you talking about?" Jack asked.

"This man is an imposter. The man he pretends to be, our friend, is dead."

"You don't know what you're talking about," Jack yelled. "I've known this man my whole life. We grew up together."

"Well, then, maybe you're an imposter, as well!"

I heard wrestling. "You're making a mistake!" Jack yelled.

Cory flicked his arms.

Delia revealed her blade. "It's time," she whispered.

Cory waved to the boys and ran toward the building. I followed close on his heels, not knowing what I was going to do. I had no idea how to use the staff—*my* staff.

Cory looked back at me. "Remember, stay back and shout out orders."

I swallowed hard and nodded.

Cory kicked open the door. The men in the stable abandoned their lively debate and stared at us, clearly taken aback. To my horror, James hung upside down from a beam. He had been badly beaten and was covered in blood.

Fury burned within me as the witch inside me came to the surface. I slowly turned to look at the men. "You will die a painful and horrible death, my lords."

Their faces twisted in shock as they realized who I was. They came at us, weapons drawn.

Cory shielded me as one man lunged at me with his sword. I stepped out of the way as Cory's blades slashed the man's face clean off. Delia struggled behind me as one of the men held a knife to her throat. Out of the blue, Fish's hooks flew at the man and sank into his back. Fish gave a hard pull, peeling the man's skin from his body.

I scrambled to James, hoping to release him from his constraints. A man stood in front of him with James's own whip in his hand. The man smiled at me, turned, and tried to strike James with it.

"Catch!" I yelled, throwing my stick at him. The man dropped the whip and reached for the stick. When he caught it, he laughed. "This is it?" he asked. "All you've got is a stick?"

I smiled and whispered, "Seek." The staff disappeared under the man's skin. Moments later, it came out of his chest, his heart speared on the tip. "Yes, that's all I've got."

"Thea, up here!" Samuel yelled. He had crawled up to the beam. He pulled out a knife and cut James down.

James fell to the ground, his head cracking against the floor.

I ran to him, rolled him onto his back, and grabbed his face. "James?" No response. I grabbed his arms and shook. "James!" Still nothing.

Above me, Joshua held back several men

with a beam. They were trying to get to me.

I reached for James's whip. "Get down!" I yelled to Joshua as I lashed out at the men. Joshua ducked, the whip passing just inches above his head. Three heads went flying as the whip found its mark. I tossed the whip to Joshua, and he swung it at the others.

I ran back to James, placed my hands on his chest, and chanted: "Heal!"

"How is he?" Jack yelled. I was surprised to see him fighting alongside the boys.

James's eyes began to open.

"James," I said breathlessly. "I'm here."

His eyes darted around the stable, taking in the chaos. He scrambled to his feet. "Joshua, my whip!" he yelled. James pushed me behind him as Joshua tossed down the whip. "Here, take this!" James kicked over an abandoned sword.

Joshua looked happy to be rid of the whip. He reached for the sword and ran to help Cory, who had been hit on the head by what looked like a steel bat. The man who had hit him now stood over him, ready to hit him again. James swung his whip and severed the man's hands, and the bat fell to the ground. Cory jumped to his feet, nodded a thanks to James, and James nodded back. Cory turned to help Fish, who was protecting Delia from whoever dared to get near her.

"Stay behind me," James said as he swung his whip at the men. I fought back the urge to shout orders. They didn't need my help. I wasn't going to allow her to control me this time, or take credit. This victory belonged to them.

I watched as they finished off the men. With one swing of the steel bat he'd swiped from the now handless man, Samuel killed the last of them. When it was over, they all stood, looking at each other and smiling. They turned to look at Jack who was also smiling, but stopped suddenly when he realized they were staring at him. The boys turned to Cory. No one knew what to do about Jack, and Jack clearly had no idea what to do about them.

James stepped forward. "Jack, it doesn't have to be like this," he said. "We don't have to kill you."

Jack looked into my eyes and then back at James.

"Don't even think about it, Jack," James warned.

The boys stepped toward Jack and raised their weapons. Jack lifted his knife.

I stepped out from behind James. "Jack?"

He eyed me nervously, the knife quivering in his shaky hand. His eyes darted back at James and the boys.

I moved to step closer to Jack, and James grabbed my arm.

"It's okay," I said. "I just want to talk to him."

When James released my arm, the boys moved closer to Jack.

I held up my hand. "Stay back," I ordered.

The boys held their places but remained

on guard.

Jack's body trembled as he waved the knife in the boys' direction.

"Jack, I'm not going to hurt you, I just want to tell you something."

He pointed the knife at me. "Don't come near me, you evil witch."

"Yes, it's true, I was an evil witch. But that's not who I am anymore."

Jack looked at James. "How could you do this to me?" he asked. "You betrayed me!"

I took another step toward him.

"Don't come any closer," he warned, his voice cracking.

"Stop pointing that knife at my wife," James said, trying again to pull me back.

Jack's face twisted. "Your wife?"

I held up my hand. "Listen, Jack, I'm sorry for whatever I might have done to you in the past. I'm not that person anymore. If I could take back every horrible thing I did, I would. But listening to Simon isn't going to give you a better life. He's lying to you about why he wants the crystal."

Jack continued to point the knife at me, his hand growing shakier. "He's going to share what you never did, show us the things you were never willing to."

"It's all a lie," James said. "He doesn't care about you. You're all his puppets. He's using you to get what he wants."

"You speak to me about lies?" Jack shouted. "I trusted you!"

As Jack addressed James, Delia quietly crept up behind him, the box in her hand.

"I promise things will be different this time," I said. "We don't need an outsider telling us how to live."

"You mean the way you did?" he shouted.

Sensing movement behind him, Jack spun around. Delia blew powder in his face and chanted: "Close your eyes and drift away, remember not the things I say. I take the memory for this time, and make you think that things are fine."

Jack's eyes closed, and he dropped to the floor.

Delia sank down and immediately began extracting memories from his head. "Quick, give me some ideas of what to put back in."

"Just make him think he found me at Thea's apartment," James said.

"Why?" Cory asked. "Why don't you want him to know you were here?"

"Because I won't be able to explain all of you," James replied. "How I happen to know you're all witches." James looked down at Delia. "Please, just do as I ask."

Delia nodded and went to work.

At that moment, a thought occurred to me. "Delia, can you erase any of the bad memories he has of me?"

"I'm already on it," she answered.

As we waited, the boys congratulated each other. "That was awesome, dude," Fish said, high-fiving Samuel. "Did you count how many of those guys we took?"

"Dude, something like twenty."

"Twenty-four," Javier said.

279

"I counted twenty five," Joshua corrected.

Cory shook his head. "None of you know how to count."

"I think I counted twenty-six," James said, looking at Cory. "Didn't you?"

Delia looked up, rolled her eyes, and resumed her task.

After a few moments of silence, James turned to the boys. "Thank you," he said. "For risking your lives to save mine."

The boys looked at Cory, anticipating his response.

Cory looked away. "We did it for Thea."

James nodded. "Nonetheless, I owe you my life."

Cory nodded and asked James what he was doing here in the first place.

James explained that they knew the man he had killed and was now pretending to be. "I didn't realize that two of the guys knew that the man was dead."

"Why are they here?" Cory asked.

"Well, a couple of their brethren are missing," James said. "I killed one at the bakery, and you killed several others—the ones who came into the bakery with Jack. But there are still two men missing. Simon's getting nervous, so he sent for these guys."

"Great," Delia said, standing. "Now he'll probably send for more men."

"Simon was apparently not aware that these guys were already here. That's why I came here tonight, to see if they'd arrived." James looked thoughtful for a moment. "I have an idea," he said, looking at Cory. "I'll tell Simon they've arrived and wait for his orders. He never talks to them directly. He'll have no idea they're dead."

Cory nodded. "We'll check the forest for new arrivals at sunup. Maybe we can pick them off as they arrive." Cory pulled out the money we found at the campsite and handed it to James.

"Where did you get this?" James asked.

"At a campsite in the woods by the lake," Cory replied. "There were two of them."

"Were?" James asked.

"We ran into them while the boys and I were out training by the lake."

I was relieved Cory didn't mention that I had been with them.

James looked at the money. "It's from Mexico."

"Simon knows witches from Mexico?" Cory asked, surprised.

"No," James replied. "These men turned to dust just like the rest of them. I suspect they've been with Simon since he fled all those years ago. I think they used to live here."

"What do you mean?" Cory asked. "They lived here in the sixteen hundreds?"

"Yeah," James replied. "A lot of warlocks left the area because they didn't want to obey . . . ." He paused, glanced at me, and continued. "Simon likely promised them freedom and riches. They think he's going to share the powers in the crystal."

My heart felt heavy as James spoke. He didn't need to say the words for me to understand. Those men fled from my cruel treatment and had come to get payback.

"Please tell me," I said. "Tell me what I did to them—why they hate me so much." They didn't answer and looked down. "So I'm the villain?" I asked, my voice quavering. "You've been protecting a villain this whole time?"

My friends stayed silent as I studied each of their pitying faces. My eyes locked on Jack still lying in a heap on the stable's floor. "Wake him up!" I ordered. "Wake him up and leave, so he can kill me!"

"It's not like that, Thea," Delia said gently. "They hated you because you defended us, the half humans."

James reached for me. I pushed him away and ran out of the stable. I sprinted toward the lake, intending to free everyone from the trouble I had caused. I would sink to the bottom and allow the water to wash away my memories. My legs had carried me almost to the shore when James caught up to me.

"Thea, stop!" he yelled, wrapping his arms around me. "Don't do this."

"I saw the hatred," I cried. "Jack had hate in his eyes."

"When you told him you were sorry, I assumed you knew something from the past."

I buried my face in his chest and wept. "I understand that I behaved horribly back then, but I still have no idea why they hate me so much."

Without warning, unfamiliar images rushed through my head; the witch inside had another message for me.

~~~

Delia and I were surrounded by several men, the boys standing off to the side.

"And what, may I ask, do my lords think they will gain if I show them a fishing spell?"

"Mistress," one of the men said, stepping forward, "the fishing has been dreadful. Perhaps thou couldst take the spell off the lake?"

"My lord is a greedy man," I replied. "These witches were here first, but my lords did not want to share the lake. You ran them off like animals. You will have to figure out how to catch the sleeping fish on your own."

They looked at each other and set off.

One man stopped and turned to face me. "It is thou who art greedy, mistress," he said. "If thou wouldst only teach us, we would not feel such anger for these witches. Thou hides spells from us, ways in which we could help ourselves—fishing, planting, and the like. Why dost thou not share?"

I laughed. "You blame me for the hate that ye carry, my lord? Dost thou not believe these witches deserve to starve, that they are not worthy enough to live among you?" I looked at Delia, smiled faintly, and called out, "Your talk of sharing is laughable, my lords."

The rest of the men stopped and turned.

"Do you not treat this land as though it belongs only to you? Indeed, why should I help you? You see, my lords, I was warned about warlocks and their self-serving ways. I do not plan on becoming a slave to any of you."

~~~

283

I exhaled in relief, taking great comfort in the fact that my ruthless behavior toward the warlocks was the result of protecting those who had been victimized by them. I feared what the future held and did what I could to protect the weak. But my actions gave the warlocks a reason to hate me and want me dead. I was too young and too arrogant to understand the divisive atmosphere I was creating. The warlocks couldn't have known my father had groomed me to detest them. They saw me only as evil and cruel. I had to find a way to make things right, to show them I had changed.

My face was still buried in James's chest.

"They hated what they couldn't understand, Thea," James said, lifting my chin with his fingers. "They didn't know what to make of you."

I was surprised he hadn't noticed that my mind had been elsewhere. "I have to make things right with them," I replied. "I have to show them I'm not the same person I used to be."

His blue eyes rested on my face. "It's not your fault they made the choice to follow Simon," he said sternly. "You have nothing to prove to them."

"Did you ever hate me?" I asked.

He kissed my head and squeezed me. "Does it feel like I ever hated you?"

I stared at him and swallowed thickly. "Then why did you wish you could take back your love?"

James went still.

"What did I do to you that day?" I asked.

He sighed and pulled away. "Of all the things for you to remember, you have to remember that."

"Was it that bad?"

"Can we please not talk about it?" He turned his back on me.

I couldn't understand why he didn't want to talk about it. I rested my head on his back and wrapped my arms around him. "If you still wish, I could erase your love when I get my powers back."

He spun around and grabbed my face. "Don't ever say that to me again," he said, shaking me. "Do not punish me by bringing up the past." He let me go, looked away, and sighed. "I need to speak to Cory. We should get back. Have Delia take you home. The boys and I will clean up here."

I nodded, and we walked to the stable. The boys—minus Cory—stood outside the building, watching for us. "Are you okay?" Samuel asked when we reached them.

I hung my head. "I'm sorry for my outburst."

James walked inside to talk to Cory. I looked up at the boys and began to cry.

"Do you want me to kick his ass?" Fish asked, taking my hand.

Laughter escaped through my tears. "You always know exactly what to say."

Chapter 16
The Steel Bat

James and Cory talked inside as the boys and I stood outside, laughing at Fish recounting his version of the fight. In Fish's mind, the body count was closer to forty, half of which he claimed to have killed single-handedly.

Cory walked out of the stable and told us he was going back for Delia's car. "It's getting too dark to walk home," he said. "I'll be back for you guys in a bit, so hurry and get everything cleaned up." They nodded, and we all headed inside the stable.

James and Delia were standing in a corner, talking quietly. "You guys didn't leave with Cory?" Delia asked.

"No, he said he was going back for your car," Samuel replied.

"Well, we have to get out of here," she said anxiously. "James and Jack will be expected back."

Samuel pulled out his phone. "I'll get him back here."

I looked at James, who seemed to be avoiding my gaze.

"Will I see you later?" I asked.

James nodded, picked up the sword he'd kicked to Joshua during the fight, and handed it to him. "You did well with this," he told him. "I think you should consider switching weapons."

Joshua took the sword from James and smiled. "It was certainly easier to use than your whip," Joshua replied. "I almost cut my own face away."

James smiled and put his hand on Joshua's shoulder. "Would you like me to put a spell on this so it never breaks on you?"

Joshua's eyes lit up. He handed the sword back to James. "Can you make it cut through anything?"

James nodded and laid the sword on the ground. "You'll be able to cut through steel and rock, and cut down trees with one swing."

"I gotta hear this spell," Javier said, walking over to join them. "Maybe it will improve my weapon."

James held out his hand. "I can do it now."

"Awesome!" Javier exclaimed, handing James his chain.

James looked at Fish. "How about you? Do your hooks need an upgrade?"

"Does King Kong have hair?" Fish set down his hooks next to Joshua's sword.

James laughed and placed Javier's chain on the ground next to the other two weapons. He chanted: "Be hard as a diamond and tough as a nail; with the might of a Titan, may your strike never fail. May nothing break or bend you as we battle in a fight; may nothing be left standing when it feels your mighty strike."

James reached down and handed each of the boys their weapons.

"Where did you learn that spell?" Fish asked.

James glanced at me. "Some witch taught it to me."

"I'm going outside to try it out," Fish said.

"Oh, no you don't," Delia yelled. "We have to leave now. I can't keep him asleep forever, you know. And it's getting late."

As the boys finished picking up, I noticed Javier whispering to Samuel. Samuel nodded, and the two approached James. "Hey, um, we just wanted to say thanks for doing that," Samuel said.

James smiled and extended his hand. "No, thank you for saving my life."

Samuel shook James's hand, and one by one, the other boys did the same.

"Okay," Delia said, gesturing to the pile of debris the boys had collected. "Take this stuff outside. We'll burn it with the stuff we found at the campsite."

As the boys began gathering up the debris, I spotted the steel bat and decided to add it to the pile. As my hand made contact with the bat's handle, searing pain shot through every fiber of my body. An ear-piercing scream escaped me as pieces of steel penetrated my skin. I collapsed as the steel bat melted into me, tearing my skin and pulling it away from my bones.

"Kill me!" I screamed.

The pain overwhelmed my senses as the weapon skinned me alive, and sharp pieces of steel stabbed me repeatedly. Delia and James chanted, but their spells were useless. The pain was so great that I only wanted to die.

"Please kill me!"

"No!" James shouted, continuing his chant.

Jagged pieces of steel entered my eyes, distorting my vision. The steel bat had disappeared into my body, searching to destroy. It was as though it had transformed into a million iron spiders that entered through my skin.

"*Release me*, Thea!" James yelled. "Say *Release me*!

"Get that sword out of here," Delia shouted to Joshua. "Don't let it touch her!"

Blood streamed from my eyes as the steel tore at them. The pain was unbearable; I could barely think.

"Thea!" James screamed. "Say *Release me*! *Release me*! Say it, Thea—*now*!"

It took every ounce of my strength to follow James's instructions. As I finally began to speak the words, my tongue filled with steel. I could no longer make sound. My eyes rolled back as pools of blood gushed from my body. My life rapidly fading, I prayed for death.

"No!" James shouted. "I'll die with you, Thea. I'll die with you."

Then the witch inside me spoke. "You can't die, Thea, for more than one life will be lost." I could feel her protecting my heart from the steel. "Say the words, Thea," she whispered.

"Say the words."

"Re . . . re . . . lea . . . se . . . me."

"Yes, darling," James said. "That's it."

I heard healing spells being chanted. The boys joined in with Delia and James. Cory's voice sounded particularly strained. "Why the hell isn't it working?"

Delia touched my head and chanted a sleeping spell. I welcomed the peace that washed over me.

"Sleep, my love," I heard James murmur before I drifted off to sleep.

When I awoke, William was smiling down at me. "Welcome back."

I was in my room at James's house. A cold, wet towel had been placed on my forehead. I tried to smile back at William, but intense pain blocked my effort. My lips felt as though they'd been sliced open. It hurt to breathe. I moaned and tried to touch my damaged lips, but I could barely move my hands.

"Don't try to move, child," William said, gently brushing a lock of wet hair away from my face. "You were hurt by a powerful spell."

Warm liquid ran down my cheek. William dabbed at with a towel. When he pulled the towel away, it was covered in blood. My questioning eyes found his.

He sensed my fear. "It was a very powerful spell," he repeated. "You are healing very slowly." He sat on the bed and took my hand. "I want you to rest. Getting upset will only serve to slow my healing spells."

I tried to squeeze his hand, but found I

couldn't without causing myself severe pain. I moaned again, and William quickly stood. "Don't try to move, child."

I heard a knock at the door. Delia popped her head in. "May I come in?"

"Yes, but stay calm, please," William warned.

I heard her tell the boys to wait outside. As Delia approached, a tentative smile spread across her face. "Hey, kid," she said, tears filling her eyes. "How are you feeling?"

William spoke up. "She can't talk yet."

Delia nodded and stepped closer to the bed. "The boys are here," she said shakily. "They wanted me to tell you they love you." She choked on a sob and drew her hand to her mouth.

William grabbed Delia's arm and abruptly escorted her out into the hallway.

"I'm so sorry," she cried. "I wasn't prepared to see her like that."

"What the hell kind of spell was that?" Cory asked.

"The kind you should be prepared to deal with," William replied. "Simon knows some extremely powerful spells, and it appears he's teaching them to the others."

"But we touched it, too," Cory said. "And nothing happened to any of us."

"Cory was hit over the head with that bat," Samuel said.

"The spells placed on those weapons were meant for her only. They would have needed something from her person to cast them. James told me that much of her hair had been pulled out when he found her in the grave. My guess is Simon is using that."

"How would someone like Simon know such a powerful spell?" Cory asked. "I've never heard of or seen anything like it."

"It wasn't a witch spell," William answered. "It was a wizard spell. Wizard spells are more powerful than anything you could ever chant." He paused. "And Simon learned it from a fool who trusted him once upon a time."

"Is she going to be okay?" Fish asked.

"I'm trying to speed up the healing with some tea recipes I found," William replied. "I'm doing everything I can to save her."

"Her eyes," Delia cried. "It's just so horrible."

"Control yourself, young Delia," William said. "This will not help her."

"May we see her?" Cory asked.

I heard William sigh. "You may see her if you promise not to upset her. Try not to react to her injuries. They are quite shocking."

"I give you my word," Cory said.

"May we see her, too?" the other boys asked.

"Yes, I only ask the same of you."

One by one, the boys appeared in the doorway. I tried to look over at them, but once again, the pain stopped me. Cory stepped into the room. He took a deep breath and forced a smile. Javier stood, glassy-eyed, at the edge of the bed. A single tear floated down Samuel's cheek and he quickly looked away. Joshua was nearly trembling but managed a warm smile. Fish took one look at me and promptly stepped

292

back out of the room.

"J . . . Ja—"

"He's been calling every five minutes," Cory said. "He'll be here as soon as he can." Tears welled up in his eyes, and he excused himself. "I'll be downstairs," he said to the others as he stepped out the door and into the hall.

Moments later, Fish appeared at the foot of the bed, one hand behind his back. "Remember this?" he asked, revealing a rock. He looked down. "That was a stupid question," he whispered to himself. He looked back up and smiled. "I use to be scared of the water because I couldn't swim. You cast a spell so that I would desperately need this rock that sat at the bottom of the lake. You said nothing was impossible if you truly believed in yourself. So I jumped in the lake, swam to the bottom, and found the rock." He walked over and placed the rock on the bedside table. "As it turns out, you never actually put a spell on me. You just made me think you did. But it was all the courage I needed to go into the water. Now I pass that courage on to you." He leaned over and kissed my cheek.

I wanted to hug him and tell them how much they all meant to me. "Th . . . ank y—"

"Shh," they all said in unison.

"We're going to let you rest now, okay?" Fish whispered.

I blinked my eyes slowly, and they headed out the door.

When they had all gone, William stepped back into the room with fresh towels and sat next to me. "James will be here soon," he said, wiping my eyes. "And Sharron is on her way, as well."

I tried to smile but managed only a quiet moan.

"I believe my spell is wearing off," William said. "Blink if you're feeling pain again."

I slowly closed and opened my eyes.

William nodded and walked out of the room. "I'll be right back," he said and closed the door behind him.

I lay still, trying not to feel the pain. The last thing I remembered was reaching for the steel bat, and the searing pain that had come soon after. I wanted to sleep, just drift away to escape the pain. I heard the faint sound of muffled voices coming from downstairs. I closed my eyes and commanded to be able to hear them.

"My spells are weak," William said. "One of you must go up there and cast a stronger one."

"I can't see her like that again," Delia said, her voice still shaky. "Please don't ask me."

"What if we keep her sleeping?" Cory asked.

"No," William said. "Then I would have no way of knowing if something is wrong. I need her conscious."

"James is going to lose his mind when he sees her," Cory said.

"She wasn't that bad when we brought her here," Delia added.

"She was covered in blood," William answered. "You had no way of knowing."

"What's taking him so long?" Delia asked. "She keeps asking for him."

"He's on his way," William said. "We must prepare him before he sees her."

"That spell was pure evil," Delia cried. "What kind of animal would do something like that?"

"And how do we fight against it?" Samuel asked.

"You don't fight against it, young man," William replied. "You protect yourself from it."

"How?" Cory asked.

"We can discuss that later. Right now, Thea is in need of a spell."

Cory spoke up. "I'll do it."

Seconds later, I heard them on the stairs. More than ever, I wondered what I looked like. They said they needed to prepare James before he saw me.

The door opened, and Cory walked in, followed by William. Cory looked down at me and smiled. "Your pain pill is here."

"M . . . mm . . . irr . . ."

Cory shot an alarmed look at William.

William smiled kindly and shook his head. "Neither I nor anyone else in this house will bring you a mirror. Upsetting you will only delay your healing." He turned to Cory. "I'm going to make a fresh batch of healing tea. Stay with her until I return."

As William left, Cory placed his hand over mine, but even his gentle touch sent stinging pain through my arm. "Does it hurt when I touch you?" he asked.

I blinked my eyes slowly, hoping he would understand.

His eyes widened. "I'm so sorry." He removed his hand, grabbed a towel from the top of the nightstand, and dabbed at my eyes. He chanted as he wiped the blood from my face: "Hear my voice with open ears, and let it dry away your tears. Feel my spell kill all your pain, and wash it away like falling rain. Like gentle snow that falls from above, I kill this pain with all my love." He smiled and winked. "I made it sound pretty, just for you."

"Th . . . an . . . k . . . y—"

"Shh. Don't try to talk. It makes your lips bleed. Is your pain any better?"

I blinked once.

"Good," he said, smiling. "William is bringing you some tea. Do you think you can sit up to drink?"

I considered his question for a moment and tried to sit up, but the pain was still too much. My tongue felt heavy as I tried to speak. "P . . . a . . . in."

"Okay, sweetie," he said. "Just stay still."

We heard a tap at the door. Cory got up and opened it.

"Hello, dear," Sharron greeted Cory. "May I come in?"

He stepped aside for her. "Hi, Sharron. Of course."

She set a bag on the floor, leaned down, and kissed me softly on the forehead. She smiled and looked at Cory. "I'm going to clean

296

her up. Do you mind waiting downstairs, dear?"

"Of course not," Cory answered, quietly stepping out of the room.

Sharron turned back to me and pulled the blanket away from my body. I was relieved when she didn't react the way the others did. She held her hands over me and chanted: "Take her skin and make it numb; don't let her feel the things to come. Let me touch and cause no pain; may she lay and not complain." She looked down and smiled. "Ready, dear? We don't have much time."

I blinked my eyes.

Sharron opened her bag, removed several bottles, and placed them on the nightstand. My eyes followed her as she placed leaves on my body and soaked them with the liquid from the bottles. She used her fingers to rub the saturated leaves into my body. When the leaves disintegrated, she reached for more and repeated the procedure. "I'll do your face last," she said, continuing her work. "Your eyes are still bleeding. I'll wait and see if it stops." She worked fast and said very little. Occasionally, she said the word *animals*. I was so happy to be out from under all the dried blood. Despite how hard she scrubbed, I couldn't feel her touch.

When she was done, she laid a clean blanket on top of me. "Now your face," she said. She pulled a pair of glasses from her bag, slipped them on, and sat on the bed.

As she leaned toward my face, I glimpsed my reflection in her glasses. My eyes didn't even look like eyes anymore. They were blood red and encircled in bruises, my lips swollen and sliced open. The skin had been pulled away from my face, and pieces of steel remained embedded in my cheeks.

Sharron must have noticed the terror in my eyes. She swiftly pulled the glasses from her face. "You're going to be fine, dear," she assured me. "It's not as bad as it looks."

I heard a knock at the door.

"I'm not finished," Sharron yelled. "Just a few minutes more, please."

"Please," James called from the other side of the door. "I beg you, let me in."

"J . . . James," I cried.

Sharron sighed, crossed the room, and opened the door. James walked briskly past her and toward the bed. When his eyes locked with mine, he looked away and closed his eyes.

Sharron placed her hand on his shoulder. "Be calm, dear," she whispered.

He nodded and tried to compose himself. He knelt down beside the bed, took my hand, and held it to his cheek.

Sharron stood by the door. "I'll give you two a moment," she said, quietly stepping into the hallway and closing the door behind her.

James kept his tear-filled eyes on me and smiled. "How is the most precious woman in my life doing?"

I gently squeezed his hand. "I . . . lo . . . ve . . . you."

Tears streamed down his face. "And I will forever love you, my angel," he said, leaning over and kissing my head.

"Ssstay," I said, my voice barely audible.

He stroked my face softly. "A million

spells couldn't keep me from your side."

I closed my eyes and breathed in his sweet scent.

"Did you know the first time I laid eyes on you, I felt my heart stop?"

I looked at him.

He nodded. "It's true. And when it started beating again, I knew I couldn't live without you."

I began to cry, knowing that if I died at this moment, I would die a happy woman because of how much he loved me.

He kissed my head and then my hand. "I love you."

Sharron walked in and asked if she could finish cleaning me.

"Yes, but I'm not leaving," James answered.

Sharron nodded. She repeated the spell, picked up the leaves, and started gently cleansing my face. I kept my eyes on James as she resumed her work. Small pieces of steel glinted among the leaves as she wiped them away from my eyes.

"I probably can't get it all," she said. "But I'll try."

James responded to a knock at the door. When he opened it, William stood on the other side, holding a tray with a pot of tea.

"Ah, Xander," Sharron said. "There you are."

"Hello, Sharron. How comes the cleaning?"

I looked at Sharron, surprised.

"Yes, dear," she said, winking. "I know

who he is." She set the tray down on a nearby table. "It's going better than I thought it would. You were right about the leaves; I'm glad I went through the trouble to find them."

William put his hand on James's shoulder. "Give her as much of this tea as she can drink. The more she drinks, the faster she will heal."

James nodded and poured some of the warm liquid into a cup. He grabbed a spoon from the tray, sat on the end of the bed, and waited for Sharron to finish. When Sharron stepped aside, James scooted up next to me and began spooning the tea into my mouth.

"Take good care of her," Sharron said to James. She turned and walked out with William, who patted James on the back before exiting the room.

James blew lightly on a spoonful of tea. "Do you think you can finish the whole pot?" he asked, offering me the first spoonful.

I smiled weakly, my cheeks finally free of the embedded pieces of steel.

He held up another spoonful of tea. "So, did you ever ask Delia about Fish's eyes," he asked. "Blink once for yes."

I blinked.

He smiled. "And were they blue?"

I blinked again.

He arched his eyebrows. "I had a feeling," he said, spooning more tea into my mouth. "I like that kid. I like all of them, but Fish makes me laugh." He stood and refilled the cup. When the pot was empty, he asked, "Up for one more pot?"

300

I blinked.

He stepped to the door and turned the knob. "I'll only be gone a moment," he said and left the room.

I felt the tea already working. I wiggled my fingers and made a fist.

James returned minutes later with Delia. "My love," he said, "I need to speak with William about the tea. I won't be long, I promise."

I looked at Delia, her eyes moist with tears.

"C . . . ry . . . ba . . . by," I murmured.

She chuckled and sat down beside me. "You'll do anything for attention, won't you?"

I was slowly reaching for her hand when I heard the murmur of voices coming from the kitchen. I commanded to hear them, closed my eyes, and listened.

"It took everything I had not to kill him today," James said. "If I had seen her first, I don't think I could have stopped myself."

"These are the kinds of spells I have been telling you about," William replied. "They're capable of killing us all. Simon knows she's half wizard."

"Is this the kind of spell he put on you?" James asked.

"Somewhat," William replied. "And look how long it has taken me to recover; nothing from this world can restore my full powers. But Thea is half witch. The tea can at least help that part of her heal quickly."

I heard liquid being poured.

"And what about the wizard part of her?" James asked.

"That will take longer," William answered. "Nothing in the human world makes much of an impact."

"Will that make her more vulnerable to Simon?" James asked, sounding worried.

"Without her powers, it would take years for her to recover," William replied. "But she can heal herself. Her powers are strong enough."

"What about you, William?" James asked. "Will she be able to heal you?"

William sighed. "No, it was not the same kind of spell. He cast a black spell on me. I need white energy to recover completely. And that, my boy, is not found in your world." There was a long pause before William spoke again. "You must be strong, my son," he said. "Don't let her see you like this."

"I won't give her reason to worry," James said shakily. "Just give me a moment, please."

"Take all the time you need. This has not been easy for any of us. One could not expect her to be alive, looking the way she does."

"Did you know about this?" James asked, his voice still quavering. "Was this something you saw coming?"

"I warned you about this," William replied. "Some things can change. I'm afraid I can do nothing to stop that. I can only prepare things for the next step."

"When will you tell me more?" James asked.

"I've already told you what you need to know, for now," William answered.

I lay there, confused, trying to make sense of their conversation. I remembered Delia telling me about how my father could sense the future. Did he know this was going to happen to me?

"Be strong, James," William said. "This is only the beginning. We have a long journey ahead."

"I can do this," James replied. "But I worry about her. I don't like seeing her suffer."

"You'll have to. It's the only way. Stay here until you compose yourself," William ordered. "She needs you."

"Can you make sure the boys are in the rooms nearest to her?" James asked. "It will make her happy to know they're here. Oh, and please make food available to them. I don't think any of them have eaten since it happened."

I heard a third person enter the kitchen. "Thank you," Cory said. "How is she doing? Is the tea working?"

"I'm bringing her a second pot right now," James replied. "We'll just have to wait and see."

"James, wait," Cory said. "Would it be possible for us to stay here for a few days?"

"Absolutely," James answered. "I wouldn't have it any other way."

"Thanks a lot, man," Cory said.

Seconds later, I heard James on the stairs. I listened as Fish stopped him and asked how I was doing.

"Would you like to come in and see her?" James asked.

Moments later, I heard James and Fish enter the room.

"I think she fell asleep," Delia told them.

"I'll let her rest, then," Fish said.

I felt Delia get up from the bed. "Come get me if you need me," she said as she stepped out of the room.

I heard the door close, and I opened my eyes. "D . . . did . . . she leave?" I asked James.

He set the tray on the nightstand and sat down next to me. "You sound much better, my love," he exclaimed. "The tea is starting to work."

I slowly reached for his hand. "S . . . stay," I whispered.

He kissed my hand and poured some tea. "If you're better by morning, we'll move you to another room."

"W . . . why?"

"Because I want to sleep next to you," he said, smiling. "And this bed is too small—I might hurt you."

"M . . . move mme . . . now."

He chuckled softly and spooned some tea into my mouth. "No, my love. In the morning, if you're better."

"I lo . . . ve y . . . ou."

"And don't you ever forget that," he replied.

James stayed by my side the entire night. I finished three pots of tea. I'm not sure how I was able to sleep with all that liquid inside me. As I drifted in and out, I felt James with me:

touching my face, kissing my head, and whispering into my ear that he loved me.

When I opened my eyes in the morning, Sharron was already there, leaves in hand. "Good morning," she said, smiling. I hadn't even felt her move my leg, which she was holding up while rubbing leaves on the underside. "Everyone's been asking if you're awake yet." She poured liquid from one of her the bottles. "How do you feel, dear? Can you talk at all?"

I moved my tongue which, to my great relief, no longer felt heavy. "I think so."

"Wonderful. I was afraid I was going to wake you when I was scrubbing your mouth."

"Where's James?" I asked.

"He's with the boys. They went to check the woods, and also to talk to Vera; she's changing her appearance and going to work in your place today."

"At the bakery?"

"Yes, dear." She lowered my leg gently to the bed. "Delia pulled memories from your head this morning. Vera knows what to do. She'll work as you until you're feeling better."

I looked up at her, my eyes wide. "You guys can do that?"

"We're witches, dear," she said, winking. "We can do anything we want." She reached for more leaves.

"I know William is my father," I said.

She kept scrubbing. "Yes, dear. He told me."

"He told you?" I asked, surprised. "How did he know?"

305

"He can read your thoughts. The wizard part of you is connected to him like that."

I was stunned. "Can he read your thoughts?"

She laughed delicately. "I'm not half wizard, dear. He can only read yours. But he's having trouble reading them clearly."

"Is it because of the spell Simon used on him—to kill him?"

She stopped working on me and sat on the bed. "That was a black spell. If Simon had killed him, he would have stayed dead."

"Then what was it?"

"What happened to your father was a spell that kept him prisoner to a grave. A piece of your mother's heart was used to call him there, and he was to sleep an endless sleep." She resumed her work and began to scrub my face. "But Simon does believe that your father is dead. He doesn't understand the secrets behind the wizard spells your father taught him. He never imagined your blood would break his spell and bring your father back. That's why Simon hides: he doesn't know what happened to your father's body, or your mother's heart. He fears your father so much that even your father's bones scare him."

"My mother's heart," I whispered to myself. Maybe that was the message James was trying to give me in those books. "Sharron, why didn't you tell me about my father? That you knew he was alive?"

"He asked me not to, dear. He said you'd figure it out when the time was right."

I was grateful to Sharron for always

306

giving it to me straight. She never beat around the bush like the others.

"How long have you known?" I asked. "About my father being alive?"

She reached for more leaves and wetted them. "Several hundred years by now," she said, smiling. "We've kept in touch by letter."

"Did he ever ask about me?"

She smiled and sighed. "All of his letters were about you. He and James both insisted on knowing your every move."

"I still can't believe James is my husband."

Sharron stood. "No more questions," she ordered. "I need to finish up."

After Sharron's magical cleansing, she helped me into the shower. "I'm going to show you how to put a spell on your hair."

I smiled, relieved. I wanted to look my best tonight. If James moved me to a room where we could be together, I wanted to be ready.

"Do you see any shards of steel on me?" I asked as Sharron dried me off.

"Very little. I'll get what's left next time." We heard someone walk into the bedroom. Sharron hurriedly closed the bathroom door. "I'm changing her," she called.

"Into what?"

Sharron and I laughed.

Delia peeked her head into the bathroom. "Oh, Thea," she exclaimed. "You look so much better."

"The tea is working fast," Sharron said, slipping a robe onto me. "Okay, now let's take care of this hair, shall we?"

"Thank God," Delia said. "I couldn't think of a spell strong enough for that disaster."

Sharron ignored her and told me to hold my hands to my head. "Once you chant this spell, it will start on its own every morning," she explained. "You can change it from straight to curly whenever you want."

I nodded excitedly.

"Now repeat after me. De—"

"Wait! What about . . ." I thought of James and how he kept telling me never to change my hair.

"Is there a problem, dear?" Sharron asked.

I dropped my hands to my sides and sighed. "When I look at James, I see his love for me in his eyes. If I fix my hair, he won't be able to see the symbol of my love. I couldn't imagine not seeing his blue eyes when he looks at me."

Sharron smiled kindly. "I completely understand, dear."

Delia rolled her eyes. "Can you at least learn how to use a brush?"

"She's in love," Sharron said. "Only her spell will work on that hair."

I smiled, making particular note of Sharron's own massive heap of knots and tangles.

"By the way," Sharron said, "I don't know if you've noticed, but Xander broke your spell."

"My spell?" I asked.

"Yes, dear. Delia and James are able to

be around each other without you having to be present."

I looked at Delia and back to Sharron. "Why did I cast such a spell in the first place?"

"Because Delia hated him," Sharron explained. "You were protecting him from her."

I looked at Delia, my eyebrows arched.

"Don't look at me like that," she said. "I don't hate him anymore." She smiled sheepishly, and I smiled back.

Sharron ushered me back into the bedroom, and Delia followed. "Sharron," I asked, "why do you call him Xander?"

"Because that's his name," Sharron replied. "William is his middle name."

At that moment, a thought occurred to me: I didn't even know James's last name. How could that be? "Sharron, do you know James's full name?"

"Of course, dear," she replied, helping me slip into some clothes. "It's James Ethan Wade."

"James Ethan Wade," I murmured. "Even his name is beautiful."

Delia rolled her eyes. "Oh please. You're going to make me throw up."

Chapter 17
The Council Meeting

After I dressed, Sharron and Delia helped me back into bed. Sharron packed her bag and readied herself to leave. "I'll be back later for the council meeting," she said. "We'll clean up the rest of those shards beforehand."

I looked up at her, surprised. "Council meeting? Here?"

"Yes, dear," she said. "You're not ready to move about, so we're bringing the meeting to you."

"What exactly happens during a council meeting?"

"You'll see. I'll be back in a few hours."

As soon as she left, I threw off the blanket and tried to sit up.

"What are you doing?" Delia asked.

"All that tea is making me anxious," I replied. "I need to get out of this bed for a while."

Delia took my arm. "There's a sitting room across the hall. Why don't we walk over and sit for a while?"

When we made it to the sitting room,

Delia sat me down next to the fireplace. She chanted a spell to start the fire and took the seat next to me. "I can't get over how much better you look today, Thea."

"I feel better."

William appeared at the door, holding another pot of tea. "I'm glad to see you up and about, madam."

I looked at the tea and made a face. "How many more of those do I have to drink?"

"As many as it takes." He set the pot on a table, poured a cup, and offered it to me. "If you do not finish two more pots, I will tell James not to move you into your new room."

I hastily reached for the cup and took a sip. William smiled and threw another log on the fire.

"Did Fish tell you about the rock he gave me?" I asked Delia.

She nodded. "Yeah. He's so sweet."

"James really likes him," I said, taking a sip of my tea. "I think you do, too."

"Yeah. I tell you what, Thea," she said dreamily, "if it wasn't for this damned bond, I'd probably throw myself at that kid."

William glanced over his shoulder at Delia, his eyebrows arched.

Delia met his gaze. "What?" she asked indignantly.

As William slowly turned back to the fire, I set down my cup and leaned back. "So you *do* have feelings for him," I said, smiling.

"You know I do," she replied. "But I'm pretty sure he's just flirting with me."

William gave Delia another curious

glance, but she didn't notice.

"If I thought he was serious about me," she continued, "I'd tell him how I feel."

William's eyes fixed on Delia. "You have feelings for this young man?"

"Yes, why?"

William was thoughtful for a moment. He stepped over to me and whispered to me something I couldn't quite understand.

I looked up at him, confused. "What?"

"I must make sure," William said.

I looked at Delia. "I'm going to free you from Simon when I kill him."

Delia's eyes narrowed. "Don't say things like that to me," she snapped. "It makes me want to hurt you."

I looked at William questioningly.

"Say it again," he said, staring at Delia.

"I'm going to kill Simon," I said.

She closed her eyes and looked away from me. This time, I felt sharp zaps on the back of my head.

"Again," William ordered.

"I'm going to kill Simon."

I clutched my head and fell from the chair. William grasped Delia's arm and almost dragged her out of the room. Their voices were faint as the stinging sensation began to subside.

"What did I do?" she asked, looking at me from the doorway.

"Wait here," William told her. He hurried back into the room and helped me into the chair. "Has it stopped?" he asked.

I nodded and looked toward the door. "What's going on?"

"I'm sorry I had to do that," William said, "but I had to confirm my suspicion."

"And exactly what was that?"

He smiled. "That Simon is very sloppy with his spells." He stepped back to the door to retrieve Delia.

"What did I do?" she asked as she reentered the room.

"Sit down," William said. "I need to ask you some questions."

Delia sat and eyed him curiously. "What's going on?"

"I was wrong about something," William admitted.

"Wrong about what?"

"When you are bonded, it is impossible to have romantic feelings for someone else."

"What are you saying?" Delia asked.

William put his hands on her shoulders. "I believe I may have misinterpreted a vision I had about you." He paused and smiled. "I do not believe you are bonded to Simon. I am almost certain that you are merely under a spell."

Her head shot up. "A spell? Is that possible?"

"Very possible, indeed, young Delia."

"How could you possibly know that?"

"Because I know him. And I know this spell."

"Wait," she said. "Why would you have a vision about me?"

He ignored her question. "I think Simon is using you to protect himself from Thea," he continued. "The spell causes Thea pain

313

whenever she feels anger for him."

He looked at me and nodded.

Wincing, I said, "Delia, I'm going to kill Simon."

She looked away and closed her eyes.

I felt the zaps immediately. Seconds later, I heard voices: "*You said this spell would work, so why can't we move it?*"

"I can hear voices," I said excitedly. "Someone is trying to move something."

"Leave the room, Delia," William said, pushing her out the door.

My voice rose. "It's Simon!"

"I know, child," William said. "I know."

"Bring her back in so I can hear more."

He knelt down in front of me. "That will not be necessary. For now, you must rest."

"But I want to help."

"You already did." He got up and motioned for Delia to come back in. "If it would not be too much trouble, young Delia, I would like permission to have a look around inside your head. Come, help me get Thea to my room so we may get started."

They helped me up, and we started down the long hallway. When we arrived at the very last door, we walked inside. William's room was a cluttered mass of open books lying about on nearly every available surface. They looked old and worn, the pages yellowed from years of use. They appeared terribly fragile. Dried plants, hung with string, dangled from a clothesline drawn from one side of the room to the other. The desk in the corner by the window looked to be reserved for maps. If I had to guess, I'd say William was trying to find something important. I couldn't help but wonder what.

"What are all these books for?" Delia asked, surveying the chaos with obvious bewilderment. Her eyes came to rest on William. "What kind of warlock are you?"

He smiled and closed the door. "I am not a warlock."

"Then what are you?" she asked.

He just smiled. "We should get started. The others will be back soon."

Delia looked at me. For a second, I thought she was putting it together. Instead, she sat in the chair William had placed in the middle of the room.

"I am going to make some smoke," he said. "Inhale as much as you can, hold it for a moment, and blow it out with your eyes closed."

"Okay," she replied.

He walked to a small table topped with different-sized jars, opened one of them, and pulled out what looked like cotton. He walked back over to Delia and set it on fire. "Remember, breathe in as much smoke as you can," her reminded her. "It will allow me to see your memories."

Delia nodded as he held the jar up to her mouth. She closed her eyes and drew a deep breath. The smoke sparkled and made little circles before proceeding into her mouth and nose. As Delia held the smoke in her lungs, her head began to glow. As she slowly exhaled, the smoke spun in circles and landed on William's extended palm. He held the smoke close to his mouth, slowly inhaled it, and closed his eyes. He stood remarkably still.

Delia looked awestruck by William's performance. Her eyes swept the room repeatedly as William searched her memories. Her eyes came to rest on me anytime she saw something that struck her as odd. "Who is this guy?" she mouthed, tilting her head ever so slightly in William's direction.

I smiled. I imagined it was, by now, okay to tell her the truth. Certainly William wouldn't have invited her to this room if the case were otherwise.

"Yes," William murmured. "I know this spell very well." He opened his eyes and looked down at Delia with one eyebrow raised. "He was very sloppy, indeed. He forgot two extremely vital words."

"What does that mean for me?" Delia asked anxiously.

He smiled widely and placed his hand on her cheek. "It means, young Delia, that I was wrong about my vision. You are still able to choose to whom you wish to be bonded."

Delia bounded from the chair and threw herself into William's arms.

"Thank you," she cried, planting a peck on each of his cheeks.

William blushed, taken aback by Delia's demonstrative display. "It will take me a few days to create a potion that will break the spell. I do not have the strength needed to remove it right now."

Delia composed herself and looked up at

316

William. "You can actually break the spell?"

He smiled and nodded.

Delia regarded him curiously. "How do you know so much about these bizarre wizard spells?" she asked.

"Like I said," William replied. "I know Simon."

"But Simon isn't a wizard," Delia said. "How is it that he's able to cast these kinds of spells?"

"While it is true that Simon is not a wizard, he *is* a witch," William replied. "With proper training, you could cast wizard spells, as well."

Delia continued to eye him inquisitively. "Who are you?"

I was surprised Delia hadn't figured it out on her own.

William glided past Delia and her questioning eyes. "We should get Thea back to her room."

Delia maintained her scrutiny of William as they helped me up. As I got to my feet, I was suddenly hit with a bout of dizziness.

"Are you all right, child?" William asked.

"Just a little light-headed. I'll be fine."

"Let's get you into bed before you pass out," Delia said.

As we exited William's room, we saw Sammy walking up the stairs.
"Hey, what's going on?" Sam asked.

"Come, Samuel," William said. "Help me get Thea into bed."

"I'll go get the tea," Delia said.

The spinning in my head slowly came to a stop. I reached for Sammy's arm and smiled weakly. "Hi."

"Hi, Boo. You feeling any better?"

"Yes, a lot better. I just got a little dizzy."

"Well, you certainly look a lot better."

We made it to my room and I got into bed. William left to help Delia with the tea.

"Mind if I stick around for a little bit?" Sammy asked.

"Sure," I replied. "Where are the rest of the boys?"

"They're still at work. Norm sent me home early. It was sort of slow."

"I'm sure he'll call you back soon."

A few minutes later, William walked in with Delia. He poured a cup of tea and handed it to me. "I'm going to make you something to eat," he said. "I'll have the young man here bring it up when it's ready. Would you care for some lunch, Samuel?"

"No, thanks, I already ate."

After Delia and William left the room, I noticed Sammy staring at me intently.

"Why are you looking at me like that?"

"I'm sorry, but I can't get over how much better you look today."

I smiled and sipped my tea. "I can't believe how much better I feel."

"Is that stuff any good?"

"For healing, yes, but it tastes awful," I said, grimacing. "But don't tell William I said that."

He smiled and placed a finger to his lips.

"I promise." He looked thoughtful for a moment. "That was some fight. It was cool of James to show the guys that spell." He paused. "I don't think James likes me."

"Did James say something to you?"

"No, it's not that. Ah, don't listen to me, I'm probably just being stupid."

"Sammy, why do you think he doesn't like you?"

Sammy didn't answer. He smiled weakly and shrugged.

I decided to change the subject. "I can't wait to get back to our training," I said, taking another sip of tea.

"You still want to train?" he asked, surprised.

"Why wouldn't I? You really think I'm ready to face a warlock all by myself?"

"No, I suppose not."

Delia returned, wearing a wide grin on her face.

"Hey, Dells," Sammy said. "You certainly look happy."

"That's because I am, you wonderful creature, you," Delia replied, planting a kiss on Samuel's cheek.

I suppressed a giggle as Sammy leaned back, obviously astounded. "Wow," he exclaimed, his eyes narrowing playfully. "Who are you, and what have you done with Delia?"

Delia just smiled and sat on the bed. "Can you go get Thea's food?" she asked him. "I think it's ready."

Sammy nodded and left the room. The moment he was gone, Delia fixed her eyes on me. "Okay, spill," she said. "Who, and more importantly, *what* is William?"

I was about to answer when Sammy reappeared in the doorway. "Room service," he said, holding up a tray.

"That was fast," Delia said.

"I intercepted William on the stairs." He placed the tray on my lap and left to help William set up for the council meeting.

When he was gone, Delia leaned closer. "Okay, let's have it."

"He's my father," I said, taking a bite of my sandwich.

Delia's eyes widened until I thought they would explode. "Are you still dizzy? I thought I heard you say he was your father."

"He is," I said matter-of-factly. "But you can't tell anyone. Oh, but Sharron already knows."

Stunned, Delia sat, her mouth agape.

"This is nice," I said, nodding. "For once, the shoe is on the other foot." I took another bite of sandwich. "Take your time. It'll sink in."

A knock at the door did little to jolt Delia from her state of shock. She was still staring into space when I yelled, "Come in."

William opened the door and brought in more tea. "If you are to attend the council meeting, this will help." He set the pot on the nightstand and looked amusedly at Delia. "Ah, I see you told her."

I took another bite and looked up. "Sheesh, not even I reacted like this," I said, giggling. "And I'm your daughter."

320

He poured me some tea. "That's because you figured it out on your own. I knew when you hugged me that first time."

I looked at him, curious. "Why didn't you want me to tell you that I knew?"

He looked at Delia, who was still staring at him. He smiled and looked back to me.

"How did you know I didn't want you telling me?"

"I don't know," I replied. "I just knew."

"And what am I thinking right now?"

I looked over to Delia and chuckled. "You're wondering if Delia is ever going to stop staring at you."

Delia finally broke free of her trance and shook her head. "I'm sorry, but this is amazing. I thought you were just some warlock James met in England." She looked at me and back to William. "So, was she right? Is that what you were thinking?"

"No," he replied. "Not even close."

I laughed and popped in the last bite of sandwich. "Got you to stop looking at him though," I said, my mouth full of tuna.

We heard the doorbell, and William left to see who it was.

"Your father, Thea," Delia said. "He's your father. Why are you not jumping for joy?"

"I am. But I can't seem too happy. I don't know why, but he doesn't want me to make a fuss."

"If you haven't discussed it with him, how do you know?"

"I just know."

She looked at me intently, eyebrows

arched.

I sighed. "I hear his voice in my head sometimes. I think I can hear his thoughts."

"You can read his thoughts?"

"I'm not sure, but I think so."

"I should have guessed. Sharron told me he knew that you and I would be good friends."

"Delia, do you think he saw what happened to me?"

"I don't know. Why?"

"I heard him talking to James. I got the impression he knew this was going to happen."

"Why don't you just ask him?"

"Because I don't think he'll tell me."

Sharron walked in. "You're just eating lunch now, dear?"

"The tea takes my appetite away."

Sharron nodded knowingly and set down her bag. "I'll set up while you finish. A few more scrubs should do the trick."

"I'll go help Sam," Delia said. "I'll see you downstairs."

I finished my food and set the tray aside.

Sharron helped me remove my clothes and got right to work. "The others will be here soon," she said as she lifted my arm. "It's the first time you'll remember being at one of these things."

I heard the murmur of voices downstairs. "How many are coming?"

"I thought it best if only a handful of us sat in tonight. Simon and his men are keeping a close eye on us. It's safest if we're not seen out and about in large groups." She finished and pulled some clean clothes from the dresser.

"Drink one more cup, and I'll help you get dressed."

I downed the last of the tea, which was now cold. Sharron helped me dress and called for Samuel to help take me downstairs.

I was surprised to see Cory in the doorway instead. "Well, look at you," he said, grinning. "You're like a new person."

Fish walked in behind him. "Did I hear you needed someone with muscles?"

I smiled. "Hey, guys. How was work?"

Fish burst out laughing.

Cory shot him a look. "Shut up. It wasn't funny."

"What happened?" I asked, concerned.

Fish failed in stifling another laugh.

Cory smacked him over the head. "What did I tell you on the way here?"

"Cory, what's going on?" I asked again.

"Fish was giving Vera a hard time today."

I gave Fish a sideways glance. "What did you do, you little stinker?"

"Nothing," he said, grinning mischievously.

Cory rolled his eyes. "He told Vera that you always dance before putting anything in the oven. He told her she should do everything you do so as not to give her real identity away."

Fish smirked. "I also told her that you call Norm 'Normie Poo.'"

Cory slapped him over the head again. "And then he told her you always slap Norm on the butt when he walks by. I thought Norm was going to have a heart attack when, sure as

323

anything, Vera followed Fish's instructions to the letter."

Laughter bubbled up inside of me. "You're a handful."

A hint of a smile appeared on Cory's face as he hit Fish over the head a third time. "By the end of the day, Norm was a nervous wreck. I can't begin to imagine what he must be thinking."

I could no longer stifle my laughter and let loose an uncontrollable bout that left me feeling winded. Cory turned his head to the side, his shoulders bouncing. Javier and Joshua arrived and knowingly joined in.

"We were just filling Sam in downstairs," Javier said. "He's pissed he missed it." He looked at me. "Holy crap, is that really you?"

"Don't be rude," Cory scolded.

"I'm sorry," Javier replied. "But look at her. She looks great."

"I can't believe I missed the best part of the day," Samuel said as he walked into the room.

"Well, we're off for the rest of the week," Cory said. "At least Vera will get a break."

"Off?" I asked. "Why?"

"The witches removed the spell, and things have slowed way down," Cory explained. "Norm said he'd call us if he needed us."

Sharron clapped her hands, abruptly ending the conversation. I'd forgotten she was even there. "That's enough, boys. Let's get

Thea downstairs. It's getting late."

As I started to sit up, Cory leaned down to help me. His eyes looked different to me now.

"Hold on to my neck," he said.

I nodded and continued looking at his eyes, which I realized were no longer blue, but green.

"You mind if I take her?"

I looked up to see two beautiful blue eyes staring at me from the doorway. "James."

Cory stepped aside and motioned for the boys to follow him out of the room. "We'll be downstairs," he said as they left.

Sharron excused herself and left with the boys. "Don't be too long, dear," she told James.

James nodded but kept his eyes on me. "I wasn't expecting to see such a dramatic transformation."

I hoped he planned to keep his promise. He was the reason I had drunk all the tea, and I wanted my reward. "I'm still a bit weak," I said.

He smiled and walked to me. "Do you feel too weak to give me a kiss?"

I felt dizzy as his blue eyes pierced through me. I grabbed his shirt and pulled him closer. "Never too weak for that," I said, pressing my lips to his.

He grabbed my arms and pulled me up, our lips never parting as I wrapped my arms around him.

"I missed you," I murmured between kisses.

"I'm sorry I took so long. I was working on getting a few days off."

"So how many days do I have you for?"

"You have me forever, my love," he whispered, kissing me again.

I heard the sound of William clearing his throat in the doorway. "Perhaps relocating Thea to another room isn't such a good idea," he said.

James quickly pulled away from me. "I'm sorry, William. I was just so pleased to see how well she's doing."

"I need a word with you," William said.

James nodded and sat me on the bed. "I'll be right back." He kissed my head and walked out of the room.

William smiled and pulled the door closed.

When the two men returned, James looked solemn. "Let's get you downstairs," he said, helping me to my feet. "We need to start this meeting."

The others waited in the living room. I was glad to see Vera; perhaps this would give us an opportunity to talk. When she smiled at me, I imagined her dancing in front of the ovens and had to suppress a giggle.

"We're happy to see you doing so well, Thea," Amanda said.

"Thank you."

She looked at James. "Do you need help with her?"

"No, I've got her, thanks."

"Sit down, Amanda," Helena snapped. "She's doing fine." Helena shot me a hostile glance and roughly pulled her sister back down into her chair.

James helped me into a chair and walked

to the middle of the room. Sharron stood beside him. As I scanned the faces in the room, I observed Amanda and Helena sneering at the boys.

"We all know why we're here," Sharron began. "We don't have time for formalities. We'll therefore skip the performing of the usual pre-meeting spells." She nodded at James.

James addressed the group. "I apologize for our presence at your council meeting, but we have a serious matter to discuss. As you know, I've been gathering information and relaying it to Sharron, and now we have a problem. Simon is trying to steal the hourglass. I didn't believe it to be of much use to him other than giving notification of the return of Thea's memory, but now he seems desperate to get his hands on it."

Amanda spoke up. "But we've cast spells on it."

"He's trying to break the spells," James replied.

Helena stood. "That's impossible," she said haughtily. "We each put our own spell on it, and those spells are unbreakable."

"The spells aren't enough to stop him," James answered.

"Why don't we just go and get it then?" she asked. "We can move it tonight."

"We can't," James explained. "They're watching the ship around the clock."

Sharron nodded. "We have to find a way to remove the hourglass without Simon knowing. We need him to believe that it's still on the ship."

"But what if he finds out we took it?" Vera asked. "What then?"

"He's not going to find out," James answered.

Helena scoffed. "And how do you propose we keep that from happening?"

"We're going to switch it," Sharron answered. "Simon can't know the real one is missing, so we'll make it easy for him to steal the fake one."

James nodded. "But first we have to think of a distraction so the boys and I can board the ship and make the switch. Each of you will need to provide us with a reverse spell so the hourglass can be removed."

"Why does he want the hourglass so badly?" Cory asked.

"We're not sure," James replied.

"Are we going to bring it here?"

"Yes," James answered.

Helena stood again. "I don't understand. Why don't we just get it now?"

"That's not possible," James replied.

"Again, why?" Helena snapped.

James locked eyes with Helena. "Because if Simon learns that the hourglass is missing, he will hunt you down and kill each and every one of you." James looked around the room. "Simon has been sending for men—warlocks with whom he's promised to share Thea's powers. They believe he's going to make them all wizards once the crystal is opened."

Helena looked at me, a disgusted expression on her face.

"This is the only way to avoid bloodshed," James continued. "Most of you aren't prepared to fight like they are. Simon has cast wizard spells on their weapons. You have no defense against them."

"And she does?" Helena said, pointing at me.

James smiled. "Once her powers are back, she'll be well prepared."

I smiled back at James and looked at Helena. "I think you've asked enough questions for one day."

Helena tilted her chin up and looked away. I couldn't understand why she hated me so much.

"We still need a distraction," James said. "We have to find a way to lure Simon's men away from the ship."

Delia erupted into laughter.

James turned to her, curious, his eyebrows arched.

"I think I know a way to distract them," Delia said, still giggling. She turned to Amanda and Helena. "But I'm not saying it in front of them."

"Don't worry, witch," Helena shot back. "We don't care to hear your plan."

"It's a good thing, hag," Delia said. "Because it involves actual work, which is not something either of you have much experience with."

Helena snorted. "Witches like you are perfectly suited to handle the dirty work. I was made for something else."

"Yes," Delia said, looking around the

room. "But I don't see any beds here."

Fish chuckled.

Helena flashed him a look. "What are you laughing at, idiot?"

Delia stood, eyeing Helena contemptuously.

"Enough!" James yelled. "This is not the time."

Sharron looked from Helena to Delia and told James to take a seat. "We must unite, sisters. We must prepare to fight for our lives. I'll understand if some of you choose to leave instead of fight. "But for those of you who choose to stay, fight training begins tomorrow."

"So this is it?" Helena asked. "We fight, then?"

"We fight or we die," Sharron replied. "Which would you prefer, dear?"

James walked over to Helena. "I've sent for help," he said. "A few friends that know of our troubles have offered their services."

"Who are these men, James?" Cory asked. "Can we trust them?"

James nodded. "I'd trust them with my life."

"They're your friends, not ours," Helena snapped. "How do we know they can be trusted, that they don't want the crystal for themselves?"

James smiled. "They would rather die than betray me."

"Why must we fight?" Vera asked. "Do you really think they would hurt us?"

James looked uneasy and cast his eyes at the floor. "Simon is not planning on leaving any of you alive," he said quietly.

The witches regarded each other with fear in their eyes.

"May I say something?" I asked, standing. All eyes were on me as James helped me to the middle of the room. I drew a deep breath and looked at each of the faces in the room. "I want you all to promise me something. You can give me your word, or I will order it from you."

"What is it, Thea?" Delia asked, clearly concerned.

I searched inside of myself for courage to say the words. "If something goes wrong, if Simon finds that you've switched the hourglass, promise me you will hand me over to him. Promise me you will escape and leave Salem."

"Oh, we promise," Helena said, sneering.

Delia was on her feet again. "Shut up, hag!"

James appeared at my side. "Thea," he said, glancing at Helena from the corner of his eye, "if anyone in this room thinks for one moment about doing that, I will kill them myself."

"This is my fault," I said, suddenly feeling exhausted. "I can't let you all fight for me—not for something I did."

"We can, and we will," Cory said, getting to his feet. "And whoever isn't with us is welcome to leave." He shot Helena a knowing look.

The rest of the boys rose from their chairs. "We stand with you, Thea," Samuel said, speaking for the group. "We'll fight till the end."

Sharron stepped up and faced me. "It's settled, dear. Not another word."

I looked at my father, who was standing in the corner of the room. "Some things cannot be changed," he said.

I bowed my head, hot tears spilling from my eyes. "I don't deserve any of you. I won't ever stop asking for your forgiveness."

James turned me to face him. "Did you not hear me?" he asked. "We're all in danger. There is nothing to forgive."

"That's right," Fish said. "Simon wants to kick all of our asses."

I smiled through my tears as the room exploded with laughter.

Chapter 18
Delia's Plan

After Sharron called the council meeting to an end, people talked amongst themselves. I repeatedly tried to catch Vera's eye, but she seemed to be avoiding my gaze. The closer I moved to her, the more nervous she appeared.

I watched as Delia approached her. "May I speak to you alone?" she asked.

Vera nodded, and the two slipped into the kitchen. My curiosity aroused, I commanded to hear them.

"What can I do for you, Delia?" Vera asked nervously.

"I don't know how to say this," Delia said, "so I'm just going to spit it out."

"What is it?" Vera asked.

Delia sighed. "I'm sorry I've been such a bitch to you. I hope you can forgive me."

I heard someone begin to cry. "It was never of my own free will," Vera said, sniffing back tears. "I hate myself for what I've done."

"I know, Vera. I should have helped you."

"I try not to talk to her in front of you,"

Vera said. "I fear what you might think." She burst into a sob.

I decided to interrupt their conversation. Now I understood why Vera was so nervous around me. In the kitchen, Delia had her arms around Vera. They both turned to me, Vera wiping her tears.

"I'm glad you two kissed and made up," I said with a smile.

Delia's eyes widened. "Thea," she said. "You're walking with no help."

I had barely noticed that my legs were no longer achy. "Yeah, I guess I am," I said, looking down at my legs.

Vera started to leave the room, but I reached out to her. "It was nice seeing you today, Vera. I hope to see you again soon."

She flashed me a shy smile. "Yes, mistress. Very soon, I'm sure." When she reached the kitchen door, she stopped and turned around. "May I ask you something?"

"Sure, what is it?"

"Why do you dance before you put things into the oven?"

I suppressed a giggle and smiled. "It makes the day go faster."

After she left, Delia asked me to explain Vera's question. After I had relayed the story of Fish's antics at the bakery, Delia nearly fell to the floor in a fit of laughter. "He's such a naughty little man," she said, wiping tears from her eyes. "I love that about him."

We were still musing about Fish and Vera when James walked in. "What's making my wife smile like that?"

"Fish," Delia replied.

James nodded knowingly. "Enough said."

I smiled, immediately lost in his big blue eyes.

He took my hand. "I see you're not limping, my love. In fact, I noticed you walking with no problem."

A pang of anxiety hit me. What if James thought I was so much better that I didn't need him to look after me? No way was I sleeping alone tonight. "Well, yes, but there's still a good bit of pain."

He squeezed my hand and looked at Delia. "They've all gone, by the way, so let's hear this plan of yours."

The three of us headed back into the living room and reunited with the boys and William.

"Okay, what's your plan, Delia?" James asked on behalf of the group.

"It's actually pretty simple," she said.

James raised an eyebrow. "Enlighten me."

"Well, no offense," Delia said, looking at James and the boys, "but you males pretty much have one-track minds. It's not all that difficult to distract you."

"That's not true," James said, appearing mildly offended.

"Really?" Delia looked around at the boys. "Well then, what did I just say?"

I hadn't noticed when she crossed her legs, exposing her bare thighs.

"What?" Fish said, his eyes rising from

335

her legs to her face.

"How about you, Joshua?" Delia asked. "Do you know what I just said?"

"Um, what?" he answered.

Delia's gaze returned to James. "Like I said: easy to distract," she said, uncrossing her legs.

James rolled his eyes. "Okay then, the plan?"

"I'm just going to stroll right by Simon's watchdogs and sit near the pier," she said. "And I'll need Thea, too."

I turned to her slowly and raised my eyebrows. *What does she need me for?*

James shook his head. "Out of the question."

"She won't be in danger," Delia said. "We're just going to walk by them—not even that close. And while they're busy ogling us, you all can go in and do your thing." Delia crossed her legs again, folded her arms, and leaned back in her chair, seemingly satisfied with herself.

James seemed to be thinking it over. "Walking by, and nothing else?"

"That's right," Delia replied. "But I need Thea because they think she's human. Witches aren't exactly in the habit of sunning themselves."

"Sunning?"

"It's been unseasonably warm," Delia explained. "Which is perfect for my plan."

James looked at me. "Are you up for this?"

"I want to help," I replied.

He looked at Delia again. "Walking by, and nothing else?" he repeated.

"Yes," she said. "But you guys need to get in and out of there fast."

"We'll be ready," Cory said.

William, who had remained quiet for most of the conversation, finally spoke. "You will be nearby if she needs you," he said to James.

James nodded and looked at Delia. "Get the spells from the other witches," he ordered. "We'll work on crafting a fake hourglass."

"Will do," Delia said.

James stood. "Good, then. The boys and I have things to discuss. We'll be in my study if you need us." The boys followed James out of the room.

Delia moved closer to me and explained the details of her plan. Once I knew what she had in mind, I wasn't so sure I was up for it. "No way, Delia," I said. "I can't do it."

"Thea, they think you're human. Witches don't do that; we have spells for that."

"No," I said emphatically. "If you think I'm wearing one of those things, you're crazy."

"Thea, it's the only way," she pleaded. "Male witches can't help themselves. It's the very best way to distract them."

I wanted to help, but didn't know how I was going to muster the courage to do what she was asking of me.

"It's no big deal, Thea. Humans do it all the time."

"Can't you think of something else—anything else?" I asked.

337

The study door opened. James and the boys filed out, smiling. "I'll show you the room," James said to them. "We'll bring your things here; it'll be safer than training her in the forest."

I shot Delia a worried glance, but she was already on her feet.   "You told him?" she asked the boys.

"James told us it would be a good idea to teach Thea to fight," Cory replied. "It seemed like an okay time to tell him that we've already started."

James shot a look at me. I felt like a kid who'd been caught stealing. "Come," he beckoned the boys. "I'll show you the room."

My nerves were instantly on edge; James was clearly angry. I'd wanted to tell him, but I assumed he wouldn't want me fighting. Delia continued telling me about her plan. I didn't want to hear any more about it; the very idea was making me feel ill.

"Think we'll be ready by tomorrow?" she asked.

Terror rushed through my body. "Tomorrow?"

"When did you think we were going to do it?"

I tried to put on a brave face. James and the boys were on their way back, and I didn't want James to see how scared I was.

"I think me and the guys will go home, after all," Cory said as they all returned to the living room. "We pack up our stuff tonight."

Delia stood up. "Then I'm leaving, too. I'll get our things ready for tomorrow."

338

I rubbed my forehead, overwhelmed by the very idea of Delia's plan.

"Are you okay?" James asked.

"She's fine," Delia answered. "She's just tired."

After Delia and the boys had gone, we retired to the sitting room. James lit a fire and sat next to me. I stared into the fire, hardly saying two words. Between Delia's plan and James's obvious disappointment in me, my nerves were frayed.

James turned to me. "May I ask you something?"

"Sure," I said absently.

James remained quiet and continued to stare at me.

I suddenly realized he was waiting for me to react. "I'm sorry. I was somewhere else."

"Why didn't you tell me about the boys training you to fight?"

I bit my lip and looked down.

"Why would you keep something like that from me?"

I finally looked up. "I didn't think you'd understand."

"Have I been a tyrant?" he asked worriedly. "Have I given you a reason to keep things from me?"

I bowed my head.

"Thea, I *want* you to be able to defend yourself."

"I'm sorry I didn't tell you. I didn't think you would want me fighting."

He sighed and looked away. "Do you have any idea how it feels to find out you've been keeping things from me? Don't you have any faith in me?"

"Why would you say that? I have complete faith in you."

"Do you?" he asked, his voice low.

"Why would you ask me something like that?"

"Do you think me not capable of helping you? Do you feel I'm not man enough?"

I couldn't understand why he was saying that. "I think you're capable of many things— most of all, keeping me safe."

"I would give my life if it meant saving yours, Thea."

"I know that. I have complete faith in you."

He gently pushed my hand off his leg. "I don't think you do," he whispered.

I could see the hurt in his eyes. It reminded me of the argument we'd had all those years ago. "What did I do to you, James? Why did we argue back then?"

James stood and stepped in front of the fireplace. He leaned his arm on the mantel and stared into the fire. "I didn't mean for these old feelings to surface," he said. "I'm sorry I overreacted."

What he'd said about taking back his love for me still hurt. "I tried to control you, like I did everyone else, didn't I?"

"Let it go, Thea."

I got up and stood beside him. "I tried to tell you what to do. I treated you like my servant, didn't I?"

"Please, Thea, stop."

"That's it, isn't it? I acted like I owned you."

He turned to me, rage in his eyes. "You lied and made a fool of me!"

I stepped back, stunned.

He drew in a deep breath. It felt like an eternity before he spoke again. "You told me you were going to see Delia. Instead, you went to fight a battle that was meant for me. And when I found you, you silenced me in front of the witches, ordered me to do as you said, to stay quiet while you fought my battle—a battle I was fighting for you, my wife!" He abruptly turned back to the fire.

I couldn't get past the fury in his eyes. I swallowed hard and remained silent.

"'Be a good boy and go home,' you said." James's face reddened. "Those are the words you spoke to your husband in front of all the witches, as though I was your puppet."

Hot tears filled my eyes and spilled down my face. "That witch was blind," I said. "She didn't know how else to handle the thought of losing you. She was willing to do whatever it took to keep you safe. I can see the idea of you getting hurt drove her mad. She thought she was protecting you." I stepped closer to him. "But she didn't see what I see. I've changed, James. I swear to you, I've changed."

He swiftly gathered me in his arms. "Don't cry, Thea. Forgive me, my love. I had no right to say that to you."

I rested my head on his chest. "I'm sorry for hurting you. I'm sorry I made you feel like less of a man." I leaned back and looked into his eyes. "Please don't ever wish you could take back your love for me."

"I would take back nothing but those words I said to you. They will forever haunt me." He wiped my tears with his thumbs and softly kissed me. I felt the resentment in his heart fly away. I knew the moment he let it all go.

The witch had wanted to put her powers away in the crystal because she thought they were the cause of her arrogance, and that that was the cause of her failed marriage. But I saw now that her arrogance was born of fear—fear of losing the one person she loved most. I was finally beginning to understand the witch inside.

"Is everything settled now?" William asked from the doorway.

Smiling, James kissed my head and nodded.

"Good, because your room is ready. I took the liberty of making a few changes."

"I thought we were sharing a room tonight," I said anxiously. "I still feel very weak."

James winked at William and eyed me amusedly. "We are, my love. Shall I show you?"

William handed James a set of keys. "It's as you intended. With just a few minor changes."

James thanked William and grabbed my hand. "Come, let's go see our room."

"Just a moment," William said. "You have something that belongs to me." He approached me and held out his hand. "May I have it now, please?"

I looked down at his hand in confusion.

"I believe Sharron gave you something a few days ago," he prompted.

I realized he was talking about his wedding ring, and my heart sank. "I left it back at my apartment."

"Can I expect it back by tomorrow?" he asked.

"Absolutely," I replied, smiling. "I'll go and pick it up."

"Then I wish you both a good evening. Remember our agreement, James. You gave me your word."

James nodded and retook my hand. "Come, my love, I'll show you our room."

"What agreement?" I asked James as we made our way down the hall.

"It's not important."

We continued down the hall until we arrived at a set of ornately carved wooden double doors. James opened them and picked me up. "I've waited so long to do this," he said, grinning.

I gasped as he carried me into the enormous suite and set me down. Two double beds seemed out of place in the sitting room. James saw me eyeing them curiously and chuckled. "That was William. Our real bed is through there." He pointed toward another set of double doors. "William thought it would be best if we slept in the sitting room, and he's probably right, but I want to show you our bedroom." He grasped my hand, and we walked to the second set of double doors, these ones glass and covered with silk curtains. "Through these doors is the master bedroom, the room I intended for us to share." He paused and smiled at me. "The room that will be waiting for us when your memory returns."

I looked back at the double beds. I hadn't planned on those.

"I know it's not what you were expecting," James said, turning my head back to face him. "But at least we can be in the same room."

I wiped the sour look off my face and mustered a smile. I didn't want to ruin this beautiful moment.

James's face was practically glowing. The happiness in his eyes shone. "Are you happy, my love?"

I reached out and touched his cheek. "Nothing could make me happier than being by your side."

He kissed the top of my head and turned to open the doors. "I hope I got everything right," he said as he swung them open.

I didn't have time to ask him what he meant. My jaw dropped at the beauty of it. I gazed around the room in awe. "Oh my God, James," I exclaimed. "I've never seen anything like this."

"Is my lady pleased?" he asked.

Without warning, my mind began to drift...

~~~

James was leading me down a path in the forest toward a cozy cottage. He looked so happy as he pulled me along behind him.

"Where is my lord taking me?" I asked.

"Allow me to surprise thee." He stopped in front of the cottage and turned to face me. He knelt on one knee and took my hand.

My eyes lit up in disbelief.

"My lady, thou hast given me happiness I've never known. I kneel before thee a poor man, with nothing to offer thee but this poor home and my heart. But if thou agrees to share this life with me as my wife, I promise to make thy life rich with love."

I looked down at him, smiling widely. "My lord, I see not a poor man when my eyes are upon thee. I see not a poor home when I see what thou offers. My eyes see only what my heart feels. I see walls of silk and floors of gold. I see fields of roses and lilies when I look into thine eyes. I would be honored to be thy wife. I would be honored to share my life with thee."

James stood and pulled me up into his arms. He kissed me, then opened the door and carried me in. I gazed around the small cottage as he set me down.

"Is my lady pleased?" he asked.

~~~

The memory faded, leaving a smile on my face.

I felt James kissing my neck. "Do you like it, my love?" he asked.

I gazed at the room with its silk-white walls and gold marble floors. Across from the foot of the bed was the biggest fireplace I had ever seen. All around the room, there were vases filled with glittering roses and lilies;

sparkles seemed to float in the air like tiny fairies flying around the flowers. The bed, massive and beautiful, was straight out of *Gone with the Wind.* On the far side of the room were French doors leading out onto a terrace that overlooked the ocean.

"It's breathtaking," I whispered.

"I spent years trying to get this room just right."

"It's like a page from a fairytale. A room fit for a princess."

"I'm pleased you like it."

"I more than like it, James," I said, throwing my arms around him. "It's perfect."

"I used a spell that William taught me on the flowers," he said. "They'll always sparkle for you and never die."

I walked to the oversized bed and turned to look at him. "Why can't we sleep here?"

He smiled and walked over to me. "I promised your father we would sleep in the beds he brought in," James said solemnly. "I can't break my promise to him."

I so wished I could sleep in this garden-like bedroom. "Is this house four hundred years old?"

"No," he replied. "I had it built the first time I came back, but as you know, Delia found out I was here and asked me to leave."

"You returned once already?" I asked, surprised.

"Several times, actually. That's how I realized Delia was keeping your mind occupied with reading. That's how I got the idea to write the books." He smiled and looked into my eyes.

"I wanted to stay connected to you."

"Did I ever see you?"

"Yes," he replied. "You reacted strongly, which is why I agreed to leave."

"And what made you return this time?"

He enfolded me in his arms. "My heart just knew it was time."

I looked into his eyes. "Get me out of this room before you have to drag me out."

"Before William has to drag both of us out," he added, taking my hand. We walked through the glass doors and back out into the sitting room. "Are you too tired to stay up for a bit, or would you rather just go to sleep?"

I looked at our matching double beds and made a face. "No, I'm not tired."

"It pleases me to see you upset because we can't sleep together." He smiled. "And it makes me happy when you say how weak and fragile you are so I'll stay with you."

I blushed. "I was afraid you'd change your mind if you thought I was feeling better."

"You're my wife, Thea. We don't need a reason to sleep in the same room. Besides, it makes my heart happy to know you still love me."

"What do you mean, still love you? I will always love you."

"And don't ever forget that."

"You always say that to me. Why?"

"Come," he said, taking my hand. "I'll tell you some other day. Let's just enjoy the night." We sat by the fireplace and talked. James laughed when I told him about Fish and Vera.

"Poor Vera," he said, shaking his head. "That kid is a handful."

"He's a stinker."

"I really like him, though. I hope he and Delia end up together. He really loves her; I can see it in his eyes."

"Delia can see it in his eyes, too," I said. "But she thinks he's too young for her."

"Seriously?" he asked, laughing. "She'll get over that soon enough."

We sat talking for a long while. James told me that he was looking forward to training with the boys. "I'll talk to them after we retrieve the hourglass. Maybe we can fit in some training tomorrow."

I felt my face flush and tried to put Delia's plan out of my mind. Suddenly, I remembered my conversation with Samuel from earlier in the day. "James, you don't dislike Samuel, do you?" I asked.

"Not at all. I have no reason to dislike him."

"I wonder why he thinks you don't like him. He did mention to me that he thought it was very nice of you to cast spells on the boys' weapons."

"I would have offered the same for Samuel's weapon, but I never saw him using one." James smiled and stood. "You look tired," he said, extending his hand to me. "It's late. I have to leave with the boys in the morning, and Delia's picking you up early."

I sighed and grabbed his hand, and he pulled me up. I tried to kiss him, but he turned his head a little and kissed my cheek.

I tried again, and he pulled away. "I think it's best if we don't go down that road tonight."

I looked at him for a moment and walked over to one of the beds. "Which one is mine?" I asked, annoyed.

"I think William laid out some pajamas on yours," James replied, heading for the door. "I'll give you a moment to change."

When he returned, I was already in bed, wearing the pajamas which happened to cover nearly every inch of my skin.

James giggled. "Are those going to be too warm?"

"I can take them off?"

He held up his hand. "No, they'll do fine, I'm sure. I think it's going to be a cold night, anyway."

He turned off the lights, pulled off his shirt, and sat on his bed. As he leaned over to remove his shoes, I stole a glance at him. The glow from the fire danced across his beautiful body. As I admired his muscled arms, I noticed several slash-like scars. I tried to look away as he stood, but my eyes were glued to him. He was so fit, I nearly gasped as he removed his pants. I clenched a fistful of sheet, the attraction so intoxicating, it took everything I had to keep from running over and jumping into his bed.

He slid into bed, turned onto his side, and looked at me. "Is the fire bothering you?"

"Um, what?" I replied absently.

"The fire, is it bothering you?"

"Oh no, not at all."

He lay on his back and tucked his hands

behind his head. "Are you tired?"

"N . . . no," I said, my eyes finally drifting away from him and up to the ceiling.

He pulled the blankets over himself. "Good night, my love."

How was he able to sleep? I pulled the blanket over my head to block his sweet scent and turned onto my side.

"Thea," James whispered.

"Yes."

"I just want you to know," he said, "only my promise to William is keeping me in this bed."

I smiled. "Thank you." I heard him laugh a little as I buried myself in the blanket. I was crazy with desire for him, but somehow managed to drift off to sleep.

When I awoke in the morning, James was already gone. I eyed his empty bed for a minute or two before jumping into it, wrapping myself in his blanket, and drinking in his sweet scent.

"Why are you still in bed?" I heard Delia say from the doorway.

"Go away," I said, burrowing deep under the covers. "I'm not going with you."

She peeled the blanket away from me and tossed a bag on the bed. "Put this on," she ordered. "And throw some normal clothes over the top for now. I'll wait for you downstairs."

My stomach lurched. I reached for the blanket and pulled it back over myself. "I don't know if I can do this, Delia," I said from under the covers.

"Okay," Delia said. "I'll just do it by

myself. I knew you'd chicken out."

I popped my head out and narrowed my eyes at her. "Fine," I said huffily. "I'll come with you, but I'm going to look like a fool."

She rolled her eyes and chanted: "Like a volcano filled with lava, you will release the witch today. You will walk and feel her guide you as we lead those men away. You will only feel her confidence when you walk along my side; you will not feel scared or nervous or want to run and hide."

Chapter 19
Wolf Eyes

I rolled down the car window and allowed the fresh air to hit my face. Delia was right; it was unseasonably warm. It wouldn't seem odd for us to be out enjoying the sun. I was still nervous, but I had to admit that the plan made sense.

Delia pulled into a parking space across the street from the pier, a good ways from the ship. "This is good," she said. "I want them to see us coming from here."

I looked toward the ship where three of Simon's men stood, at least for the moment, firmly planted at their posts.

Delia pulled two folding beach chairs from the trunk. "Here, take one."

As I reached for the chair, I scanned the area for James and the boys. I finally spotted them standing near a closed concession stand. Fish was eating what looked like a pickle, and James was laughing at something Sammy was saying.

"I see James and the boys," I told Delia.

"Good, take off that sweater," she

ordered.

I swallowed down my rising panic. Relief washed over me as I felt Delia's spell kick in.

As I peeled off my sweater, Delia's eyebrows arched. "Good lord, Thea," she said. "You're going to give James a heart attack."

"Well, Fish might just have one, too," I said, looking her over.

She smiled and grabbed a small bag from the wagon. I admired her long legs as she threw the bag over her shoulder. I envied the way her tiny white bikini accentuated her perfectly proportioned body.

I straightened, hoping to convey as much confidence as Delia. My bikini, black and covering a little more skin, hugged me in all the right places. "Do we have to wear heels?" I asked.

"They're beach sandals, Thea," Delia replied. "And yes, we have to wear them."

I glanced at James and the boys, who were still laughing—this time apparently at Fish.

"We'll walk by the pier and set up our chairs on the sand," Delia said. "Those idiots will probably follow us all the way there."

We clutched our chairs and started walking. I felt like a teen-movie cliché: the girl walking down the street in slow motion, a breeze blowing back her hair as the music plays. I couldn't help giggling. I was enjoying this moment in spite of myself.

Delia flipped her hair and smiled from ear to ear as she strutted. She looked at me and shook her head. "I wish I could take a picture of James's face when he sees you in that."

I started to wonder if Delia was right about my curves. Was I not the ugly monster I thought myself to be? James always made me feel so beautiful—my weight never seemed to bother him. Delia used the word *voluptuous* to describe my body. *How come I don't see what they see?*

"You really think those men are going to follow us?" I asked.

"Oh, please," she replied. "Warlocks drool at the sight of a bare ankle."

I looked back to where James and the boys stood. James had his back to us, and Fish was directing the pickle up to his mouth. When Fish spotted us, the pickle slipped from his grasp, and he froze. The others turned to see what he was gawking at. James did a double-take, and they all stood, mouths agape.

"Look at them," Delia said as we walked. "Did I not tell you? Geez, they'd better not forget they have work to do."

We sauntered by Simon's men, and Delia even pulled on her bikini bottom. I saw one of them elbow another, and just like that, they fell in behind us.

"They're behind us," I said quietly from the corner of my mouth.

"That's the plan," Delia replied.

Once past the pier, we stepped onto the beach. Delia set down her chair and glanced over her shoulder. "Showtime," she said. She opened her chair and looked at me. "Bend down a lot, flip your hair, stuff like that. We have to keep them focused on us."

I bent over slowly, placing my chair next to hers.

"That's a good little witch," Delia said, smiling.

The men moved closer. They had all but forgotten about the ship. Delia's plan was working. I could hear them whispering to one another, and one of the men even wolf-whistled. From the corner of my eye, I spied them leaning against the closed ticket booth. Delia periodically jumped out of her chair, stooped over, and pretended to search for something inside her bag.

I could no longer see James and the boys. "Delia, I think they went inside."

Delia glanced over to where they'd been standing. "Look again," she said, laughing. "They're still there. I'm pretty sure James has forgotten how to close his mouth."

I looked over my shoulder again just in time to see Cory grab James and Fish by their collars and pull them away. "I think they're going in now," I said, giggling.

"Okay. We have to keep these men here."

We sat for what seemed like forever: rubbing on suntan lotion, chatting and laughing. Bored, we finally walked down to the shore and got our feet wet. "What's taking them so long?" Delia said. "The clouds are coming in."

I was starting to get cold and reached for my sweater.

"Not until they come out," Delia said, snatching the sweater from my hand.

At that moment, I happened to catch James and the boys from the corner of my eye. They were running from the ship and disappeared around a corner.

"Okay, they're out," I announced.

Delia quickly stood and folded her chair. "Let's get the hell out of here," she said, throwing her bag over her shoulder. "I'm freezing."

As we walked past Simon's men, they said, "Hello, ladies."

We kept walking.

"You need help with those chairs?" one of them asked.

Delia stopped and turned. "Do you need help going to hell?"

We heard them laughing as we walked away. For a moment, we worried they would follow us, but we were relieved when we saw them head back toward the ship. When we reached the car, we hurriedly threw the chairs and the bag into the back.

"James said to meet back at your apartment," Delia said. She grabbed her sweater and wrapped it around herself. "It's getting so cold."

The temperature had dropped quickly. It was hard to believe how warm it had been earlier. Delia's phone rang as I blew into my hands. She answered it and quickly hung up.

"Who was that?" I asked, opening the passenger door. "You didn't even say hello."

She slid behind the wheel and pulled her door shut. "It was your husband. He said for you to put some clothes on and hung up."

I threw on my sweater and blew into my hands again.

Delia started the car, and we headed out. "They must have had trouble with the reverse spells," Delia said. "It took them a lot longer than I anticipated."

I flipped on the heater and held my hands to the vent. "Do you think they were able to get it?"

She turned up the heater, pulled out her phone, and hit the speed dial. "Okay, you can stop now," she yelled into the phone. She snapped it shut and rolled her eyes. "He's such an idiot."

"Who's an idiot?"

"Your husband," she replied, glancing at me. "Only a spell can make the temperature drop this fast."

I smiled to myself. The thought of James being jealous was silly, but it made me feel good nonetheless.

When we made it back to my apartment, we quickly ran into the building and up the stairs. I couldn't wait to throw on a pair of jogging pants and warm up. "You want some warmer clothes?" I asked Delia.

"Yes, it's freezing."

When we walked through the door, James and the boys were already there.

"Really, James—weather spells?" Delia said, rolling her eyes.

He ignored her and looked at me, an odd expression on his face.

"Did you guys make the switch?" Delia asked him.

357

James remained silent, continuing to stare at me. I looked at the boys. They, too, seemed as if in a trance. Fish's eyes were glued to Delia, following her every move. I was about to ask if everything was okay when James took two steps forward, reached for my face, and kissed me passionately. He moaned as he pulled me closer.

I tried to step away, uncomfortable with this open display in front of the group.

James pulled me back into his arms. "Kiss me," he said, again crushing his lips to mine.

I felt his hands slip under my sweater, and I forcefully pushed him away. "James, don't—not here."

Delia looked at James, her eyebrows arched. "So is someone going to answer my—"

Before she could say another word, Fish pulled Delia into his arms and kissed her. She started to push him away at first but quickly gave in to his kiss. Feeling emboldened by Fish's passionate advance, James pulled me into his arms again and kissed me so hard it hurt. I felt a stream of water hit the side of my cheek.

Cory stood across the room with a spray bottle in his hand. "Wake up, guys," he said. "You're just making it harder on the rest of us."

.James shook his head, seemingly trying to regroup.

Fish let go of Delia, who was smiling from ear to ear for the second time that day.

"I think we'd better leave now," James said.

Fish tried to grab Delia again but Samuel

grabbed him by the shirt. "Come on, Romeo, you need to take a cold shower," he said, pulling Fish away.

Delia laughed and looked at James. "I think you'd better go take one, too," she said. "We'll meet you back at the house later."

As they made their way out of my apartment, James eyed me over his shoulder with that same strange look on his face, as though he was undressing me with his eyes.

Joshua walked over to Delia, and she quickly put her hands up. "No more kisses."

"I was only going to say that we made the switch," he said, looking down.

"Oh, sorry," she said. "It's just that I know how you guys get."

Joshua smiled sheepishly and followed the others out the door.

Delia hurried over and locked the door. "I think we'd better stay here for a good few hours before we head back to the house."

"What the hell was all that?" I asked.

She laughed and collapsed onto the sofa. "Now you know why they seek out human women."

I sat on the other end of the couch. "What do you mean?"

"It's a male witch thing," she explained. "When they see us like they did today, it's like they go into heat or something."

I started thinking about last night, how I had to clutch the sheet to hold myself back. I wanted James last night exactly the same way he wanted me just now.

I went in search of warmer clothes. I

handed Delia a pair of jogging pants, and we decided to order some food.

"I'll call William and tell him we'll be over in a few hours," Delia said, grabbing her phone.

We ate and talked for hours. Delia elaborated on this trance-like thing that happens to male witches.

"It's actually painful for them?" I asked.

"Yes, that's why most stick to human girls—no risk of getting bonded, and their manly parts remain free to date as many women as they want. I suppose they feel they have too much to lose with us." She rolled her eyes.

"Delia, you do that a lot," I said, taking a bite of pizza.

"Do what?"

"Roll your eyes. You do it all the time."

She seemed surprised. "What are you talking about? I never roll my eyes."

I burst into laughter.

She continued to look at me, confused. "I roll my eyes?"

"All the time," I said, laughing harder.

"Since when?"

I fell to the floor, laughing. Sure enough, Delia rolled her eyes. My laughter was uncontrollable for several minutes as Delia looked on, mystified.

"So tell me more about this pain," I said, attempting to compose myself.

Delia rolled her eyes, and I stifled a giggle. "Why do you think I'm half human?" she asked.

"Cory told me that males don't want to

become bonded so they fool around with human girls."

"Yeah," she replied. "That, and they want to ease their pain."

"What do you mean?"

"Well, take my father, for instance," she said. "He had a girlfriend—a witch—but he wasn't sure if he loved her enough to become bonded to her. When they were together and things got heated, he felt physical pain because they weren't bonded. That's where my human mother comes in: no bonding, no pain. It's an easy way out for them."

I wondered if that was the reason James didn't want to touch me. But we were married, so it didn't make much sense.

"But when they bond with a witch," Delia continued, "the attraction is like no other; neither can live without each other. Even if no love is shared, she won't think of another man the way she does him, and he won't have control of his body anymore; it belongs to her forever." She looked at me. "But you, you're half wizard. I've always wondered if the same rules apply."

"What do you mean, rules?"

"You never bonded with James," she explained. "You wouldn't have been able to stay away from him. Even with your memory loss, your mind would have gone mad without him."

This reminded me of something I had thought about. "Delia, do you think James didn't want to bond with me?"

She burst into laughter.

I wasn't sure what was so funny.

"Thea, do you not see the way he looks at you?" Delia asked. "Even back then we all saw that look in his eyes. He wanted you, trust me."

I decided to change the subject. "And what happened to your mother? Where is she?"

Delia seemed suddenly sad, a faraway look in her eyes.   "Well, that's the unfortunate part about witches loving humans. My father loved my mother, but he outlived her—by a long shot. He tried to keep her alive with potions, but they don't take on humans the way they do with us. He didn't stay alone for long, though. They never do."

"Is your father still alive?"

She looked away.

"I'm sorry, Delia. I didn't mean to upset you."

"That's okay," she said, looking back at me. "He's dead. He was killed by warlocks for being a human-lover."

"So have you ever bonded?" I asked.

She rolled her eyes again, and I burst into laughter.

Sometime during our conversation, the sun had gone down. "You think it's safe to leave yet?" I asked.

"Yeah. They should be back to normal by now."

I got up, grabbed some clothes, and packed William's ring.

From the front room, Delia yelled, "Hurry, I have to feed my pet!"

"What are you talking about?" I asked,

362

closing the bedroom door.

"Never mind, just hurry."

I locked up and we headed home. William met us in the foyer when we arrived. "Did you remember to bring what I asked for?"

I nodded, retrieved the ring from my bag, and handed it to William. "It's a beautiful wedding ring."

"It's not a wedding ring," he answered.

I was taken aback. "Oh? What is it, then?"

He ignored my question. "Are you ladies hungry?" he asked. "I'm afraid we've already had dinner."

"We already had something," Delia answered. "Where are the boys?"

"They've gone to check the forest for new arrivals."

I didn't like the thought of them searching the forest. I had seen firsthand how dangerous warlocks could be. "How long have they been gone?" I asked.

"A few hours," William replied. "I wish to speak to you before they return."

"What is it?"

"Please, follow me," he said. "Both of you."

We walked into a room I'd never been in before—a kind of training room.

"So this is where the boys put their equipment," Delia said, looking around. "I was wondering where they were going to show you how to fight."

William closed the door behind us. "Please, sit," he said, motioning toward some chairs. "I need to ask you something."

"Is everything okay?" I asked.

"It's the hourglass, isn't it?" Delia asked.

He nodded. "The glass has a spell I can't make out. I was hoping you could tell me the spell you put on it."

"How could I possibly tell you?" I asked. "I can't remember anything."

Delia stood abruptly. "I was there. I know the spell."

"Can you relay it to me?"

She nodded and closed her eyes: "Keep the time, keep the day, do not let a moment slip away. Move your sands with my mind, until the crystal I can find. Save for thee what I give now, so that you may always show me how. Do not move until I say, for I shall always find a way."

William looked at me and smiled. After a moment, he looked back at Delia. "Did she chant any other spells?"

"Yes, she put one on herself." Delia closed her eyes again. "To the witch that lives inside, I order you to go and hide. Speak to me at any cost, let me hear thy voice when hope is lost."

"Thank you, young Delia," William said, pacing the room. "Now, what spell did Simon put on it?" he asked himself.

"A spell to warn him when Thea remembers," Delia answered.

William shook his head. "I don't think so."

"Why not?" I asked.

"Simon is definitely hiding a spell in it,

but it's not the spell we thought." He smiled at me. "Don't worry," he said. "I'll find a way to break it."

I didn't have time to ask him anything more. We heard James and the others in the hallway. William turned and left the room.

"Hello, William," I heard James say.

My heart raced when I heard his voice, all my worries quickly forgotten. The boys walked in first. I saw Fish scanning the room for Delia.

"Thank God you two put some clothes on," Sammy said.

Fish found Delia and couldn't seem to take his eyes off of her.

"Did you bring the spray bottle?" Delia asked, noting Fish's ardent gaze.

Cory laughed and shoved Fish. "He's been bragging to us about how you threw yourself at him."

Delia crossed her arms and looked at Fish. "Is that how you remember it?"

He smiled and walked over to her. "Will you marry me?"

Cory and the boys laughed.

James walked in, seeming confused. "Did I miss something?"

"Fish just asked me to marry him," Delia replied.

James smiled and looked at me, and I smiled back. His eyes traveled up and down my body before he slowly looked away. "Let's put him over there and see how she does with him," he said to Cory.

I sensed James was avoiding me. I

headed over to talk to him, but Delia reached him first, with Fish on her heels.

"Fish, get to work," Cory yelled.

"Who are you putting in the corner?" Delia asked.

Cory turned and smiled at her. "Like I said a few days ago, we have a tool now."

"You brought my pet here?" Delia asked, her eyes widening.

"It's the only safe place to train Thea," James said. "The forest is too dangerous."

"What are you guys talking about?" I asked.

I heard something being dragged behind me. When I turned around, Javier and Sammy were pulling a large chest across the room.

"You ready to do some training?" Cory asked.

I looked at him, surprised. "Right now?"

"The sooner, the better."

Sammy handed me my stick. "Let's see what else you can do with this thing."

I took hold of the stick and wondered what the hell was going on. James walked over to me, seeming nervous. "I'll be right over there," he said, attempting to reassure me.

I was about to question him, but he turned and walked away.

I looked at Delia but she, too, seemed confused. "What the hell did you guys find out there?" she asked.

James and the boys looked around at each other and remained silent. Cory walked over and whispered something in Delia's ear. The look of alarm on Delia's face was of no comfort to me. "Thea, you have to get as much practice as possible," she said.

I narrowed my eyes. How stupid did they think I was? It was obvious they'd found more warlocks in the woods. Cory slowly opened the chest. I swallowed hard. Sitting inside, mouth taped shut and hands chained together, was James's imposter.

I shot a glance at Cory, who hurried over to me. "I kept him alive so you could fight him," he explained. "This is a perfect test. There's a lot of them, Thea, and you have to get good at this fast."

"You found more?" I asked.

He didn't answer and ordered Joshua to remove the tape from the man's mouth.

"You dirty witch," the man yelled as Joshua removed the tape. "I'm going to kill you!"

"You can do this," Cory whispered to me. I looked into all their eyes. They were as scared as I was, and it wasn't because they were worried I couldn't fight this one man. There was something more, something they weren't telling me.

"Stand back," I said. "I have some fighting to do." Cory walked away as I turned to face Joshua. "Release him," I ordered.

The chains broke open, and the man bounded from the chest and ran at me.

I tightened my grip on the stick and held my breath. "Come on, witch," I whispered to myself. "Show me what I can do." I ran across the room, planted the end of the stick on the floor, and vaulted over him. I struck him across the face as I flew over his head. I landed on my feet and smiled at the man. "Give him a weapon," I ordered.

"No!" James yelled.

I looked down at James's pocket and held out my hand. "Whip," I yelled. The whip flew from his pocket and into my hand. I looked at the fake James and shook the whip so that it opened for me. "A gift for thee," I said, tossing him the whip.

The man picked it up, a malevolent grin on his face. "I'm going to enjoy this even more than the first time I felt your blood on my hands," he whispered.

"And I shall enjoy this more than the first time you failed to break me," I replied.

The smile left his face and he ran at me, swinging the whip. I moved my head to one side as the whip clipped a strand of my hair. From the corner of my eyes, I saw the boys hold James back as he tried to run and help me. I smiled at the fake James as he took another swing.

"Release spell," I whispered, looking at the whip.

I held up my stick, and the whip wrapped itself around it. I ran up the wall and gave the stick a hard pull, and the fake James flew across the room. I jumped off and untangled the whip. "Let's try that again, shall we?" I said, throwing him the whip again. He picked it up and began to swing, the whip missing me by inches. I spun the stick in my hands and hit him across the face.

He spit out blood and threw the whip on

the floor. "I'm going to kill you with my bare hands," he shouted.

I smiled and dropped the stick. "I was hoping thou would say that." I stood on my hands as he ran at me. As he neared, I wrapped my legs around his neck and yelled, "Over!" My body turned itself over, pulling him with me and tossing him across the room. I ran up the wall and came down on his leg with my knee. He screamed and reached over, trying to grab my leg. "Stick!" I yelled before his hands reached me. It flew into my hand, and I whispered, "Blades." The stick turned into two small swords, resembling Cory's blades. I spun them around and cut into his arm.

He screamed as he rolled over and got to his feet. He ran for the whip, and I shouted, "Arrow!" One part of the stick turned into an arrow. I held the other part, now a bow, up to my cheek. I pulled back and released, hitting his leg. He fell to the ground in a heap. I walked to the middle of the room and held up what was left of the stick. "Hook," I whispered as I flung it at him. At once, it turned into Fish's hooks. A piece of wire was still in my hand as the hooks caught him on the back. He screamed in agony as the hooks pulled the skin from his body.

All went quiet.

I walked over as he was turning to dust. "Rot in hell, my lord."

I slowly turned to the others, their mouths agape. "Is that what my lord wanted to see?" I asked Cory.

He didn't answer. No one seemed to know what to say.

James took a step toward me. "Thea?" he asked. "Is that you?"

"Who do you wish it to be?" I replied.

He walked over to me, searching my eyes for a sign. He pulled me to him and kissed me.

I dropped the wire and wrapped my arms around his neck. "My lord," I whispered as I kissed him back.

William started across the room. "Stop!"

I felt the witch inside drift away as James stepped back to address William. "She wants to come back. She's ready to return."

"A word with you," William replied sternly. "Outside."

James turned to look at me; I could see he thought she was still there.

"You should go," I whispered. "She's gone."

James stared at the wall and said nothing before following William out of the room.

Tears streaked my face as I realized how much he wanted her—and not me. The look in his eyes . . . He couldn't help but to reach out and take her. I felt defeated, knowing I could never be the witch I once was. Was I prepared to let her take me over when my memory came back? Was I going to stand aside as she reclaimed her man? If today was any indication of what was to come, I had already lost that fight; James had made his choice.

I turned to Delia. "Take me home."

She walked over to me. "Thea, I think you should stay here."

I ran for the door. I couldn't stand there a

moment longer. He could come get me when his true love returned.

"Thea!" Cory yelled. "Stop!"

I ignored him and ran out of the house. The image of James's face when he thought I was her was burned on my brain. He had never wanted me. All this time, he'd been waiting for her. I ran across the yard and tried to open the massive gate. "No!" I yelled when it wouldn't open.

"Thea!" James called from the door.

"Open this damn gate!" I yelled. "I need to get out of here!" I slid to the ground, sobbing.

James ran to me and tried to pull me into his arms.

"No!" I shouted, pushing him away.

"Thea, I don't understand," James said. "Why do you want to leave?"

"So I can get away from you," I cried.

He took a step back. "What have I done? I don't understand."

"Don't worry," I replied. "I'll stay in my apartment until her memory returns. Then you can go look for her and be happy. You'll never have to bother with me again." I turned and tried again, in vain, to pull open the gate.

"What are you talking about?" he asked, grabbing me from behind. He wrapped his arms around me and pried my fingers from the gate. I felt his breath on the back of my neck as he held me. "Thea, please don't do this."

"Your eyes," I cried, "I saw them. You want her, not me."

"Thea, please. I love you—both of you.

You're everything I have, everything I live for. I can't love her without you. You're who she turned herself into. I can't live without you."

"Lies!" I cried.

He spun me around and grabbed my face. "If she came back and I couldn't see you anymore, I would lose all hope of finding true happiness. I can no longer love her without you being a part of who she is." He wiped away my tears. "The way you fidget and bite your nails, the way you get nervous when you see me—all of this is new to me, but I've become accustomed to it. I couldn't live without it."

I looked down.

He raised my head. "You changed who she was, Thea. You don't have the fears she did. You don't have to prove yourself to anyone. You are who she always wished she could be, don't you see that?"

"And who do you want me to be?" I asked, looking down again.

"You can't change a soul, Thea," James replied. "I'm connected to your soul, no matter how you might change." He tilted my head up to face him. "I love all the things about you, past and present."

I felt so foolish for being jealous of myself. Once again, I had jumped to conclusions.

"Do you still wish to leave?" he asked.

I threw myself into his arms.

"Thea," he said wrapping his arms around me.

"Is there a spell to remove stupidity?" I asked.

He chuckled. "Maybe we can find one and use it on Fish."

I smiled and looked up at him. "I love you."

"And don't ever forget that."

I felt my heart come to life again. He loved me—this me. He loved who I was and who I am. I pressed myself into him.

He leaned his head on mine and sighed. "This is not a good time to hold you like this."

"What do you mean?"

"Thea, I've been avoiding you," he confessed. "It's getting harder to hold myself back. Most of the time, I just want to drag you to our room and take you."

"I'd go willingly."

"I can't, Thea."

"Why?"

He stepped away and reached for my hand. "We should get back inside."

When we walked back into the house, William pulled James aside. "Delia's waiting for you," he said to me.

I returned to the room. Javier was sweeping the dust from the floor. Cory and Delia were talking in the corner.

"You used our weapons," Fish said excitedly. "You turned your stick into my hooks."

"Yeah, but I didn't see mine," Javier yelled from the top of the room.

Sammy walked over. "You did good, Thea. Real good."

I smiled shyly. "I'm sorry I act so foolish sometimes."

Delia rolled her eyes and smiled playfully. "Of all the people to be jealous of," she said, "you're jealous of yourself."

The boys laughed. I bowed my head, embarrassed.

"You want to be jealous of someone?" Delia continued. "Be jealous of Helena. Oh, I mean, *Helen.*"

"Delia!" Cory snapped.

I turned to her, confused. "Helena?"

"Never mind," Cory said, giving Delia a sideways glance. "Let's just practice."

Delia rolled her eyes at him and looked at me. "Because out of all the witches you know, she's the only one he ever dated."

"He dated Helena?" I asked.

"Yes," Delia replied. "That's why she hates you so much."

Cory tried to pull her away, but Delia pushed him back. "No, Cory," she said. "Helena's going to be here learning how to fight with the rest of us. Thea has a right to know who she's dealing with."

"Why?" Cory asked. "So she can drive herself crazy thinking about it?"

I wondered why James hadn't mentioned that he'd dated Helena, but I wasn't particularly bothered by it; he never so much as gave her second glance. "It's okay, Cory," I said. "It really doesn't bother me."

"Good," Cory said, shooting Delia another look. "We have more important things to worry about." He ordered the boys to come forward and resume my training.

Delia rolled her eyes and looked at me.

"She and Amanda are coming tonight, with Maya from the diner."

"Delia, can I ask you something?"

"What?"

"What did James and the boys find in the woods today?"

Delia sighed heavily, jutted out her chin, and looked at me intently. "Warlocks. Hundreds of them."

"Hundreds?"

She nodded. "Scattered all throughout the woods."

I looked toward the boys. I wasn't going to let anyone die. Now, more than ever, I needed to talk to Vera. She was the one person who could help me.

"Javier," I called, "show me how to use that thing."

Chapter 20
Shinobi Shozoku

It was late by the time we finished up. Maya, Amanda, and even Vera had done well. Helena injured herself early and had to sit out the rest of the evening. I offered to heal her, but she said she was already tired and preferred to sit. James never so much as glanced at Helena the entire evening; it was clear he had moved on long ago.

I sidled up to Vera as the evening came to a close. "Come to the bakery," she said, passing me a small bottle. "Take this potion. It will allow you to go unnoticed."

I slipped the bottle into my pocket. "I'll be there tomorrow."

She said good night and followed the other witches out the door.

The boys and Delia were getting ready to leave when James asked them to wait. "I have a gift for Samuel," he said, walking over to the wall.

Sammy arched his eyebrows. "Me?"

"Yes," James replied. "And one for Joshua, as well."

Joshua looked at Samuel and shrugged.

James tapped the wall and it slid to one side, revealing a glass cabinet. He pulled a set of keys from his pocket, unlocked it, and stepped inside.

Sammy looked at me questioningly.

I don't know, I mouthed to him.

James returned holding a beautiful sword and what looked like a black cloth draped over one shoulder. He offered Joshua the sword. "I still think you could use another weapon in addition to your bow and arrow," he said. "And since the last sword had to be destroyed, I hereby offer you this one. I've already put my spell on it."

Joshua took the sword and gazed at it. "This is even better than the one from the stable. Thanks, James."

James smiled, turned to Sammy, and pulled the cloth from his shoulder. "I thought long and hard about what weapon would suit you, Samuel, but I realized your strongest asset is your bravery. I've seen you climb walls and do amazing things with that spell, and then it came to me." He handed Samuel the cloth.

"What is it?" Sammy asked, taking it from him.

"It's called a Shinobi Shozoku, a gift from a rice farmer friend of mine in Japan. He told me only men of honor could wear it. It's the clothing of a ninja. William put a spell on it, one that will render you invisible whenever you're in the shadows or darkness, making you one with the night as you crawl about in search of your enemy."

James walked back to the cabinet, pulled out a small box, and walked back to Sammy. "You'll find several little pockets in the suit," he said, handing the box to Sammy. "Place these inside of them. I've already put my spell on them, as well."

Sammy took the box and opened it. Inside were ten silver stars with extremely sharp edges. "Ninja stars?" Sammy asked.

"Yes," James replied. "And with the sound of your voice, they'll fly back to you. Just hold out your palm." James removed one of the stars from Samuel's hand and threw it at the wall.

"What do I say?" Sammy asked, holding out his hand. Before James could answer, the star flew back and landed on Sammy's palm. "Holy shit!" he yelled. "That's awesome."

"I'm pleased you like it," James said.

Sammy shook James's hand. "Thank you."

James smiled. "You've watched over my wife for many years. It is I who should be thanking you."

Sammy smiled and quickly turned to show the others his gift. "Can you believe it?" he exclaimed. "A real ninja suit, stars and all."

"Go put it on," Javier said. "Let's see what you can do with it."

Sammy ran to change as Joshua swung his sword.

"Thanks for that, man," Cory said to James.

"My pleasure."

Cory went to check out Joshua's sword.

James smiled as he watched Joshua trying it out.

Delia walked over to James. "That was very nice of you."

"I owe them much more than that."

"Please," Delia said. "Stop already. I might actually start to like you."

We spent nearly an hour watching Sammy climb the walls. He would vanish completely when any kind of darkness hit him. He repeatedly snuck up on Fish, smacked his head, and laughed. "This is so cool," he shouted.

"We should put that thing on Thea and have her go reclaim the crystal," Delia said.

"It will only work for him," James replied. "He's its master."

James and I finally said good night to the crew and headed off to bed. I had so many questions for my husband.

"Good night," he said when we reached our room.

I was taken aback. "Where are you going?"

"To my room."

"But why?' I asked. "I'll be good, I promise."

He smiled and kissed my head. "I can't make the same promise." He walked away, careful not to look back.

I stepped inside our room and slammed the door behind me. After trudging to the bed, I picked up the pajamas and pitched them across the room. "What's the point?" I began to remove my clothes.

The door opened suddenly. "Thea, I'm sor . . ."

I looked up to find James staring at my half naked body. He stood, as if in a trance, for several long moments before backing out of the room and closing the door.

Deeply frustrated, I crawled into bed, turned off the lamp, and pulled up the covers. The first part of my night was an endless series of tosses and turns, barely skimming the surface of sleep.

Sometime after midnight, I heard the door open and close. My eyes popped open as James's sweet scent filled the room. My back was to him as he crawled in bed beside me. I drew a deep breath when his hand touched my leg and traveled up my thigh. I started to turn toward him as he kissed my neck. I looked over my shoulder to find he wasn't wearing a shirt. He looked into my eyes, turned me over, and sat me on top of him. I wrapped my legs around his waist.

He leaned back against the headboard and sat, staring at me, his eyes drifting down to my breasts and back up to my face. He gently threaded his fingers through my hair as he stared into my eyes. I didn't say a word as he touched my face and lips, his touch nearly burning my skin.

"How I've suffered without you, Thea," he whispered. He leaned forward and pulled my lips to his, moaning as I wrapped my legs tighter around him. He scooted to the edge of the bed and picked me up, our lips never parting as he walked to our bedroom door, opened it, and carried me to our bed. He lay me down and removed his pants.

The sight of his naked body overwhelmed me. I trembled with desire as he leaned over and kissed me again. "James," I whispered, pulling him into the bed.

"Oh Thea, my Thea." His hand caressed my breast as he kissed my neck. He reached his other hand up and around my neck and squeezed more tightly than was comfortable.

"James," I whispered, "you're hurting me, my love." When he didn't respond, I pulled at his hand.

He looked into my eyes. "What?" He looked down at his hand, horror instantly filling his eyes. "No, no," he murmured.

Suddenly, his other hand clamped onto my neck.

"James, stop," I said. "You're hurting me."

His face reddened as he tried with all his strength to pull his hands away.
"Oh God, no!"

I pulled desperately at his hands.

"No!" James shouted.

As I lay beneath him, gasping for air, the spell Simon had chanted while I was in the grave appeared in my mind. I could still hear him laughing as he spit out the words: "*Body to body, heat to heat, release my spell when these two meet. May she never warn him, may she never tell, may she never find a way to ever break my spell.*"

In a flash, I knew why I had sent James away; he would never be able to live with himself if he killed me. I looked into his panic-filled eyes, touched his face, and tried to kiss him one last time before I died.

"Thea, no!" he cried as I pulled him closer. "Don't leave me!"

He continued trying to pull his hands from my neck, chanting spells repeatedly, but Simon's spell was too strong. My eyes rolled back as James forced the life from me.

"Thea, no!"

The last thing I saw as I drifted into darkness was William entering the room. "Release!" he shouted.

I felt James's hands fly from my neck, the force of William's spell thrusting him backward. He landed on the floor with a thud. I sensed William at my side. He opened my mouth and blew in a spell. Seconds later, I was breathing.

I was vaguely aware of being wrapped in a blanket and pulled to the floor. "I'm so sorry, Thea," James cried into my ear. "I'm so sorry."

"You gave me your word!" William yelled.

James ignored him. "Open your eyes, Thea," he pleaded. "Please open your eyes!"

William spoke again. "I warned you—"

"Just save her—*now!*" James shouted.

"She'll be fine," William said. "My spell is already working. I will go and fetch you both some clothes."

My eyes fluttered open.

James pulled me closer. "Thea, I didn't know," he sobbed. "I'm so sorry, I didn't know."

I reached up and touched his cheek. "It wasn't your fault. It was Simon."

"Please forgive me," he said, tears rolling down his face.

William returned and laid our clothes on the bed. "I will stay with her while you dress."

James nodded and lifted me to the bed. "I'll be right back."

"She's leaving with Delia," William said, looking over his shoulder at James. "She cannot stay in this house until I find a way to break Simon's spell."

"It won't happen again," James shot back.

"Still, I don't think she shou—"

"I said, it won't happen again," James shouted. "She stays here."

William regarded him for a moment and nodded. "As you wish."

James dressed quickly and returned. He lifted me from the bed and started for the door.

"Where are you taking her?" William asked.

"To the sitting room," James replied. "We'll stay there from now on."

William followed him. "But you can't. Think about what just happened."

James set me down on one of the beds and turned to face William. "I can and I will. She's my wife, and I will stay by her side."

William stared at James intently. "What do you fear, James? What is going through that head of yours?"

James looked away.

William placed a hand on James's

shoulder. "That spell was meant for you only."

James pushed his hand away. "How do you know? What if Simon cast a spell on Delia, too? Any one or more of you could be walking around here under Simon's spell, and we wouldn't know it until it was too late." He looked at me and back to William. "She stays with me."

William didn't answer and started for the door.

"William?"

William stopped and turned.

"It won't happen again, I place my honor on it."

William nodded and solemnly walked from the room.

James knelt by my side, smiled, and took my hand. "Please forgive me, my love."

"It wasn't your fault," I whispered.

James rested his head on the edge of the bed.

"Will you still kiss me?" I asked.

He smiled and kissed my head. "Always, my love. Always."

I was pleasantly surprised by James's reaction to the circumstances. I'd expected him to back way off and refuse to come near me.

"Will you be okay for a little while?" he asked. "I have something I need to take care of."

I nodded.

He kissed my head again. "I love you," he whispered and walked out of the room.

Moments later, I heard yelling in the foyer.

"You will put her in more danger if you leave now," William said. "Don't be foolish, James!"

I jumped out of bed and ran for the door. From the top of the stairs, I saw James attempting to leave the house, his whip in hand. William was holding him back.

"Get out of my way," James yelled. "I'm going to end this now."

"And then what?" William asked. "Lead them right to her? Do you really think you can kill all of them before they get here? Do you think Simon will not put two and two together?"

I stood, motionless, at the top of the stairs, hoping William would find a way to stop James. If he got past William and to the door, I was prepared to stop him myself.

"I have to kill him," James said desperately. "He nearly made me kill my own wife!"

"James, Simon has been expecting you for a very long time. He will be ready." William released his grip on James. "You will lose, my son."

"Take care of her, William," James said. "Leave tonight and take her far away."

As James turned toward the door, William revealed a small dagger. He made a thin cut on his wrist, reached for James's arm, cut into him, and held their wrists together.

James froze, and his eyes suddenly looked distant.

I descended the stairs in a panic. "What are you doing to him?"

"I am showing him your vision," William replied.

As I reached the bottom of the stairs, I saw James smile briefly before an expression of terror crept across his face. "No!" he shouted.

"William, stop this," I pleaded.

"I must show him," William replied. "It is the only way."

I looked at James, his eyes filled with fear, his body trembling. He looked at me and dropped the whip.

William released him. "Now do you understand?"

James slowly made his way to me. He looked into my eyes and took my face in his hands. "Forgive me if I've ever doubted your reasons," he said, tears filling his eyes. "I will never doubt you again."

I searched his eyes. "What did you s—"

"I love you, Thea," he said, cutting me off. "I've never been so happy and horrified at the same time."

I tried to make sense of his words as he wrapped his arms around me.

William pulled me out of his grasp. "I think it's best if you put on some clothes," he said, looking the other way.

I was suddenly, horrifyingly aware that I was only half-dressed.

James quickly removed his shirt and covered my torso. "Is it bad that I didn't even notice?" he asked, smiling sheepishly.

I refused to be distracted by James's smile and turned to William. "Show me the vision, too."

"No," James answered.

"I have no intention of showing her anything," William said to James.

"Why?" My eyes drifted to the scars on James's arms. It was clear this wasn't the first time William had shown him something.

"No, Thea," James said, shaking his head.

"Fine. I'm going to bed." I glared at James. "Alone." I climbed the stairs two at a time, never looking back. I stomped into our suite and slammed the door behind me for the second time that night. After gathering my things, I headed for my original bedroom and nearly crashed into James in the hallway.

"What are you doing?" he asked.

"I'm going to my room."

"Thea, wait," he said, reaching for my arm. "You have to understand."

I pulled my arm from his grasp and kept walking. "Leave me alone," I said bitterly. "Why don't you go to Helena? Maybe you can tell *her* what you saw." When I reached my old room, I dropped my things on the floor and locked the door.

"Thea, please," James said from the other side of the door. "It's not something you want to know or remember. It would shock your memory back."

"Go away!" I yelled. "I don't want to talk to you right now."

I heard William's voice. "Please stand aside, James. I will handle this."

"I'll be downstairs," James said.

I double-checked the lock and waited for

William to knock. I was startled when he easily threw open the door and strode into the room. "You think a simple lock can keep me out?" he asked.

I turned my back on him. "I don't want to talk to you, either. You lied to me."

"Child, get dressed," William ordered. "I will wait here."

With a defiant glare at William, I snatched some clothes from the floor and stepped into the bathroom to change. When I returned, he was still waiting.

"What do you want?" I asked irritably.

He pointed to the bed. "You will sit and change your tone, child."

I sat, purposely avoiding his stern gaze. "What do you want?" I repeated.

"It appears I have upset you somehow. It cannot be the fact that I showed James your vision. Or perhaps I should have allowed him to go on a suicide mission. Or perhaps I should have allowed young Delia and the boys to die in vain. Or maybe you would rather they come here and kill me."

I looked at him. "How can you say that?"

"Because I'm tired," William said. "Tired of your constant outbursts. I'm tired of seeing those who care about you having to run after you every time you feel you've been the victim of even the slightest injustice. I will not stand by and watch you hurt those who love you, those putting their lives on the line for you. They have done nothing but follow your orders." He sighed and sat beside me. "That man downstairs has suffered unspeakable torment because he could not be by your side. He has spent four hundred years waiting to return to you. He has asked for nothing except to be allowed to protect you. He has earned the right to know the truth. You will do well to remember that the next time you are tempted to jump to conclusions."

I bowed my head in shame. How could I have been so selfish? My father was right; I'd been acting like a spoiled brat, never taking into account how my actions were affecting the others—most of all, James. I attempted to apologize.

William raised his hand. "You will wait until I'm finished."

"Yes, Father."

He looked at me for a moment with an expression I couldn't quite decipher. "When you sent James away, it took me months to get him out of Salem. I had to keep changing what he looked like so he wouldn't be found. He kept running back to you and begging you to let him stay, but by that time you had no idea who he was." He looked at me. "I've seen him suffer, Thea—almost die of a broken heart. I will not stand by and watch you be controlled by fear."

"What do you mean?"

"Why do you think you are so insecure, child? Why do you think you cannot understand why he loves you?"

"Because," I said, gesturing to my body. "Look at me. Why would he?"

"I showed him your vision because I needed to stop him. But your secret is still your own. I did not show him your fears—your worries about whether his love for you is real. But I will tell you this: I have seen with my own eyes that his love for you is genuine."

"I don't understand."

"But the witch inside of you does," William said. "She needed to hear that. She has been restless, worrying and wondering about his love."

The rage inside of me began to recede. I looked at my father. "Why won't you show me the vision?"

"It is too dangerous."

"You keep saying that," I said, frustrated. "Why is it too dangerous?"

"I cannot speak the words," he replied. "If Simon ever learns of what you saw in your vision, he would come to realize that he has no use for you. And if he has no use for you . . ."

"What are you talking about?"

"Simon believes everything is going according to his plan, that all he needs now is for you to tell him how to open the crystal. As you know, he is not aware that only you can open it. He is also not aware that you deposited more into the crystal than just your powers. This is the secret you are hiding from him."

"That's not true," I said. "Vera told him about the crystal."

"He put spells on that poor woman to help him, but he already knew about the crystal."

"So he knew I was going to put half my powers into it? How?"

William sighed. "When we found your mother dead, her heart missing, I knew Simon's plan was already in the works. He needed me out of the way in order to implement it, and sure enough, when I finally realized what was happening, it was too late to stop it. So, I put spells on you to make you arrogant and cold."

My eyes filled. His words gave me the permission I needed to forgive myself. "How could that have ever helped me?" I cried.

"My intention was to make you strong and independent. I knew it would make it more difficult for Simon to carry out his plan if he had a formidable opponent, one who could protect those he wished to destroy." He sighed and looked down. "But neither I nor Simon saw it coming."

"What?" I asked desperately. "What didn't you see coming?"

William looked at me, his eyes intense. "He does not know, Thea. Simon does not know the true reason you transferred your powers into the crystal. To this day, he still believes you did it because of his plan."

With every revelation my father offered, I became more confused. "What plan?"

"A plan I saw coming," he admitted. "A plan that had to happen."

William's evasive explanation offered me little understanding. My frustration mounted as so many unanswered questions churned in my mind.

William stood. "And that, my child, is all I will tell you. I must insist you go downstairs and speak to James; he needs you, now more than ever."

I shook my head. "No, wait. How did

Simon know I was going to relinquish my powers to the crystal?"

William placed his hand on my shoulder. "You will find out soon enough." He turned to leave and stopped at the door. "Oh, I suggest you forget about your plan. I have already spoken to Vera. She will not be creating any more changing potions for you. And I have destroyed the one she already gave you."

I sat, silently, my mouth agape.

A slow smile spread across my father's face. "I am more connected to you than you know," he said, walking out the door.

Chapter 21
The Real Simon

I couldn't get William's words out of my head. How could Simon have known I was going to transfer my powers to the crystal? I thought of James's suffering. Why would the witch doubt his love?

I was leaving my room to confront James when I heard Delia downstairs. "What's going on now?" she asked. "I came as fast as I could."

I made my way to the top of the stairs and stood, listening.

"Did you say something to Thea about Helena?" James asked.

"Yeah, why?" Delia asked. "What's the big deal?"

"Why would you do that? There was no reason for her to know about Helena."

Delia laughed. "Don't tell me she's jealous of that thing."

I hurried down the stairs.

Delia stopped laughing when she saw me. "What did you do, try to kill her?"

James stepped to my side. "Thea, please—"

"I'm sorry," I said, cutting him off. "I

didn't mean to hurt you. Please just slap me next time I say or do something stupid." I bowed my head.

I felt his fingers on my chin. "How about I kiss you instead?"

I searched his eyes for any sign of anger or disappointment, but found none. "I don't deserve your kiss."

"No," he said, pulling me toward him. "You deserve more than that."

I threw my arms around his neck, my earlier mood returning in a rush. "Let's go upstairs," I whispered into his ear.

He pushed me away, alarm flashing in his eyes. "Thea, don't you remember what just happened? Are you crazy?"

I sighed and smiled. "I just wanted you to help me bring my things back into our room."

His scent filled my head as he kissed me. I wanted to become one with him, to lose myself in his arms.

"Can you guys tone it down?" Delia asked. "You're making me sick."

James grinned. "Did you hear someone talking?"

"I didn't hear a sound," I replied, kissing him.

William stepped out from the kitchen. "James, a word please?"

"I'll be upstairs," Delia said, passing us on her way to the stairs.

"You're staying?" I asked.

"Yes, she is," William interjected. "James and I have things to do."

"I'll see you in the morning," James whispered.

I smiled and headed up the stairs. Delia was waiting in the sitting room.

"What happened?" she asked, obviously eager to learn why she'd been summoned.

We sat at the fireplace as I relayed the grisly details of my ill-fated rendezvous with James.

"Wow, I didn't see that coming," she said, staring into the fire. "No wonder you kept telling me not to let him touch you."

We were silent for a moment before I decided to satisfy my curiosity about a lesser matter. "I wonder why James didn't want you telling me about Helena," I said. "How long did they date?"

"I'm not sure. But there was a short-lived rumor that he was actually thinking about marrying her. I only saw them together a few times. From what I hear, she took the breakup pretty hard."

I was taken aback. "He was going to ask her to marry him?"

"That's what I heard."

A thought occurred to me. "Delia, did you bring the memory box?"

"Uh-uh. I know what you're thinking, and the answer is no."

"Come on," I pleaded. "I can freeze him. I just want to see them together, that's all."

"No way, Thea," she said. "James would kill me."

I sat for a long moment, stewing. I was determined to find out why the witch inside doubted James's love. Maybe it had something to do with Helena.

"Oh, never mind," I said, sighing. "It was a stupid idea anyway."

"You cannot be jealous of that sourpuss."

"No, it's not that. Just forget it."

"He loves you, Thea," Delia said. "Trust me, you have nothing to worry about."

"I told you, it's not that. Let's just change the subject."

Delia and I talked for a few more minutes before heading off to bed. As I lay sleepless, my mind repeatedly conjured images of James and Helena together. I wasn't jealous, but William's cryptic words had me reeling. I was still rolling it all over in my mind when I heard voices downstairs. I commanded to hear them.

"And you're sure Vera isn't going to help her?" James asked.

My eyes narrowed. *So nice of William to rat me out to James.*

"Yes, I'm sure," William replied. "And Vera had no idea what Thea's plans were."

"What did Thea think she was going to do?" James asked. "Just walk in and ask for the crystal?"

"Here," William said. "Drink some more. It's the last of it."

I sat up and glanced over at Delia, who was snoring quietly. I slowly stood, tiptoed to the door, and opened it. As I started down the hall, I noticed William's door ajar. A shiny object lying on one of his tables glinted and caught my eye. I crept into his room and saw that it was the glass ring. I picked it up and slipped it onto my finger.

At once, I felt myself falling, as if I'd been thrown into a deep hole. Sparkly, dust-like specks surrounded me, gently pelting my face as I descended. When I reached out to touch them, I fell faster. As I retracted my hand, I suddenly felt ground beneath my feet.

I marveled at the beauty all around me. Flowers, like the ones James had placed in our room, grew everywhere, sparkling as a strange light hit them. Above me, I located the source of the light. It was the sun, but not the sun I knew. The rays were such that I could look at it without hurting my eyes. It almost appeared as if I was standing behind the sun somehow. I gasped as I turned and saw a huge, picturesque lake, smooth as glass and crystal clear. From where I stood, I could see fish swimming under the water.

This was no vision or flashback; the ring had taken me to this strange and magical place. My eyes widened as a flower bloomed in front of me. I smiled and reached out to touch it. As I ran my fingers along its pedals, the sparkles stuck to my fingers. "What is this place?" I murmured.

Suddenly, it dawned on me: this was my father's world. The ring was some kind of transporter. I wondered why my father chose to live in our world rather than this one.

The garden was like nothing I had ever seen before. The forest, though obviously magical, reminded me of Salem. Out of nowhere, something huge flew at me. I couldn't make out what it was, only that it was enormous. I panicked and pulled the ring from my finger. Instantly, I had the sensation of being pulled backward and around, as though I was returning to the other side of the sun.

Before I knew it, I was back in William's room. I set the ring on the table, but planned to return later. I was eager to learn more about my father's world.

I headed down the stairs and met James and William, who were on their way up. "Thea, you're awake," James exclaimed.

I shrugged. "Couldn't sleep. I'm just heading down for some warm milk."

William held his hand out to me. "Come, I will have some with you."

When I reached for his hand, William stepped back, a look of alarm on his face. I looked down at my hand and found that it was still covered in sparkles from the flowers I had touched. William quickly looked up at me.

"Is everything okay?" James asked.

William tore his eyes away from mine. "Yes, everything is fine," he said, quickly composing himself. "I just need a word with Thea."

James remained on the stairs as we slipped into the kitchen. William spun to face me. "What have you done?" He lifted my hand to his nose and sniffed it. "How did you get there?"

"The ring," I replied. "I just put it on. I didn't know—"

"And it worked?"

"I guess. It took me to some strange place, like behind the sun or something."

"Did you speak to anyone?" he asked, gripping my shoulders. It was obvious he had no idea the ring still worked.

"I didn't see anyone. There was a big something or other that flew at me, but I pulled off the ring before it reached me."

He smiled. "So, he still waits."

"Who still waits?"

He didn't answer and seemed lost in thought.

"Is that your home?" I asked.

"Yes. A world I left many years ago."

"It's beautiful," I exclaimed. "Why did you leave?"

He reached out and touched my cheek. "Why else? Love."

"So you could be with my mother?"

"So I could marry your mother."

"Why don't you go back now?"

He ignored my question and held out his hand. "The ring?"

"I left it in your room." He turned to leave, but I stopped him. "Why don't you go there and get that white energy you told James about?"

"The ring does not work for me, Thea," he replied. "And we have more pressing issues to get through first. Besides, I do not want to add to your problems right now."

"What do you mean you don't want to add to my problems?"

"Do you know why Simon wants your powers so badly? Have you ever stopped to think about why one man would be willing to kill so many for something he wants?"

"I thought it was because he hates that he's half human."

"Simple-minded witches," he said, shaking his head. "He hates that part of himself, yes, but that is not why he wants your powers."

"Why, then?"

"Because I was a fool," he replied, running his hands through his hair. "I took him to my world. I took a boy I thought I was helping, a boy who grew into the evil man who now hunts my child."

I began to question him further, but he cut me off.

"Enough, child," he said sternly. "I will answer no more questions." He walked out of the kitchen and headed for the stairs.

"Is everything okay?" James asked, popping his head out from his study.

"I need to talk to you."

He motioned for me to join him. "What's going on?" he asked, closing the door.

"I need to get out of this house. I'm getting anxious." I paused and drew a deep breath. "I want to go back to work." What I really wanted was to talk to Sharron, and I didn't want William near me when I did.

"No," James replied flatly. "I know what you were planning, Thea, and I won't let you do it."

"It was a stupid idea, I know. I'm not even thinking about that. Really, I just need to get out of this house." He seemed to be thinking it over, but I thought I would give him a little push. "Being stuck here has me constantly wondering and drawing all sorts of ridiculous conclusions. I think being at work will help keep my mind occupied." I sighed. "I'll follow any rules you lay out for me, just let me out of this house."

He thought it over for a moment and relented. "Well, maybe it isn't such a bad idea. I can have Norm call Sharron and the boys back, as well."

"Thank you, James," I said, embracing him.

"I'll let William know in the morning. And I'll have the boys stay close by until Norm calls them back." He squeezed me and kissed my head. "Thank you for asking me first."

We said our goodnights and I headed off to bed. When I awoke in the early morning, it was still dark. I jumped into the shower, wondering if James had already told Vera that I'd be returning to work today.

By the time I finished my shower, Delia was awake. "So, going back to work today, huh?" she asked. "James told me."

"Yes, I need to get out of this house."

She stretched her arms above her head and jumped out of bed. "Good, I can get back to my stand. I've only been able to keep it open a few hours a day, and this week is going to be busy."

Delia showered, and we headed downstairs together. James was waiting in the foyer as we reached the bottom of the stairs. "Good morning, my love."

"Good morning," I said, hugging him.

"I just talked to the boys. Cory and Fish will be at the bakery today. I'll make sure the others are called back by the end of the day."

I nodded and we headed out.

Delia dropped me off at the bakery. "I'll come by later," she said out the window as she drove away.

I walked into the bakery and breathed in the smell of fresh muffins and coffee cake. I was tying my apron when Norm appeared from the back room.

"Thea, you're here," he said, giving me a strange look.

"Morning, Norm. Busy day today?"

"Um, yes," he said, keeping his distance. "Very busy."

I suddenly remembered the tricks Fish had played on Vera. I smiled and reached for the day's orders. Norm scratched his head and quickly made his way past me, turning sideways.

Without warning, the smell hit me. I scanned the bakery but saw no one but Norm. I discreetly stepped up behind him and breathed deeply, the smell filling my head.

Cory and Fish breezed through the door. "Morning," Cory said. When he saw the look of alarm on my face, he motioned for me to follow him to the back room. "What is it?" he asked.

"It's Norm. He smells like a witch."

"We're not even having coffee?" Fish asked, striding into the back room. "I'm barely awake yet."

"Are you sure?" Cory asked me.

I nodded.

He turned to Fish. "Stay alert," he whispered.

"What's going on?"

"I'm not sure yet," Cory replied.

Norm walked in and began turning on the rest of the ovens. "Start the cookies first," he ordered. "We've got a ton of them to deliver today." He seemed like the same old Norm—business as usual.

Cory and I glanced at each other and began working.

"It doesn't make any sense," Cory whispered. "Get close to him and make sure."

I nodded and walked over to Norm with an order form. "Norm, is this an S or an eight?" I asked, and breathed in deeply.

Norm looked down at the paper. "It's an eight, Thea. Do you need glasses?"

"Thanks," I said, walking back to Cory. "It's faint, but it's there."

For the rest of the day we kept a close eye on Norm, but he never did anything out of the ordinary. He even left for lunch at his usual time.

After lunch, James walked into the bakery. "Hello, Norm, how are you?"

"Fine, fine, James," Norm replied, walking up behind the counter. "What can I do for you today?"

Delia slipped in through the back door, snuck up behind Norm, and chanted: "Fall asleep and do not twitch; let us see if you're a witch."

As Norm closed his eyes and began to drift off, Cory and Fish broke his fall and dragged him into the back. Delia followed, opened the box, and went to work.

I watched as she sorted through Norm's memories. "I don't understand," Delia said. "What made you think he was a witch?"

"Because he smells like one."

"Well, he's human." Delia shrugged and looked at James.

An alarm went off in my head as I realized what had been right in front of my nose the entire time: I couldn't smell witches—I could smell those who had been near Simon. William smelled the strongest because he'd been around Simon for the longest period of time. I recalled the memory when I had first seen the boys. It wasn't them I smelled; it was the men who wanted us to leave the lake. The boys—Delia told me Simon didn't even know what they looked like. That explained why they never carried the foul scent. I wondered why James didn't smell like the others. He'd been around Simon numerous times.

I looked down at Norm. "I can't smell witches," I told them. "I can smell Simon."

"You mean he was here?" Delia asked. "In the bakery?"

I nodded.

Delia looked at James. "It makes sense," she said.

Cory and Fish dragged Norm back to the counter and propped him up. James walked around to the front of the counter and nodded at Delia.

Delia chanted for Norm to wake up and then disappeared into the back.

James smiled as Norm opened his eyes. "I'll take one of those chocolate cakes," James said, reaching into his pocket.

Norm looked dazed. "I'll have Thea box one up for you right away." Norm turned to me, rubbing his head. "Thea, will you box up one of the chocolate cakes for James, please?"

"Just one?" I asked.

He nodded.

I stepped up behind the counter, removed a cake from the case, and quickly boxed it up. James paid for the cake and left the bakery, glancing at me over his shoulder as he walked out.

"Thea," Norm called.

"Yes, Norm?"

"Get the big order ready. And then have the boys start the deliveries."

"Right away, Norm."

I moved into the back room. "Norm wants you guys to start the deliveries."

Cory untied his apron and threw it across the room. "I'm getting tired of this," he said. He shot a glance at me, and I stepped back. "We're getting paranoid," he said. "We can't be putting everyone we think might be a witch to sleep. Humans are bound to get near Simon from time to time. I'm tired of waiting around for him and his thugs to find you. We need a plan to beat them to the punch." He kicked a stool and walked out, Fish following closely on his heels.

I'd barely had time to process Cory's words when Norm called me again. "Coming, Norm," I yelled.

For the rest of the day, Cory and Fish

405

were in and out on deliveries. I had to hurry to keep up with them. I was relieved when we came to the last order for delivery. "The big order stays here," I told Cory. "The customer is picking it up."

Cory looked at the sheet for the delivery. "This one's pretty far out. I'll call Sam to come and walk you home." With that, he was off again.

I started the evening cleanup. Norm left before closing, looking particularly exhausted.

I was folding boxes for the next day when I smelled him. The door opened and closed.

"Ah, splendid," the short man said, strolling in. "You're still open."

I walked behind the counter and breathed deeply, trying to stay calm. "May I help you?"

He approached the counter. "I called in a large order earlier today. Is it ready?"

The door opened again and a tall man strode in, his stench sending shockwaves through my body. I looked at him and swallowed hard, my heart racing as he and I locked eyes. The witch inside me screamed. My eyes fixed on him while he perused the bakery. When our eyes met again, images furiously raced through my mind. I tried to make them stop, but the witch inside wouldn't have it.

~~~

They dragged me down into a cellar. I was bound and flanked by two men chanting spells to keep me from casting any of my own.

A tall, angular man slowly made his way down the stairs. "Where did you find her?"

406

"She was headed back to the house, my lord."

"And James?"

"She was alone, my lord."

The tall man looked at me and back to his men. "Go," he ordered. "Bring me the witch, Vera. Find out if it be true of James."

The men nodded and ran out.

He turned to me again. "Tell me, wast thou running back to thy home to get this?" He held up the crystal.

My eyes widened in shock.

He laughed as two of his men dragged me backward and tied me to a pole. "I never thought thou wouldst do it so quickly," he said. "James did a good job. I may just forgive him for his treachery."

"My lord, thou mustn't let her touch the crystal," said the short man—the man we had all mistaken for Simon.

The real Simon turned on the short man, disdain in his eyes. "Dost thou think me a fool?" he bellowed. "I won't even allow thee to touch it!" He looked at me again. "Tell me, witch, what is the chant that opens this crystal?"

"Rot in hell, Simon," I replied. "I will tell thee nothing."

He straightened, slapped me hard across the face, and leaned forward. "Did you think James really loved you? Didst thou really believe he wanted to be with thee? Thou foolish witch, he is my servant."

"James is nothing like thee," I replied. "Thou art pure evil."

407

He laughed and turned to the others. "Did you hear that, my brothers? The witch says James is nothing like me." He looked back at me. "I find it humorous what a love spell can do to a man—make him think he cannot live without a woman." Simon leaned closer and grazed my cheek with his fingers. "Make him think he wants her more than his own life, make her give to him what she will give no other."

He looked at the crystal, walked across the room, and turned to face me. "Love is predictable," he said. "And I needed an act of love. Only love can do what nothing else can. I learned that from thy father, by the way—a very wise man, thy father."

"Do not mention my father," I spat. "And what couldst thou know of love? Thou hast no one to love thee."

He laughed. "Oh, but I do, witch. You see, your father and I spent many years together. He introduced me to his world—a world to which I plan to return. But I need this." He gazed at the crystal, turning it in his hands. "I need powers to make that world my home. In his world, I can be who I was born to be, rich beyond anything money could ever provide. And before I leave to fulfill my destiny, I will share my riches with my brothers here." He gestured to his men, who looked at each other and smiled. "So, thou must tell me now, what is the chant that opens this crystal?"

His lie about sharing the powers disgusted me. "I would rather die than tell thee."

"As thou wishes," he said.

He nodded at his men.

They dragged me to a barrel filled with water, forced me to my knees, and repeatedly dunked my head and held it under. I was still gasping for air when one of the men fastened a rope around my neck and pulled it tight, obviously deriving pleasure from my pain. Another man removed my shoes. I screamed as needles pierced the bottoms of my feet.

Simon held up his hand, and the men halted their torture. "It will go no further if thou will divulge the spell," he told me.

"I will tell thee the spell," I said hoarsely.

Simon towered above me, glaring. "I am waiting."

I looked up at him defiantly and chanted: "Stench of rot, scent of thee, may this always stay with me."

Simon's eyes widened with rage. The sting of his slap lingered on my cheek as he gathered a fistful of my hair and yanked. "I will show you a spell, witch!"

I laughed. "You fool. I have spells to grow that back!"

He brushed the hair from his hands, leaned over me, and glowered. "My spell worked better than expected; thou truly loves him, dost thou not? I believe I will reward James when he comes back. I am sure he will be most grateful to have the spell lifted."

"Thou art lying," I yelled.

"Am I? I forgave him for setting thee free this morning; I could hardly hold him responsible for the love spell's doing. But even

409

if not for the spell, I could hardly kill my own son." A sinister smile spread across Simon's face.

"Liar!" I shouted.

"Tell me the chant, witch!" His voice thundered through the dark, dank cellar.

When I remained silent, Simon nodded to his men, and the torture resumed.

I screamed as handfuls of my hair were yanked from my scalp and needles again pierced the bottoms of my feet.

"Bring me the bag!" he yelled.

The short man approached Simon. "My lord, the potion is ready. We cannot allow the witch, Vera, to know what thou looks like."

Simon downed the potion and ordered the men to bring him the longer needles.

~~~

The sound of my screams rang in my ears as the short man waited for an answer. "Your order is in the back," I managed to say. "I'll go and put it together."

I walked into the back room and clamped my hand to my mouth. My eyes filled. I leaned against the wall and tried to compose myself, but the tears began to spill over. I now understood why the witch inside needed to hear William's words of reassurance about James's love.

She knew James loved her only because of a spell. This whole time, it had been only a spell. I swallowed down my rising panic. I couldn't allow myself to lose focus right now—not with Simon himself standing a few feet away.

"Miss?"

I cleared my throat and wiped my face. "I'm coming." I gathered as much of the order as I could carry, returned to the front, and placed the boxes on the counter.

Simon's scent was so strong, it stung my eyes. "Do you need some help?" he asked.

The short man spoke up. "Don't bother. I can help the girl."

"There are just a few more boxes," I said.

Simon's dark brown eyes and dark hair seemed to be features in keeping with that of a villain. The resemblance between Simon and James was striking. James had his father's thick, dark eyebrows and strong facial features, and like his father, James was also tall. Simon looked too young to have a son James's age.

He eyed me up and down with an expression of disgust. "How much do I owe you?"

"I'll get the rest of your order and ring it up."

I walked to the back and breathed deeply, trying to stay in control. The witch inside was furious, however, making it difficult to calm myself.

I was relieved to hear Sammy's voice. "Oh, hello."

"Back here!" I yelled. I grabbed several more boxes and carried them to the counter. "Can you go and get the rest of their order?" I asked Sammy.

"Sure," he said, glancing at the two men.

Simon stared at me as I rang up the

order. I wondered why he had chosen to finally show his true identity.

After paying for the order, Sammy helped the men carry out the boxes. When he returned to the bakery, I broke down.

Sammy ran to my side. "What's wrong, Thea?"

I couldn't answer him; the disturbing revelations from my flashback flooded my mind. I slid to the floor, sobbing.

Sammy sank to the floor and sat beside me. "Thea, did those men do something to you?"

I shook my head and threw myself into his arms. "Erase my memory, Sammy," I sobbed. "Erase everything."

Sammy looked alarmed. "Is your memory back?"

I shook my head. "I should have let them take me. I should have told them who I was."

Sammy enfolded me in his arms. "Thea, what's the matter?"

Cory and Fish walked back in.

"Over here," Sammy yelled from behind the counter.

"What's going on?" Cory asked.

Sammy shook his head. "I don't know. She started crying after those men left."

"Men?" Cory asked. "What men?" He knelt down in front of me. "Thea, what happened?"

I wrapped my arms around his neck. "Just take me home," I cried. "Please."

"I will," Cory said. "But I need you to tell me what happened first."

Unable to answer, I continued sobbing uncontrollably.

Cory looked at Sammy. "What men?"

"It was that short, bald guy," Sammy replied. "He was with some other guy. They just picked up an order."

Cory put his hands on my shoulders. "Thea, what did they say to you?"

I looked up at him as tears continued to stream down my face. "Was your love for me a spell, too?" I asked.

Cory's face twisted in confusion. "What?" He looked at Sammy and Fish, who just looked at each other and shrugged.

"I'm lost," Fish said.

"Lock up," Cory said. "I'm taking her home. I'll meet you at James's house." He lifted me off the floor. "Hold on to me, Thea," he whispered.

I was still crying when we arrived at the house. I needed to talk to William. I prayed he would tell me that the love spell Simon cast on James had long since been broken. But if it remained unbroken, I would leave tonight. I planned on taking William's ring with me.

I was determined to find out more about this world that Simon was willing to do so much for—even using his own son to do his dirty work. I tried to imagine a life without James. Perhaps this was all too good to be true.

"Come on, Thea," Cory said, opening my car door.

"It was a love spell, Cory," I cried. "Only a spell."

As Cory carried me through the door,

William came running. "What happened?"

"I don't know," Cory replied. "She just keeps crying and talking about love spells. She even asked if I had a love spell on me."

My heart was shattered. I could never make sense of why James loved me, and now I knew why. The way he looked at me was too much; no one could love another person that much.

"I was afraid she would learn about that," William said.

Cory set me down on the sofa. "You mean this love spell stuff she's going on about is true?" he asked.

William looked at me and nodded.

Cory's eyes widened. "You mean, James?"

William didn't answer.

Cory knelt down and took my hand. "Thea, no spell ever made me love you. I've always loved you. Leave with me now, and I'll show you how much."

"What are you doing?" William asked.

Cory dropped my hand and stood. "Giving her a choice."

William lifted my head up. "Do you want to leave, child?"

"Is it true?" I asked.

"Yes," he replied.

I searched his eyes, waiting for him to say that he broke the spell years ago, but he looked away and said nothing.

"Why didn't you tell me?" I asked, trembling. "Why did you let him near me?"

"Because I believe he truly loves you."

"Lies!" I screamed. "You knew it was a spell. All this time, you allowed me to believe he really cared about me."

Cory placed his hand on my back. "Thea, come away with me. You don't have to stay here."

"Stop this at once!" William ordered.

I shot William a disgusted look. "Wait here, Cory. I'm going with you."

Chapter 22
They Found Me

I bolted up the stairs to our room and slammed the door behind me. William had confirmed it: it was a spell. James's kisses, his touch, and all the rest, all only a spell. I thought of all the times he'd kissed me on the head, and wondered if he did so only because he couldn't stand to kiss my lips. The horror of the truth broke me, crushed my heart, and as much as I hated to admit it, I knew I couldn't live without him.

I leaned back against the door and slid to the floor. This world held no meaning for me without James. If I couldn't be with him, I didn't want to live. As I stared through tears at our bedroom doors, a thought occurred to me: if I died, my powers would die with me or stay trapped in the crystal forever. Simon would have no powers to steal, nothing to kill for. The witches could resume their lives.

I walked to the doors and threw them open. The flowers glittered brilliantly as if calling to me. I withdrew one from a vase. "You, too, live only because of a spell," I whispered as the flower slipped from my grasp and onto the floor. I reached for the vase and pitched it at the fireplace. It exploded on impact, spraying jagged pieces of glass across the room. "All lies!" I screamed as I reached for another vase. I wanted to destroy everything that was him. Anything he had touched, I wanted gone. "How could you do this to me?" I cried, sinking to the floor in tears. After several long minutes, I rose and began to gather my things, shards of glass crunching beneath my feet as I made my way to the closet.

I heard someone on the stairs. Assuming it was Cory coming to fetch me, I opened the door.

I was startled to see James running toward our room. "Thea!"

I slammed the door, locked it, and hurried to the window, desperate to escape. When I reached the window, my heart fell. Cory was driving away.

"Please, Thea," James called. "Open the door!"

I opened the window, but it slammed shut again. Someone—probably William—was trying to prevent me from leaving. I searched the room frantically for somewhere to hide.

James kicked open the door.

"Leave me alone!" I shouted.

"Thea, please," he said, slowly walking toward me. "Let me explain."

"I don't want to hear your lies!"

"Thea, Simon's spell had no effect on me," he said. "By the time he'd cast it, I was already completely in love with you."

"Liar!"

"Go ahead, break the spell," James challenged. "Say the words and learn the truth." He stepped closer. "I never asked William to break the spell because I wanted you to do it. I needed you to see for yourself that nothing had changed. I will still want you, Thea. I will still love you."

I eyed James suspiciously, unconvinced. But I needed to know the truth, even if the truth would be the death of me. I swallowed thickly, my eyes locked on his. "Release spell," I whispered. "Now go find Helena, your true love," I added bitterly through my tears.

He stepped forward and gathered me into his arms. "I already found my true love."

His touch melted my heart. I gave in and threw my arms around him. "I don't care if you love me because of a spell. I can't live without you," I cried.

He squeezed me tighter and kissed my head. "You don't have to, you silly, stupid girl," he said, looking into my tear-filled eyes. "No spell could make me love you more."

I felt my heart putting itself back together. The pain of believing he didn't truly love me hurt more than anything Simon could ever do to me. *Simon!* "Oh, James," I cried. "Simon, he's yo—"

He placed his finger to my lips. "I don't want to talk about my father right now." He lifted me into his arms, walked over to the door, kicked it shut, and started for the bedroom.

"What are you doing?" I asked.

He set me on my feet next to the bed and

took my face in his hands. "Simon's love spell wasn't the only spell broken today," he said. He began to unbutton my blouse, and I knew my father had broken the spell. "My wife, my love, my life," he whispered, pulling me into his arms. We became one as he finally took me. I had never felt anything so pure and perfect. He kissed me like he couldn't get enough of me, and I kissed him back as though my life depended on it. Every kiss felt like magic; every touch took me to another world. I trembled with desire as he ran his hands along my naked body. "Thea," he whispered.

"Kiss me again," I answered, pulling him closer.

As dawn approached, James wrapped a sheet around me and carried me to the terrace. We sat, enveloped in each other's arms, and watched the sun rise.

He kissed my head.

"How I love when you do that," I said.

"Are you happy, my love?"

I looked up at him and smiled. "I am, when I'm with you."

He kissed me passionately, and the sheet fell away. I melted into his arms, and he took me again.

We spent the rest of the morning in our room, temporarily forgetting about work, the other witches, and Simon's despicable quest. Nothing could pull us away from each other. We laughed when James turned off his phone and flung it across the room. "The world can wait!" he said.

"Yes," I murmured.

"Are you hungry?" he asked, pulling away from my lips. His eyes were bluer than ever.

"I'm starving."

He bounded out of bed. "I don't think I've ever been so hungry," he said, pulling on a pair of pants.

I admired his muscled body. "You and the boys are all so fit," I said, sitting up.

He smiled as he buttoned his pants. "Four hundred years of training will do that." He jumped on the bed and straddled me. "So you've noticed Cory's body, too, huh?" he asked, kissing my neck.

"Cory who?" I said, finding his lips again.

He kissed my lips, nose, and both of my cheeks. "We're going to waste away to nothing if we don't tear ourselves away from this bed."

"Looks like we're going to starve, then," I replied, pulling him closer.

There was a knock at the door.

"Hold on!" James yelled. He jumped out of bed and threw the sheets over me. "Don't get dressed," he said, bounding through the sitting room to the door.

I smiled as I watched him. "Please don't wake up from this one, Thea," I whispered to myself.

"Thank you," I heard James say. "I was just coming down."

"May I speak to her?" William asked.

"Just a moment," James replied. Seconds later, he walked through the bedroom door holding a tray of food. He set it down on the end of the bed and pointed at the dresser. "First drawer, nightgown. Put it on."

I rolled off the bed, grabbed the garment, and slipped it over my head. "Is everything okay?"

"I'm sure it's fine, love," he said. He called William into the room.

William entered holding a cup in his hand. "Good afternoon."

"Hello, William."

"Forgive me for interrupting, but I need you to drink this." He offered me the cup.

"Now?" James asked, seeming miffed.

"We agreed," William replied.

I peered into the cup. "What is it?"

"But she'll be knocked out for the rest of the day," James whined.

"Tomorrow will be too late," William said.

I looked from one to the other. "What are you two talking about?"

James seized the cup from William and turned to me. "Do you trust me?"

"Yes, why?" I replied.

"Because," he said, "I need you to drink this without asking why."

I searched his deep blue eyes, reached for the cup, and drank the contents.

"How long do I have?" James asked.

"One hour and not a minute more," William replied, turning to leave.

"William," I called. "I'm so sorry."

William smiled. "Go, enjoy your time with your husband, child." He shot James a look and slipped quietly from the room.

"Come, my love," James said, reaching for my hand. "Please eat something."

We sat on the bed and began to eat. I was desperately curious to know what the tea was for, but I kept my promise and didn't ask questions.

"I was going to take you for a walk on the beach today," James said. "Maybe tomorrow?"

"You'll be home tomorrow?" I asked excitedly.

"For half the day, anyway. I'm heading out today, as well."

"Because I'll be sleeping?"

"Yes, but I'll be back when you wake up." He took a bite of his sandwich and looked at me. "You know, we never had a honeymoon. When all this is over, how does Aruba sound?"

"Today feels like a honeymoon," I answered.

"And so will tonight," he said, grinning. He leaned over and kissed me. We quickly forgot about the food as we fell back on the bed.

When I opened my eyes, I was alone. It was dark outside. "What time is it?" I muttered to myself. The clock read five thirty. I was relieved to see that it wasn't particularly late. I was out of clean clothes and needed to pick some up. I took a shower and quickly got dressed, hoping to find James downstairs. Perhaps he would drive me to my apartment. I stepped into my shoes and headed for the door.

As I walked by William's room, I heard him yelling. "Another useless spell!"

I quietly pushed open the door. "Is

everything okay?"

Startled, he looked up, and our eyes met. He was obviously distressed. "Please leave me, child." The hourglass sat on the table in front of him.

I stepped into the room and closed the door. "What is it? What spell did you find?"

He stared down at the hourglass and sighed in frustration. "I cannot remove Simon's spells without removing the one you put on it. I do not possess adequate energy to separate them."

"What kind of spell did I use?"

He lifted the hourglass and turned it in his hands. "The question is, what spell did Simon put on it?"

I studied the hourglass. The sands appeared to be trying to escape their confines and shifted in my direction.

William eyed it curiously and set it down. "Walk to my other side," he ordered.

I did as he said and kept my eyes on the sands, which shifted again toward me.

"Now, leave the room," he said quietly.

I hurried out into the hall and waited.

"Okay, come back in," William called.

From the doorway, the sands appeared to be still. When I reentered the room, they began circulating in my direction again.

William lifted the hourglass and eyed it thoughtfully. "He's trying to trap your memory."

"What do you mean?"

"Do you not see, child? He wants the hourglass to warn him when the sands run out, but he wants to control when you remember who you are. He must be confident that he will have captured you by then. His spell would have led him right to you."

"Why? Is my memory in the hourglass?"

"No, but the spell to bring back your memory is."

"I put a spell on it. Is that what it's set for, a spell?"

"Yes, I figured that out today."

William seemed more at ease, exuding his usual confidence. He returned his attention to the hourglass. "No more questions, child," he said, waving me away. "I have work to do, and I do not have much time."

"Oh, I was hoping you could walk me to my place. I need to pick up some clean clothes, and I don't think James is home yet."

He set down the hourglass and spoke earnestly. "For reasons I will not share with you, I cannot leave this house—not even for one second."

I was deeply curious as to the reason for this, but realized it wasn't the time to ask questions. I pecked him on the cheek, noticing him tremble slightly as I did so.

Without warning, my father reached for me, closed his eyes, and bowed his head. I was astounded when he pulled me into his arms and hugged me tightly. "I would stop it if I could," he whispered.

"Stop what?" I asked, pulling away from him. "What's wrong?"

His eyes filled as his shaky hands pulled me into another embrace. "Be strong, Thea.

You can get through this."

"Get through what?"

He didn't answer, but continued to hold me. Finally, he kissed the top of my head and pushed me away. "Go. I'll be waiting when you come back to me."

"Are you okay?"

He nodded. "Yes, now go. Your destiny waits."

I regarded him curiously. "You're scaring me."

"It takes much more than this to scare you."

I stared at him, puzzled, unable to decode his cryptic message. I backed out of the room slowly and closed the door behind me. As I made my way toward the stairs, I heard him pound on the table. His actions and his words were a complete mystery to me. I decided to leave him alone for now and hoped that, sometime later, he would explain.

I descended the stairs quickly and headed for the door. I wanted to hurry back and clean up the broken glass in our room—a simple command should take care of it. I couldn't wait for my second night with my husband. I wanted to be in his arms, kiss him like I did last night, and lose all track of time again.

I slipped out the door and headed for my apartment, wishing it weren't so dark. The streets were flooded with tourists, which put me somewhat at ease. The reason for my anxiety escaped me; I walked home from work after dark all the time. Maybe Cory was right, we were becoming paranoid.

I remembered Delia telling me she'd be at her stand tonight and decided to pay her a visit.

On the way to Delia's alley, I found myself on the same street as the bakery and decided to check in with the boys. When I finally made my way through the throng of tourists and across the street to the shop, I froze. Simon and his men were walking out of the bakery with another large order. When our eyes met, Simon seemed momentarily taken aback. He looked into the bakery and slowly back at me, glaring. I looked into the bakery to see what he was looking at. My heart almost exploded when I saw Vera working, pretending to be me.

Simon whispered something to one of his men. I watched as the man walked back into the bakery. I spun on my heel and hurried in the direction of Delia's stand. I wanted to run, but the mass of tourists made it impossible. I sensed Simon's men following me and crossed the street again. As the gap between us started to close, I broke into a run. I glanced over my shoulder as one of the men reached for me. I gripped his hand and ran up the side of the nearest building, spinning until I heard his arm break.

I had resumed running toward Delia's alley when someone grabbed my hair. I ducked, spun to face him, kicked him in the stomach, and yelled "Fly!" The man soared backward for nearly a block before he disappeared from view. People applauded, assuming it was some kind of show.

I ran as fast as I could. I couldn't allow

Simon to get to James. By now, Simon had surely figured out that James was not the man he pretended to be. As more of Simon's men closed in, I began bounding off trees—anything to keep me one step ahead of them. At the entrance to the alley, I had Delia in my sights, but she was surrounded by tourists.

"Turn!" I ordered her.

Her head snapped in my direction, searching the crowd for my face.

"Hear me," I ordered from the top of a tree. "They found me."

I was attempting to jump from the tree when a rope wrapped itself around my ankles. I stumbled but managed to grab a branch to steady myself. "Release," I shouted, but the rope wouldn't budge. My feet were paralyzed. I felt a rope around my neck. With one hard yank, I fell from the tree. "Release," I yelled again, to no avail.

Three men appeared and wrapped another rope around my wrists. They covered my head with a bag, dragged me a short distance, and shoved me into a car. The men chanted spells, just as they had in my flashback, to prevent me from casting any of my own. But I didn't know any spells. I could feel the car speeding through town when I heard a sudden thump on the roof.

"What the hell was that?" one of the men asked.

"I don't see anything," another man said. "Someone must have thrown something at us."

I tried to free myself, but the ropes had been fortified with spells. I couldn't move an inch and could barely breathe.

I heard someone laugh. "I thought he said this was going to be hard," the man said, kicking my leg. "She's not that tough."

The rest of the men laughed. "We did in two minutes what he hasn't been able to do in four hundred years." I heard a round of high-fives before receiving another hard kick.

I needed the witch inside to rise to the surface, but she was nowhere to be found. I had no strength to draw on—no witch, not even a flashback. Why?

"I can't believe she's the one," one of the men said. "I've seen her a million times." A foot pressed into my back. "She's always reading. Maybe she was looking for new spells." More laughter.

When we'd been driving about thirty minutes, the car turned and the road surface changed from smooth to bumpy.

"Peter, he's following us. Does he think we're going to drive away with her?"

"I don't know, Randy," the man named Peter replied. "But I don't trust him. His reasons for wanting this witch don't add up."

"He didn't even live around here back then," Randy said. "How does he know so much about her?"

"This witch was arrogant," Peter said. "But I never saw her do the things he says she did. Like I said, it doesn't add up."

I wanted desperately to tell them they were being lied to, that Simon was using them, but the man's chants prevented me from speaking.

"And how does he plan on sharing with so many of us?" Peter continued. "This witch never had that much power. There's something he's not telling us."

"What do you want to do?" Randy asked.

I closed my eyes and commanded to be free of the ropes, but I remained bound. I had to at least try to talk to them. They were already suspicious of Simon; maybe I could convince them to let me go. I was trying to talk when the car came to a stop.

"Keep your eyes and ears open," Peter told the others. "I want to know what Simon's up to."

The door opened and someone pulled my feet. My head smacked the door frame as they yanked me from the car and dropped me on the ground.

"Not so fast," Peter warned.

Someone picked me up, slammed me against the car, and lifted the bag from my head. I found myself face to face with Simon.

"Well, look what the cat dragged in," he said, a wicked smile spreading across his face.

Peter spoke up. "Not so fast, Simon, I want to know—"

All went quiet. When I turned to look, a man emerged from the car holding the handle of a long knife which he pulled from the man named Peter's chest. Peter fell to the ground with a thud.

"Sorry, my lord," another man said. "But this man was untrusting of you. He was attempting to poison the others against you."

I didn't recognize the man's voice from

the car; he must have purposely remained quiet. My heart sank as I realized he had just killed any hope I had of these men helping me.

Simon grabbed my face roughly. "It's her. She's been casting spells at them." He made a fist and struck me hard across the face.

I heard movement near the car.

Simon didn't appear to have noticed. "Anyone else feel like saving this witch?" he asked.

I couldn't understand why I was so calm. Simon's slap hardly fazed me. There was no fear, no tears, nothing but steel nerves. I scanned my surroundings; we were in some sort of campsite. Hundreds of men stood regarding each other as Simon waited for their answer. Behind Simon stood several old cabins. I recognized this place. Norm and I had taken a shortcut through here on the way to Fall River to pick up some specialty items for the bakery. My eyes were still focused beyond Simon when he struck me again. Startled, I nearly fell to the ground.

He grabbed my hair. "We have some unfinished business, witch."

A sort of numbness washed over me; nothing Simon did or said had any effect on me.

"Take her inside," Simon said to his men.

The men dragged me across the campsite.

Simon followed close behind. "When they get here, tell them to come inside with Vera," he ordered. "Jack, bring the needles. I have a memory to restore."

430

Chapter 23
The Bevel Needles

Hearing Jack's name prompted me to look over my shoulder. I desperately wanted to shout out and ask him about James, but he quickly disappeared into one of the cabins.

"They just called, my lord." It was the short man speaking. "The house is empty."

We arrived at one of the cabins. The men dragged me inside and threw me across the floor. I felt detached, as though I was watching a scene from Delia's memory box.

"Tell them to keep looking," Simon ordered. "Find out if that witch, Delia, is with him."

"As you wish, my lord," the short man replied.

"It appears your friends have left you to fend for yourself," Simon said, walking over to me. "Even your husband has gone missing."

I closed my eyes and sighed in relief. If they had fled, I could die happy, knowing they were safe.

Simon reached down, grabbed a handful of my hair, and yanked my head back to face him. "What kind of spell did you put on James?" he demanded. "You will remove it before you die, witch." He shoved me back and looked over his shoulder. "Put the chains on her. And remove the ropes. I want her to feel everything."

Two of Simon's men dragged me across the floor of the small cabin toward a steel pole in the corner. A survey of the room revealed that the cabin had been converted into a torture chamber. Hooks and leather straps hung from the walls. A blowtorch sat under a table.

I closed my eyes, wondering why I wasn't screaming. I was about to die a painful death, but knowing my loved ones had escaped made my death feel necessary and useful. The power to free them gave me peace.

They leaned me up against the pole and wrapped chains around my neck and waist.

I commanded to break free of them, but their spells were too strong.

"Remove her shoes," Simon ordered.

Anger surged through me. "I thought by now you'd have come up with better ways of making me talk," I said with a smirk. "I've seen this all before, Simon."

Simon tilted his head. "Is that you? Have you come to play?" He leaned over and revealed the crystal.

I tried to free my hands and reach for it, but the chains wouldn't budge.

Simon held it in front of me for a moment before pulling it away. He laughed. "You had me there for a moment. I thought my old friend had come to say hello."

I watched as he returned the crystal to the velvet bag. He slipped the bag into his pocket. "I do need you to remember who you are," he said. "How else will you be able to tell me what I need to know?" He walked over to a table, opened a box, and pulled out the fake hourglass. "This will help us take a little trip down memory lane." He set it down next to me, brushed his hand across my cheek, and moved to the door. "It's time," he yelled to the men outside.

Five men, including the short man, ran into the cabin.

"Stay close to her," Simon ordered. "And don't stop chanting. Her memory will likely make her stronger."

The men took their places, closed their eyes, and began to chant. Two men, holding hunting knives, stood on either side of me.

Simon faced me. He raised his hands and chanted: "I break the spell I cast on thee. I take her memory and set it free. Allow the sands to release her mind. Allow the hourglass to run out of time." He lowered his hands and smiled at me, confident that he had released my memory.

I smiled and shook my head. "Sorry. Maybe you should try another spell."

Simon's face twisted in confusion. He pulled the crystal from the velvet bag and held it near me, but the crystal remained dormant. "Impossible!"

"Huh," I said. "I wonder what happened?"

Simon's hand came from nowhere and struck me across the face, but I didn't flinch. I

433

felt strong, as though the witch inside was here but not letting me feel her. I spit in his face.

Simon's rage mounted as he wiped his face and smeared the contents of his hand on my cheek. "I'm going to enjoy killing you. Nothing will give me more pleasure than to see your blood on my hands."

The short man looked nervous. "My lord, what do we do now?"

Simon finally tore his eyes away from me. "They must have switched the hourglass," he hissed. "We'll have to proceed without it." He looked at me and smiled. "I believe we can shock her memory back." He walked to the door, called for Jack, and returned his attention to me. "Remove her socks."

Jack strode in holding a long wooden box. He avoided looking at me as he handed the box to Simon.

"Make sure the chains are secure," Simon ordered, taking the box from Jack.

Jack hurried over to me and pulled on the chains. "They can't find him," he said to me, his voice barely audible.

I glanced at Simon. "Thank you," I whispered.

Jack gave me a quick glance and walked over to Simon. "She's secure."

Simon waved him off and removed several long needles with wooden handles from the box. I wondered why Simon wasn't angry with Jack, hadn't killed him for standing up for James. Then it hit me: Simon didn't know about Delia's spell. He had no way of knowing that Jack thought he and James were good friends.

Perhaps Simon thought Jack had also been fooled by James, or maybe he assumed Jack had been friends with the man James pretended to be.

Simon placed a chair in front of me and sat down, two of the needles in his hand. "Do you know what these are?" he asked. "They're called beveled needles. They're not usually this large, but I had these made special, just for you. They are used for surgical suturing. They're very sharp, and do not break like my old ones did." He reached down and grasped my ankle. "I wonder if they're as painful," he said, lifting my foot.

As the needle penetrated the bottom of my foot, I closed my eyes and clutched the chains. I refused to give Simon the pleasure of hearing me scream.

"I see," Simon said, holding out his hand. "Lucky for you, I saved the dull ones. Perhaps they'll make you happy."

The short man took the beveled needles from Simon and carefully placed a new set of needles onto his open palm.

"Say when," Simon said, pushing the needle into my foot.

A scream rose within me and escaped my lips.

Simon looked at his men and smiled. "I think that's a 'when.'"

The men laughed.

Simon held up another needle. "Now, where were we? Oh yes, where can I find the heart?"

I didn't answer.

435

He inserted another needle.

"No!" I screamed.

Simon laughed and extended his hand for another needle. "I'm not going to bother asking how to open the crystal," he said as he pierced my foot a fourth time. "I'll settle for knowing where the heart is."

I tried to yank my foot away, but Simon pulled it closer. "If you keep pulling away, I'll be forced to break your leg."

"Rot in hell, Simon," I shot back.

He dropped my foot, pulled out the crystal, and once again held it near me.

"Don't let her touch it, my lord," the short man whispered.

"Silence, you fool!" Simon yelled. "I only need to hold it near her." When the crystal refused to glow for him, Simon stood and kicked over the chair. "Maybe this will help you remember."

I screamed as the needle plunged into my foot.

Simon waited, holding the crystal next to my head. "Show thy face, witch!"

I resumed my silence as Simon turned to grab a leather strap from the wall. "You will not make a fool out of me again!" He lashed at me repeatedly with the strap. I could feel welts already forming on my face and legs.

"Simon!" Jack yelled.

Simon stopped and looked at him.

"If you kill her," Jack said, "all of this will be for nothing. Have you forgotten what you promised us?"

Simon looked away and flung the strap

across the room. He righted the chair, sat down in front of me again, and sighed. "Forgive my impatience. You see, I've been searching for you for a very long time. I never imagined those witches were hiding you right under my nose. Imagine my dismay when I realized I could have had you long ago." He leaned back. "When I left you in that grave, I thought it was over. I foolishly believed I would find the heart, and in it, the spell to open the crystal. But I was wrong."

He extended his hand to the short man, who immediately handed him another needle. Simon reached for my other foot. "I don't plan on making the same mistake twice."

I screamed in agony as the needle entered my foot. He twisted the wooden handle, smiling as I shrieked.

"I will tell you nothing!" I screamed.

"Show your face, witch!"

I heard someone being dragged into the room. Simon looked over his shoulder and smiled. "Ah, my old friend Vera," he said, releasing my foot.

Vera, crying and trembling, had been badly beaten. Simon strode over to her.

"Leave her alone!" I shouted.

Vera looked at me. "It wasn't me, mistress. I told them nothing."

"Silence!" Simon ordered, glaring at Vera. "Your death will not be quick, witch. I have dreamed of smelling your burning skin." He looked at the short man. "Take her into the next cabin. Find out what she knows." He paused and smiled wickedly. "Take some needles with you."

"No!" Vera screamed. She managed to wriggle from the man's grasp and made a run for the door. Another man grabbed her by the hair and threw her to the floor.

My rage grew as I watched the men pull Vera up by her hair. I prayed for the witch inside to come forth and give me the strength to break free of the chains. I closed my eyes as they dragged Vera away, her screams ringing in my ears like sirens.

Simon seemed pleased with himself. He sauntered back to me, grinning. "I have a feeling that witch is more motivated to talk than you are."

One of his men walked in, looking anxious. "My lord, there is something you need to see."

"What is it?" Simon asked.

"It's Peter's body. It's turned to dust. And there are five other dust piles nearby."

Simon shot a glance at me and walked out behind the man. I wondered how and when five others had been killed. *Is Jack helping me?* Several minutes passed before Simon reentered the cabin, his face contorted in anger. "How are you still able to cast spells?" he asked, grabbing a fistful of my hair. "How, witch?" He made a fist and struck the left side of my face. He hastily removed the chains and pulled the needles from my feet.

"What are you doing?" Jack asked.

"Forcing this witch out," he said as he dragged me toward the door.

Outside the cabin, I heard Vera's

screams. I tried to get to my feet, but Simon was walking too fast.

"Tie her at the top of the camp," Simon ordered. "And throw some wood under her feet."

The man who killed Peter ran over and grabbed me. "Remember me, witch?" he asked, yanking my hair.

I studied his face and remembered him from one of my flashbacks. He was the one who had asked me to share my spells. He dragged me up to a platform and tied me to a pole. "I bet you wish you would have shared some of those fishing spells now." He slapped my face and tossed several small logs under my feet.

I heard Simon speaking to his men. "Be well, my brothers," he said. "I only mean to force out the witch, for she is the one who holds the secret to our riches. She will provide us powers you've never imagined, and we will bring the world to its knees with a simple wave of the hand. Let us set her ablaze and wait for her cries for mercy."

"Burn her!" the men chanted.

Simon smiled.

Panic set in as the fire ignited. I closed my eyes and thought of James. "I love you," I whispered to the image of him in my head. The heat came quickly, the pain searing as the fire reached my feet and swiftly rose. I should have been screaming as the smell of my burning flesh drifted into the air.

I squeezed my eyes closed and waited for death to take me.

"Burn her!"

The camp was filled with warlocks out for my blood. They stood, weapons in hand, waiting for me to burn. My body trembled from the unbearable heat. I tried not to scream from the pain as layers of my skin peeled away.

So this was how I would die, burning while those I loved were far away and safe. I couldn't think of a better way for my life to end. I would die for those who had tried to save me. It would end with me. No longer would they be hunted. No more innocent blood lost.

I vowed not to scream for mercy. My secret would die with me and forever keep Simon from opening the crystal. I allowed the image of James to take me away from the pain. I could smell the flowers as my mind drifted.

~~~

James and I lay in each other's arms under a tree near the lake. I was wearing the dress from the painting.

James kissed me gently on the cheek as I gazed at my wedding ring. "Art thou happy, my love?" he asked.

I smiled and looked into his eyes. "I am when I'm with you, my lord."

He brushed his fingers across my cheek and began undressing me.

~~~

My eyes snapped open. I suddenly realized why James and I couldn't live without each other, why his love for me was so intense, and why Cory's kiss had felt so awkward. James and I were already bonded. I remembered the time he told Cory it had been over for quite some time, and when he told me I had already

440

showed him how much I loved him. It was as though a veil had been lifted from my eyes. I tried to stay calm as I took in the images that flooded my head. I was at our cottage in the woods, about to transfer my powers into the crystal, and the terrifying vision came to me— the vision that held the answers to my questions . . .

I was walking through the forest, pregnant and due any day. I picked some wildflowers and placed them in my hair. I rubbed my stomach and smiled, oblivious to the two men emerging from the trees—Simon and the short man.

They wrapped a rope around my neck, and I froze. Simon tied my hands together, threw me to the ground, and stood over me. The short man chanted as Simon revealed a knife. "I don't need you anymore, witch," Simon said. "Your child shall provide what you have denied me." He leaned over and made an incision, attempting to steal the child from my womb. I tried to shout a command, but the short man's spells restricted me.

The vision flashed forward in time. My son was now twelve years old and looked like James. He thought Simon was his father.

The boy held the crystal, with Simon at his side. "Remember, my son," Simon said, "You must use the spell I taught you. It will allow you to open the crystal."

My son looked at the crystal and back up at Simon. "And these powers will save your life, father?"

"Yes, son," Simon lied. "I shall die if

you fail to give them to me."

I watched in horror as my son transferred his powers to the crystal and handed it to Simon.

Simon's face lit up as the powers flowed into him. "I never dreamed the love spell I put on James would give me so much," Simon said. His body sent visible waves into the air as he raised his arms and laughed. "At last, I can go back to where I belong."

The vision charged forward again. Simon was killing everyone I loved, burning Delia, Cory, and the rest of the boys alive. Simon sought to destroy all evidence of what he'd done. He wanted everyone to think he was a true wizard.

Again, the vision changed. I saw the body of my dead son, killed by Simon. Simon cut out my son's heart and dropped it into a velvet bag.

"No!" I opened my eyes and tried to free myself. I knew now that, along with my powers, I had placed my unborn son in the crystal. I was going to give James a son, a half-wizard son, a son Simon could use to gain the powers he so desperately wanted. I panicked when Simon cast a spell on the heart because it would have revealed my secret.

William had left with James after he rescued me from the grave, because he, too, wanted to protect my son. The tea William gave me this morning made sense now: it was to prevent me from having another child. He couldn't risk giving the vision another opportunity to prevail. My fury escalated as the truth revealed itself to me.

"Where are you, witch?" I yelled.

I needed my memory to return. I couldn't die and forever trap my son in the crystal. The witch inside knew this all too well. That day at the stable, she wasn't protecting me; she was protecting her son.

Blisters formed on my body, popping as my skin peeled away. "James!" I shouted desperately, realizing that death was near. Why had he left me to die like this? William had shown him the vision; he knew what was at stake.

Suddenly, a bag floated by, emptying its powdery contents onto the fire and promptly dousing it.

"Light it again!" Simon shouted. The smoke blocked Simon's view of the bag.

A man ran over with a torch to relight the fire, and that's when I saw it: James's whip. The hand of the man carrying the torch flew away.

"James!" As my eyes searched, I felt a tugging sensation. I looked over my shoulder and saw Fish's hooks poised on the ropes that bound my hands. In front of me, Joshua stood in the trees behind Simon, his bow and arrow pointing directly above me. I heard a rustling noise to the side of me. I turned and saw Delia in the trees, handing off the hourglass.

When I saw the hourglass floating, suspended in air, I knew she had handed it to Sammy. It was Sammy who had killed those other men, and who had doused the fire. It was Sammy who had thumped the top of the car.

I heard James's voice. "She cannot give you what you seek!"

My head spun in the direction of his voice. He was walking out from the trees. "I have what you're looking for," he yelled to Simon.

"James, no!" I yelled.

Simon's men ran at James. "Stop!" he commanded. "Do not attack until I say."

James walked to the middle of the camp and smiled at Simon. "It's been a long time, Father."

Simon smiled but remained still. "Too long, my son. I've missed you."

I realized James had removed the spell I had taught him; Simon could see his true face. Jack seemed confused as to who James was.

James glanced at me and back to Simon. "I've come for my wife," he said. "She has nothing you want."

Simon smiled and stepped forward. "I'm afraid, my son, that I cannot allow that. I have unfinished business with her."

"She no longer has what you seek, Father. Your unfinished business is now with me. And if you kill me, the heart dies the moment my own stops beating."

Simon appeared flustered. "What have you done, James? Where is the heart?"

"I made sure I would walk out of here alive." James smiled. "Rest assured, the heart is in a very safe place," he said, patting his chest. "You see, Father, when you put that spell on me, I was already in love with her. But the spell did help me: it made me see who you really

444

were and what you were capable of. I knew you would kill me after I convinced Thea to use the crystal, just like you killed my mother when she gave birth to me."

Simon was visibly shaken.

"Yes, Father, I know about that. You bonded yourself to her in the hope that she would give you a son whose only purpose was to make this witch fall in love with him. What you didn't count on was me actually falling in love. You thought she would use the crystal to give me her powers, and you planned to steal them and kill me before I could make the powers mine. But you see, Father, I always told her I didn't want her powers. You never counted on the one emotion you know nothing about—that you have never even felt—getting in your way."

Simon smiled and shook his head. "I see I was mistaken about this witch putting a spell on you. But you're mistaken if you think I've never loved. I have always loved you. Give me the heart, James, and we can begin a new life as father and son. I will show you a world that will make us both more powerful than you ever dreamed."

As Simon talked, Joshua's bow remained at the ready. Fish's hooks were still poised behind me, and Cory remained, waiting behind a tree.

"You're not understanding me, Father," James shouted. "The only way to get the heart from me is to kill me. And that will kill any chance of you ever getting your hands on it."

Simon's faced twisted in confusion. He

was growing visibly nervous.

"You see, Father," James continued, "I, too, have learned some wizard spells. And if I die, so does the heart, and any information it ever took from her."

Simon laughed. "And how do you intend to kill a heart that is already dead? Did you bring her mother's heart back to life?"

James smiled.

Simon stopped laughing. "What have you done, James?"

"You knew this witch would never talk, didn't you, Father? You knew she would choose death before she would ever tell you how to open the crystal. That's why you want the heart so badly. It's the only way you'll ever get what you want." James unbuttoned his shirt. "Well, come and get it."

Simon's eyes widened as James's revelation set in. "No!"

James pulled out his whip and began lashing at the men surrounding him.

"Don't kill him," Simon shouted. "I need him alive!"

I screamed as more and more men stormed my husband. "Behind you!" I shouted.

Chapter 24
The Battle

The boys remained in their holding pattern. What were they waiting for? I screamed as more than a dozen men attacked James and seized his whip.

"Take him to my quarters!" Simon yelled.

As they hauled him away, my panic escalated. "James!"

"Light that fire and keep it going until she talks," Simon ordered.

"I'm going to kill you," I shouted as the men relit the fire.

Simon glared at me and pulled out the velvet bag, his fury soaring now that the heart was out of his reach. I was his only hope. I trembled, the pain becoming more intense as the fire roared around me.

"How do I open the crystal, witch?" Simon yelled, holding up the bag.

At once, Joshua released his arrow, sending it through the velvet bag.

Simon shrieked as the bag glided from his grasp, the arrow carrying it to a target directly above my head. When the arrow struck, Fish slashed the ropes with his hooks. Sammy threw the hourglass to the ground, where it shattered, sending the sands flying toward me. It sounded like a deck of cards being shuffled as the sands released my spell.

My life experiences came back to me in an instant. I remembered everything. Every moment, every spell—they all returned. I understood now why I couldn't feel the witch inside; she was waiting for the hourglass to release her spell. As the sands ran out, she became part of me, and I was ready to embrace her.

Clouds from Delia's box closed in around me. I sensed her nearby, transferring memories back into my head. Cory and Delia ran out from the trees and were quickly joined by the rest of the boys, Sharron, and the other witches. I reached up, tore the bag from Joshua's arrow, and withdrew the crystal. The others fought as I held it up. "Give to me what lies inside, I leave my son for you to hide. Protect him as I kill these men, do not open until I say when." I held the crystal to my heart, and it began to glow.

"No!" Simon yelled. "Kill her!"

His men ran at me, weapons drawn. Cory, Delia, and Javier formed a united front at the foot of the stake and fought off Simon's minions.

"Kill them all!" Simon yelled, disappearing into one of the cabins.

My hands trembling, I returned my attention to the crystal. "Hurry!"

A surge of energy blasted through me, sending out a shockwave that caused the nearby trees to lose their leaves. The ground beneath me rippled as my body's energy radiated. Birds left their nests, and dust lifted from the ground. I ceased to feel the pain of the fire as it continued to burn my flesh. The crystal's glow dimmed and shut down, my son safely tucked inside. I reached for the flames, which formed a ball of fire in my hand. The fire that once burned under me now spun in my open palm.

I smiled at the men who fought for Simon. "Time to play, my lords," I said, throwing the fireball into the center of the battle. I watched as it jumped over my friends to find its targets.

Simon's hapless soldiers screamed as I walked down from the platform. My wounds healed without a verbal command, my body able to read my mind. My clothes lifted from the ashes and flew back onto my frame. New skin formed, and bruises faded. The pain in my feet subsided.

As several men charged up on my left, my eyes zoomed in on their feet. I waved my hand in a spinning motion, and their ankles twisted. I left them screaming in pain and ran to where I'd seen Simon's men take James. Determined to reach my destination, I began weaving my way through the hundreds of men. To my right, I spied a pack of soldiers going after Cory. I pounded my fists together and the men sank into the earth, leaving only their heads above ground. Cory nodded and continued fighting.

I was about to start off again when I heard Delia shouting. "Who wants to die first?" Several men surrounded her. I focused on an enormous tree, raised my hand, and spread my fingers. The leaves broke from the tree and waited, suspended, for my command. With a wave of my hand, I turned them hard as iron and sent them flying. I watched as they sank into the men and killed them.

Delia turned. "Catch!" she shouted, tossing me my stick.

I caught it, spun it in my hands, and placed it between my legs. "Fly," I commanded. The wind whipped up under me and took me with it, blowing through my hair as I raced to help James. His heart directed me to him, a heart that now beat with my mother's heart inside of it.

A spell hit my back and knocked me off my stick. I landed on my feet and spun around to find several warlocks charging me. They stopped a short distance away, and one stepped forward. "We are not half human, witch," he said. "We can kill you." He spat spells into his hand and blasted them at me like shooting stars. He narrowed the gap between us, the others quickly following suit.

I looked at the man and smiled as their spells halted inches from my body. "And you're also not half wizard," I replied. A flick of my finger sent their spells flying back to them. They took off running but the spells quickly caught up, sending them spinning up into the air, twisting them nearly in half, and killing them. I reached for my stick as more soldiers ran at me. This time, there were no less than fifty. I couldn't believe they continued to fight. *Do these warlocks have a death wish?*

I held out my hand, and my stick flew into it. One by one, the trees around me came to life as I pointed to each of them with the stick. I spun the stick and pounded it on the ground. The men fell quickly as branches and roots encircled them and tore at their bodies.

More men came running up behind me. I blew into my hand, held it over the ground, and sent dirt spinning into the air. With a wave of my hand, the swirling earth ravaged the men, leaving only their bones behind when the dust had settled.

Another wave of men stormed me. "Surround her!" one yelled.

I remained motionless as they encircled me, keeping my head down as they took their places. "You're willing to die for a man who cares nothing about you, my lords?"

"Who said we're dying?" one replied.

My head shot up. "I did."

They came at me, swords and bats swinging. I knew those bats all too well. I pointed my stick toward a cloud; a stream of lightning descended and entered it. I spun it in my hand and held it to my head, the surge flowing through me instantly. As I raised my hand, the lightning jetted from my fingers. One by one, the men sailed into the air, quaking from the shock. My eyes glowed white as I blasted them again. When they finally came down to the ground, smoke rose from their bodies and they writhed in pain.

451

One man stood, trembling, still holding his bat. Upon close examination, I was stunned to realize that he was only a boy. I slowly approached him.

His eyes widened in terror. "Please don't kill me," he cried.

"How old are you?" I asked.

"F . . . fourteen."

"Don't be scared," I said. "I'm not going to hurt you."

He nodded, but didn't drop the bat.

"Let go of that bat," I ordered gently.

As he allowed the bat to slide to the ground, I noticed the front of his pants were wet.

"Why are you here?" I asked.

"My father made me come. He said he would kill me if I didn't."

"Who is your father?"

"The one who lit the fire."

Anger surged through me. I carefully placed my hands on the boy's head and learned that he had no mother, and that he didn't understand why he was here. I used my power to erase his memory; he was better off without such a father, a man I aimed to kill as soon as I found him.

The boy seemed dazed for a moment and looked up at me.

"I want you to run to the lake and wait for me there, understand?"

He nodded and disappeared through the trees. I felt better knowing he would be safe, and realized I would have to keep my eyes open for more sons who had been cruelly thrown into this despicable battle.

I refocused on finding James. As I began to run in his direction, a mass of spinning warlock spells flew past. I spun my stick, successfully repelling the spells and sending them back.

As more men approached me from behind, I turned to attack. I was stunned when their spells whizzed past me toward the men I had just been fighting. These men, at least twenty of them, were helping me.

"Tu eres Thea?" one of them asked. I was relieved to realize that these were James's friends, the ones he had told Cory about.

"Yes, I'm Thea," I replied.

The man nodded and ran toward the men who had been attacking me.

"Wait! I have friends fighting. Please don't hurt them."

"Marcalos!" he replied, continuing on toward Simon's soldiers.

I raised my hand and tossed a spell into the air, marking my friends as the man had asked. With no men charging me for the moment, I ran into the cabin where they had taken James. There had obviously been a struggle; most of the furniture had been turned over, and powder littered every surface. I saw a man, his skin torn away, and knew at once that Fish had been here and had managed to rescue James. Back outside the cabin, I spotted Jack fighting a few yards away. He was attacking one of Simon's men. After finishing him off, Jack looked at me, and our eyes met.

He flashed his weapon as I stepped

closer to him. "Put it down, Jack," I said. "I mean you no harm."

He carefully put his weapon down and looked toward the men still fighting. "Now what?" he asked, looking back at me.

"Now you tell them," I replied. "Tell them to stop or die."

"What's does Simon want with your powers?" he asked. "What are we really fighting for here?"

I walked over to him. He stumbled back as I placed my hands on his head. "I'm just going to show you something," I said. I closed my eyes and exposed Simon's plan, making sure to include the part where he would kill them all once my powers were in his grasp. I opened my eyes and stepped back. "Now, go tell them, Jack."

He nodded and took off running. I hoped Jack's word would help prevent further bloodshed. They needed to know they were fighting for a lie. Some of these men wanted me dead regardless—their hatred for me was a powerful motivator. I was a threat to their world, someone to fear. Warlocks had little tolerance for fear.

I scanned the chaos for the others. I spotted Delia close by, struggling with several men. My fingers still charged with lightning, I dropped the stick and blasted the men, sending them flying across the camp. I smiled at Delia. "Hello, old friend."

She smiled back. "Hello, witch. Took you long enough."

There was no time for catching up; I

needed to find James. I extended my hand, and my stick flew into it.

"I wonder what wild stories we'll hear this time after people see you on that thing," Delia said.

I chuckled. "I was seen one time by human eyes, and I've never heard the end of it." I mounted the stick and flew off.

Immediately, I heard crying and spotted Helena stooped over Amanda, who lay on the ground. Sharron stood nearby, trying to prevent several of Simon's men from approaching. I flew by Sharron. "Get down!"

Sharron looked up for a moment and threw herself onto the ground. I waved my hand and blasted spells at the men, sending piles of dust drifting into the air. I dismounted and hurried to Amanda, but it was too late.

"Get away from her!" Helena sobbed. "This is your fault!"

I backed away. "I'm truly sorry, Helena."

"I hate you!"

Sharron placed her hand on Helena's shoulder. "Helena, we all knew the danger. There's nothing she could have done."

Helena pushed Sharron away. "She's taken everything from me," Helena shouted. "And now I've lost my sister, too, because of her."

"There was no other way, Helena," Sharron said. "We all would have died had we not fought."

"Why didn't they kill her?" Helena said, pointing at me. She turned and continued sobbing over Amanda's lifeless body.

Sharron looked at me. "Go, dear. I'll stay with her."

I nodded, holding my hand out for the stick. I looked at Helena one last time. I wanted to be able to bring back her sister, but Sharron was right, there was nothing I could have done. All of us would be dead if Simon had gotten his way. But Helena wasn't thinking about that now. The way she saw it, I had taken James from her, and now her sister was dead, also because of me.

As I flew off to find James, I couldn't help wondering about his relationship with Helena. I knew how much he loved me, but why had he never told me about her? This was no time to think about that, though; I had a fight to win.

Many of the men had begun fleeing into the woods. Simon hadn't shown his face since disappearing into one of the cabins. It wasn't like him to back down from a fight. He was still here, lurking, I was sure, ready to unleash the powerful wizard spells my father had taught him. Simon needed me alive. He still needed something from me beyond opening the crystal, but what?

In the vision, he was cutting out my son's heart, but I didn't understand why he needed it. My father would have to answer that question. We could speak freely now, without the fear of my memory coming back. I knew now that my father resisted holding me because he feared his heart would speak to mine—a special bond that wizards share.

My search for James came to an end when I spotted him fighting alongside the Spanish warlocks. His eyes darted wildly about the surrounding area; he was looking for me.

Before I could fly to him, I heard Vera screaming. I raced to the cabin where she was being held and blasted the door open as I approached. I flew inside and found Vera, needles protruding from the bottoms of her feet. I hopped off my stick and blasted the two men standing over her, sending them crashing into the wall. I rushed to Vera, carefully removed the needles, and waved my hand to heal her feet.

I gathered up the needles and turned to face the men who were still glued to the wall. "I know a better place for these," I said, waving my hand. Their shirts ripped open, and I smiled at Vera. "Care to play darts, Vera?"

When I looked back to the men, I realized one of them was the short man. "Has your master left you behind?" As he opened his mouth to answer, I threw a needle and sank it deep into the right side of his face. "Oh, I'm sorry," I said. "That was rude. What were you going to say?"

The man hanging next to him was the man who had wanted me to share my spells, the man who had lit the fire, the father of the boy I had sent to the lake. "Oh, there you are," I said, stepping close to him. "As it turns out, I do want to share a spell with you. Want to hear it?" I touched his head. "I set a fire inside your head, may you suffer until you're dead. You will scream and you will shout, but nothing shall put my fire out."

I left him screaming as I stepped over to the short man, who trembled as I approached. "Bring me the needles, Vera."

Vera threw herself at my feet, needles in hand.

"Stand tall, Vera," I said. "All is forgiven." I grabbed the needles and helped her to her feet.

"Mistress," she cried, "I told them nothing."

"I know. Do you know where Simon is?"

She pointed to the cabin next door. "I heard him chanting a little while ago, mistress, but it's been quiet since."

I eyed the short man.

"Please, no spells," he begged.

"Who said anything about a spell for you, my lord?" I spun the needles and waved my hand. They floated toward his feet. "Remove his shoes, Vera."

Vera hastily pulled off the short man's shoes.

I looked up at him and smiled. "You see, no spell for you. Just a little spell for the needles."

With another wave of my hand, the needles shifted, poised for entry into the bottom of the man's feet.

He gasped as I stepped up to face him. "No, please," he cried.

"Where did Simon go?"

"H . . . he changed himself and fled."

"Into who?" I asked, my voice rising.

The needles pressed against his skin, and

the man screamed instead of answering.

"Longer," I whispered.

"No!" he screamed again as the needles sank into his feet.

"I'm only going to ask you once more: who did Simon change himself into?"

"I . . . I don't know," he stammered. "I swear."

I turned and grabbed Vera's hand. "Come, let's go end this."

I glanced over my shoulder as we left the cabin. I waved my hand, lengthening the needles. The man shrieked in pain as I stepped outside. I paused at the door until his screams faded—until I knew his heart had stopped— ending his part of my vision.

I instructed Vera to find Sharron and stay with her, then raced to help the others. As I flew above the waning battle, I saw that many of the men had already fled. The camp was nearly empty; Simon's troops had clearly heeded Jack's words.

When I spotted James, I dismounted my stick. "James!" He turned abruptly, and our eyes locked. We sprinted toward each other.

"Mistress, look out!" Vera shouted.

I waved my hand incessantly as I made my way to James. Nothing could stop me from getting to him—not even warlock spells. I passed the boys, who attacked any man who tried to approach me. The Spanish warlocks ran behind James, taking down everyone in their path. Arrows and spells flew all around us, but I didn't care. It was a reunion four hundred years in the making. I just wanted to touch my husband again, feel the man who never treated me like a witch, never wanted anything from me except to love me.

When we'd finally managed to close the distance between us, I threw myself into James's arms. He lifted me up, and our lips met. Everyone and everything else around us vanished as we held each other, as if we were the only two in the world. I melted into his arms, and we kissed over and over again.

When he finally set me down, he stared at me with his big blue eyes. "Welcome home," he said, grinning widely.

I touched his face. "My lord."

He kissed me again, his sweet scent—the scent I had marked him with—filling my head. I reached my arms around his neck as he lifted me up and kissed me harder. We couldn't get close enough. My hand tingled as I ran my fingers through his hair. He set me down again, and an odd feeling came over me. His eyes seemed different somehow, his touch not the same. I backed away when I noticed that he was covered in powder. Simon had cast a spell on him. I lifted my hand to break the spell.

"Delia, look out!" Cory shouted.

Fish threw himself in front of Delia, taking the spell that was meant for her.

"Fish!" Delia shouted.

Fish collapsed, writhing in pain. "Make it stop!"

Delia dropped to her knees and chanted, but it didn't help. "What did you do, you fool?" she screamed.

Joshua aimed his arrow. "Find," I

whispered as he released it.

I looked down at Fish and waved my hand, releasing him from the spell. His body went limp.

"Fish, why did you do that?" Delia screamed. "Wake up, wake up!" She leaned over him, tears streaming from her eyes. "Fish," she whispered.

I started to tell her that he would be okay, but before I could get the words out, Fish opened his eyes and winked at me. He quickly closed them again and began to moan.

"Fish," Delia cried. "Please don't die. You can't leave me."

He slowly raised his hand and pulled her toward him. "There you go again," he said. "Throwing yourself at me."

She gasped and leaned back. Fish raised his head and smiled.

"You stupid kid," Delia said. She grabbed his shirt, pulled him to her, and kissed him. Delia was finally free of Simon's spell— the work of my dear father, no doubt.

I returned my attention to James, raising my hand to break the spell.

Vera came forward. "Don't do it," she said, blocking my arm. "I heard Simon's chant, Thea. If you break the spell, James will die."

"What spell?" James asked.

Fish and Delia jumped to their feet. "James, you're covered in powder," Delia said.

James looked down and shot his head back up. "What spell?" he asked again.

I knew the spell. I had known the moment Vera touched me. We had to get James

461

home, get him to my father so he could tell me how to remove it. I had to stop it before it took effect. I couldn't tell James about the spell. I knew what he would do if he knew what it was.

I looked at Vera, hoping she would play along. "It's nothing," I said. "Nothing we need to worry about right now."

James stepped closer and searched my eyes. He didn't believe me. "What did Simon do, Thea?"

I smiled and touched his cheek. "Sleep," I whispered.

He closed his eyes, and I called to the boys to help me lay him down. They carefully laid James on the ground and looked up at me. "Why did you do that?" Cory asked. "What the hell is going on?"

I ignored him and told Javier and Joshua to go find the boy I'd sent to the lake. "Take him to the house," I ordered.

"What's going on, Thea?" Delia asked.

"Put James in the car," I said. "We need to get him home."

Jack stepped up and helped the boys lift James. The Spanish warlocks left to check the forest for any stragglers from Simon's army.

Delia grabbed my hand and looked at me intently. "What's going on?"

I yanked my hand away. "Amanda was killed."

"And what about James?" Delia asked. "Is he going to die, too?"

I looked toward the car. "No."

Chapter 25
Simon's Spell

His head resting in my lap, I brushed my fingers through James's hair as we sped back to the house. Cory peppered me with questions, but I remained silently focused on James as we drove.

"So you're not even going to tell us what's going on?" Delia asked.

"Silence, witch," I replied. "I will tell you nothing—not until I have spoken to my father."

Jack reached over and covered my hand with his own.

I looked at him and smiled weakly.

"He's going to be fine," he whispered. "You'll see."

I turned my hand over and squeezed his. "Thank you."

"Are you sure James won't mind that I'm in his home?"

"He would expect you to be there, Jack."

"That's the kind of man he is, isn't he?"

I looked down at James and smiled. "That's what I love about him—he's noble."

When we finally made it home, we took James inside. William paced in the foyer as we came through the door. I ran to him and threw my arms around him. "Father," I whispered.

He sighed and kissed my head. "My child, fate has allowed you to return to me."

"I feared they had found you, Father."

"Do not worry about me, my child," he said. "For I shall find them."

I buried my face in his chest and started to cry. "He got away," I said. "He got away."

"His death is not your burden," William replied, "for my hands shall be the ones to end his life." He pulled away and looked at James, who was draped over Cory and Jack's shoulders. "Take him to my room."

"Please find a way, Father," I said. "I can't lose him."

"I will do everything I can, my child. I give you my word."

He followed the boys up the stairs as tears rolled down my face.

"Thea, what's going on?" Delia asked.

"I can't remove the spell," I said. "If I do, I'll kill him."

"What spell? What kind of spell did Simon put on him?"

I was about to explain when the doorbell rang. I opened the door to find the Spanish warlocks waiting on the other side.

"Tenemos que hablar," one of them said to me.

"What did he say?" Delia asked.

"He said we need to talk."

"Please forgive me," the man said. "I

forget where I am sometimes."

I motioned for them to come in.

"What happened to James?" he asked.

"Simon cast a spell on him," I said.

The warlock nodded. "His father knows many spells. You must be careful how you remove them. James told me Simon has been practicing the spells on humans."

"What?" Delia asked, incredulous.

I heard the boys coming down the stairs. "What's going on?" Cory asked.

"These are James's friends," I said. "They helped us out today."

Cory shook the man's hand and waved politely at the others. "Thank you," he said. "I saw you fighting—you guys are good."

"Thank you. My name is Ciro, and these are my brothers, Elias and Galo. We are at your service." The rest of the warlocks stepped forward and introduced themselves. We all shook hands, and they shared all they knew about Simon.

Ciro told us that Simon tried to recruit them several weeks ago. "That is how we found out about your troubles. We wanted to help James; he is my friend and a man of honor."

"Thank you, Ciro," I said.

He nodded and looked at Cory. "I am afraid your troubles are not over. Several men followed Simon north. I fear he is trying to recruit more warlocks. You must stay alert and ready."

"We'll be waiting for him," Cory replied.

Ciro looked back to me. "Please, if you ever need our help again, know that we are at your service."

"James is very fortunate to have friends like you," I said.

"I will call later to speak to James. In the meantime, please tell him that I agree." He gave a small nod and walked out. The other warlocks said good-bye and followed him.

Jack looked thoughtful. "I wonder which men would have stayed with Simon?"

"Where do you think he's going?" Cory asked.

"I don't know," Jack replied. "I didn't even know who he was; I thought David was Simon."

"Who's David?" Delia asked.

"The short, bald guy. I didn't even know what the real Simon looked like until yesterday when he finally started walking around as himself."

My mind drifted as they talked. I was so worried about James. What was taking my father so long?

I felt Cory's hand on my shoulder. "He's going to be fine, Thea," he said. "William will know what to do."

I looked into his green eyes. "I'm afraid it's not that easy this time, old friend."

William called from the top of the stairs, asking Jack to stay behind.

As Jack nodded to William, I ran up the stairs with Delia, Cory, and Sammy on my heels. I didn't like the look on my father's face.

When I entered the room, James was still sleeping. I ran to his side. "My lord," I murmured.

Sammy stepped into the room, looking worried. "Is he going to be okay?"

I looked up at him and smiled weakly. "He's fine," I lied. "He's just sleeping."

I couldn't bear to tell Sammy the truth, that Simon's spell was still active. My father had not, as of yet, been able to remove it.

I kissed James's cheek as my father put his hand on my shoulder. "I tried, my child," he said. "But there is nothing to be done."

Tears streamed down my cheeks as my father put his arms around me.

"What do I do, Father?"

Cory stepped forward. "Can you please tell us what's going on now?" he asked.

"Have a seat," William said, motioning to Delia and the boys.

They all sat and looked at him intently. William started at the beginning. He told the boys that he was my father, explained my reasons for putting my powers into the crystal, and described the spell Simon had cast on my mother's heart. "That is why Thea had you erase her memory," he explained. "The heart would have nothing to steal if she couldn't remember who she was."

"Where is the heart now?" Cory asked. "Is the spell no longer in effect?"

"Many years ago," William said, "I found a way to stop the spell Simon had placed on the heart, but it had to be enclosed by love. It was the only way to stop the enchanted heart from releasing Thea's secrets to Simon." William paused and bowed his head. "But I was too weak to enclose it."

"What do you mean, enclose it?" Cory asked.

"Surround it by pure love," William replied. "In the one place the soul feels every emotion: in one's heart. The spell Simon used can be stopped by love. Even though I loved Thea enough, I was—am—too weak to stop such a spell."

"So how did you stop it then?" Cory asked.

My father looked at James. "There was another who loved her enough. And without knowing the reasons, he agreed to help. He was willing to die to protect my daughter. That is when I knew Simon's spell hadn't worked— only pure love could bestow a sacrifice like that."

"I don't understand," Cory said.

"It is a wizard's spell," William explained. "Simon used my wife's heart to drain Thea's memories. But if you surround the heart with pure love, the spell is rendered useless."

"You mean Thea's mother's heart is beating inside of his?" Cory asked, pointing at James.

William nodded. "Yes. And today Simon tried to cut it out. But James's love for Thea is protecting it. Simon can't touch it as long as James still loves her."

I started to weep because I knew what he was going to say next. I took James's hand and held it to my cheek.

"Today Simon put a spell on James, to make him stop loving Thea." William sighed. "He made sure she wouldn't be able to break it.

Once his love for her is gone, Simon will have access to the heart, killing his own son in the process."

Sammy stepped forward. "So he's not going to love her when he wakes up?"

"It does not work that way. His love for her will diminish gradually. I assume Simon planned it that way to give himself plenty of time. The fact that James has the heart must have caught him by surprise, but I have no doubt that he will return."

"But Thea has the crystal," Cory said. "Isn't that the whole reason he wants the heart? So it can tell him how to open it?"

"He knows I'm hiding something," I said quietly. I released James's hand and walked over to Delia. "Give me the box."

She removed the box from her pocket and handed it to me. I walked back to James and held the box to his head. "This memory is from today," I told the others. I opened the box, and the memory cloud hovered over our heads. "Come, stand next to me. This was going on while we were outside fighting."

"You think this will stop me?" Simon asked James in the memory. *"I would rather see you dead than loving the likes of her."*

Simon slapped James across the face and pulled out a knife.

"Go ahead," James yelled. *"I'll die happy knowing you'll never get what you want."*

Simon leaned back and regarded James for a long moment. Suddenly, he lurched forward and tried to cut out the heart, but the knife flew out of his hand. Simon reached for the knife and tried again.

James laughed as the knife escaped Simon's grasp a second time. *"Like I said, Father, I made sure I would walk out of here alive."*

Simon leaned back and tilted his head. *"What is she hiding, my son? What are you willing to die for?"*

James looked away as Simon studied him curiously.

Simon pulled out a bag of powder and dumped its entire contents over James. He held up his hands and chanted: *"With all the power I can find, I put a spell inside his mind. Take the love inside his heart, make it fade and fall apart. Replace the love with bitter hate, bring him death if my spell they break. May he kill her when his heart is free, and bring the crystal back to me."*

Simon grabbed a bottle and downed a potion, once again changing his appearance. He ordered two of his men to stay with James, and fled.

I reached for the cloud and pulled us from the memory.

Tears filled my eyes again, and Cory put his arms around me. "Thea, I know James," he said. "He'll do anything he can to stop it."

I pulled away from him. "No, you can't tell him," I warned. "None of you can."

"But why?" Cory asked. "He'd want to know."

"And what do you think he's going to do when he finds out he's going to slowly grow to

470

hate me, and then kill me?"

Cory bowed his head. "He'd kill himself before he would ever put you through it."

"Now you see my problem," I said.

Sammy walked over to William. "Can't you do anything?" he asked. "I thought you were a powerful wizard. Help him!"

William smiled kindly. "That is exactly what I plan to do, my son."

I hurried to William's side. "Father, what have you found? Please tell me."

He placed his hands on my shoulders. "The boy is right. I am a wizard. The time has come for me to do something. I have found a way to restore my powers, and once that happens, I can remove Simon's spell."

I searched his eyes. "How?" I asked excitedly. "What do you need me to do?"

"I need white energy. It can only be found in my world—a world *you* can get to. Now that you possess your full powers, you will be able to retrieve what I need."

"Give me the ring," I said, holding out my hand. "I'll go at once."

"I need a few days to prepare the capsule you will need to fill, but you will not be going alone." He looked around at all the faces in the room. "You will need your friends."

"Just say when," Cory said.

"Count me in," Sammy added.

Fish arrived at the doorway. "I'm in, and I know Javier and Joshua will say the same."

I looked at Delia.

"Like you even have to ask," she said, rolling her eyes.

I smiled and looked at William. "When do we leave?"

"Five days," he said. "The capsule will be ready by then."

"And Simon's spell, how much time do I have until he . . ." I couldn't finish the sentence; I couldn't bear the thought of James hating me.

"You'll be gone before the spell has a chance to progress too far," he replied. "I will make a potion to slow it down."

"And you, Father," I said, "will you be safe here alone with him?"

"The spell pertains only to you," he explained. "His feelings for me and the others will not change. I will be safe, I assure you." William walked over and opened the door. "I will give the rest of you more details tomorrow. Right now, if you don't mind, I need to speak to my daughter."

As the others filed out of the room, I sat at James's side. I stroked his face and leaned down to kiss his lips. "Always be with me, my lord."

I felt my father's hand on my shoulder. "There is something I must tell you."

"What is it?" I asked, standing.

"Your vision. I must explain why Simon wanted your son's heart. Simon knows a spell to get into my world, but he needs wizard powers, and a wizard's heart—living or dead—to utilize it."

My eyes widened in shock. "That's why he didn't kill me today. He needs my heart."

William nodded. "He does not know about your son, so yes, he was going to take yours."

"Father, what if I left tonight and hunted Simon? He could be dead by morning."

"And so would James. You think Simon is that stupid? If he dies, James dies. Killing him will have to wait."

My father picked up Delia's box, walked over to James, and began to pull out memories.

"What are you doing?" I asked.

"I am removing the memory of your vision. James must not know about your son if he comes to hate you. It is too dangerous."

I watched him pull several other memories, as well, but I didn't question him. I sensed he didn't want me to know. I could feel him blocking his thoughts from me.

"It is safe to sleep beside your husband for now," he said. "But do not forget to drink the tea."

"How long will it take for the spell to take effect?"

"His heart will fight it at first," William explained. "But you will start to see small changes before too long."

"Won't the bond stop him from hurting me?"

"He can hurt you if he hates you. You are half wizard, which means the bond works differently for you. It is possible that your bond to him will be severed as his love for you wanes."

"Wait, what does that mean for me?"

He looked at James and didn't answer. He was trying very hard to block his mind from mine.

"Why won't you tell me?"

"Not now, Thea."

"When?"

"When you leave to my world, and not a minute sooner."

"What are you trying to hide from me, Father?"

"Nothing. We will talk another time."

"Tell me now."

He ignored my request and called the boys and Delia back into the room. "It has been a long day for everyone," he said. "Go, rest, and we will talk tomorrow."

They nodded and looked at me. "You going to be okay?" Delia asked.

I nodded and bowed my head slowly. "When I asked Delia to erase my memory, I didn't know who would still be around when my memory came back. I want you all to know that I remember everything, every night you watched over me, every minute you spent by my side. I am forever blessed and want to thank you for standing by me. I promise to give back to you what I can. If not for you, I wouldn't be alive."

"We would be dead if not for you," Cory replied. "You owe us nothing."

I looked up and smiled. "I am proud and honored to possess such friends as you all."

"Oh, stop," Delia said. "Don't get all mushy on me now. Go and get some rest. We'll wait for the kid. We can talk tomorrow."

I stepped forward and threw my arms around them. "Thank you, all."

"Welcome home, mistress," Sammy

474

said.

I pulled away with tears in my eyes. "Please don't call me that. I liked it when you all just called me Thea."

Sammy smiled. "I liked it, too, Thea."

I asked them to bring James into our room. I wanted to be alone with him, even if he was sleeping. I waved my hand as the boys carried him in and cleaned up the broken glass on the floor.

"We'll see you in the morning," Delia said. "Get some rest."

I closed the door and looked around the room. The broken vases had repaired themselves, the flowers glittering inside of them once more. I smiled as my eyes settled on James's beautiful face. I climbed in bed beside him and wrapped my arm around his body. I started to cry as I thought of what was to come. I felt helpless, even though William had offered me hope. My thoughts drifted to our son, whose soul remained trapped in the crystal, waiting for his mother to set him free. But his little soul would have to wait. I wanted my son to have the life I never had, a life filled with happiness and joy, not torment and fear. I held fast to James and tried not to think. I needed him to hold me and tell me everything was going to be okay.

Suddenly, I felt James's arms embracing me tightly and lifted my head. "And why is my wife crying?" he asked.

I tried to sit up, but he pulled me back into his arms. "And where do you think you're going?"

"My lord, you're awake."

He kissed my head and drew me closer. "Yes, but the question is, why was I asleep to begin with?"

"I thought you were hurt, my lord. Forgive me if I panicked." I found it odd that he didn't ask me about the spell and then realized that my father must have removed the memory. It was better this way.

He rolled over and on top of me and wiped my tears, smiling. "Well, as you can see, my love, I'm not hurt. I'm deliriously happy, in fact, because you're here."

I reached up and brushed his cheek with my fingers. "Tell me you love me, my lord."

"I will always love you. Don't you know that?"

"Promise to tell me every day, my lord. Promise me."

He stared deeply into my eyes. "I should be the one asking that of you." He kissed me before I could ask him what he meant. I wrapped my arms around him.

"Ciro was here," I said between kisses. "He said to tell you he agrees."

James raised his head and smiled. "I knew he would."

"And what does he agree with, my lord?"

He started kissing my neck. "I always told him how beautiful my wife was." He raised his head again. "And now I would like to welcome my beautiful wife home properly."

Our clothes fell quickly to the floor as my husband took me in his arms. "I love you," he said, pulling me against him. I closed my

476

eyes and committed his words to memory. I would need to recall them as Simon's spell progressed. I put the spell out of my mind for now and allowed myself to drift away in James's arms.

For the next five days, I would spend as much time as I could with my husband, memorizing every detail of his love for me.

"Hold me closer," he whispered.

I wrapped my legs around him. "Tell me you love me."

"Forever, my love. Forever."

Epilogue
The Ugly Spell

I sat in the garden, longing for solitude. I had planned to spend the next five days with James, but Simon's ugly spell had other plans.

James was already becoming easily agitated with me. In just three days, the way he looked at me was changing. Even his kisses felt forced at times. His eyes turned an ugly gray when his mood changed, covering the beautiful blue I loved so much. He had left our bedroom, opting for one of the guest rooms instead. I pleaded with him to stay, but the spell had control of him now. My James was fast becoming a stranger.

I, too, had changed. My regard for my father's plan rose and fell along with James's mood. My father was giving him a potion in an attempt to slow the spell's effects, but it helped very little, if at all. In two days, I would travel to my father's world and bring back the white energy he needed to restore his powers and remove Simon's spell. I was anxious to move along with the plan, if for no other reason than to escape the hell of living with a man who couldn't remember that he loved me. I had waited so long to hold James, to wake up next to him every day, and Simon had mercilessly taken that dream away.

For the next two days, I would do little else but plan Simon's death. As soon as my father broke the spell, I planned to hunt him down and kill him slowly, just as his cruelty was killing me now.

Delia and the boys were causing me pain, as well. James had insisted everyone stay here, and even though the house was big, I felt suffocated nonetheless. The boys and Delia were all so worried about me, and though I appreciated their concern, I was growing weary of their repeated inquiries as to how I was doing. Their concern only served as a constant reminder of the disturbing circumstances that surrounded us all.

Strangely, they seemed untroubled by what was to come. Having my powers back seemed to give them a solid sense of security. My father had also given them hope, which appeared to set them ever more at ease.

But my heart didn't understand hope. It only knew that James was changing, and it was killing me. I tried to stay positive around my husband, but the often cold tone of his voice repeatedly drew me back to the garden in search of some measure of solace. It was my only escape from the horror and my exhaustion from having to keep up a brave face for everyone all the time.

Every time James snapped at me, I had to remind myself—and everyone else—about the spell. My friends were clearly troubled by his erratic behavior, especially Cory.

My relationship with Cory had deepened over the last three days. He acted like my protector now. He seemed to be the only one remembering how dangerous the situation still was. He watched James's every move, stepping between us whenever James became surly.

Delia and Fish seemed to be trying to figure out their budding relationship. The kiss they had shared when Delia thought Fish was dying was the only thing Fish ever talked about anymore.

"I know you love me," he'd say to her.

Delia kept telling him he was taking things too fast. "I thought you were dying," she'd reply. "It was a pity kiss."

Fish was determined to win her over, telling her they would be together forever. I could see that Delia saw the boy in him and feared that his feelings were merely a crush, something he would soon get over. But I knew Delia; she feared love. She worried it would make her act foolish. She feared she'd have her heart broken. Right now, I could understand that fear.

I was determined to stay strong and not let James's behavior upset me. I walked back into the house in search of my father. I asked him each day if the capsule was ready, and each day I received the same answer.

I walked into the kitchen hoping for good news, but my father was already shaking his head at me. "I told you, child," he said. "Five days. It will be ready in two more days."

I bowed my head and broke into tears. My father quickly wrapped his arms around me. "Thea, human air will destroy the white energy. The capsule will protect it. It's important that I get it just right."

"But why two days?" I whined. "I'll lose him by then."

"Do you not think I would work faster if I could? To see you in such pain kills me."

"He's starting to hate me, Father," I cried. "I can feel it."

William put his fingers under my chin and tilted my head to face him. "So you think I would allow that?"

"What do you mean?"

He wiped my tears and smiled. "Do not forget, Thea, there are things I've always known would happen."

I looked into his eyes and tried to understand, but I wasn't sure what he was trying to tell me.

He just hugged me again. "Be strong, my daughter, for in the end you will understand."

I heard someone walk in. "Oh, I'm sorry," James said to William. "I thought you were alone."

I looked at him, but he looked away. "Is my tea ready?" he asked William.

My father pulled away from me and walked to the counter. "It's almost done, James."

James glanced at me from the corner of his eye. "I'll come back when it's ready." He turned to leave.

"James, wait," I said.

He stopped and looked at me, his expression devoid of emotion.

I still had tears in my eyes as I approached him. "I was thinking maybe we could go for a walk," I said. "It's very nice outside."

He looked into my tear-filled eyes, made a fist, and turned to my father. "There has to be another way."

"I will call you when your tea is ready," my father replied.

James looked at me again and walked out. I heard him hit the wall before walking into his study.

I started to run after him when my father stopped me. "It will not help to pester him. Leave him to his thoughts."

But I knew there was something he wasn't telling me. I saw it in James's eyes; he was upset to see me crying. He was worried about me—I sensed it.

"Father, let me go talk to him, please. I think the tea is working."

"No, Thea," he replied. "He's helping Helena with the funeral arrangements. You can talk to him later, when he's had more tea."

"Why is he helping her?"

"Because she asked him to. Now leave so I may finish preparing his tea."

I stormed out of the kitchen. It made me enormously uncomfortable that James was helping Helena. I still didn't understand why he'd never told me about her.

I ran up the stairs and knocked on Delia's door. "Did you know James was helping Helena?" I asked, walking in.

"Helping Helena with what?" she asked.

"So you didn't know?"

She looked over at me, confused. "Know what?"

I sighed and closed the door. "Helena asked James to help her with the funeral arrangements."

"Why James?"

I heard the boys knock. "Thea, you in there?" Cory asked.

I opened the door. Steven, the boy I had rescued the night of the fight, was with him. I had brought him here to live with us. We had erased his past: taken every memory, transferred them to Delia's box, and given him all new ones. He thought he was my little brother—one that had been away at school and was now home to stay.

He thought Delia was his aunt, and he already adored her. His face lit up every time she walked into a room. "Who's the most beautiful aunt in the world?" she would ask him.

"You are, Auntie Delia," he'd answer.

"You're a smart kid."

I already felt love for this boy. I saw my son's face every time I looked at him. He calmed and lifted my spirits. He had a gentle way about him, and a heart of gold.

"There she is," Cory told Steven.

"Were you looking for me?" I asked.

"Why can't I go outside?" Steven asked. "Cory says you don't want me to. I won't go far, I promise."

Though I had changed what he looked like, I still wasn't comfortable with him wandering around outside. We still had no clue as to Simon's whereabouts, and I couldn't take the risk.

"I told you, sweetie, you can go outside in two more days," I replied.

"How about us, Mommy?" Delia asked, smirking. "When do we get to go outside?"

I knew they were all tired of being stuck in the house; I had ordered everyone to stay indoors. It troubled me how little regard they had for the danger we were in. Simon was still a very real threat.

"You know the dangers, Delia," Cory snapped.

She rolled her eyes and reached for Steven's hand. "Come on, sweetie, Auntie Delia will play video games with you."

They headed for Fish's room while I headed back downstairs. I spotted James walking out of the house on my way down.

"That tea your father is giving him, is it working?" Cory asked from behind me.

"I don't think so." I walked over to the window and watched James leave. I thought I saw flowers in the front seat.

"Has Jack called you?" Cory asked.

"No, have you heard from him?" I replied, still gazing outside.

"No, but I don't trust him. I don't like him coming here."

We still didn't know where Jack stood. Delia had removed the false memories she'd put into his head, and he'd left the house that very

day, refusing to stay here with us. We didn't
know where he was staying now, but he and
James seemed to be getting along fine. They
appeared to be forming a solid friendship.

All the same, the boys didn't trust him.
Cory didn't like the fact that Jack wouldn't tell
us where he was staying. He stopped by
randomly to speak to James privately in his
study, and would leave without a word to
anyone.

"We'll just have to be careful around
him, Cory," I said.

Cory didn't answer and went upstairs. I
walked into the kitchen, where my father was
cooking.

"He left," he told me.

"To help Helena?"

"Yes."

"He needs to bring her flowers?"

"Does that bother you?" he asked as he
chopped an onion.

Without answering, I returned to the
garden, my only place to cry alone. I sat for
what seemed like hours, until I heard the boys
behind me. I glanced over my shoulder. They
appeared nervous.

"What's going on?" I asked.

Sammy glanced at Cory and looked
down. "I don't know how to say this."

Delia stormed into the garden. "Tell her,
Samuel," she yelled. "She needs to know."

Sammy's eyes darted around nervously.
The other boys continued to gaze anywhere but
in my direction.

"Oh, for heaven's sake," Delia yelled.

I stood. "What's going on?"

Delia rolled her eyes and looked at me. "These two went out today," she said, pointing at Sammy and Javier. Before I could respond, she held up her hand. "Wait, that's not it. Tell her what you saw," she told the boys.

"We saw James," Javier said, his voice barely audible.

"Where?" I asked.

Javier glanced at Sammy. "You tell her."

"Just tell me!"

"He was in his car with Helena," Sammy finally answered.

"That's it?" I asked. "That's what you couldn't tell me?"

Sammy slowly looked up at me. "He was kissing her."

I felt my heart shatter into a million pieces. Cory reached for me.

"No!" I said, pushing him away.

I stormed into the house and yelled for my stick.

Delia and the boys came running in behind me. "What are you going to do?" Delia asked.

"I'm going to kill them both!" I caught my stick as it flew into the kitchen. I turned to leave, but my father stopped me.

"Put it down," he ordered.

"Get out of my way," I said, clenching my jaw.

"Make me," he hissed.

I raised my hand to wave it, wishing to toss him across the kitchen.

Delia gasped. "Thea!"

"You dare raise your hand to me!" my father yelled.

I looked into his eyes and dropped the stick. I bowed my head and started to cry.

My father enfolded me in his arms. "Thea, things are not what they seem. James loves you. Don't ever forget that."

I pushed him away, wiped my tears, and fled to my garden. I sat, thinking of how much pleasure Simon's death was going to give me. Now, more than ever, I wanted to kill him.

Two more days until I could exact my revenge.

Why had James gone running back to Helena? I couldn't lose him to her. I had to find a way to get him back. I also had to find a way to keep my son a secret from Simon.

I closed my eyes and began to cry.

"Two more days, Thea," I whispered. "Two more days."